Susan Alexander

ISBN: 1-4392-1279-1
ISBN-13: 9781439212790

Visit www.booksurge.com to order additional copies.

FOR MEREDITH AND LESLIE

with endless thanks

and

FOR HERB

forever in my heart

I never hear the word "escape"
Without a quicker blood,
A sudden expectation,
A flying attitude!

– Emily Dickinson, *Escape* (Poem 77)

I left the woods for as good a reason as I went there. Perhaps it seemed to me that I had several more lives to live, and could not spare any more time for that one.

– Henry David Thoreau, *Walden*

PROLOGUE

"Karen, Karen...."

A voice was calling her name, over and over. The voice was nasal, annoying. *Why didn't it stop?*

Karen's head was aching. Why didn't the nasal voice go away and leave her alone? Then maybe the terrible pounding in her head would stop.

"Karen, Karen...," the voice persisted.

Karen slowly opened her eyes. The sudden light was blinding.

A gray-haired woman in a white dress was peering at Karen, her forehead furrowed with concern.

Go away, go away.

"Karen? Are you awake?"

Karen stared at the woman's name tag and tried to focus on it. Finally, the bold black letters began to make sense. "CHICAGO GENERAL HOSPITAL," it said. Underneath, in smaller red letters, she read "THERESA DUNN, R.N."

Chicago?

"Karen, I'm Theresa. You had a bad fall, you hit your head. But you're better now, aren't you?"

Karen glanced around the room. It was clearly a hospital room, a bare-bones antiseptic cubicle, with the one obligatory framed artwork on the wall facing the adjustable bed.

What am I doing here?

Suddenly Karen had a mental picture of a young woman's face, a heart-shaped face, framed by lustrous dark hair.

Who was she? And what happened to her?

CHAPTER ONE

Karen Clark was hot. Steaming, sweltering, broiling hot.

The August sun's rays, only slightly obscured by the layers of dirt coating the airport-bus window, were hitting her face and trickling down her arm. Karen took a deep breath and tried to relax.

Just my luck. First the delays at La Guardia and O'Hare. Now the air conditioning on this damned bus is broken.

She felt pools of sweat bubbling beneath her breasts and dribbling down her midriff. Her white linen blouse, crisp when she left New York, was wilting in the heat, sticking to her skin, soaked with sweat. Her head pounding, she gazed out the filthy window at the mass of cars and trucks surrounding the lumbering bus.

Get moving! Get to my hotel before I die of heatstroke on this goddamned bus!

The driver of a semi, two days' worth of stubble on his face, pulled alongside and began leering at Karen.

Great. Just what I need right now. A creep like you giving me the once-over.

For the hundredth time, she wondered what she was doing on this hellish bus. Karen was impulsive, she was the first to admit it, but this decision had to be one of her all-time worst.

If only the air conditioning on this damned bus worked!

If only...if only Jason hadn't been such a bastard. If only he hadn't...

Oh, hell. Face it, Karen: Jason *is* a bastard. A genuine, one-hundred-percent, all-American bastard.

Karen sighed. How much longer would this bus ride take? It seemed like hours, days, since she'd climbed onto the bus at O'Hare.

I didn't even want to come to this absurd convention. I've never had the slightest desire to see a zillion American lawyers, all packed into one overheated city for the better part of a week.

And none of the partners pushed me to go. The only one who pushed was Jason.

Jason had been to, what, two NLA conventions? Couldn't wait to tell Karen story after story of high-powered seminars and extravagant cocktail parties. The contacts would help, he insisted. Help her climb the notoriously shaky law-firm ladder.

Now Karen peered through the bus window, thinking how traffic on the Kennedy looked like traffic in Manhattan. Too many cars, too little space. Just one of the delightful features of life in New York City.

No, life in New York wasn't quite the magical existence she'd expected, was it? She had hoped her prestige-heavy job, her inflated salary would insulate her from the nastier side of life in the city. But they hadn't, not really. She hated the crowds, the noise, the dirt. The sweltering subway. The pathetic homeless men begging on the street.

Her work at the firm wasn't the heady intellectual exercise she'd expected, either. In truth, she'd already come to hate the work at Garrity & Costello. The endless boring memoranda ground out for the endless line of demanding corporate clients. The crushing burden of nights and weekends spent in front of her computer.

She tried to have a life outside of work, but the reality was that the firm "owned" her. "That's the bargain," Jason told her over steaming cups of coffee at their favorite coffee shop on Broadway. "That's what they're paying you for."

Karen nodded, knowing Jason was right.

Eighty-five thousand a year. A lot of bucks right now, the kind of salary most people would kill for. But was it worth it? Three years after leaving Harvard, Karen felt like the stereotypical burned-out Wall Street lawyer: *Karen B. Clark, Cliché at Law.*

Still, her existence wasn't a total horror show. She'd grown more or less accustomed to the pattern of her daily life. The nice little apartment in the East 80s she shared with Jason. The camaraderie with some of the other associates at Garrity & Costello. The occasional weekends in East Hampton, where she and Jason shared a house with three other young lawyers at the firm.

So despite Jason's urging, she'd resisted the notion of flying to Chicago in the August heat. The convention was an annual event. Maybe she'd go next year. This year, she'd stay in New York.

But Jason kept urging her to go.

What a fool I was. Nearsighted–no, blind!–not to see what was going on. Until Thursday night. Thursday night, when Jason stumbled into the apartment at midnight, claiming he'd been at the office, working late.

Karen knew he was lying. That he must have been lying to her for weeks.

She stormed out of the apartment at two a.m. and hailed a cab for La Guardia. Anything, even hours of waiting at La Guardia for her hastily-arranged flight, was better than staying in the apartment for another minute. Staying in the apartment, looking at Jason's chin.

Reliving the fight with Jason now, Karen felt profoundly depressed. Her slender face, surrounded by thick masses of reddish-brown hair, was thoughtful. Maybe she'd been too quick to walk out. Maybe she should have stayed in New York, talked to Jason, come to some sort of rational conclusion.

They could have hashed things out in a calm, lawyer-like way. Instead, Karen had been hot-headed and impulsive.

One more stupid mistake in a long series of stupid mistakes. She always tried so hard to be disciplined, rational, purposeful. Once again, she'd failed.

Had she overreacted? Karen reflected on the two years she'd shared with Jason. A lot of it had been good. Very good. Maybe she *had* overreacted.

There was a lot to salvage there–a two-year-long relationship filled with laughter and good times. Something she shouldn't throw away so fast, so impulsively. She'd call Jason as soon as she got to the hotel.

Sure, Jason was a bastard, but what guy wasn't?

CHAPTER TWO

The airport bus lumbered at last into the driveway of Karen's hotel. She descended into the August heat, dragging her carry-on suitcase, and ducked into the air-conditioned lobby, a high-ceilinged atrium filled with exotic greenery. Relieved to hit an air temperature somewhere below 95 degrees, Karen glanced around the busy lobby.

A large green banner read "WELCOME TO THE 1993 NATIONAL LAWYERS ALLIANCE CONVENTION." Hundreds of people, most wearing NLA name tags, were milling around.

The noise level was jarring, sound waves crashing into everything and everybody. Her head still pounding, Karen checked in quickly and went directly to her room.

She glanced at her watch. 3:50 p.m. What was that in New York? 4:50? Too early to call Jason at home. But no point in calling him at the firm either. Friday afternoons in summer, Jason moved heaven and earth to leave the office by 4:30, 4:45 at the latest.

Karen tried phoning the apartment. She got the answering machine and left a deliberately non-committal message: "Jason, it's Karen. I want to talk to you. I'll call back later."

Should I call the house in the Hamptons? No. Too many people, too many questions. I'll keep trying the apartment and call the Hamptons later if I have to.

Exhausted from the heat, the trip, the lack of sleep, Karen showered and crawled into bed. Slipping between the cool sheets, she sank into a deep sleep.

When she awakened at dawn, Karen was disoriented, unsure where she was and why she was there. A minute later, she remembered, and a wave of depression washed over her. Again she reviewed her impulsive decision to walk out on Jason, the hectic, hot trip that led to this hotel room.

Maybe I should pack my things right now, rush back to New York, reconcile with Jason.

She hesitated, remembering Jason's chin. She had to talk to him first.

Karen found her suitcase and rummaged through it, searching for the convention materials she'd almost forgotten in her haste to leave the apartment. The green brochure with the schedule of events finally surfaced. Karen skimmed it quickly. She'd arrived so late, there wasn't much left to the convention. A few remaining seminars that morning, a speech in the afternoon, the closing banquet that evening.

Karen dressed in a fresh white blouse and the only summer suit she'd packed–her favorite, a blue-and-white striped seersucker. Perfect for August in Chicago. She grabbed the brochure, stuffed it into her already-stuffed-to-capacity shoulder bag, and headed for the hotel lobby.

The elevator was crowded with lawyers, all wearing green NLA name tags pinned to their jacket lapels. No one looked familiar.

In the enormous lobby, a sign above a small table said "NLA Registration." A young woman with curly blond hair sat behind the table, filing her nails. As Karen approached, the woman looked up. Her green name tag read "Cindi."

"Yes?" Cindi said, making a valiant effort to look helpful.

"I want to register," Karen said.

"It's kinda late, you know. Last day. You have to pay the full fee even though it's...."

"That's all right," Karen said. "I'll pay it. I want to go to one or two seminars and the speech and the banquet. No, wait, I'm not sure about the banquet...."

"You don't have to decide about the banquet now anyways," Cindi said. "The reservations were due last week. But we always get some no-shows. You can pay at the door."

Karen nodded, thinking she might prefer to go to a really good restaurant instead. Especially if she ran into someone she knew, and she wouldn't have to eat alone. She signed up for two seminars, then made her way to the hotel coffee shop for breakfast.

Still no familiar faces. Not in the coffee shop, and not in the seminar room on the third floor, where she arrived early. A Cindi-clone sat at the doorway, poised to check off the names on her list.

"Name, please?" Phony smile, bored-looking eyes, too-curly hair, dangling earrings. Another green name tag said "Tammi."

"Karen Clark. But I don't think I'm on your list. I just registered twenty minutes ago."

Tammi looked at a computer-generated list of names. "Is that Karen B. Clark?

"Yes."

"Well, you're down here. Karen B. Clark."

Amazing. If this was an example of NLA efficiency....

"Just go on in and take a seat," Tammi said. "The seminar will start in ten minutes."

Karen entered the room and found a seat near the front. A few other lawyers were already in the room. Two balding young men who looked like some of her friends at Garrity & Costello were sitting together a couple of rows ahead of her. Closer inspection revealed them to be strangers.

Karen reminded herself that a lot of the male lawyers she knew seemed to look alike. Many were balding. A few of those wore beards to show they had hair elsewhere on their heads. Some were thin and ectomorphic, or overweight with double chins. Many were wired, hyper personalities, especially the litigators.

Others began filtering into the room. A pair of lawyers who seemed to know each other entered, talking, but most were silent, rustling papers they pulled out of briefcases, or making notes on yellow legal pads.

Suddenly Karen heard two women's voices just outside the room. Raised voices, discussing something, disputing something. Karen thought she heard her name mentioned. Puzzled, she rose and walked back to the doorway.

"Look, here's my ID," a young dark-haired woman was telling Tammi. "See, my name is Karen B. Clark. I'm registered for this seminar. Now what's the problem?"

"Well, miss, I told you, another lady by that name checked in a minute ago," Tammi was saying. "I can't let you go in if...."

Karen interrupted. "Maybe I can help out here. I'm the other Karen Clark."

The dark-haired woman turned to look at Karen. "Your name is Karen Clark?" She seemed startled by the coincidence.

"Yes, it is. Sorry!" Karen smiled, hoping that would ease the tension. "Have I caused some kind of problem here?"

"Well," Tammi said, "I only have one Karen B. Clark on this list." She waved the list in Karen's direction.

"Okay, okay. I can explain this," Karen said. "Remember how I told you I just registered? This list was probably made up some time ago. And this other Karen Clark probably signed up before I did. So it's her name on the list. If the list hasn't been updated in the past half-hour, my name isn't there."

"Oh," Tammi said, nodding vacantly. "I guess you're right. Well...," Tammi paused, "well..., you can both go in then, I guess."

Karen and the dark-haired woman looked at each other. "Shall we?" Karen asked.

The other woman smiled at Karen. Her smile lit up a delicately-featured heart-shaped face. "Why not?"

They entered the room together, unsure of what came next. "Do you want to sit with me?" Karen asked.

"Sure," the other woman answered.

Karen took a seat in the back this time. The other woman followed and seated herself next to Karen.

Karen wanted to say something but wasn't sure how to begin. "We really should get to know each other," she said finally. "Obviously, I'm Karen Clark. I'm with Garrity & Costello in Manhattan, doing corporate work."

The other Karen nodded. "I've heard of Garrity & Costello. Thought about interviewing with them at law school."

"But you didn't?"

"No. No, I didn't. Do you like it?"

"Not much. It's pretty boring, actually. A lot of hours and a lot of really dull corporate stuff. I'm starting to feel burned out, in fact."

"That's too bad." The other Karen looked sympathetic.

"Now tell me about you," Karen said.

"Oh...well, there's not much to tell. I just finished law school in June."

"Where?"

The other Karen paused. "Harvard," she said finally. She looked almost embarrassed to have said it.

Karen knew how she felt. She'd met countless lawyers whose envy-tinged comments about Harvard made her squirm. She sometimes tried to avoid that reaction by steering people away from questions about where she went to law school. "I went there, too," she said, hoping to put the other woman at ease.

"Did you?" The other Karen looked at her, wide-eyed at one more coincidence.

"We must have just missed each other," Karen said. "I graduated three years ago."

The other Karen paused, looking hard at Karen. Finally she spoke again. "You know, I think I heard about you. Some people in the class ahead of me must have known you. They told me there was another Karen Clark, but I forgot till just now."

"Oh...." Karen was flattered to hear that younger students at the law school had remembered her, had talked about her after she left. Her success in the moot court competition must have meant something after all.

Just then Tammi approached, waving a piece of paper. "I just got this note from downstairs. Everything's okay, you're registered now, too," she said, looking at Karen.

Tammi turned and walked away, her too-curly hair bouncing as she walked. Karen looked at the other Karen, and they both burst into laughter. "As if anyone cares...!" Karen blurted out.

They laughed a moment longer, then stopped abruptly as the electronic buzz of a switched-on microphone suddenly filled the room. A graying middle-aged lawyer appeared behind the microphone and self-importantly announced that the seminar was about to begin.

Three smug-looking law professors and two almost equally smug-looking practitioners seated themselves behind a long table, composing the panel on "Tort Recovery: Where Are We Headed?" Karen and the other Karen leaned forward to listen to the latest developments in the law of torts.

CHAPTER THREE

The seminar turned out to be livelier than Karen expected. By the time the panelists finished their spiels, then handled some spirited questions from the audience, it was nearly eleven o'clock. As the seminar room emptied, Karen glanced at the other Karen. "Where are you going now?"

The other Karen looked at her brochure. "Umm...I think I'm free now. What about you?"

"I was supposed to go to another seminar, but I think I'll skip it. Maybe go to lunch."

"Where?"

"I don't know. Somewhere good. Want to join me?"

"Sure," the other Karen nodded. "Should we stay in the hotel?"

"No, let's go out." Karen had been in Chicago once before. She remembered that Michigan Avenue and the adjacent side streets were filled with terrific little restaurants.

Together the two Karens left the hotel. A blast of August heat hit them as they emerged into the sunshine and headed towards Michigan Avenue. They finally settled on a small Italian place on Huron Street, ordered esoteric forms of pasta, and sat back to evaluate each other while they waited for the food.

"So your name is really Karen B. Clark? Not just Karen Clark, but Karen B. Clark?" Karen asked. The other Karen nodded. "Amazing. Of course, Karen's not an unusual name, and neither is Clark, but...."

"Tell me," the other Karen said, "what does 'B.' stand for?"

"Bailey," Karen answered. "My mother's maiden name. She always liked the way it sounded: Karen Bailey Clark. She really loved my name. Not surprising, considering that her parents stuck her with Thelma." Karen suddenly felt sad, thinking about her mother.

"Mine's Beatrice," the other Karen was saying. "But my mother refused to pronounce it the usual way. She adored 'The Divine Comedy'–by Dante?"

Karen nodded.

"She named me for the heroine, and she insisted on pronouncing it the Italian way: Bay-ah-tree-chay, with emphasis on 'tree.'"

"Bay-ah-tree-chay." Karen said the four syllables out loud. "That's beautiful. Much nicer than Bailey."

"It *is* pretty, pronounced like that," the other woman agreed. "But everyone says Bee-ah-triss. My mother was the only one who ever said Bay-ah-tree-chay." Suddenly her gray-blue eyes looked away.

"Is your mother dead?" Karen asked. The other Karen talked about her mother in the past tense, just as Karen had.

"My mom and dad are both dead. They died together, in a commuter plane crash, coming home from Disney World a couple years ago." The gray-blue eyes, filled now with tears, looked back at Karen.

"My mother's dead, too," Karen said. "She died of cancer seven years ago, my senior year in college. I think about her all the time."

"And your father?"

"He remarried a few years ago, right after he retired. We've kind of lost touch. They live in Florida, and they travel a lot...."

The other Karen looked genuinely sympathetic. Karen wasn't surprised. Being orphaned, losing even one parent at an early age, changed people. She realized she had still another bond with this woman. They shared not only their names but also the loss of their mothers, the absence of their fathers in their lives.

"Any brothers or sisters?" Karen asked.

"Nope. Just me."

"Me, too," Karen responded.

It had been a lonely childhood, growing up in the two-story colonial in Summit with no brothers or sisters. Neighborhood kids weren't much company for a brainy kid like Karen, easily bored by their juvenile jokes and endless games of Monopoly and Clue. She preferred to be alone in her pink-and-white bedroom, reading or copying pictures of horses from her favorite books.

Summers and school holidays, her mother would drive the Olds into downtown Newark. The trip always ended with a hotly anticipated elevator ride to her father's law office. Karen remembered her father looking oh-so-important, sitting behind a massive oak desk, either too busy to talk to her, or else making a huge fuss over her, telling his aging overworked secretary that his "little princess" had arrived.

In her mind's eye, she could still see her father's dusty office and the countless identically-bound books, lined up on the bookshelves that reached to the ceiling. Official-looking legal documents lay everywhere in intimidating piles, and a small framed photograph of her father, shaking the hand of the mayor of Newark, smiled down on her from its place of honor on the wall behind her father's desk.

Karen had decided at age twelve to pattern herself after her father. To become a lawyer and have her own paper-strewn office where *she* would sit behind a massive desk, looking oh-so-important. She soon discovered that being brainy would help her get there. After graduating at the top of her high school class, Karen went on to Princeton, then Harvard Law.

And Harvard had led to Garrity & Costello. Now Karen often wondered whether she'd made the right decision after all.

The pasta finally arrived, and the two women ate with gusto, savoring the subtle flavors the chef had managed to create. Finishing their meal, they left the restaurant and strolled back toward the hotel.

"Karen...should I call you Karen?" Karen asked. "This could get to be confusing."

"You could call me by my middle name. Pronounced the Italian way, of course," the other Karen said, smiling.

"Okay. Bay-ah-tree-chay. That's kind of long, though. How's just plain 'Bay'? Or 'Bee'?"

"No, sorry. I don't think so," she laughed.

"Okay, okay. How about 'K.B.'? Your initials."

The other Karen thought about it. "I guess that's okay," she said. "So now I'll be K.B. What about you?"

"Mmm...I'll be Karen. If that's okay with you."

The other Karen looked away, shifting her gaze to the traffic on Michigan Avenue. "That doesn't seem fair somehow. You get to be Karen, and I don't." She was smiling a half-smile, but Karen suspected that she resented the way Karen had manipulated her.

"Well, I'm older than you, right?" Karen said. "I'll pull rank, or whatever they call it."

The other Karen smiled more broadly. This time it was a genuine smile. "I'll bet you're not older than me. Not if you went to law school right after college."

"I did. Didn't you?"

"No," K.B. said, shaking her head. "I worked for four years before law school."

"Where?"

"In a law firm, as a paralegal. That's when I starting thinking about law school."

"Where was this?"

"Cleveland. After Oberlin."

"Oberlin?"

"I majored in political science at Oberlin. Then, when I graduated, I didn't have a clue what to do with the rest of my life. I finally decided to look for a job in Cleveland."

"Cleveland? Why Cleveland?"

K.B. laughed. "It seemed like a good idea at the time. It's a pretty big city, not too far from Oberlin."

Karen nodded.

K.B. went on. "I answered an ad and ended up working as a paralegal for three years before I even thought about law school."

"What happened then?"

"One of the partners encouraged me to apply. When I got in, I left the firm and became a student again."

"So that makes you what? 28 or 29?"

"Right. 29. I turn 30 this fall. The big three-oh."

"I'm 28. So I guess *you* can pull rank on *me*. Want to call me Bailey?" Karen laughed.

"No, no, that's okay. I was just kidding before. I kind of like 'K.B.' Why don't we stick with that?"

They were crossing the Michigan Avenue bridge, approaching the vast hotel looming ahead of them just east of Michigan Avenue. Entering the lobby, they were gratefully immersed in air-conditioning again. "So where do you go now?" Karen asked.

"The closing speech by the new president. In the grand ballroom," K.B. said.

"Mind if I join you?"

"Of course not! I don't know a single person here. A few people have been friendly, but I really haven't gotten to know anyone. Till now."

Karen nodded. "Did your firm send you?" she asked K.B. as they walked to the elevators.

"No, no. I...." An elevator arrived, and K.B. signaled to Karen that she'd explain later. They joined the crowd heading for the grand ballroom and found seats towards the back of the huge room.

"This isn't a very good place to talk," K.B. said.

"Want to get together again later?"

K.B. hesitated. "Why not?" she smiled at last.

"A drink at the bar?" Karen asked.

"Umm, I don't drink much."

"What about dinner?"

"Dinner?"

"Or are you signed up for the banquet tonight?"

K.B. looked pained. "Oh, God, that's right. I guess I have to go to that."

"You don't really *have* to. Why don't we go somewhere else, somewhere really nice? We can have a good dinner, and we can talk. I want to find out what's been happening at Harvard, what job you're starting, that kind of stuff."

K.B. paused.

"If it's the money you're worried about, I'll treat for dinner. I can afford it," Karen added hastily. "That way you won't lose anything."

K.B.'s face brightened. "Are you sure you want to? I dread going to that banquet alone, but it's paid for, and I'm kind of short of cash right now till...."

A loud voice broke in. The outgoing president of the NLA had stepped up to the podium and begun speaking, preparing to introduce the new president. The audience fell silent.

"Good," Karen whispered, nodding at K.B. She pulled a note pad out of her shoulder bag and wrote a message: "Meet me in the lobby at 6:30. I'll make a reservation somewhere." K.B. glanced at the note, then nodded.

The speech began, and halfway through, Karen suddenly remembered Jason. As the speech droned on, failing to spark her interest, she decided to try calling him again. Waving at K.B., she quietly rose from her seat and headed for her room.

CHAPTER FOUR

Karen first tried calling the apartment on East 86th Street. Still no answer. She left another message, then steeled herself to call the house in East Hampton.

"Yeah?" a voice answered.

"Hi, this is Karen." No response. "Karen Clark."

"Oh, hi, Karen. It's Katie." Katie? Katie Roberts? One of the relentlessly perky young secretaries at Garrity & Costello–young women who made Karen feel tired just to look at them. Rumor had it that Katie was living with Arthur Danowitz, a thirty-ish associate at the firm. Karen remembered now; she'd run into Katie and Arthur at the house one weekend in July.

"Hi, Katie. Have you seen Jason?"

"Umm...nope. Pretty sure he's not here this weekend."

"Oh. Well, if you see him, will you tell him I called?"

"Sure, Karen. See ya." Katie hung up.

Jason wasn't home, and he wasn't at East Hampton. Where was he? With...with...?

She put that ugly thought out of her mind and pondered what to do next. She could try phoning him at the firm. Maybe he'd gone in to work on his big tax case, the one he'd talked about for the last six months. Karen was sick of hearing about it.

She decided not to bother and put down the phone. She'd be back in New York tomorrow anyway. She'd probably feel less stressed by then. Able to discuss things with Jason in a calm, reasonable manner. They'd review their options, they'd discuss the alternatives....

Oh, shit, Karen thought. I dread it. I dread having to discuss our relationship when I get back. I'm not sure I even want to live with Jason anymore. I'm not sure about anything.

She glanced at her watch. If she wanted a reservation at a fairly good restaurant, she had to get cracking. She needed a phone book, a magazine, something with restaurant listings.

In a desk drawer, she found the hotel's magazine. She leafed through it, noting its array of some of Chicago's best restaurants, along with many of its other attractions. Finally she started calling nearby restaurants.

But getting a reservation wasn't easy. After a number of unsuccessful phone calls, she finally managed to reach La Maison Carrée, a French restaurant in an obscure neighborhood on the North Side, where a 6:45 reservation was still available. She booked a table for two, making a note of the restaurant's address.

After a quick shower, Karen slipped into the only dinner dress she'd brought along–a slinky black silk number. Sliding into her high-heeled pumps, she looked at her watch. Six o'clock. If K.B. was ready, they could get an early start.

After Karen cleared up some understandable confusion with the hotel operator, who finally found the other Karen Clark's room number, she jotted down the number and called K.B.

K.B. answered on the first ring.

"Are you ready?" Karen asked.

"Yes, are you?"

"Uh-huh. Why don't you come by my room? We can leave from here. The lobby's probably a zoo on Saturday night."

"Okay. Be there in a minute."

"Good. I'm in Room 612."

Five minutes later, K.B. knocked at the door. Her low-cut royal blue dress showed off her tan shoulders. On her feet, high-heeled black patent sandals looked dusty but slinky nevertheless.

"Wow," Karen said."You look terrific."

"Saturday night in the big city, right?" K.B. said. "This is my one decent dress. I'm lucky it was clean."

"I'll just get my bag, and we'll go," Karen said. She reached for her shoulder bag, perched on the desk, and pulled it toward her. Suddenly the strap on the bag tore, and the bag fell to the floor, scattering its contents in every direction.

"Oh, shit," Karen said. "Shit, shit, shit."

K.B. chuckled. "C'mon," she said, "it's not that bad. I'll help you pick it up." She kneeled on the floor, picking up a hairbrush that had bounced under the bed.

"No, no, forget it," Karen said, grabbing K.B.'s elbow and pulling her upright. "If we try to pick it all up, we'll be late for dinner. Just leave it. I can manage without most of this junk for a few hours."

"Okay," K.B. said, "if you say so."

"I'll just take my room key and my credit cards," Karen said. She searched for a moment, finding the plastic key-card and her credit-card case. "Now let's go. Oh, what about the cab fare? Some of them don't take credit cards."

"I'll pay for the cab," K.B. said. "I've got enough cash to cover it, don't worry."

"Okay," Karen said, guiding K.B. out of the room. "Hey, can you hold these things till we get back? This stupid dress doesn't have any pockets."

"Sure," K.B. said, opening her handbag.

Karen dropped the key-card and the credit-card case inside K.B.'s black patent handbag. "Why don't women's clothes have pockets?" she ranted. "I mean *all* women's clothes, not just some of them? It's absurd!"

K.B. laughed at Karen's sudden burst of outrage, but she nodded in agreement just the same. All women's clothes *should* have pockets. When would fashion designers get that idea through their stylishly-coiffed but very thick skulls?

CHAPTER FIVE

The hotel doorman hailed a cab, and Karen and K.B. quickly jumped inside. The cabbie made several wrong turns before he found La Maison Carrée. It was on a quiet side street only two blocks long, and the cabbie had never heard of it.

The two women climbed out of the cab and rushed inside, hoping they weren't too late to get the table they'd reserved.

They weren't. But the restaurant was extremely small—the French word *intime* came to Karen's mind–and she realized just how lucky they were. When the maitre d' led them to their table, she noticed that every one of the eight other tables was already filled.

She and K.B. perused the menu, amazed at the unusual offerings it described. They both selected *canard aux olives,* duck in an olive sauce, a dish Karen had discovered in France but rarely found in American restaurants, even in Manhattan. At K.B.'s insistence, Karen also selected the wine–her favorite red, Chateauneuf du Pape.

"You know a lot about French food," K.B. said when the waiter left.

"Not that much. I've been to France a couple of times, and I have some French cookbooks. But I never have time to cook."

K.B. nodded.

"Jason and I–we like to go out for French food."

"Jason? Is that your boyfriend?"

"Uh...yes. At least I think so. We just had a fight, so right now I'm not really sure where we stand."

"Oh, sorry," K.B. said quickly. "I don't want to pry...."

"That's okay. That's what this dinner is for, right? To find out about each other," Karen said. "But I don't think I want to talk about Jason right now."

"Fine. I don't mind."

The waiter arrived with the bottle of wine, and Karen tasted it. Perfect. She nodded, and the waiter filled both glasses.

"Now tell me about your job," Karen said. "I'm assuming you *have* a job."

K.B. smiled. "That's funny. Not funny ha-ha. I mean, funny you should say that. Because I just barely have a job."

Karen was puzzled. "What?"

"I'll explain. First of all, I did pretty well at Harvard. Not top of the class, or law review, but well enough." Karen nodded, and K.B. continued. "While everybody was lining up jobs with law firms, my dream job was a clerkship with a federal judge. So I applied to a whole bunch of judges, and I actually got a clerkship."

"Great," Karen said. A clerkship with a federal judge was always a plum. "Which judge?"

K.B. paused for a split-second. "Rodriguez. Luis Rodriguez, in San Francisco."

"Fantastic!" Karen had never heard of Luis Rodriguez, but getting a clerkship with *any* federal judge in San Francisco had to be a major coup. "So what happened?"

"I guess you didn't hear about it."

"Hear about what?"

"Well, in June, right after commencement, right before I packed up to leave for San Francisco, I got a phone call. Judge Rodriguez had died suddenly. A heart attack."

"Oh, my God. What did you do?"

"Well, there I was, jobless. And you probably remember what things are like in June. The firms have already hired anyone they're going to hire, and all the judges have had their clerks lined up for a year."

"Couldn't some other judge take you on, as an extra clerk or something?"

"I thought about that, and I went to the law school placement office right away to see if they could help me find something. But they weren't very helpful," K.B. said, shaking her head. "They gave me some phone numbers to call in San Francisco, and the names of some new judges. But I called, and everything was already locked up."

"How awful!"

"It really was. Really awful."

"So what did you do?"

"Well, I went back to the placement office. They were a little more sympathetic by that time, but they didn't hold out much hope. The law firms wouldn't be coming through to interview again till the fall. All they could suggest was sending letters to a bunch of law firms and government agencies in whatever cities I was willing to work in."

"Incredible."

"I know," K.B. nodded. "Then something really strange happened. While I was sitting in the placement office, a phone call came in. From this law firm in a little town in Wisconsin. The head partner said they needed somebody. He thought he might as well try to get the best, so he called Harvard. And there I was, desperate for a job. Any job. The placement director–Judy Montana, remember her?

Karen nodded.

"Well, she called me over to the phone. Asked if I'd consider going out to Wisconsin, sight unseen, to work for this firm. I didn't know what to say."

"Unbelievable!" Karen said.

"I know. Finally I got on the phone and talked to the man. He sounded okay. Kind of brusque, all business, you know? But he described the firm and the town and, well, it all sounded somewhat idyllic. A small-town practice. The kind a lot of lawyers used to have. The kind they never talk about at Harvard."

Karen nodded again. K.B. was right. Harvard prepared its students for Wall Street, D.C., and the glittering mover-and-shaker world of the other big cities. Hardly anyone from Harvard wound up in a small firm in a small town, in Wisconsin or anywhere else.

"So you took the job?" she asked.

"Well, I told him I'd think about it and call him back. I was up all night thinking it over. I finally decided I couldn't face going through a job search again. The kind the placement office told me I'd have to do to get something else. Besides, I liked the idea of being a small-town lawyer. I'm actually kind of excited about it. So I called him back and told him I'd take the job."

"So that's where you are now? This firm in Wisconsin?"

"No. Not yet. I haven't started there yet."

"Well, how did you wind up here? At the convention?"

K.B. looked down at the sparkling white tablecloth, then up again at Karen. "The firm didn't want me to start till the middle of August. So I hung around Cambridge for a while. Then I heard about somebody who was driving to Cleveland, and I asked if I could go with him. I figured I'd stop off there on my way to Wisconsin. Get a chance to see my old friends at the law firm." K.B. looked down at the table again. This time she carefully moved the silverware in front of her so the knife, fork, and spoon all lined up perfectly.

"Did you?"

K.B. looked up again and nodded. "While I was there, I saw my old boss, and he offered to pay my way to the convention if I wanted to go."

"Nice."

"Yeah. He also said they'd try to find space for me as soon as they evaluated the new associates they just hired. So...if things don't work out in Wisconsin, I could possibly go back there next fall."

"So things didn't work out that badly after all," Karen said, smiling.

"No, I guess not," K.B. said, the half-smile on her heart-shaped face trying valiantly to match Karen's.

The food finally arrived, and the two women feasted on *canard* until their stomachs ached, sipping the wine and sampling the delicious fresh bread and butter between mouthfuls of duck. Karen never ate real butter except in French restaurants, where she always felt she had a special dispensation from calories and cholesterol decreed by the President of France himself.

Their plates clean, their stomachs full, Karen paid the bill with a credit card extracted from the case K.B. fished out of her handbag.

"Thanks for dinner, Karen. Fabulous meal!" K.B. said when they finally pushed their chairs away from the table.

"My pleasure," Karen said. She suddenly noticed that K.B., walking ahead of Karen toward the door, was unsteady on her feet. "Are you okay?"

"It's the wine," K.B. said. "I'm not used to it." She giggled. The giggle sounded odd. Not like K.B.'s usual laugh. Fleetingly, Karen felt guilty about foisting wine on a young woman who was obviously unaware of its effect. But by now Karen was herself a bit high from the wine, in a delicious haze in which the world seemed far more benevolent than usual. So what if K.B. was a bit high, too?

Leaving the restaurant, K.B. tripped over the doorway threshold and giggled some more. Karen, following her out the door, used her hand to steady K.B., then felt herself nearly trip over the same spot. "We're quite a pair," she muttered to K.B. "Now let's see if we can find a cab." K.B. giggled again as they emerged into the warm night air.

Karen looked up and down the street in front of the restaurant. The quiet street had no traffic, no sign of any cars moving, let alone a cab. "We'll have to go back inside and call for a cab," she said, turning towards K.B. But K.B. had started walking and was already halfway down the block. Karen heard her calling out in a soft voice, "Taxi, taxi," as she moved unsteadily toward the corner.

Karen took off after K.B. Her high-heeled pumps kept her from moving as quickly as usual, but K.B. was in high heels, too, and wasn't far ahead. Again, Karen felt a pang of guilt for having induced K.B. to drink so much wine with dinner.

K.B. had reached the corner, with Karen several yards behind, when a car suddenly appeared on the cross street. It swerved as it slowed down to turn the corner, flashing its headlights in their faces. K.B. turned to call to Karen. "Maybe there's a taxi here...," K.B. said, stepping off the curb.

The car accelerated as it turned the corner. It moved quickly. Too quickly. As Karen watched, her mouth agape, the car struck K.B., throwing her to the street.

"K.B.!" Karen ran quickly to the corner. The car's driver, sensing trouble, floored the accelerator. Zooming down the street to the next corner, the car turned again and, tires squealing, disappeared from sight.

Karen rushed to K.B., lying sprawled on the dirty asphalt street. "K.B.!" Karen said, but there was no response.

Karen wished now that she had taken CPR, or knew how to take a pulse, or something. K.B. appeared to be unconscious, and Karen suspected that her new friend was seriously injured. She was suddenly afraid to even touch her.

She looked around. No one. No people, no cars. No other witnesses.

Her heart was pounding. *What should I do?*

Look for help, of course. But where? The restaurant? She was already nearly a block away.

Karen heard a sound and looked up. Another car was coming down the cross street. It stopped about half a block away.

Still in a daze, a daze compounded now by shock, Karen robotically grabbed K.B.'s handbag and began to run toward the car. As she approached it, the car started to move again.

"Stop! Stop!" Karen shouted. "Someone's hurt! She needs help!"

The car kept moving.

Karen felt dizzy now, dizzy and scared. But she had to find help for K.B.

She began to run down the cross street. At least there was some traffic on this street. Another car would come along soon, it had to. Someone would come along and help K.B.

Running in these shoes is a bitch. Sure, I'm used to jogging in Central Park, but I'm not up to running in high heels.

Her feet, her legs began to ache, and she stumbled once or twice as she ran.

The cross street was quiet now. No other cars had come into view.

Where is everybody?

Karen was sorry now she hadn't gone back to the restaurant. She was running farther and farther away from it, farther and farther away from K.B. She was tired and groggy, and she didn't know where she was going.

Still Karen kept running. *I have to find help, find help for K.B.*

Suddenly her heel caught on a piece of uneven sidewalk. She tripped, falling clumsily onto the pavement, striking her head.

Suddenly everything was black.

CHAPTER SIX

"Karen, Karen...."

A voice was calling her name, over and over. The voice was nasal, annoying. Why didn't it stop?

Karen's head was aching. She wanted the nasal voice to go away and leave her alone. Then maybe the pounding in her head would stop.

"Karen, Karen...," the voice persisted. Karen slowly opened her eyes. The sudden light was blinding, and she blinked for a moment until she could open her eyes and leave them open.

The owner of the voice, a gray-haired woman in a white dress, was peering at Karen, her forehead furrowed with concern.

Go away, go away.

"Karen? Are you awake?"

Karen stared at the name tag pinned to the woman's dress and tried to focus on it. Finally, the bold black letters began to make sense. "CHICAGO GENERAL HOSPITAL," it said. Underneath, in smaller red letters, she read "THERESA DUNN, R.N."

Chicago? I'm in a hospital in Chicago?

"Karen, I'm Theresa. You had a bad fall, you hit your head. But you're better now, aren't you?"

Karen glanced around the room. It was clearly a hospital room, a bare-bones antiseptic cubicle, with the obligatory framed artwork on the wall facing the adjustable bed.

What am I doing here?

Theresa began talking again. "Do you remember what happened last night? Anything at all?"

Karen shook her head. Shaking it made her headache feel even worse.

Gently, Theresa took Karen's hand. "Karen dear, you were found unconscious last night."

Unconscious? Karen's heart began to race. "Where did I fall? Who found me?"

"The police found you, dear. Lying on a sidewalk on the North Side somewhere. You had a head injury. They brought you here to CGH right away."

Startled, Karen stared at Theresa.

Where was I last night? How did I wind up on a sidewalk, unconscious?

"Now that you're conscious again," Theresa was saying, "a doctor will be in to check you. If you're okay, you might even be released this morning."

Karen looked at her watch, or tried to, but her watch wasn't on her arm. A hospital bracelet circled her wrist instead. "What time is it?" she asked.

Theresa consulted her watch. "Quarter to ten. And don't worry about your watch. All your valuables are under lock and key at the nurses' station. And your clothes are all in here." Theresa walked over to a narrow metal door located on one wall of the room. She opened it and pointed to the clothes hanging inside.

Karen saw a black dinner dress, filthy and torn, hanging on a hook. Suddenly some glimmers of the night before began filtering into her brain.

She remembered running, running, then tripping on some broken sidewalk.

But where was I? And why was I running? Think, think! I was running to find something, find...what?

Her mind was a blank.

Okay, Karen, okay. Back up a little. What were you doing on that street, wherever it was? You must have been...eating dinner, right?

Wait. I was eating dinner in a little French restaurant. That's right. Now who was I with? Who...?

Suddenly Karen had a mental picture of a young woman's face, a heart-shaped face, framed by lustrous dark hair. Who was she? And what had happened to her?

"Is my friend here, too?" she asked Theresa, her heart beginning to pound again.

"Friend? Did you have a friend with you?"

"Yes. Well, she wasn't exactly with me. She was maybe a block or two away...I'm not sure...." Karen's voice drifted off.

K.B. Was her name K.B.?

"Sorry, I don't know anything about a friend," Theresa said. "Check with the police on that, honey."

"The police? Did you say the police brought me here?"

"Ginny in the E.R. said somebody saw you on the sidewalk and called the police, but I'm not sure exactly what...."

Just then a young physician with thick black hair and honey-brown skin entered the room. Theresa stopped talking immediately. "Good morning, Dr. Patel," she murmured and ducked out of the room.

The doctor smiled warmly at Karen. "Well, how are you doing this morning?"

Karen looked at him blankly. She didn't feel like smiling back. "Okay, I guess, except for this headache."

"Where are you from, Karen?"

Her head was finally beginning to clear. "New York. I live in New York." Yes, that sounded right.

Dr. Patel proceeded to examine her, gently touching her bruised flesh, checking her neurological responses, finally announcing that she could leave the hospital as soon as she felt like getting dressed. "The headache is normal," he assured her. "Just take some Tylenol till it subsides. But if you get any symptoms like dizziness or nausea, be sure to see your doctor right away," he warned.

Karen assured him she would, and he briskly left the room. She thought of Marilyn Hogan, her Manhattan gynecologist, the only doctor she'd seen in the last three years. She almost smiled, wondering how Marilyn would deal with a head injury.

Karen slowly rose from the bed. Clearly she had to leave the hospital. She had a hotel room somewhere, didn't she? She'd try to figure out where it was and get back there. She began to dress herself in the things she found inside the closet.

Not very appropriate for ten o'clock in the morning, but they'd have to do. She brushed some dirt off the black dress and pulled it on. The tears on the front weren't as noticeable as she had feared. But her pantyhose were so badly torn, she dropped them into the wastebasket and put her high-heeled pumps onto bare feet.

Now what? Something was missing. Her watch, and whatever else Theresa had meant by "her valuables." She looked around for a buzzer or some other way to call Theresa, but before she could find one, Theresa entered the room. "Here's your bag," she said, handing Karen K.B's bag. "Everything's inside."

"This? But this isn't my bag," Karen said, shaking her head. Her headache got suddenly worse.

"Sure it is, honey. That's your bag all right. Your memory's just not what it should be," Theresa clucked. "Don't worry about it," she added, noticing the stricken look on Karen's face. "You'll get it all back. Here, maybe you should sit down again for a minute."

"No, no, I'm all right. I'll be fine," Karen said. She felt pretty good, except for the headache. Strong enough to leave the hospital and get back to her hotel, at least. Clutching K.B.'s bag, she left the room.

Theresa hurried down the hospital hallway after her. She took hold of Karen's elbow and gently guided her toward the elevators. "I'm supposed to put you in a wheelchair, honey," she said.

"Don't bother," Karen said. "I'm all right."

"Well, don't tell anybody," Theresa muttered under her breath. "By the way," she added, "you're lucky you had that health insurance card in your wallet."

"Insurance card?"

"You know, the card from Harvard. It covers emergency care, anywhere in the country. That's a great deal, honey. Better than a lot of students get."

"Oh, yeah, sure," Karen said, her head spinning. The people in E.R. must have taken that card out of K.B.'s bag last night, checking for health insurance before they provided any medical care. Lucky for me it was there, she thought.

But what happened to K.B.?

Theresa accompanied Karen to an elevator bank and waited with her for the next elevator. As Karen entered it, Theresa waved goodbye. "Bye now, honey," she smiled. "Take care of yourself."

"Thanks," Karen said, the elevator doors shutting out her view of Theresa.

Surrounded by other patients and medical staff, Karen nevertheless felt very much alone. Her mind was racing, trying to process everything that had happened. The convention, she had gone to the NLA convention. She had met K.B.

Wait a minute. Not K.B., idiot. Karen B. Clark. A woman with the same name as you.

They'd hit it off. They had lunch, then dinner....

Just then, the elevator doors opened on the ground floor. Karen exited and headed toward the revolving door that led outside. She stumbled through the door and looked around. Traffic and noise assaulted her from every direction.

Karen suddenly remembered the bag she was clutching. K.B's bag. A medium-sized black patent bag with two short straps, the kind a woman carries in her hand or over her wrist. The kind the Queen of England always carried.

Karen preferred large shoulder bags, big enough to stuff full of her essentials. She liked the ease of a shoulder bag, the way it left her hands free, and she always puzzled over women who carried the kind K.B. had chosen. Didn't they want the freedom a shoulder bag allowed? Now Karen looked down at K.B.'s bag and began to fumble with the clasp.

A man jostled Karen as he walked by. She couldn't stay there, in the middle of the sidewalk, opening the bag while people brushed past her. She walked back through the hospital doors and collapsed into an empty chair in the lobby. Then she opened the bag and looked inside.

She felt vaguely uneasy, looking through another woman's handbag, but she had no choice. First she searched for her own things. She found her credit-card case and what looked like her plastic room key-card (fortunately identifying the hotel), and the watch she'd been wearing the night before. That was all. Everything else was K.B.'s.

Rummaging through the bag, she found another plastic key-card, one that looked just like Karen's, and a well-worn red leather wallet. Karen quickly looked through the wallet. Inside was a Massachusetts driver's license with a fuzzy picture of K.B., a Social Security card, and the student health card Theresa had mentioned. Looking further, Karen found $207 in bills and some coins in the wallet. Not much money to travel on. No checkbook, no travelers' checks, no credit cards.

Besides the wallet, key-card, and the usual assortment of make-up, facial tissues, and breath mints, K.B.'s bag contained only two items: a bus ticket to Walden, Wisconsin, and a letter from her new employers. Karen scanned the engraved letterhead on the envelope: Fuller, Fuller & Chase, 100 Main Street, Walden, Wisconsin.

Karen didn't open the envelope. Looking at the letter itself would be an invasion of K.B.'s privacy Karen wasn't prepared to make. Not yet.

Once again Karen exited the lobby through the revolving door. Between her credit cards and K.B's cash, she could get back to the hotel all right. Once there, she'd try to find out what had happened to K.B.

She hailed a cab and headed back to the sanctuary of the hotel.

CHAPTER SEVEN

As Karen pushed her way through the hotel's revolving door, the noise in the atrium lobby seemed almost comforting. At least the hotel was safe, secure. Nothing bad could happen here, could it? She walked shakily through the lobby, aware that her tattered cocktail dress and bare legs invited incredulous stares from the Sunday-morning crowd on its way to brunch.

In the elevator, Karen hesitated, unsure of her room number. Three men in business suits stared at her until she pressed 6, hoping it was right. She got off the elevator when it reached 6, and found herself walking to room 612.

Was this the right room? She fished the two key-cards out of K.B.'s bag and tried one. It worked. Karen silently thanked her subconscious for directing her to both the right room and the right key.

The bed was still made up from the day before. She lay down on it, carefully, not wanting to jar her head any more than necessary. Lying on her side, Karen groaned when she saw the jumble of items piled on the floor. The contents of her shoulder bag were still strewn all over the carpet, and the bag itself lay beside them.

Karen knew she had to pick it all up, but oh God, not now. For now she just wanted to rest. Her head was throbbing. Did she have any Tylenol in her suitcase? She couldn't remember. But maybe a quick shower would help her head.

Karen stumbled into the bathroom and showered. The hot water felt good on her aching muscles, but it made her headache even worse. She emerged quickly and searched for Tylenol in her travel kit. Thank God she had packed some. She swallowed a couple of tablets and headed back to bed.

Karen tried to clear her mind and fall asleep, but a million crazy thoughts crowded into her head, crashing around, making sleep impossible. At least her headache had begun to subside.

I can't keep lying here like this, she thought. I'll get dressed. Maybe getting dressed will help me get back on my feet.

Rummaging through the few remaining things in her suitcase, she slipped on a lightweight summer dress and a pair of summer sandals she found buried at the bottom of the case.

Now what? Call the police, of course. Try to find out what happened to K.B.

Karen called the front desk and asked to be connected to the police. But instead of putting the call through, the woman at the desk demanded to know if something was wrong.

"Nothing. Nothing's wrong," Karen said quickly. "I just want to make an inquiry."

The woman finally connected her with Chicago police headquarters. When someone answered after fourteen rings, Karen hesitated, then blurted out, "Was a woman, a young woman, found injured last night?"

"Where would that be, miss? We find a lot of injured women in this city," an exasperated voice answered.

"Uh, on the North Side somewhere, uh, on a street corner where...."

"Just a minute, miss. Hold on, please" the voice responded.

Karen was put on hold, then connected to another voice, then put on hold again, then disconnected. Frustrated, she hung up and decided to try again later.

Karen walked over to the window. It faced south, and Karen's view of the city was spectacular. The sky was cloudless again; another blazing hot day in Chicago. Karen suddenly thought about the living room window in her apartment. It faced south, too. Karen wondered if the weather in New York was hot, as hot as Chicago's was right now.

New York....New York! She had totally forgotten about New York! Wasn't she supposed to take a return flight sometime that afternoon? She rushed over to the pile of things on the floor. There it was, her return ticket to New York. What was her departure time? *Quick, quick, find it.* There, right there: 2:00 p.m.

Could she still make it? Karen glanced at her watch. It was almost 12:30. If she rushed, threw her things together, caught a fast cab, she might be able to make it.

But did she want to? Did she really want to make a mad dash for the airport?

Not with this headache. I'll call the airline and change my flight.

No problem. Why rush back to New York? The city would be there. No need to hurry.

Karen reached for the phone. She'd request an evening flight. She'd have time to relax, eat something before leaving for the airport. She'd get to the apartment pretty late, but so what?

The apartment....

Karen suddenly had a vision of the apartment, a vision of Jason standing in it, watching her pack, his chin jutting out at her.

Jason, that bastard. I have to talk to him, have to clear the air before I go back to New York.

Karen gritted her teeth and phoned the apartment. No answer. Now what? Where would he be? The firm? East Hampton?

Karen closed her eyes and envisioned Jason on the deck of the house in East Hampton, jutting his chin toward the ocean. When she phoned, Arthur Danowitz answered.

"Uh, Karen, uh, yeah, Jason's here," Arthur said. He was trying to conceal something, but he wasn't doing a very good job of it.

"Is he there with Joan?" Karen asked.

Arthur paused.

"Don't worry, Arthur. I know about Joan. You can tell me."

"Well, yeah, Karen. He's here with Joan. Do you still want to talk to him?"

Karen's heart sank. She had suspected that Joan would be there, but hearing Arthur confirm her suspicions upset her nonetheless. Arthur coughed, waiting for a reply.

"Yes, yes, I do. Please get him. Tell him I have to talk to him." Karen's mouth suddenly felt dry. She wished she'd gotten a drink, a Coke, anything, before she made this call.

Waiting, Karen recalled the last time she saw Jason. Thursday night. The night he got back to the apartment at midnight, claiming he'd been at the office, working on a motion he had to file on Friday.

Karen knew he was lying. She had phoned the office, left a message on his voicemail, then called some of the other associates. No one had seen him there all evening.

"Where were you, Jason?" she had asked.

"What do you mean? I was working."

"I know you weren't at the office, Jason. I called."

Jason paused, glancing out the window at the traffic in the street below. Finally he said, "Okay, okay, I wasn't at the office."

Karen waited.

"Okay, Karen, you win. I was with Joan."

"Joan?" A mental picture of Joan Granger, tall, slim, blonde, hit Karen's consciousness. A summer associate at the firm, a whiz kid from Columbia Law, a few years younger than Karen. "What... where...where were you?"

"At her place." Instead of looking sheepish, the way Karen thought he should, he looked belligerent. Daring her to start a fight.

"Oh." Karen's heart was racing. She could barely breathe. "When...when did this start?"

"A couple weeks ago." Jason lifted his chin aggressively, daring Karen again.

Karen walked away from Jason, then turned to face him again. "What do you want to do now?"

Jason paused. "Do? Nothing. Why?"

"Why?" Karen almost laughed. How stupid, how insensitive, how incredibly rotten could he be? "Jason, this changes everything. I can't go on living here with you...."

"Why not?" he interrupted. "Joan isn't that important to me. Let's forget it."

"Forget it? Forget it?" Karen's voice began to rise, to sound almost shrill. The shock had subsided, and anger took over. "No, I *won't* forget it! No, Jason. *You* can do the forgetting. Forget about living with me!"

Karen's heart pounded. Jason just stood there, staring at her. Karen's fury welled up inside her again. "After two years, two years together!" she erupted. Karen knew she sounded hysterical, like the stereotypical jilted woman, but she couldn't stop. "You're right, Jason. I'll forget. I'll forget *you,* you shit!"

Karen stormed into the bedroom. She grabbed a small suitcase, the one she usually took to East Hampton, from under the bed. She went to the closet, pulled some summer clothes off their hangers, and began throwing them into the case.

Jason followed her into the bedroom and watched, his chin raised again. "What are you doing?"

Karen didn't look up. "You wanted me to go to the convention, I'm going to the convention. Now you can take Joan up here and... and fuck her here, on our bed!" Karen felt her face flushing. She didn't say any more but kept packing. Jason continued to watch her, his arms folded, saying nothing.

By 1:30, Karen was dressed, packed, and ready to leave. Suddenly she remembered she had no plane ticket, no reservation at a hotel. Jason coolly watched her as she called an airline, got a reservation on a morning flight, then called the convention headquarters hotel and booked a single room. By 2:00, she was out the door, on her way to La Guardia.

Now Karen sat in her hotel room in Chicago, clinging to a phone. Remembering the fight with Jason had set off the pounding in her head again.

Finally Jason came on the line. "Karen? Where are you?"

"Still in Chicago. I was in an accident here."

"Oh." No questions, no concern.

He doesn't care if I live or die. "I just thought I'd ask you...I'd ask how you feel about...about me. Do you want me to come back?"

A long pause.

"Jason?"

"I'm here."

"Well?"

"Look, Karen, you've got to do what's right for you. If you want to come back here, if you want to try living together again, fine. Maybe we can work it out. I don't know."

Karen paused, her mouth so dry she could hardly speak. "What about Joan?"

"Yeah, well, Joan and I have hit it off pretty well. I...I don't really want to jeopardize that...."

Karen's stomach turned over. There was no hope of reconciling. "So, in other words, you're telling me you don't really want me to come back. Right?"

"Well, it's your apartment, too. I realize that. You haven't got any other place to stay. I guess I can move out. You...."

"Don't bother!" Karen slammed down the receiver, hard, her heart pounding. She stormed around the room, furious again with Jason. Just like Thursday night, only now it was worse. Now she was in Chicago, she was recovering from an accident, she felt displaced and shaky and her nerves were a mess.

Karen couldn't stay in the room another minute. She would suffocate if she did. She grabbed K.B.'s handbag, made sure the room keys were still in it, and bolted from the room, heading for the lobby.

* * *

Somehow Karen made her way to the hotel's coffee shop, fell into a booth, and ordered a Coke. While she waited for it, her eye fell on a pile of Sunday newspapers near the cashier. She searched for some money in K.B.'s wallet, paid for a paper, and carried it back to her table.

She quickly scanned the first section for a story about K.B. Nothing. Features about the decline of the American family, exposés of local members of Congress, the latest news from the Middle East. But nothing about a hit-and-run accident on the North Side.

Karen began to take the heavy Sunday paper apart. She flipped through section after section till she found a headline on page five of section seven: "Collision Victim Awaits ID."

The story was brief and to the point. The body of a woman in her late twenties or early thirties had been found on a North Side street Saturday night, the apparent victim of a hit-and-run driver. The woman had no identification, and police were attempting to discover who she was. The police requested that any witnesses come forward.

"Here's your Coke, dear." Karen looked up. A waitress with a smiling middle-aged face was holding a glass filled with bubbly brown liquid. "If you move some of that paper, I'll put it down."

Karen hastily moved the newspaper out of the way. She gulped down the Coke, then grabbed the newspaper and read the story again.

The hit-and-run victim...she had to be K.B.

So K.B. was dead. Dead!

Karen had hoped that K.B. had been found, injured, just as Karen had. Then rushed to a hospital where she'd recovered, just as Karen had.

But that hadn't happened. Instead, K.B., the sparkling young woman with the same name as hers, was dead. K.B. was gone, along with the brand new life she had described at dinner.

Where was it again that K.B. was supposed to go? Karen opened K.B.'s handbag and searched for the letter. There it was. Walden, Wisconsin. The firm of Fuller, Fuller & Chase. K.B. had been excited, elated about starting her career. About being a lawyer in a small town, working in the sort of small-town practice most lawyers never got the chance to try these days. Now she wouldn't get the chance to try it either.

Karen ordered another Coke and a BLT on toast. When the food arrived, Karen bolted it down, suddenly aware of how hungry she was. She tore the news item out of page five, leaving the rest of the paper for the table's next occupant. Then she left the coffee shop and wandered through the enormous lobby.

What next? What next?

Call the police again, of course. She had to return to her room and try calling the police again.

Karen collapsed into a Barcelona chair along one wall. Yes, yes, she should call the police again. But what would happen if she *didn't*?

Maybe I should just keep quiet. If I come forward, the police will easily solve the mystery of the unidentified accident victim. They'll discover that K.B. was the woman they found lying on a North Side street.

But who really needs to know? K.B. had no parents, no siblings, to wonder about her whereabouts, to notify the police that she was missing.

Do I really want to get involved? Do I really want to be a witness to a homicide, maybe have to stay in Chicago while I make a statement? Maybe even have to return for a trial?

If I don't come forward, I won't get embroiled in all of that. I can leave Chicago free and clear. No one would ever know.

Karen wasn't sure what course to take. Her head had started pounding again, and she wasn't sure of anything anymore.

Suddenly Karen remembered she had the key to K.B.'s room. If she saw K.B.'s bed, K.B.'s things, maybe she could sort everything out. She jumped out of the Barcelona chair and headed for the elevators.

Waiting for an elevator, Karen searched K.B.'s bag for the two room keys. Two almost identical plastic cards. She'd used one of them to get into her own room. The other one was K.B.'s, sure, but it gave no indication of K.B.'s room number.

How could Karen learn the room number? A security-obsessed front desk would never tell her.

Suddenly she remembered calling K.B.'s room the night before. Calling to suggest they leave for the restaurant a few minutes early. She had jotted down K.B.'s room number, hadn't she?

Karen took the elevator to the sixth floor and hurried back to her room. Look, there, beside the telephone, on that pad! She rushed over to look at it.

"1841" was scribbled on the pad. That's it, Karen thought. 1841.

Karen took an elevator to 18, found room 1841, then held her breath while she used one of the room keys. It didn't work. She tried the other one. It worked.

She cautiously pushed the door open. The room was dark. Karen flipped the light switch and walked in.

A large shabby-looking suitcase sat on a table near the bed. Karen opened it. Unlike Karen's suitcase, packed for a short weekend, it held a large quantity of clothes, enough to last a couple of weeks.

Two smaller cases stood on the floor of the closet. Karen pulled them out and quickly looked through them. Toiletries, books, a hair dryer, an electric shaver. K.B. had packed all her worldly goods for her move to Walden, Wisconsin.

Karen suddenly felt a chill and shuddered involuntarily. It was macabre, being in a dead woman's room, looking through a dead woman's things. She fled K.B.'s room and headed back to her own.

Her head was throbbing when she arrived at room 612. Uneasy, uncertain, she began to pace back and forth in the room.

Jason's chin resurfaced in her brain. The thought of seeing him again, living with him again, was repellent. She couldn't, wouldn't go back to Jason.

She wouldn't go back to that apartment either, with or without Jason. Too many bad memories.

And how in God's name could she go back to Garrity & Costello? Jason and Joan would be an item by now. A hot item. Everyone at the firm would know that Jason had dumped her, discarded her in favor of the tall, blonde, lovely Joan.

She couldn't go back there and face them. Face the smirking visages she would have to face. She couldn't do it. Not now. Not for a while.

But could she do *this*? This...whatever it was she was thinking about. Could she really do it?

Karen walked into the bathroom and looked at herself in the mirror. Karen B. Clark, what are you thinking?

She stared at her reflection. What *am* I thinking? Am I really thinking of becoming K.B.? Jettisoning my lousy life in New York and starting a new one somewhere else?

Come on, Karen! You can't be serious!

Well, why not?

Give up everything you've worked for? A great job, a great apartment, a guy you could probably get back if you really wanted to? *You can't just throw it all away.*

But wait a minute, Karen thought. I don't have to throw it all away. Not yet. That associate at the firm, Liz Casanis–she took a medical leave last year after an appendectomy that went terribly wrong. I could do the same thing. I could go on medical leave. That way I wouldn't have to cut all my ties to Garrity & Costello, to my life in New York. Not yet.

If I took a medical leave, I could bend the ties, not cut them. Bend them just long enough to try life in Walden, Wisconsin. Try it–and go running back to New York as soon as things turn sour.

K.B. had viewed life in Walden as idyllic. Hell, even the name of the place was idyllic. Walden. As in Walden Pond. Karen always *had* liked Thoreau.

Why not thoreau my old life aside for a while? she thought, smiling wryly at her own joke. Why not show up in Walden as Karen B. Clark? I *am* Karen B. Clark.

I don't have to tell anyone I'm a different Karen B. Clark. What difference would it make to them anyway?

I'm a lawyer, just like K.B. I've got three years of experience working as a lawyer that K.B. didn't have. Fuller, Fuller & Chase will be getting *more* for their money, not less.

Karen grabbed K.B.'s handbag and opened it. She found the envelope from the law firm, ripped it open, and pulled out the letter.

"Welcome to our firm," it said. "Mrs. Belinda Binnington, secretary to Mr. Charles W. Fuller, Sr., will meet you at the bus stop on Sunday evening, August 15th. She will help you get settled in Walden. We look forward to your beginning work on Monday, August 16th." The letter was signed, "Charles W. (Chad) Fuller, Jr."

Chad. Karen's heart skipped a beat. She'd had a law school classmate named Chad. Bright, good-looking, sexy. She'd had an enormous crush on him.

Chad. She realized that she was influenced by the name, she admitted it to herself, and she took it as an omen. She was meant to go to Walden, Wisconsin. To meet Chad and the other members of the firm of Fuller, Fuller & Chase.

Karen got up and paced some more. *Am I crazy? Probably. Maybe it's this pounding in my head that's keeping me from thinking clearly.*

But why not do it? *Why not?*

I'll try it for a week. Or a month. Try living a different life, a life without Jason, a life without Garrity & Costello. The life K.B. had mapped out for herself.

Karen called the front desk and asked them to prepare the bills for both Karen B. Clarks. Her friend, the other Karen Clark, had been called home to deal with an emergency. "I'll be paying for both rooms," Karen said. "And I'll need some help with all of our bags."

The man at the desk didn't question her statement. Thirty minutes later Karen walked through the hotel's doors and hailed a cab to the bus station.

Karen B. Clark was dead. Long live Karen B. Clark.

CHAPTER EIGHT

The bus to Walden left the sterile bus terminal south of the Loop late Sunday afternoon. Karen managed to get a choice window seat, hoping to get the best possible view from the vehicle's elevated seats.

Back on a bus, she thought. At least the air-conditioning works on this one.

Was it only two days ago that I sat on a bus like this? Agitated over my fight with Jason, worrying where I stood with him.

This time, instead of obsessing about Jason, focusing on what's already happened, I'm looking ahead, looking forward.

Looking forward to what? Karen had to admit she wasn't sure what she was looking forward to. The idyllic life in Wisconsin she'd pictured while she paced around her hotel room? Or a boring existence in some godforsaken town where she knew no one and had no idea what to expect?

Gazing out the window, high above the traffic, Karen was surrounded by cars and trucks much like the ones she'd noticed on Friday afternoon. But now the tumult on the expressways seemed distant, remote, as though some sort of shield surrounded the bus, protecting it from the noise and fumes the other vehicles were generating. Maybe this feeling is another omen, she thought. An omen of a fresh new start in Walden.

As the bus traveled north, the landscape began to change. First, the urban congestion vanished, and neatly manicured suburban lawns arose alongside the highway. Then less populated wooded areas began to appear. After a brief stopover in Milwaukee, the bus made more frequent stops, at towns that seemed to get smaller and smaller. Karen checked the bus schedule she'd picked up in Chicago: she was due to arrive in Walden at 9:25 p.m.

Now the bus was cutting a swath through genuine countryside. It whizzed by some dairy farms, where black-and-white cows grazed placidly near the road. Karen smiled, thinking how the word "grazing" had come to have a very different meaning in sophisticated New York circles. Here was grazing in the original sense of the word.

Karen closed her eyes for a few minutes. She felt excited, apprehensive, but the motion of the bus was soporific. Her headache had subsided, and she suddenly realized how tired she was.

Maybe I can catch a few winks....

"Miss, miss...." Someone was jostling her arm. Karen awoke from a deep sleep, unsure where she was. She looked up to see a concerned young man's face with a Greyhound cap above it. "Miss, we're in Walden. Didn't you give me a ticket for Walden?"

Karen looked around. Only two other passengers remained on the bus. The summer sky had turned dark, and a few bright lights twinkled outside the bus's windows.

"Oh, I'm sorry," she said. "I must have fallen asleep."

"You have to leave the bus now, miss, or I'll get behind schedule."

Karen quickly climbed out of her seat. Feeling shaky, she nearly tripped down the stairs of the bus. The driver's hand caught her just in time. He looked annoyed and hurried over to remove her suitcases from the belly of the bus.

They had stopped at the fringes of a district harboring a few small shops and offices. The downtown district of a small town. An old-fashioned lamppost shone a circle of light around the bus stop. Karen squinted in the bright light and tried to make out the names of some of the shops.

Suddenly she heard brisk footsteps on the pavement. A tall, solidly-built woman was striding toward her. The woman cocked her head and scrutinized Karen. "Ms. Clark?" she asked.

"Yes, I'm Karen Clark," Karen answered. I am, she thought. I really am.

The woman smiled and put out her hand. "I'm Belinda Binnington. Happy to meet you, Karen. Welcome to Walden." The skin crinkled around her eyes and mouth when she smiled, and Karen guessed that Belinda was in her 40s, maybe even her 50s.

Belinda's handshake was vigorous."Thanks for coming to meet me," Karen said.

"Well, Mr. Fuller thought it would be a good idea. So you would have someone here to greet you. It's hard to start out in a town when you don't know anyone, isn't it?" Belinda grabbed two of Karen's larger cases, and Karen picked up the rest.

"I guess so," she said.

Belinda began walking in the direction of a not-very-new station wagon. "Well, here's my car," she said. "Hop in."

"Where are we going?" Karen asked, stashing her bags in the back, then sliding into the front seat next to Belinda.

"I've rented a small house for you, a little ways out of town. There wasn't a thing available in town right now. But Walden's so small, you're only ten minutes from the office by car. Will you have a car?"

"No," Karen said. Oh my God, she thought. I'm so used to being car-less in New York, I totally forgot I might need a car in a town like this.

Belinda seemed to be reading her thoughts. "Well, you won't need one right away. You can walk into town in about twenty, thirty minutes. It's that close."

Karen breathed easier. She didn't want to face the complications of getting a car. Not just now. Maybe after she settled in, after she saw a bit of life in Walden, after she decided to stay. Maybe then she'd get a car.

Besides, she liked to jog. What better place to jog than down a country road? The fresh air, the leafy trees, the roads free of heavy traffic. Perfect. I can jog to the office and change there, she thought. It would be a damn sight better than taking the subway to work every morning, then jogging at night in Central Park.

Belinda's car left the center of town and headed into the countryside. It was too dark by now to see very much. Karen noticed one ugly yellow sign at a lighted crossroads. Bold black lettering spelled out:

Every Wednesday
Chicken Fry
All You Can Eat $5.75

A big black arrow pointed to a small one-story restaurant. The parking lot was full, and Karen could see groups of five or six people ambling near the cars. My future clients, she thought. Maybe.

Five minutes later Belinda pulled into a driveway next to a small frame house. Even in the darkness, Karen could see that the paint on the outside walls had begun to peel. "This is it," Belinda said. She and Karen went around to the back of the car, grabbed the suitcases, and walked up the short walkway to the house. Belinda rummaged in her purse until she found a housekey. Then she climbed the three wooden steps to the large front porch, crossed the porch, and turned the key in the lock. Karen followed her inside.

"Here's the key, before I leave and forget to give it to you," Belinda said, smiling. Karen took the key and stashed it inside the new shoulder bag she'd bought at the bus station in Chicago. Tacky white vinyl, but it would have to do till she could shop for a new one. She had put everything from her old shoulder bag inside it, along with everything she'd found in K.B.'s handbag.

Karen looked around. They were standing in a small foyer just inside the front door. A stale smell pervaded the house, as though the windows had been shut for a long time. Belinda began walking through the house, turning on some lights as she went. "This is the living room," she said, entering a medium-sized room in the front of the house.

Karen followed. A shabby old sofa and two threadbare chairs framed the front window. A walnut coffee table marked with water rings and cigarette burns sat between the sofa and chairs.

Again Belinda read Karen's mind. "The furniture's not much, but it comes with the house, so you don't have to bother shopping right away. And the price is right: $300 a month."

Karen's mouth fell open. $300 a month for a house? A furnished house? She and Jason had been paying $1400 a month for a cramped one-bedroom apartment in New York. Even her student apartment in Cambridge, a run-down studio over a bagel bakery, had cost more than $300 a month.

Something was wrong. There had to be something wrong with the house. Someone had died here, right? Maybe been murdered. That was the only explanation.

"You look surprised," Belinda said. "Does that seem too high for this house?"

"High?" Karen was astounded. Did Belinda really think she found the price too high?

"It's a pretty good deal, considering all the room you have here. Plus the garden in the back and the garage. I don't think you'll be sorry."

Karen realized that Belinda wasn't kidding. The older woman was concerned that Karen was unhappy with the house she had found for her. Karen rushed to reassure her. "Oh, no, I don't think the price is too high. Not at all. In fact, it seems too low to me. I'm used to such high rents in New York, this is a real bargain!"

"New York?" Belinda looked puzzled. "Are you from New York? I thought you just finished up at Harvard."

Karen's heart started pounding. *Tripped up. Already.* "You're right, I did!"

"Then you're from New York originally?"

Quick, where did K.B. say she was from? Karen's mind raced, going over everything K.B. had said, but she couldn't remember. Still, she was certain K.B. had never mentioned living in New York. "No, no, I'm not from New York."

Hurry, say something else. Don't give Belinda a chance to ask where you *are* from. Not till you have time to think about it. "It's just that some of my friends at school were New Yorkers, and they talked about the rents there, and I just...."

"Oh, I've read about those rents in New York!" Belinda said, nodding. Thank God she had shifted neatly onto that track. "They really are something, aren't they? Well, Walden sure isn't New York. We're not even like Milwaukee or Madison," she went on. "Walden's a real small town. None of those high rents and none of the crime you have in the cities today. It's a real nice life here." Belinda smiled again. "I just hope you won't get bored here. A lot of our young people leave, you know. They find there's not much to do here at night. Or weekends."

Karen nodded. "I know. But I think I'll like it here. In fact, I expect to like it very much." She gave Belinda a reassuring smile.

"Good. Now let's look at the rest of the house."

Belinda ushered Karen through the other rooms: a remarkably out-of-date kitchen and a small dining room downstairs, two tiny bedrooms and a bathroom upstairs.

"It's just fine," Karen said as they walked back downstairs. She did feel absurdly happy in the house. It was more room than she'd ever had completely to herself. Her family's house in New Jersey, her student apartments, the apartment she shared with Jason–none of them had offered her the combination of space and privacy this house did. The shabby furniture and the stale smell, those things didn't matter. Life in Walden was already as good as she had hoped. Maybe better.

"If you have any problems here," Belinda was saying, "you can call the real estate people. Andrews Realty in town. Ask for Betty."

"Oh, I'm sure I won't have any problems," Karen responded. "The house is terrific, really."

"Well, goodbye now, dear," Belinda said, walking to the front door with Karen. "I'll see you in the morning. I'll pick you up at eight o'clock and take you out for breakfast before we go to the office. How does that sound?"

"Oh, I don't want you to bother. I'll...."

"It's no bother, dear. I know you haven't had a chance to get any groceries. I bought you a few things, just some bread and milk, and left them in the kitchen, but you should have a proper breakfast tomorrow." Belinda stopped talking and peered at Karen. "Maybe you'd like to have something to eat right now. I'll bet you're hungry after your trip."

"I'm just tired right now," Karen said quickly, eager for Belinda to leave. All Karen wanted to do now was to collapse in bed. "I think I'll go to bed right away. I'm exhausted."

Belinda squinted, looking carefully at Karen. "Yes, I can see that. Well, have a good night's sleep. I'll be back at eight tomorrow." She paused for a second. "I wrote my phone number down in the kitchen if you need to reach me. Don't hesitate to call."

"Okay. Thanks for everything. I'll see you in the morning."

Karen locked the door behind Belinda. Then she slowly climbed the stairs to one of the tiny bedrooms, threw herself onto the bed, and promptly fell asleep.

CHAPTER NINE

Karen awoke at about six o'clock the next morning, totally disoriented, her head throbbing. She was still dressed in the summer dress she'd put on Sunday morning in Chicago.

Chicago. It seemed like years ago and a million miles away.

The dress was damp and sticking to her body. Karen shed it quickly and headed for the tiny bathroom. Its walls were an ugly mustard yellow, and the paint above the bathtub was peeling badly. A few thin towels hung on a cheap towel rack on one of the mustard-yellow walls. The tub itself was an old-fashioned type, complete with feet, and the porcelain was worn, but luckily it was equipped with a showerhead and a shower curtain. Karen nervously turned on the hot-water tap, not sure what to expect. There was a loud sputter, then rust-colored water burst from the showerhead. Finally the water turned clear, and Karen stepped into the tub.

Karen felt better the moment the water hit her body. The hot water loosened her muscles, and she began to think about the day that stretched ahead of her.

Was she really in Walden, Wisconsin? The reality of the impulsive decision she'd made in Chicago began to sink in. She couldn't quite believe she'd done it. Really done it. Left New York for a weekend, then gone and transported herself to a small town in the Midwest. A small town where she knew no one, where she was about to begin work at a law firm she knew nothing about. What was she thinking when she left the hotel and boarded that bus?

I must have been bonkers after that fall I took—in some kind of daze, stunned and confused. Maybe that blow to my head was more serious than I thought.

Then thoughts of Jason filtered into her brain. Jason, Garrity & Costello, everything about her wretched life in New York.

Okay, okay, maybe I was half-rational when I did it. Maybe I wasn't completely Looney Tunes. I had my reasons.

Karen stepped out of the tub, wrapped her body in a towel, and looked at herself in the small mirror on the medicine cabinet. *Well, I'm here now, and I might as well make the best of it.* I have a job to go to and people to meet. And if I don't like it, I can always leave.

Karen immediately confronted her first challenge of the day—what to wear. She had worn, and sweated in, all the clothes she'd brought to Chicago. Maybe, if it still looked decent, she could wear her favorite summer suit again. Otherwise she'd have to begin sorting through K.B.'s clothes and hope that something fit.

Karen wandered back to the bedroom, looking for the suitcases, finally remembering that she had left them downstairs the night before. Still clad in a skimpy towel, Karen descended to the first floor and began dragging the cases upstairs.

On her second trip, she thought she heard a noise outside. She stopped for a moment at the bottom of the stairs, certain she had heard something in the bushes just outside the kitchen window. But it was perfectly silent now. If anything had been there, it was gone.

Karen returned to the bedroom and began looking through the cases. Her summer suit looked okay. A bit wrinkled, but it would do. All her other clothes looked dirty and rumpled. They needed washing or cleaning before she could wear them again. Where? How?

Sighing, Karen turned to K.B.'s suitcases. In the large one, she found a few well-worn clothes that just might fit. She selected a white short-sleeved blouse and tried it on.

In the spotted mirror above the old mahogany dresser, Karen could see inches of extra fabric billowing around her body.

She smiled. Too-big clothes were much better than too-small. If K.B.'s clothes had been too small, they'd have been worthless. Thank God law students made a habit of snacking on sugary, fat-laden foods when they crammed for finals, she thought. The happy result was that K.B.'s clothes were ample, big enough for Karen to wear. Still, if she stayed here more than a few days, she'd have to get to a store and buy a few new things.

What about her clothes in New York? The Anne Klein suits, the Liz Claiborne dresses. Should she, could she contact Jason? Ask him to send her things to Walden? Karen was reluctant to talk to him again anytime soon. She could and would put off that decision.

Dressed for the office in her wrinkled suit and K.B.'s blouse, Karen went downstairs. She suddenly realized how hungry she was; she hadn't eaten since a yogurt shake she bought in the bus terminal yesterday afternoon. Would the kitchen have anything to eat or drink?

True to her word, Belinda had brought over some groceries the day before, and Karen set to work immediately. In the creaky wooden cabinets, she found a few battered pots and pans, along with some Wal-Mart-quality dishes, glasses, and flatware. A shiny chrome toaster sat on the chipped formica counter. It looked at least forty years old.

Probably weighs a ton, Karen thought. And it's probably worth a pile of money in some pretentious Manhattan antiques shop.

Karen made instant coffee and a slice of toast, smeared some strawberry jelly on the toast, and sat down to eat. The kitchen table and chairs—a dinette set circa 1950—had seen better days, but they were sturdy and clean, and she found herself beginning to relax.

Well, I did it. I'm here. I'm in Walden, Wisconsin. In a house. My house. I've escaped from New York.

A movie title flashed through her mind: "Escape from New York." Not to mention Garrity & Costello. And Jason.

A car horn sounded. Karen ran to the living room window and peered outside. Belinda's station wagon loomed in the driveway. Karen grabbed her white vinyl shoulder bag and ran outside, eager to begin her new life.

CHAPTER TEN

Belinda drove into town, taking the same route she'd taken the night before. This time, in the daylight, Karen could see much more than the all-you-can-eat chicken-fry restaurant. Two small farms and some thickly wooded areas filled the space between her house and the first scattering of houses at the edge of town.

A hand-painted sign in front of one of the farms advertised:

FOR SALE
DRESSED RABBITS

Karen immediately had a mental picture of fluffy rabbits decked out in cute little outfits like Peter Rabbit's. On reflection, she realized what the sign meant: the rabbits had been butchered. The notion that someone had killed a bunch of helpless rabbits disturbed her. Did people around here really kill rabbits and eat them?

Belinda's car whizzed past the city limits sign, and Karen began to get a look at the town of Walden itself. It was dominated by modest one- and two-story houses, some brick, some stucco, but most with the kind of wood siding she had noticed on her own house. The color-of-the-month was apparently light gray, although a few other colors popped up here and there.

Why this love of light gray, Karen wondered. In the leafy green of mid-August, gray was harmless enough. But during a dreary January, what could be more depressing?

The car approached the center of Walden, and Karen noticed a feed store and a Tastee Freez across from a small official-looking brick building. An American flag was flying on a pole stuck in the patch of lawn in front of the building.

"That's our city hall," Belinda was saying. "And that's where the firm's office is," she added, pointing to a two-story office building on the corner of the next block. "Charlie–Mr. Fuller–he's had his office in that spot for the past 35 years. Ever since he finished law school at Madison and came back to Walden to practice."

"I see," Karen said. That would make Charlie Fuller about 59 or 60. And that would make Chad Fuller what? Anywhere from 25 to 40. Belinda would know. "How long has Chad Fuller been with the firm?"

"Oh, let me see. Chad must have joined the firm about five or six years ago. He's 32 now, I think."

"Did he join the firm right after law school, too?"

Belinda paused. "Hmm, let's see," she said. "No, he worked in Milwaukee for a year or so before he came back here. I thought he might come back with a wife, but he didn't. He's still single."

Hmmm, Karen thought. Still single. "What about Chad's mother? Does she work in town, too?"

"Oh, no," Belinda said. "Charlie's wife passed away years ago. He's never remarried." Belinda pulled up in front of a group of stores. "Let's go get some breakfast. You must be starved."

Karen emerged from the station wagon and followed Belinda down the street to a storefront restaurant. The neatly-lettered sign outside said "Walden Cafe." Once inside, the women were shown to a red phony-leather-covered booth. Karen confessed that she'd already eaten, but Belinda insisted that she get some "real breakfast" now. They ordered bacon and eggs from a friendly waitress and sat back to wait for their food.

"This is the best place to eat in Walden," Belinda said. "Except for Hutter's. That's a lot fancier, though. Tablecloths and dark lighting. But this is it otherwise. Outside town, there's a couple of other places. But don't try Josie's Place down the street. Poisonous."

Belinda grinned, crinkling the skin around her deep-set brown eyes and wide mouth.

Karen forced herself to smile back, but she was inwardly dismayed to hear Belinda's run-down of the restaurants in Walden. After New York and the Hamptons, even Cambridge, the offerings in Walden were mighty slim.

Can I survive here?

Of course you can, Karen, she assured herself. You wanted to get away from all that, remember? Along with the great restaurants, you've got the repellent subway, the street crime, the miserably dull work at the firm. Have you forgotten?

"So, Karen, tell me something about yourself." Karen cleared her head. What did this woman want to know? "I've seen your résumé, of course, and your transcript from Harvard. You're some smart lady," Belinda smiled. "But what about your hometown, your folks, that kind of thing? And why did you pick Walden?"

Karen's heart began to pound again, the way it had the night before, when Belinda asked about New York. A dozen questions roared through her brain.

What did K.B. tell me about her hometown? I can't remember! How much does Belinda know already? How much will I have to fabricate to create a persona I know almost nothing about?

Just then the waitress arrived with their food, and Karen had a minute to pull herself together. She thought quickly. Maybe all Belinda knew was what K.B. had put on her résumé. That and her law school transcript. Okay. Karen remembered a little: K.B. had gone to college somewhere in the Midwest, in Ohio. She'd mentioned the name. Which one was it? Karen searched the recesses of her mind. Was it Antioch? Miami? No, no, it was Oberlin. K.B. had definitely said Oberlin.

Then what? She had worked somewhere for a law firm. Some city in Ohio. Columbus or Cincinnati or...was it Cleveland? Damn, all those cities in Ohio started with "C," and they were all interchangeable as far as Karen was concerned. She couldn't remember which one it was.

"So, Karen, tell me...."

Afraid that Belinda would begin probing again, Karen interrupted. "Well, I really loved Oberlin, you know. I hated to graduate, especially since I wasn't sure what I wanted to do after college."

"That's when you went to work in Cleveland, wasn't it?"

Cleveland! That was it. Karen nodded, smiling. Belinda would never know how much distress she had just spared Karen. "That's right."

"Did you like Cleveland? You hear so many jokes about it, you know." Belinda's brown eyes looked down at her food as she talked. Her hair was blond-going-gray, brushed back from her face in a simple easy-to-care-for style.

"Oh, I know. I've heard those jokes." Karen tried to remember one of them. Finally, it surfaced. "'The mistake on the lake!'" she said. Belinda laughed, crinkling her skin once again. "But it was really a pretty good place to live," Karen added, not knowing whether it was or not.

"And then you went to Harvard? You must be pretty smart, to go to Harvard. What's it like?"

At last Karen felt comfortable with one of Belinda's questions. She plunged into a discussion of Harvard Law School, its good points and bad, then began to describe life in Cambridge. In the middle of a description of Harvard Square street entertainers, Belinda looked at her watch. Then she looked up and broke into Karen's nervous chatter.

"Karen, it's almost nine o'clock. We really have to be getting to work. Mr. Fuller will be looking for me. You, too, I imagine." Belinda grabbed the check before Karen could, and walked over to the cashier to pay it.

Karen took a deep breath. This is it, she thought. The moment of truth. My first morning at Fuller, Fuller & Chase as the other Karen B. Clark. Suddenly she felt a enormous wave of nausea engulf her. She stood up and frantically looked around for a women's room.

The waitress noticed Karen looking pale and shaky, and guided her to a door marked "Washroom." "This is it, dear," she said kindly. "It's the only one we've got."

Karen pushed the door open and rushed to the toilet, lifting the seat just in time. The bacon and eggs, the toast and strawberry jam, the entire contents of her stomach rose inside her and hurtled into the toilet bowl. She felt wretched, her stomach emptying into a not-quite-clean toilet bowl in the stifling cramped washroom.

Her stomach finally empty, Karen felt a little better. She sponged off her face with a batch of wet toilet paper and rinsed her mouth in the rust-stained sink. Then she lowered the toilet seat and sat down for a moment, waiting till she felt less shaky, more in control.

What am I doing here? Am I crazy?

No, Karen, you're not crazy, she told herself. You made a wild, impulsive decision, and now you have to deal with it. But all you need to do right now is get through one day. Just one day. Then we'll see what happens next.

I can do that. I can get through one day here. I got through three miserable years at Garrity & Costello, I can get through one day here.

Finally she felt strong enough to leave the washroom. She opened the door, looking for Belinda. The older woman was waiting near the cafe's entrance. "Are you okay, Karen?" she asked, looking concerned.

"Yes, yes, I'm fine," Karen assured her. Shakily, she followed Belinda out of the cafe, and together they walked to the office building on the corner.

Karen licked her lips and took another deep breath.

Fuller, Fuller & Chase, here I come.

CHAPTER ELEVEN

Karen approached the office building just behind Belinda. They pushed open the heavy wooden door and climbed the stairway to the second floor. The linoleum-covered stairs were well-worn, and Karen couldn't help comparing them to the elegant carpeted stairway connecting the 45th and 46th floors at Garrity & Costello.

The stairwell itself was utilitarian gray, with metal banisters and peeling paint. Was everything in Walden covered with peeling gray paint? It certainly seemed to be the hometown favorite.

As she approached the door to the law office, Karen felt herself trembling.

Don't worry. Piece of cake. Look, you've held your own in a demanding Wall Street law firm for three years. You can do the same thing here.

Still, her heart was pounding as Belinda unlocked the door, turned the tarnished brass doorknob, then held the door open for Karen.

"Anyone here?" Belinda shouted as they entered. She looked around the dark outer office, then turned to Karen. "Guess not. We must be the first ones here." Belinda walked through the small waiting area toward a large oak desk in a corner of the outer office. "Come on back," she said to Karen. "This is my desk. I'll just turn on the lights and show you around the office."

Karen threaded her way through the outer office as Belinda turned on the lights and the air conditioning. The lights revealed a pleasant-enough outer office, furnished with Belinda's desk, one other oak desk, and a wall of battered green metal file cabinets. In the waiting area, a small upholstered sofa and a few upright chairs surrounded a coffee table covered with old magazines. A couple of large color photographs of rural scenes hung, framed, on the waiting room's walls. It all struck Karen as both comfortable and appropriate for a small law firm in a small town.

The air in the office was stifling. Nothing unusual about that, either. Monday mornings in summer, offices were invariably hot until the air-conditioning got going. Except, of course, in well-appointed, centrally air-conditioned offices like Garrity & Costello, where the air temperature never varied.

Belinda took Karen's arm and began a tour of the office. "This is Mr. Fuller's office," she said, directing Karen to a large corner office. Nice furnishings, nice view of downtown Walden, such as it was. A few diplomas and a state bar license hung among some photographs on one of the walls. "Charles Fuller, Sr., that is. He's my boss. I do all his secretarial work." Karen nodded. "Charlie's head of the firm. But then I guess you know that already. He hired you, didn't he?"

Karen paused for a few seconds, thinking back to what K.B. had said. "Oh, yes," she answered finally. "Over the phone."

"That's right," Belinda said. "Over the phone." She paused. "So you haven't met him yet, is that right?"

"Right."

"Well, you'll meet him soon enough." Belinda looked at her watch.

Karen wanted to ask Belinda about Charlie, but she wasn't sure how the older woman would react. Would she think Karen rude, overly nosy? Karen hesitated, then plunged ahead. "What's he like?"

Belinda looked startled by the question, and Karen was sorry she had asked it. Then Belinda shrugged and began to speak. "Charlie? Oh, he's all right. Kind of old-fashioned. But he's basically all right. Been a widower for a long time. I've always thought he'd be better off if he remarried. Maybe relax a bit, you know?"

Karen nodded.

"Well, he should be here any minute. You'll see for yourself when he shows up." Belinda smiled. "You'll be meeting Harold, too."

"Harold?"

"Harold Chase. He's another partner in the firm," Belinda said, leading Karen down the hall to another office. "Here's his office." It resembled Charlie Fuller's, but it was smaller, and its view–of the rooftops of the stores across the street–was less expansive than the view the corner office provided. "He's been with the firm about... about twelve years. He practiced for a while somewhere else in Wisconsin. Burlington, I think. Then he decided to make a switch, and Charlie hired him."

Karen nodded, looking at her watch. 9:15. When would the lawyers finally show up? This place was certainly nothing like Garrity & Costello, where the hot dogs were in the office by seven a.m. Everyone seems to drift in here well after nine. I think I'm going to like being a small-town lawyer.

"Martha does Harold's typing," Belinda was saying. "Martha Morgan. She's on vacation this week. So's Chad. She does his work, too."

Karen was suddenly much more interested in what Belinda was saying. Nutty, to be curious about someone just because of his name.

"Chad takes a long vacation every summer," Belinda said. "Goes fishing up north. Martha takes off a week or so while he's gone, and I do Harold's work if he needs me."

Karen nodded again. Belinda walked her past another empty office. "This is your office. We'll come back to it in a minute.

I want you to see Chad's office first." Belinda led the way to another corner office. It was the same size as Charlie Fuller's but had an entirely different view. Through the windows, Karen could see farms stretching out in the distance. A lovely pastoral view for a lawyer's office, she thought. If my colleagues at Garrity & Costello could see me now....

"See," Belinda was saying, pointing to some photographs on a wall, "here's Chad with some of the fish he's caught." Karen came closer to the pictures, squinting to make out Chad's face in the photos. The pictures weren't large enough or clear enough to show his face very well, but Karen could tell that Chad, happily displaying some inordinately large fish, was tall, blond, and handsome. Karen was eager to get a better look at him. In person.

"When will Chad be back?"

"Umm, not till after Labor Day, I think. This is...let's see, the second week he's been gone. But we won't see him again till September. Look, Karen," Belinda said, pointing to some other photographs, "Chad took these pictures himself. He took the ones in the outer office, too."

Karen looked at the pictures. More rural scenery, nicely shot. Chad was apparently an avid amateur photographer, the sort who likes to enlarge and frame his favorite shots. The scenes he'd framed were quite good–leafy green shots, some with brilliant wildflowers, others featuring dilapidated farmhouses and equipment. "Does he take these around here?" she asked.

"Oh, yes, I think so. Pretty talented, don't you think?"

"Definitely," Karen said. She had to stifle a smile as she said it. Compared to the photographs she'd seen in art galleries in Manhattan, these pictures were nothing special. But she supposed they represented top-notch amateur photography in these parts.

"Now, on to your office," Belinda said, leading Karen back down the hall to the office they had passed on the way to Chad's. "Here it is."

Karen crossed the threshold into her new office. She felt suddenly nervous. So this was it. The office where I'll spend most of my waking hours for the next...what? Week? Six months? Twenty years?

The office was empty except for the ubiquitous oak desk, a worn wooden desk chair, some metal file cabinets, and a phone. The single window looked out on Main Street, and a framed photograph of a Victorian farmhouse hung on the wall opposite the desk. "That's one of Chad's pictures," Belinda said. "The walls just looked so bare, I thought I'd put up something. You don't have to leave it there if you don't want to."

"That's okay," Karen said, peering at the farmhouse scene. "I like it."

"Well, here's your desk. I cleaned out all the drawers last week. No one's used this office for a while, but there were the usual pens and pencils, stuff like that, in the drawers. I left most of the good stuff." She turned toward the file cabinets in the corner. "The file drawers are empty, too. You can start using them right away."

Karen nodded. She felt distracted, unable to concentrate on Belinda's chatter. This is my office, she kept thinking. Not the posh carpeted quarters I had at Garrity & Costello, with the latest telephone technology at my fingertips and an impressive law library down the hall. No glittering light fixtures, no Scandinavian teak desk and matching file cabinets. It's strictly bare bones now. Forget central air-conditioning. Forget the marbled women's washroom.

Farewell, sumptuous; hello, utilitarian.

Karen swallowed. Well, she'd made her choice. Now she would have to live with it.

But did she? She'd just left Garrity & Costello last week. All she had to do was phone her secretary this morning and say she was delayed in Chicago, she'd be back soon, in a few days, in a week, in a month. No problem. This firm, this town, maybe they weren't right for her. Maybe she belonged back in New York. All it would take is a short phone call....

"Karen?" Belinda was looking at Karen, a puzzled expression on her face. "Are you okay?"

Karen collected herself fast. "Sure, I'm fine. I was thinking about something else. Sorry."

"Good. Now, I really have to get to work. Charlie and Harold will be walking in any minute. Can I get anything for you? Supplies, files, anything?"

Karen shook her head. "Just show me the supply cabinet. I'll get everything myself. As for files.... I really don't know what to begin working on. Do you have anything for me?"

"Let's see," Belinda said, leaving Karen's office. She returned a minute later. "Here are some files Charlie left for you. Just some routine leases to look over, I think. He also left you this book about the law of trusts and estates in Wisconsin," she said, handing over a heavy book. "Look it over. I think he wants you to start writing some wills."

Great, Karen thought. Leases and wills. Almost as boring as corporate charters. "Thanks, Belinda," she said, seating herself at her desk. She began leafing through the book. Some of the topic headings looked fairly interesting.

Maybe working with clients on everyday problems, like store leases and wills, would be okay. At least she'd get to talk to real people, to human beings with real problems. Her client-contact at Garrity & Costello had been mainly with corporate executives, low-echelon ones at that.

This was something else again. A typical small-town practice with typical small-town clients who had typical small-town problems. It was possible, maybe even probable, that she could make a difference in their lives.

Working at Fuller, Fuller & Chase...maybe it would be all right. Karen sat back in her wooden desk chair and read some more, learning the ins and outs of the Wisconsin law of wills and, much to her surprise, liking it.

CHAPTER TWELVE

About 9:30, Belinda stuck her head into Karen's office. "Looks like it's just us chickens today, Karen," she said. "Charlie just called. He got an emergency call from Mrs. Baker, that's one of his clients, and he had to go out to her house for the day. And wouldn't you know it, Harold called, too. He's feeling sick today. Too many barbecued ribs at his cousin's house yesterday," Belinda chuckled.

Karen felt relieved. She wouldn't have to meet anyone else today. So much was happening already: new town, new home, new office. She didn't mind waiting to meet the members of her new firm. Even Chad. She nodded at Belinda and returned to her reading.

About 11:45, Belinda appeared again. "I'm going out for lunch now, Karen. You're welcome to join me, but I gotta warn you, I've gotta bunch of errands to run."

"Oh, that's okay," Karen said. "You run along. I'm not hungry." Karen welcomed the opportunity to be alone in the office for a while. She'd have a chance to poke around. And to call Melissa Cohen. She had to call someone in New York, and her secretary at Garrity & Costello was the least threatening person she could think of.

As soon as Belinda ducked out of the office, telling Karen she'd be back around one o'clock, Karen knew she had to call New York right away. Melissa usually took lunch at one o'clock New York time; she'd be leaving her desk any minute.

Karen picked up the phone, then hesitated. She couldn't dial direct; the call would show up on the firm's phone bill. She placed a collect call instead.

Melissa accepted the charges immediately. "Karen, where are you? Phil Hendrix has been looking for you all morning."

Karen pictured Melissa in her mind's eye. Curly red hair, impossible to control, an enormous barrette assigned to the hopeless task of restraining the curls. Melissa's plump figure, the bane of her existence, was probably stuffed into one of her bright-colored summer dresses, her chubby upper arms looking pink and freckled where they burst out of the sleeves.

"It's a long story, Melissa. I went to the NLA convention in Chicago Thursday after work, and...."

"Right. I got your message on my voicemail Friday morning. But I thought you'd be back today...."

"Well, I had an accident Saturday night." That much was true.

"An accident? Was it serious? Are you all right?" Melissa sounded genuinely concerned. A lot more concerned than Jason had been. "How did it happen?"

"I fell down and hit my head. Got knocked unconscious and wound up in a hospital overnight."

"Oh, my God...." Karen pictured Melissa's eyes opening wide, her bright curls struggling to escape the barrette.

"It wasn't that bad. They released me Sunday morning, and...."

"How do you feel? Are you okay?" Melissa interrupted.

Karen hesitated. She had to make this sound plausible. "I...I feel pretty good. But the doctors say I have to stay off my feet for a while. So I'm staying here in...in Chicago...for a while. . .at...at my cousin's house. Till I'm completely recovered," Karen improvised.

Belinda's mention of Harold Chase's cousin had come in handy. Karen hadn't prepared a story for Melissa and had to blurt out something. Now she realized she had to start planning what to say before she made any more phone calls like this one.

"Your cousin's house? You never told me you had a cousin in Chicago." Melissa sounded hurt that Karen hadn't disclosed the location of every member of Karen's family in the three years they had worked together.

"Well, I do, and I'll be staying here for a while."

"Okay. That sounds like the smart thing to do. I'll tell Mr. Hendrix and anyone else who asks."

Phil Hendrix, that pompous ass. I won't miss seeing him and his arrogant sneer for a while. For ever?

"Give me your phone number so I can let you know what's happening," Melissa was saying.

"Oh...." Karen paused. "I don't think I can do that."

"Why not?"

Karen's mind raced. What possible excuse could she give Melissa? "Uhh...my cousin has an unlisted number, and she made me swear not to give it out." Lame, lame.

"What? You can't even give it to *me*?" Melissa was incredulous.

"Well, I'll talk to her about it, Melissa. Maybe I can get her to change her mind. In the meantime, I'll call you every...oh, every few days, I guess. I'll keep in touch."

"Well..., okay. You're the boss. Remember to call me as often as you can. I'll probably have Hendrix on my neck till you get back."

"Sorry about that. I'll call when I can."

"Okay, Karen. Take care of yourself. And feel better!"

"Thanks." Karen hung up quickly, her hand shaking as she put down the receiver. She'd forgotten about Phil Hendrix and the two complicated projects he had foisted on her. Phil Hendrix–Garrity & Costello's "acquisition king"–had lassoed Karen into working on a complex multi-party joint venture and an only somewhat simpler single-party acquisition. She'd begun researching both projects, and all the talk of spin-offs and other dispositions of unwanted operations, along with structuring, financing, and refinancing, made Karen's head swim.

Well, the hell with Phil Hendrix and his mind-numbing projects. He could reassign them, get someone else to do the deadly research and write the elaborate memoranda he wanted. If everything went well in Walden, she'd tell Melissa she was never coming back.

Karen knew it wouldn't really matter if she didn't go back. She had no illusions about her status at the law firm. Garrity & Costello would never miss her, not after the first week or so. She was what the law calls "fungible goods," an interchangeable commodity, easily replaceable by a thousand other young New York lawyers. Any one of them could take over her work, and would, without missing more than a few beats.

Karen got up and began to wander around the office. Might as well take a look around, she thought. Especially while no one's here.

She felt drawn first to Charlie Fuller's office. Belinda was right. According to the diploma and law license hanging on the wall, he'd been admitted to the bar about 35 years earlier. That made him about 60. The photographs on the wall showed Charlie shaking hands with an array of overweight middle-aged-to-elderly white males. Local businessmen and lawyers, no doubt, maybe even political types. Small-town cronyism at its finest.

Well, nothing wrong with that, Karen. He brings in the clients that way. If he didn't, you wouldn't have a job.

Two jobs, she reminded herself, thinking of Melissa and Phil Hendrix back in New York. You're going to have to make a break with Garrity & Costello eventually. You can't keep two jobs like these for very long.

Or could she? Karen suddenly remembered her plan to ask for medical leave for an extended period. Six months or even a year.

It had gone right out of her head when she talked to Melissa. But at least she'd laid the foundation for it when she told Melissa about her accident. She'd mention the idea of medical leave next time she called.

Karen approached Harold Chase's office, peering into it briefly. Anything of interest in there? Doubtful. But Chad's office, that was another...kettle of fish? Karen laughed quietly at her own joke.

She walked past Harold's office and entered Chad's, wondering what to look at first. The desk? Nothing on the surface except the phone, a Rolodex, and a framed photograph of a pretty woman in a '60s-style minidress. Who was that? And when was it taken? Could have been anytime, she realized. Those minidresses were back in style. Otherwise, the desktop was bare. No doubt Chad had cleared it off before leaving on vacation.

Karen considered, then dismissed the idea of looking through the desk's drawers. Too great an intrusion into Chad's privacy. But the photographs on the walls were worth a second look. Karen stared at the photos of Chad and his catches-of-the-day. Yes, her first impression was confirmed. Chad was indeed a good-looking guy. His crooked smile was endearing, and even under a fisherman's cap, his tousled blond hair looked thick and finger-running good. Karen always had been a sucker for tall blonds.

Interesting. In some of the pictures Chad looked a bit heavier than he did in the others. Karen couldn't tell which ones were more recent. Had he recently lost his earlier chubbiness, or had he gained the weight in recent years? No way of knowing till she met him in the flesh. Firm *or* flabby. She could hardly wait.

Karen heard the outer door open and rushed back into the hallway, quickly walking the few steps to the outer office. "It's just me," Belinda called out. "Anything happen while I was gone?"

Karen shook her head as she approached Belinda. "No, nothing. Very quiet."

"Good. I was afraid something would happen and you wouldn't know what to do. But it's pretty quiet here in August. Especially at lunchtime."

Belinda and Karen both returned to their desks. Karen resumed reading about the law of wills and, by four o'clock, when Belinda suggested that they both go home, Karen was happy to leave the nearly-silent office.

Emerging together into the hot August afternoon, Belinda turned to Karen. "How about a ride to the grocery store? You can pick up whatever you need, and I'll drop you off at home."

"Oh, I can't let you do that," Karen said. "You've been so terrific to...."

"I have to get some groceries anyway. And the store is on the way to your place. Come on." Belinda pointed down the street to her station wagon. "Get in."

"Well, if you're sure you're going anyway...."

"I'm sure."

Karen climbed into the station wagon, grateful for Belinda's kindness. After a short drive, they arrived at Brennan's, a medium-sized supermarket at the edge of town. Karen and Belinda zipped through the aisles, paid the cashier, and were nearly out the door when Belinda stopped. "Karen, if you don't have a car, you ought to make some arrangement with Roy to have your groceries delivered."

"Roy?"

"Roy Brennan. He owns this place." Belinda let go of her shopping cart. "Wait here." She walked back towards the rear of the store and returned a moment later, accompanied by a tall, balding man with pock-marked skin. Lines creased his scarred forehead. "This is Roy. Roy, meet Karen Clark, a new member of our firm."

"Pleased to meet you, Karen," Roy smiled. "Belinda tells me you want to have your groceries delivered."

"Right," Karen said. "I don't have a car yet, and my house is... where exactly *is* my house, Belinda?"

"It's a couple miles down Route 195," Belinda explained. "The old Parker house."

"Oh, the Parker house. That's been vacant for a while, right?"

"You can deliver there, can't you?" Belinda asked.

"Oh, sure," Roy said. "Tim can drive out there anytime."

"Tim? That your son?" Belinda asked.

"Yeah. Tim's 17 now. Helps a lot around this place," Roy smiled. "He's here now." Roy turned and called out, "Tim? Tim?"

Karen turned, too, looking for Tim. A gangly young man was walking toward them through the cereal-and-juice aisle. He seemed awkward, ill at ease, his face covered with a bad case of adolescent acne.

"Hey, Tim," his father said. "You know Mrs. Binnington, don't you?"

Tim had a dim look on his face, looking from Karen to Belinda and back, unsure who it was his father meant.

"Hi, Tim," Belinda volunteered, breaking the awkward silence. "I think we've met before. A long time ago. I don't expect you to remember." She laughed gently to put the awkward boy at ease.

"Well, Tim, now I want you to meet this pretty young lady who's new in town," Roy said. "This is Miss...? What was your name again, Miss?"

"Clark. Karen Clark." Karen tried to smile at the boy, but his edginess made her nervous. All she could muster was a tight half-smile.

The boy's expression changed. He stuck out his hand in Karen's direction, a wide smile coming over his face. "Happy to meet you, Miss," he said, smiling broadly, nervously, his head bobbing up and down. Karen took his hand and shook it, feeling slightly uneasy. This awkward boy was too eager, too excited to meet her. His hand felt sweaty, and his head still bobbed, his eyes darting all over her body.

"You'll be able to take some groceries out to Miss Clark's place now and then, won't you, Tim?" Roy said. "She doesn't have a car, and we'll be making deliveries out there."

"I'll be glad to," Tim said, still smiling goofily at Karen. She withdrew her hand, now unpleasantly moist, and turned to Belinda.

"Well, we'd better be going. Thanks."

"Yes, we'll be going now," Belinda said. She pushed the grocery cart out the door and led Karen back to the station wagon. "That pathetic boy," she said, loading the groceries and climbing into the car. "He looks so...so...gawky, doesn't he? And that skin!"

"Yes," Karen agreed.

"He sure looked happy to meet you, though," Belinda laughed. "Probably all the girls around here have rejected him. You're someone new, and he's got his hopes up again." Her laugh tinkled through the car.

"I guess so. But don't you think I'm a little old for him?" Karen said, trying to make her voice light. She felt unaccountably disturbed by her meeting with the awkward teenage boy.

"Well, *I* think so. The question is, does *he*?" Belinda laughed again.

Karen changed the subject. "Are we on Route 195 now?" she asked, looking carefully at the road and its surroundings. They were passing the all-you-can-eat chicken restaurant.

"Right. This is the road you'll take to town and back. You can walk it in about twenty or thirty minutes, if you walk briskly. But if the weather gets bad, just give me a call and I'll pick you up."

"Isn't it out of your way? I wouldn't want you...."

"It's a bit out of my way, but don't worry about it. Until you get a car, I'll be happy to pick you up, because of the weather or whatever. Just give me a call."

Belinda pulled into the driveway of Karen's house, and Karen climbed out of the station wagon. "Thanks again for everything," Karen said.

"Don't mention it. I'll see you in the office tomorrow–about nine o'clock. Charlie and Harold should be there."

"Okay. See you then."

Taking her bag of groceries, Karen waved goodbye as Belinda drove off. She climbed the front steps, entered the house, put her groceries away, and sank into a threadbare chair.

Her first day in Walden had been...what?

Nice, Karen thought. Nice. And quiet.

Just the way she wanted it.

CHAPTER THIRTEEN

After a quick kitchen-table dinner of canned tuna on toast, followed by two late-summer peaches, Karen felt energetic enough to explore her new home. She would be living here, for a while at least. She needed to know exactly what the house contained and where everything was. For one thing, she was desperate to know whether the house had a washer and dryer, so she could start laundering the dirty clothes she had brought from Chicago.

Karen began her exploration in the kitchen. She had already inspected the tired-looking cabinets and appliances before leaving for work. But now Karen found a door she hadn't noticed before. It appeared to be the only door in the kitchen. Did it lead outside?

Cautiously, she opened it. It led to a basement, not outside.

Odd, no door going outside. Maybe someone had long ago boarded it up. But the idea of a basement was promising. Could there be laundry equipment down there?

Slowly Karen descended the stairs to a dark, damp basement. Sure enough, in a dim corner Karen spied an out-of-date Maytag washer and dryer, both decorated with myriad spider webs.

Karen took a closer look. Several spiders were happily crawling over their handiwork, coating smaller insects with their special substance, saving them for colder, hungrier days. Karen felt a sense of revulsion; insects always terrified her. She would have to screw up her courage and wipe the spiders away before she used the machines. But at least she now knew she could begin washing her dirty clothes.

Still, she would have to get some new things to wear. She couldn't get by much longer with the few garments she'd thrown into her suitcase in New York–even with K.B.'s well-worn items added to the bargain. Tomorrow she'd ask Belinda where she could shop for clothes. There had to be some stores in the area, maybe even a shopping mall, where working women bought appropriate clothing. Belinda would know.

Karen took a fast look around the rest of the basement. Except for the appliances, it was nearly empty. Creepy, too. Dark and quiet, with no one but the spiders to keep her company. I'll bet I could die down here, she thought, and no one would discover me for days. She shivered and turned to go back upstairs.

Karen was relieved to return to the kitchen, dumpy though it was, and set out to explore the rest of the house. She discovered a guest closet near the front door that she hadn't noticed before. It was empty except for an old vinyl poncho and some bent wire hangers. On the second floor, she discovered more empty closets and a door in the hallway that led upstairs to an attic.

Karen boldly walked up the dusty stairs to the attic. She couldn't put off this part of her search; she had to know what was above the bedroom where she slept every night. To her relief, the attic, like the basement, was almost completely empty.

A rickety pine bookcase stood in one corner, partially filled with some musty old books. Karen looked at the titles. Mostly classics, a few she had never read. Some reading for the next few months, she thought–if I'm still here.

She surveyed the rest of the furniture. A stuffed chair, covered in torn green velvet, was pushed up against the attic's single window, and a large mahogany chest of drawers stood against one wall. Karen approached the chest and looked through its drawers. Only one drawer, the bottom one, contained anything–several bunches of old letters, tied up in faded brown ribbons.

Karen pulled out a bunch of the letters and slid off the faded ribbon. They were addressed to Mr. Gerald Parker, to Mrs. Gerald Parker, or to both. Karen suddenly felt guilty, prying into other people's mail, and she stuffed the letters back inside the drawer, unopened. She remembered hearing Belinda tell Roy Brennan that this was "the old Parker house" and wondered briefly who the Parkers were and why they moved. The house had been vacant for a while, but there certainly didn't seem to be anything wrong with it.

Probably just a depressed housing market, she concluded. In New York, something like this would be snapped up in a minute. But this was Walden, Wisconsin, not New York.

Karen wandered back downstairs and out the front door. She walked all around the house, following the dusty dirt driveway along the side of the house toward the rear. The house looked pretty solid. Peeling gray paint, per usual. But everything else seemed in order. Some ropes hung down from the roof in the rear of the house. Probably used by some workmen, maybe roofers trying to patch up the roof last spring. She'd get the painters to take them down when–and if–she ever got around to painting the place.

Karen strolled over to the detached garage at the end of the driveway–a ramshackle one-car garage that, like the house, badly needed a coat of paint. Karen tried the garage door; it moved up easily. Inside she found a couple of battered old bikes and a bicycle tire pump, along with some rusty garden tools and a beat-up push lawnmower. Would she have to mow the lawn? She hoped not; just thinking about it made her muscles ache. Maybe she could hire a local teenager to do it.

As she turned to leave the garage, she had a sudden inspiration. The bicycles! They were a possible means of transportation. Thank God she knew how to ride a bike.

The tires on one of the bikes were completely flat, but those on the other looked okay, just a bit deflated. She tried the tire pump on the second bike. The tires inflated, and she jumped on the old bike and took it for a spin inside the garage.

It worked! Karen was delighted to have a form of transportation other than her feet. Now she could pedal down the highway to work and shopping. Maybe even bring home some groceries. That way she could avoid dealing with that creepy kid, Tim Brennan, any more than necessary.

Karen rode the bicycle out of the garage and down the driveway. Still okay. Karen felt a sense of triumph at her accomplishment: She had fixed the bike well enough to ride it anywhere she liked.

Feeling highly competent, Karen left the bike in the garage and went back inside the house. That little taste of exercise reminded her that she needed more, much more. After all, she was used to jogging in New York two or three times a week. She and Jason would jog together around the Upper East Side, often going into Central Park to jog on its paths through the only large expanse of greenery nearby.

Now she was surrounded by greenery, and she felt the urge to jog again. The stiffness from her fall had begun to subside, and riding the bike felt good. But Karen hadn't brought her running shoes to Chicago, and she didn't want to ask Jason to send them. She was still far from sure what she was going to do about her "stuff"—all the things she had left behind in their apartment. For now, she would simply buy some new shoes. Belinda would know where to get them.

Karen fixed herself a cup of herb tea and took it out onto the front porch. Two large wicker chairs, their white paint drifting off in dainty white flakes, faced the road, and Karen sank into one of them. Now she noticed the sun descending rapidly in the western sky.

She watched the bright coral-colored circle fall towards the earth, unobscured by anything in her view. Only the field across the road stood between her and the setting sun. Some sort of crop was planted in the field, but thankfully it wasn't tall enough to block her view of the coral-colored sun.

Karen watched the sun lower itself, then disappear, till the sky turned dark. She felt completely, unutterably tranquil. It was a feeling she hadn't known for as long as she could remember.

CHAPTER FOURTEEN

Tuesday morning dawned sunny and warm. With bright sunshine streaming into her small bedroom through thin muslin curtains, Karen stirred in her bed. She had hoped to awaken early, but without an alarm clock, she had no way to make sure that would happen.

No problem, she thought. I couldn't keep the sun out if I tried, not with such pathetically thin curtains. She stretched, trying to determine if everything felt okay. It did.

She glanced at her watch and smiled. 7:45. Enough time to ride her bicycle to town–or at least, to attempt to ride it there. She hoped the bike would make it all the way, but in case it didn't, she would need extra time to walk it into town from wherever it broke down. She showered and dressed in the seersucker suit again, this time with another one of K.B.'s billowing blouses. She gulped down breakfast, eager to get out and on the road. Today she would meet Charlie Fuller and Harold Chase, and she would probably need to freshen up at the office before they arrived.

Riding the bike down the highway felt strange at first, but Karen soon got used to it. Traffic was light, and after a while she stopped looking over her shoulder for passing cars and began to relax. As she rode along the wooded areas, tall trees shaded the road, and a breeze rippled through the trees. Karen felt tranquil, much the way she'd felt on her porch the night before.

She speeded up when she came alongside the neighboring farms, where the lack of shade made the sun feel hot on her back. As she pedaled the rickety bike, she surveyed the landscape, noticing an occasional piece of rusting farm equipment near the road. Soon the bike crossed the city limits. As the highway flowed into Main Street, Karen found herself riding into town.

Main Street was completely residential for several blocks, then it suddenly turned into a commercial street as it got closer to the center of town. Small shops and offices dotted the commercial area. Karen thought she saw a sign for Andrews Realty squeezed between a hardware store and a small pharmacy.

Approaching the corner where her office building stood, she alighted from the bike and walked it to the entrance. Now what? She pushed the bike through the doorway, maneuvered it through the small lobby, and parked it behind the staircase leading to the second floor. She would have to take her chances till she got a bike lock. If the bike was stolen in the meantime, so be it. Easy come, easy go.

Karen looked at her watch. 8:45. Quickly she ran up the stairs to the second-floor office, wondering whether Belinda would be there to let her in. She needed a few minutes in the women's room first. Karen ducked inside the women's room, just down the hallway from the law office, and took a quick look in the mirror. Fortunately, the bike ride hadn't done much damage. Karen washed her face and combed her hair, then walked back down the hallway to the office, feeling presentable enough to meet her new boss.

The door was unlocked, and Belinda was already seated behind her desk. "Good morning!" Belinda called out. "I just remembered, you need a key to the office in case you get here early. Or if you want to come in on a weekend." Karen nodded. "Here, take this one." Belinda handed Karen a large brass key, and Karen stashed it in her white vinyl bag.

"How's everything going?" Belinda asked. "How's the house working out?"

"The house is great," Karen answered. "I explored it last night. The garage, too. I found a bike in the garage, and I rode it to work this morning."

"You did?" Belinda looked impressed. "My, you're a resourceful young person," she said, smiling. "Now you won't need a car right away, will you?"

"Right," Karen said. Suddenly she thought of a question she had for Belinda. "Belinda, about the house. Yesterday I heard you say it had been vacant for...."

Just then the door opened, and a middle-aged man appeared. He was medium height, a bit overweight, with dark brown hair balding down the middle, wire-rimmed glasses, and a small brown mustache flecked with gray. Dressed in a heavy dark blue suit, complete with jacket, he looked hot, his face shining with sweat.

"Oh, Harold, I'm glad you're here. Feeling better?" Belinda asked. "I want you to meet Karen...."

"Yes, I feel better," the man responded, approaching Karen. His wire-rimmed glasses reflected light from the ceiling fixture, obscuring his pale gray eyes. "So you're Karen Clark, our Harvard grad," he said without smiling. He extended his hand toward Karen's. "Welcome to the firm. I'm Harold Chase."

His face was impassive. No smile, no warmth behind the welcoming words. Karen took his hand and shook it. "Happy to meet you, Mr. Chase."

His face remained expressionless. "I think you'll be working with Charlie Fuller for the most part. But if you get stuck with any of my cases and you run into any problems, just let me know."

"Thanks, I will."

Harold turned and walked into his office, closing the door behind him. Karen looked at Belinda.

Belinda read Karen's mind. "Don't worry about it. He's always like that. It's nothing personal. That's just Harold."

Somewhat shaken, Karen retreated to her own office. Harold's demeanor was troubling and unexpected. Weren't small-town lawyers supposed to be friendly, congenial glad-handers? Especially with their fellow lawyers? Harold was as taciturn and standoffish as any senior lawyer she'd met at Garrity & Costello, and in this small office in the small town of Walden, Wisconsin, his cold shoulder seemed particularly chilly.

Karen resumed reading about the law of wills, but she couldn't concentrate on it. Her mind was racing, questions bouncing back and forth inside her head.

Why did I come here? What am I doing in this town, in this firm, when the first lawyer I meet is as rude as anyone I've ever worked with in New York?

Then her rational self took over. Hold on, Karen, wait a minute. Don't jump to conclusions. You've spent exactly thirty seconds talking to this man. Maybe he's shy, a withdrawn personality, an introvert. Maybe he's really delightful once you get to know him, and you'll end up adoring him, clamoring to work with him, begging for the chance to assist him on his most difficult cases. Maybe....

Belinda popped her head into Karen's office. "Charlie just walked in. He wants to see you." Karen looked carefully at Belinda's face but couldn't decipher any special message on it.

"Thanks, Belinda." Karen walked slowly out of her office, taking a deep breath as she approached Charlie Fuller's corner office.

Don't panic. He's just another small-town lawyer. You've handled high-powered senior partners at Garrity & Costello. You can deal with Charlie Fuller.

Charlie Fuller was sitting behind his desk, leafing through some files, as Karen walked in. He looked up. His lined face looked every bit of his sixty years. Large, puffy pouches were visible under his small but very blue eyes, and a scar under his right eye descended down his cheek until it stopped abruptly near his mouth. He wore his surprisingly full head of white hair in a '50s-style crew cut.

"Sit down, sit down, Ms. Clark. Or may I call you Karen?" Charlie's brusque tone was tempered with a hint of humor, and the trace of a smile darted around his thin lips. Compared with Harold Chase, he was Mr. Warmth.

"Karen, please."

"All right, then, Karen it is. Well, Karen, welcome to Fuller, Fuller & Chase. I want to tell you a little bit about our firm. I know I spoke to you at length over the phone about your duties, but it won't hurt to go over them again briefly, will it?"

"No, not at all." Karen was relieved that Fuller chose to review what he had already told K.B. As she listened to his description of the firm and what would be expected of her, she was grateful that he was just anal enough to lay out exactly what she would be doing. Now she had a clear picture of her role at the firm, and she knew she could handle most of the work with little difficulty. Some of her duties would be new to her, things she'd never tackled before, but they would sooner or later include the kind of client-contact she'd always wanted, the kind she never got in New York.

"You're not worried about taking the bar exam, are you?" Fuller asked. The bar exam.... Karen hadn't even thought about that hurdle. Taking it in New York had been an exhausting ordeal. "You can take it the next time it's offered," Fuller said.

Karen relaxed. She could put off for a while the burden of taking the bar exam. Everything was going to work out just fine.

"Now, then, Karen, are you settled in that house Belinda found for you?"

"Oh, yes, Mr. Fuller. It's...."

"That's Charlie, Karen. I feel old when my colleagues call me 'Mr. Fuller,' and I don't like feeling old!" Charlie laughed heartily, and Karen felt compelled to join in. "Besides, Chad'll be back in a couple of weeks, and it gets too confusing around here when people start calling one of us 'Mr. Fuller.' I told you about Chad, didn't I?"

Karen wasn't sure how to respond. Had Charlie told K.B. about Chad? She hesitated, smiling. Fortunately, Charlie didn't wait for an answer.

"Yes, of course, I'm sure I told you about Chad. Well, he'll be back from his fishing trip in a couple of weeks, and you'll get a chance to get to know each other then. I always like to see Chad meet a lovely young girl like you," Charlie smiled.

What was Charlie hinting at? A possible liaison between Karen and Chad?

Well, why not? At sixty, he was probably eager to see his son married and producing grandchildren. Nothing strange about that. Karen was happy to confess, to herself if no one else, that she didn't need any prompting. She was as eager to meet Chad as Charlie was to have her meet him. No encouragement from Charlie was needed. None at all.

"Well, I've already missed a day in the office this week, going out to see Laverne Baker, so I've got to get to work. You have those files I left for you?" Charlie asked.

Karen nodded.

"Good. I'm sure we have more than enough work to keep you busy. A small town like Walden produces plenty of legal work, plenty to keep all of us lawyers in town busy." He looked out his large corner window for a moment, then back at Karen. "I know Harvard prepares its students for a big-city practice, but you won't regret coming to Walden. A couple of lawyers I know in Milwaukee tell me they'd change places with me in a minute."

Karen smiled, thinking of the hundreds of lawyers slaving away at Garrity & Costello at that very moment. She was certain that dozens of them would change places with her in a *second.*

"You don't believe me, do you?" Charlie had misinterpreted her smile and now appeared offended.

"Oh, no. I mean, yes, I do believe you. I'm sure at least half of my classmates would be happy to trade places with me," Karen hurried to assure Charlie. Or they will, she thought, after a few more years at the pressure-cooker law firms they've joined.

"Well, I'm certainly happy to hear that. I don't want you thinking you made a bad decision, coming here." Charlie rose from behind his desk and extended his hand. Karen shook it. "Now, let's get to work."

"Yes. Thanks,...Charlie," Karen said, turning to leave Charlie's office. She returned to her office, chiding herself for being so nervous about meeting Charlie. He really wasn't all that bad. A bit blustery and certainly sexist. But she'd worked with a lot of older male lawyers like him, and she knew she could deal with him well enough.

She gazed thoughtfully out her window at the shingled rooftops of Walden, Wisconsin. Life at Fuller, Fuller & Chase was going to be all right.

CHAPTER FIFTEEN

Just before noon, Karen left her desk and approached Belinda. "Where can I do a little shopping?" she asked.

"Shopping? What kind of shopping?"

"I need some new clothes," Karen said. "I didn't bring very much with me. I...I...didn't have a lot of clothes at school," she added quickly.

"Well, Karen, you asked the right person," Belinda answered, smiling broadly. "I'm what you call a shopaholic. I know every store between here and Madison, and I think I know just the place you're looking for. Why don't we hop in my car and go to the Windscape Mall? There's a couple of good shops there."

The two women left the office and headed to a small shopping mall on Highway 195 about fifteen miles outside Walden. While Belinda browsed, Karen dashed through the stores, finding a bike lock and alarm clock at one place and some running shoes at another. Twenty minutes in a large clothing store called Patricia's was long enough for Karen to find appropriate clothes for work: a couple of neat blazers and skirts, a few tailored blouses, a pair of low-heeled pumps, pantyhose, a new leather shoulder bag to replace the tacky white vinyl one. Adding some casual pants, shorts, and tops to the pile, she finally felt comfortable about her wardrobe. Now she'd have enough for the next few weeks, or even months.

When the cashier totaled up her purchases, Karen pulled out her wallet, then realized that her cash was running out. She would have to use a credit card. Karen's wallet was filled with credit cards, but there was an obvious problem: the bills for all of them went to her New York address.

Karen felt panicky. The bored cashier was staring at her. An overweight teenager with greasy-looking hair, the cashier twice repeated the mantra of bored cashiers everywhere: "Cash, check, or credit card?"

Karen reached for a card, then hesitated. Maybe it was better not to let anyone know where she was–not even an impersonal credit card company. Karen had seen enough movies and TV dramas to know that the police and private detectives can track missing people by using the trail of credit card receipts they leave in their wake. The fewer people who knew where she was, the better. Besides, if the bills went to New York, they'd just go to the apartment...and Jason.

But how could she pay for everything?

Suddenly Karen had a flash. "Does this store have its own charge accounts?" she asked. The cashier nodded. Karen smiled. "I'd like to open one. Can you do it right away?"

"Sure," the cashier said. "Just fill out this form," she added, pulling out an application form from behind the counter. Five minutes later, Karen walked out of Patricia's with two shopping bags filled with her new clothes.

Belinda offered to drop off Karen's packages after work, and at five o'clock, with both Charlie and Harold already gone, Karen and Belinda left the office together. As Belinda drove off, promising to leave the packages on the front porch, Karen hopped on her bicycle and pedaled home.

Approaching Brennan's, Karen considered going in to buy groceries. The few things she'd bought the day before wouldn't last much longer. She needed to make a complete tour of the store and stock up on food. Karen turned into the parking lot and parked her bike.

She whizzed through the store, searching every aisle for her favorite foods. In line at the cash register, she again remembered the rapidly declining wad of bills in her wallet and looked around for Roy Brennan. Fortunately, she spotted him supervising the cashier in the next aisle.

"Mr. Brennan?"

Roy Brennan looked over toward her. "Yes, ma'am?"

"I'm Karen Clark, Belinda Binnington's friend. We met yesterday."

"Oh yes," Roy smiled. "What can I do for you?"

"I was wondering...this is a little embarrassing. I haven't gotten a paycheck yet, and I was wondering...."

"Whether you might get credit here?"

"Yes."

"No problem. If you'll just jot down your name and address, I can arrange that." Roy thrust a piece of paper in Karen's direction.

"Fine, fine," Roy said as Karen filled out the form. "I suppose you'll want that load of groceries delivered."

Karen gulped. She had bought much more than she'd planned to–supermarkets always seemed to have that effect on her. Now her purchases would have to be delivered, and the delivery would be made by Roy's son, Tim. She had forgotten all about the gawky teenaged boy.

Roy turned his head toward the rear of the store. "Tim!" he barked.

Tim appeared a moment later. "Yeah?"

"You remember Miss Clark?" She's got some groceries to be delivered."

The teenager's eyes swept Karen's body, and she felt the same disgust she had felt the day before. The kid gave her the creeps, no question about it. He reminded her of slimy Mr. Mehlman, the elderly man who lived down the hall from her apartment in New York. He scrutinized her body every time they shared the elevator, and she never failed to be revolted by his gaze.

"Sure," Tim was saying. "I'll take care of it in about fifteen minutes, as soon as I finish...."

"Great," Roy interrupted. "Well, then, Karen, you'll have your groceries in fifteen minutes. How's that?"

"Fine. Thanks."

Roy looked back at the cashier he was supervising, clearly indicating that he had other business to attend to. Karen left her groceries in the hands of her cashier, who was busily packing them into cartons as Karen emerged from the store and hopped on her bicycle.

Pedaling down the highway, Karen felt tranquility creep back into her psyche. Traffic was light, and she could relax and survey her pastoral surroundings. Some chestnut-colored horses were standing in a meadow next to a big red barn. A weatherbeaten sign advertised "Horses for Sale."

How much would a horse like that cost? And how much work would keeping it involve? Karen hadn't been on a horse since overnight camp when she was 14, but she'd always thought she might like to try riding again. Maybe even have her own horse someday. Well, why not? Now that she was in Walden, it didn't seem like such a crazy idea.

As the bicycle turned into her driveway, Karen was relieved to see that her packages from Patricia's and the other shops were on the porch, just as Belinda had promised. Karen couldn't wait to carry them upstairs and try everything on again. She climbed the stairs quickly and was reconsidering a navy blue blazer in front of her bedroom mirror when she heard a car pull into the driveway below.

Karen dashed down the stairs just as Tim rang the doorbell. He carried the cartons of groceries inside, then hesitated near the door. Karen grabbed her purse and pulled out a dollar.

"This is for you," she said, thrusting the money toward him.

Tim shook his head. "Oh, no. I don't want any money." He continued to stand by the door.

"Well, uh, thanks, Tim. See you next time," Karen attempted.

Tim's eyes were riveted on Karen's torso. He was staring so hard that Karen was glad she was still wearing the navy blue blazer. Clearly he would have preferred that she wore nothing at all.

Too damn bad, Karen thought. Now get out of my house, damn it. "Tim, don't you think you should be getting back to the store?" she said sternly.

Tim looked up and met her gaze. "Uh, yeah, sure," he stammered. "Gotta get back." He turned and, still looking at Karen, missed the doorway and walked into the door frame instead. Karen heard his head hit the wooden frame. She winced, feeling sorry for the gawky boy. He was creepy, but she didn't wish him any harm. She just wanted him to clear out of her house.

He found the open doorway on his second attempt, and she rushed to lock the door behind him. As the delivery truck roared down the driveway, Karen put the groceries away. Then she mounted the stairs to her bedroom and resumed trying on her new clothes.

She was uncertain about the tomato-red rayon blouse she had bought. Was it conservative enough for Walden? Karen wasn't sure what rules applied to women professionals in a small town like Walden.

Removing the blouse, she was about to slip into her nightgown when she heard a noise outside. Clutching the nightgown to her chest, she looked out the bedroom window. Had Tim returned to get another glimpse of her? She saw nothing. No one.

She slipped into the nightgown and began to hang away all her purchases. But a moment later she thought she heard noises again. What *were* those noises? She put the new clothes down and listened. It sounded like twigs snapping, or maybe dry leaves crunching under the weight of someone's shoes. She flew to the window, but again she saw nothing, only her bike in the deserted driveway.

I'm used to city noises, like ambulance sirens and car alarms, she thought. I guess I'm just not used to these country noises yet.

She liked her solitude, she loved the house, but it was worlds away from her hectic, noisy life in Manhattan. It would take a little while to get used to.

Karen didn't expect it to take very long.

CHAPTER SIXTEEN

The next two weeks sped by. Riding the bike to work each day, Karen felt stronger and healthier than she'd ever felt before. Jogging in New York a few times a week had never toned her body the way the daily biking did.

Now, riding in the summer sun, she acquired a light golden tan and began wearing a sunhat Belinda lent her, to keep some of the strongest rays off her face. Her golden arms and legs, her lightly tanned face, gave her a glow she had never acquired in the city.

At the law firm, Karen fell into a rhythm, learning what she needed to know about Wisconsin law, mastering the rules that applied to wills and real estate transactions, the two areas Charlie wanted her to focus on. The work was challenging but not so arduous or time-consuming that it forced Karen to work late or on weekends, as her work at Garrity & Costello usually had. She savored having the extra time to herself, sleeping more than she'd ever allowed herself in New York, or just sitting on her front porch, sipping iced tea and taking pleasure in the tranquility that surrounded her. She thought about New York now and then, but immediately put it out of her mind, preferring to focus on the green and sunny world around her in Walden.

Karen hadn't met any clients yet; Charlie seemed to want the client-contact all to himself for a while longer. But she did get the feeling that her work at the firm was helping people. Little people. Farmers and small shopkeepers and unsophisticated widows who had been homemakers all their lives.

Contact with the corporate world, with the avaricious corporate clients Garrity & Costello specialized in, was totally absent. No more hand-holding with the kind of people who'd stab their buddies in the back if it meant an extra buck or two in their own pockets. That type of client had always made Karen feel uncomfortable. Now Karen was helping a different kind of client. Clients who, without her help, couldn't pay off their mortgages, couldn't pass all their hard-earned savings on to their children. She knew the work she was doing for Charlie was helping these people, and that knowledge gave her a satisfaction she'd never felt before.

Karen found that, despite his idiosyncrasies, she got along pretty well with Charlie. True, he could be difficult–testy and demanding. Karen also thought he was a bit of a misogynist. With Belinda, he was polite and gentlemanly. "Belinda," he'd say, "would you please go through your files and find the Cartright matter? Thank you very much, my dear." With Karen, he was coy and charming, almost flirtatious. "Now, Karen, you're the brightest young thing I've ever met," he'd say. "And the prettiest." Karen's cheeks would flush. In the politically correct world she was used to, men didn't say things like that to the women they worked with, and although on one level she enjoyed Charlie's flattering remarks, she also felt distinctly uncomfortable hearing them.

But Charlie was unpredictable. Suddenly he would do or say something totally different. The moment a problem arose–Karen couldn't find a file he wanted, Belinda didn't type a letter fast enough–his temper rose, and he exploded. "Goddammit!" he'd yell, his face turning purple, the veins on his forehead popping out.

Belinda knew just how to placate him, and after a few moments of her soothing, he'd settle down, and his ruffled feathers once again would be unruffled. Karen was beginning to sense how to manage him, just as Belinda did. "Now, Charlie," she'd say, "you don't want to get upset about such a small matter, do you?" Although she felt a bit uncomfortable playing this role, the tactic seemed to work, and his temper worried her less and less each day.

Only Harold Chase still made her feel truly uneasy. He was distant, cool, and totally uninterested in her. His demeanor made her feel like a cipher, a non-entity, sitting in the office next door to his own. Karen kept smiling, greeting him with "Good morning, Harold" every morning, but no matter what she did, none of it seemed to matter. He remained aloof, merely nodding at her now and then.

Her first weekend in Walden, Karen had slept almost endlessly, awakening late that Saturday afternoon feeling lazy and groggy. Maybe, she thought, it was a delayed reaction to the accident in Chicago. All week, adrenaline had pumped through her body, keeping her alert, stimulated, while she tried to cope with her new home and her new job. But now her body's staved-off needs had overwhelmed the adrenaline, demanding a marathon sleep so she could recover from the shock and damage she had sustained.

All day Sunday, too, she dozed on and off. Belinda telephoned, awakening her in mid-afternoon, inviting her to an informal barbeque in the Binnington back yard, but Karen begged off and went back to sleep. By Monday, Karen thankfully felt nearly back to normal.

That Monday, Martha Morgan, back from vacation, was sitting at her cluttered desk in the outer office when Karen arrived. Belinda hastened to make introductions.

As Karen shook Martha's hand, she evaluated the older woman. Fifty-five-plus, with a few extra pounds around her puffy waist and a gelatinous double-chin. But Martha was trying awfully hard to look younger than she was. She had unnaturally dark red hair, arranged in a too-youthful, dated style that hung to her shoulders.

A quarter-inch of white roots next to her scalp made it plain that Martha colored her hair, covering gray-gone-totally-white.

Karen had no quarrel with hair coloring. Her mother had gone prematurely gray and spent the rest of her life coloring it, pretending it was still its original chestnut-brown. Karen hadn't blamed her a bit. But Martha was another story. Her attempts to look younger weren't working. She was wearing heavy pancake makeup, and crudely-applied blusher struggled to add contour to her cheeks. Dark brown penciled-in eyebrows and thick black eyeliner circling her eyes were the finishing touches.

Karen wanted to grab Martha Morgan and shake her, tell her how much better, how much more vibrant she would look without all the artifice. Not younger, maybe...but Martha didn't look any younger this way either. Instead, Karen simply shook Martha's hand and said "Happy to meet you." Martha gave her a cool smile in return.

Her second Saturday in Walden, Karen awoke to a cooler, overcast morning. A good morning to start jogging again. She treasured her bike rides every weekday, and at the end of each evening she'd been too tired to even think about jogging. But she was beginning to miss the exhilaration of a good jog. Now at last she had the time and the energy to run again. She threw on a shirt and shorts, gulped down a cup of coffee, zoomed out the door, and headed towards town.

These last two weeks, preoccupied with work and home, she hadn't done much exploring, and the town of Walden was still largely unknown to her. Now she ran up and down the quiet streets, dotted with houses and shops and schools, wondering whether she could ever call this small Midwestern town "home."

As she ran down a shady street between Main Street and Second Avenue, Karen noticed another young woman jogging a short distance ahead of her. The other woman was tall, very slender, with long brown hair pulled back in a ponytail. Wearing comfortable old jogging clothes, the slender woman maintained a slow, steady pace, and Karen was able to catch up to her after a couple of blocks.

The woman glanced at Karen as she came running alongside her. She gave Karen an inquisitive look, then smiled a half-smile, cocking her head in Karen's direction. "Hi," she called out.

"Hi," Karen responded, smiling a tentative smile.

They ran alongside each other for a moment. Finally the slender woman spoke. "Want to get a Coke?"

"Sure," Karen answered.

"Follow me," the woman said, turning at the next corner, slowing her pace, turning again, finally stopping in front of the Walden Cafe. "This okay?"

Karen nodded. Truthfully, she would have preferred another spot. She had avoided the cafe ever since her first morning in Walden, the morning she was sick in the cafe's wretched bathroom. But she didn't have a good reason to avoid it any longer.

Seated in one of the café's red leatherette booths, the two women ordered Cokes, then sat back and scrutinized each other.

The slender woman's dark eyes, set into a long, thin face, were warm and friendly. "I'm Nedra Bailey," she said at last, breaking the silence. "I'm an accountant here in Walden."

"Bailey? That's my...my...," Karen began, then caught herself. "I mean, that's...that's...a great name," she said quickly.

Nedra looked puzzled by Karen's odd reaction to her name. Karen's face was hot with embarrassment, but she couldn't think of anything else to say. Finally Nedra spoke again. "Thanks. And you are...?"

"Oh, sorry! Karen Clark." Karen smiled, hoping Nedra would overlook the awkward beginning to their conversation. "I just moved here. I'm a lawyer with Fuller, Fuller & Chase."

"The Fuller firm," Nedra nodded approvingly. "I've done some work with them. Good firm."

"I like it pretty well so far."

"Have you met Chad yet?" Nedra's dark eyes sparkled when she mentioned Chad Fuller.

"No...."

"Wait till you do! He's what I call a hunk!" Nedra laughed.

Karen smiled, unsure whether she should laugh or not.

"I've never gone out with him, more's the pity. But I've sure thought about it a lot!" Nedra went on, still laughing.

"He's on vacation right now," Karen said. "He'll be back soon, I think."

The Cokes arrived, and Karen and Nedra began sipping while they continued to talk, discovering they had a lot in common as young women professionals in Walden. Nedra did most of the talking, telling Karen about the town and some of its other young people. "It's pretty quiet here, but people are really warm and friendly," Nedra said. "At least, most of them are."

Karen nodded, saying just enough to keep the conversation going, trying to stick to what she knew about K.B., filling in with tidbits of information about herself she considered harmless, or at least consistent with her new persona.

Nedra's bright brown eyes were riveted on Karen as she talked. She had lived in Walden for nearly two years, she told Karen. She'd grown up in Highland Falls, a small town near Walden, gone off to college, then taken a job with an elderly male accountant in Walden who intended to turn over his practice to her when he retired. "Joe's a great guy. You'll have to meet him," Nedra said. "Joseph J.

Featherstone. He's become almost a father-figure to me. My own Dad's been dead for years."

"Mine, too," Karen said, thinking of her father and stepmother in Florida. "My parents died together in a plane crash," she added, pretty certain K.B. had told her that much.

"How awful for you," Nedra said sympathetically. "Listen, Karen, I've got to run. But...would you like to go to a party to-night?"

"A party?"

Nedra nodded. "A friend of mine is giving a party at his house tonight. A great place for you to meet people."

Karen hesitated. Was she ready to meet a lot of new people? A second later, she nodded at Nedra. She felt ready. "Sure. But I don't have a car...."

"No problem. I'll pick you up."

"Would you?" People in this town really *were* friendly. She gave Nedra directions to her house as they left the cafe. Nedra jogged off, waving goodbye and Karen resumed jogging, this time headed home, her mind suddenly focused on the critical question of what she would wear to the party.

Karen spent the afternoon doing some long-neglected house-cleaning, then relaxed with a couple of old magazines she'd found in the basement. Later, after a long, relaxing bath, Karen looked through her closet again. She had almost nothing for evening wear. When she'd shopped at Patricia's, she didn't think to buy anything to wear to a party. And she'd left her torn black cocktail dress in a hotel wastebasket in Chicago.

After considering, then rejecting, several creative combinations of her workday and her casual clothes, Karen finally pulled one of K.B.'s battered suitcases out of the back of the closet. She had left a couple of things in the case, unsure whether she'd ever wear them.

Sure enough, the case held the answer to Karen's problem: a black cotton knit dress that was simple enough to go anywhere. Cinched by Karen's black patent belt, it fit perfectly.

She pulled off the dress and hung it up, then lifted the suitcase to return it to the closet. She heard a soft noise, as though there was something moving around inside the case. Karen opened it again. Nothing. She closed the case, picked it up, and shook it. There was that noise again.

What is that noise? She opened the case one more time and poked and prodded it until she noticed a small tab on one side. She pulled on the tab. That lifted a panel, revealing that the case had a false bottom.

Below the panel, at the true bottom of the case, was a small gun.

A gun? Why would K.B. have had a gun?

Karen was frightened and curious at the same time. Why would a law student like K.B. carry a gun around in her suitcase? Karen remembered occasional street crime in Cambridge. Had things gotten worse in three years, so much worse that K.B. didn't feel safe on the streets of Cambridge without a gun? Or had K.B. been fearful about coming to a strange place, a small town where she imagined that the residents might all be packing guns?

Shaking, Karen reached inside the case and extracted the gun. Handling it gingerly, she carried it by the butt to the nightstand beside her bed. Carefully, she placed it inside the drawer of the nightstand.

Okay, so K.B. had a gun. Well, now it's mine. It might even come in handy sometime. Maybe I could use it on creepy Tim Brennan! She had to laugh, thinking about the gawky teenage boy.

Karen lay down on her bed and tried to nap, but she was too agitated to sleep. After a restless hour tossing and turning in bed, she arose and began to dress for the party. Her hand shook slightly as she applied her lipstick, and she was suddenly aware how nervous she was. Nervous about a party where she would know absolutely no one but a fellow jogger she'd only just met.

CHAPTER SEVENTEEN

At five after eight, Karen heard a car horn honking. She rushed to the door. Nedra was behind the wheel of a white Chevy Lumina. "Ready?" Nedra shouted.

"Ready!" Karen answered. She grabbed her shoulder bag and left the house, her high-heeled shoes clattering on the wooden porch stairs. Nedra drove off in a cloud of dust.

Karen glanced at Nedra. Her new friend looked different. The ponytail had vanished, replaced by a glamorous fall of shiny dark brown hair, and make-up glistened on her face. "We haven't had much rain this month," she was saying. "Look at the dust!"

"It's been great," Karen said. "I've been riding a bike to work every day. If it ever rains, I'll have to call Charlie Fuller's secretary for a ride."

"You've been riding a bike every day?"

"Uh-huh."

"Don't you want to get a car?" Nedra asked.

"Not yet," Karen said. "I like riding my bike into town."

"Well, it's okay for now, but what about when the weather changes? Living out here, you'll have to get a car."

"I know." Karen preferred not to think about her need for a car. So far she'd been amazingly lucky, looking out her bedroom window each morning to see another bright, sunny day, knowing she could climb on her bike and ride it to work one more time. But the good weather wouldn't last forever.

"In the meantime, if you ever need a ride, you can call *me*," Nedra was saying. "I drive to work every day. Have to. Some of our clients live out in the country. But you have to call me early in the morning. I get to work about 7:30."

"Why so early?" Karen would need to plan ahead to get a ride with Nedra. She hadn't even been getting out of bed until 7:30 or 8:00.

"I like to get to the office before Joe does. Then I can work in peace and quiet before all the phone calls begin and Joe starts interrupting me. I get most of my work done before nine o'clock. Then, if I don't get much done the rest of the day, it doesn't matter."

"Do you stay in the office till five?"

"Sure. Sometimes later." Nedra's day sounded like the day of a lawyer at Garrity & Costello. "But I don't *have* to work such long hours. I do it because I love it. And because I plan to take over Joe's practice in the next couple of years. I want to know everything about it when I do."

Now Nedra sounded less like a regimented Wall Street lawyer and more like a self-motivated entrepreneur. Karen admired Nedra's enthusiasm, her direction. For all of her intelligence and ability, Karen had always lacked the kind of drive Nedra appeared to have. In spades.

Nedra pulled up in front of a large frame house on the edge of town. It looked like Karen's house, but a bigger, more prosperous version. A sign on the front lawn said:

Medical Office
L. J. Smith, M.D.

Karen turned to Nedra. "A medical office?"

"Right. It's Jon's office. But don't worry, it's his home, too."

"Oh, I see." Karen recalled hearing that small-town doctors sometimes used part of their homes as their offices.

"Now, don't worry, Karen. Jon hasn't thrown any parties in his examining rooms. Not lately!" Nedra laughed, her brown eyes sparkling.

Karen and Nedra climbed out of the Lumina, and Nedra guided Karen to the back entrance to the house. The door was open, and the sound of light rock music filtered out the doorway. A young man and woman were standing just inside the door.

"Jon!" Nedra said to the man. "I want you to meet Karen Clark. I told you about her on the phone."

The young man turned towards Karen. He was tall, with light brown hair and hazel eyes in an unremarkable face. Nice but unremarkable. "So you're Karen." He thrust his hand out and grabbed Karen's. "Happy to meet you, Karen. I'm Jon."

"Hello, Jon."

"Welcome to Walden. Nedra tells me you've just arrived," Jon said. His face radiated warmth, friendliness.

"That's right. I've been here about two weeks."

"Two weeks. Well, I want you to meet some of the other people here, starting with Jackie." Jon turned to the blonde standing next to him. "Jackie Berlinghof, meet Karen...Karen Clark?"

Karen and Jackie nodded at each other, and Nedra pushed both of them inside. Jon went off to get everyone cold drinks, while Karen and Nedra searched for a place to sit. It was hot inside the old frame house. Karen stayed close to Nedra's side, and the two women finally found a cooler spot on the large side porch facing a leafy yard.

Nedra got busy introducing Karen to almost everyone on the porch. Karen forgot most of their names on the spot, but she remembered Jackie Berlinghof, who turned up on the porch a short time later.

"So, Karen, tell me what brings you to Walden," Jackie asked, seating herself in the wicker chair next to Karen that Nedra had just vacated.

"A job," Karen began. She couldn't avoid questions like that forever. Karen launched into a breezy discussion of her work, trying to avoid more personal questions about her background and her life before Walden. It was getting confusing, trying to remember what she had said before, trying to be consistent. She realized she had to make more of an effort to create a living, breathing persona she could live with. This other way, this ad hoc recreation of a life, was becoming too stressful.

After a couple of friendly questions, Jackie's piercing blue eyes narrowed, and she evolved into a cold-blooded inquisitor. Her questions became more detailed, more demanding. "Why exactly did you think Charlie Fuller would be a good boss?" she asked. "Do you hope to become a partner at the firm?" Karen felt uneasy being grilled this way.

She tried to deflect some of the questions by asking Jackie about herself. "I own the Gift Hutch on Main Street," Jackie answered. "A gift shop. I try to carry high-quality gift items. Lladro, Wedgwood, Steuben glass."

"Sounds nice," Karen said.

"I do custom picture-framing, too. In the back of the store. Come in sometime and I'll show you around the shop."

"I will."

"I didn't set out to run a gift shop, in case you're wondering," Jackie said. "I was an art history major at Madison. Stayed there for a couple years after I graduated and tried to get a job in my field. But there weren't any, so I went to work in an art supplies store. That's where I learned picture-framing."

Karen nodded.

"Then my mother got sick, and I came back here. My parents owned The Gift Hutch ever since I was a little girl, and my mother was running it by herself by that time. I finally took it over. Been running it myself about four years now. I added the picture-framing to pull in more business."

"Great," Karen said. Jackie didn't sound exactly ecstatic about her store and the life she had created for herself in Walden. Karen thought she would stroke her a little, try to make her feel better about it. "The items you carry in the store sound lovely. And the framing business–that's really very creative, isn't it?"

"It can be," Jackie agreed.

"I've always found that people who do picture-framing are very creative. There's this little shop in Manhattan where I used to...." Karen stopped, suddenly aware that she had said too much.

"Manhattan?" Jackie asked, looking askance at Karen.

Just then Jon arrived on the porch carrying a tray of cold drinks. Karen noticed Jackie's head turn towards Jon, an excited smile on her face. "Jon, you're back!" she said, suddenly breathing much faster. She rose to help Jon find a clear spot for the tray of drinks.

So that was it! Jackie was interested, very interested in Jon. No wonder she'd been giving Karen the third-degree. She viewed Karen as a threat, a new woman in town who just might appeal to Jon.

Karen didn't want to get entangled in this particular web. She rose and abruptly left the porch, looking for Nedra. She found her near the front door.

"When do you think you'll be leaving?" she asked.

"Actually, I've got a crashing headache," Nedra answered. "I took a couple aspirin in the kitchen, but they haven't helped. I'm ready to go whenever you are."

"Good. Let's go."

Nedra waved goodbye at Jon, and they clattered down the wooden back stairs of Jon's house. The old house was still filled with noisy partygoers as the two women drove off in the Lumina. They rode in silence for a while. Finally Nedra spoke.

"Well, what did you think?" she asked.

"Nice party. Nice people."

"Jon's a great guy. Did you get to talk to him?"

"Barely. The only person I talked to for more than a minute was Jackie."

"Jackie Berlinghof?"

Karen nodded.

"And...?"

"She seemed okay. Has the hots for Jon, as far as I could tell."

Nedra chuckled. "Right. She does." Nedra pulled into Karen's driveway. "Well, here we are." Karen began to open the car door. Nedra placed her hand on Karen's arm to stop her. "Remember," she said, "give me a call if you need a ride to work."

"I will."

"And let's get together sometime. Maybe we could have lunch next week."

"That sounds great. Thanks for the ride, and for inviting me to the party," Karen said, climbing out of the Lumina.

"Don't mention it. See ya!"

Nedra drove off, and Karen watched the lights of the Lumina get smaller and smaller as the car headed towards town. Karen finally climbed the stairs and went inside.

She poured herself a large Coke and sat down at the kitchen table to drink it. Suddenly she heard that noise again. The sound of twigs snapping just outside her open window.

Karen froze. During daylight, the sound hadn't worried her. But alone, at night, she was terrified.

Stop it, Karen, she chided herself. It's just country noises. Squirrels or rabbits, maybe even a skunk. They prowl at night, and they're attracted to light.

Slowly, she arose from her chair and walked to the light switch. She turned off the light, then tiptoed to the window and looked outside. Nothing. Quickly she closed the window and went upstairs to undress for bed.

In her bedroom, she undressed in the dark. No more lights to attract animals. Animals that made scary noises. She groped her way around the room until she found a nightgown in the dresser drawer. Pulling it on, she collapsed into bed.

Karen felt exhausted. But her head was filled with thoughts and images, of the party, of Nedra, of Jon and Jackie, and it was nearly an hour before she fell asleep.

CHAPTER EIGHTEEN

After a quiet Sunday, Karen arrived at work Monday morning to find Charlie waiting for her in a huff. "Where have you been?" he demanded.

"Charlie, I'm sorry, but it's just 9:05," Karen said. Why was Charlie so upset with her?

"I told you Arnold Hays was coming this morning. I wanted to brief you on his situation before he got here."

Karen had never heard the name Arnold Hays before, but Charlie seemed so irritated, so annoyed with her, she was afraid to tell him. She decided to take a different tack. "Well, I'm here now, Charlie. What did you want me to know?"

Karen's confident tone had the effect she'd hoped for. Charlie calmed down, seating himself in the small chair across from her desk. "Okay, Karen. It's kind of a touchy situation. Arnold's got himself in some trouble with one of his brothers. There are three brothers. They run a hardware store here, the one on Main Street. You've seen it." Karen nodded. "Well, Bill, he's the oldest, he and the other brother, Kenny, they want Arnold out of the business."

"And Arnold doesn't want out?"

"Right."

"Well, why do they want him out?" Karen asked.

"Bill, Bill...." Charlie jumped up and began pacing the small office.

Karen waited patiently for Charlie to collect himself. Finally he sat down again. "Bill thinks Arnold's been fooling around with Kathryn. That's Bill's wife."

Charlie waited for Karen to say something. "Oh," she said, trying desperately to come up with the kind of reaction Charlie was waiting for. "Is it true?"

"God, woman, I don't know if it's true!" Charlie snapped. "He'll be here in a few minutes, ask him yourself." Charlie stormed out of Karen's office and headed for his own.

Did I say the wrong thing? I must have, Karen thought. But why was Charlie so agitated? Was he merely concerned that he would lose a client, this Arnold Hays, or even all three Hays brothers, if he didn't handle things the right way? Or was there some other reason?

A moment later, Karen heard Belinda's buzz. She rose and greeted a heavy-set man in the outer office. "Mr. Hays?" she asked.

"Yes. But call me Arnold," Hays said. He was tall and obese, with a straggly dark-brown mustache and glasses. Karen suspected that he would have a damp handshake, and she was right. She ushered Hays into her office and briskly began to interview him. After a couple of minutes, Hays interrupted her.

"You're a very lovely young woman, Ms. Clark. Or may I call you Karen?" he said. His eyes were glittering behind his glasses, and Karen could have sworn she saw drool forming at the sides of his mouth.

"You can call me Karen," she said reluctantly. Charlie probably wanted her to be on a first-name basis with this man, but she felt uneasy about making the relationship any more personal than it had to be. She attempted to resume the interview, but a moment later, Hays leapt out of his chair and grabbed her hand. "Karen, let's discuss this over coffee. I know a nice little restaurant where we can talk...talk privately." His tone was suddenly hushed, a feeble attempt at sounding romantic.

"I'd rather not. I have a lot of other work to get to this morning."

Hays looked dejected, but without missing a beat, he said, "Well, how about dinner tonight?"

God, didn't the man know when a woman wasn't interested? Karen found it hard to believe that any woman, including his brother Bill's wife, could find this guy appealing.

"Sorry, I'm busy tonight. Why don't we get back to the interview now? I wanted to...."

Hays jumped up, his double chin quivering. "Well, I'm not sure you're the person I want to talk to about this matter," he said huffily. "I think I'll tell Charlie I want him to represent me on this after all."

"But...."

Hays stormed out of Karen's office before she could utter another word. She rushed after him, but by the time she got to her office doorway, the outer office door had slammed behind him.

"What was *that* all about?" Belinda asked.

"He made a pass at me," Karen said. "When I turned him down, he jumped up and left."

"No!" Belinda looked shocked. "Arnold?"

"Yes," Karen said, shuddering. "Revolting!" She turned to return to her office.

"To tell the truth," Belinda offered, "now that you mention it, I *have* heard some stories about Arnold."

Karen turned back toward Belinda. "Stories?"

"They say he tries to make time with a lot of the young women around here. Goes after them even when they make it pretty clear they're not interested."

Karen nodded. "That's exactly what he tried with me."

"Well, don't worry about it," Belinda said. "I'm sure he's harmless. If he calls you again, just tell him you're busy."

"But what about Charlie? He wanted me to...."

"I'll take care of it," Belinda said, smiling.

"You...you'll...?"

"I'll talk to Charlie about it. He'll understand."

"Are you sure?"

"Of course I'm sure. You don't work with a man for twenty years and not know how he thinks. I'll tell him what happened, and he'll talk to Arnold. Don't worry about it. Charlie must have tried to get Chad to take on at least a dozen clients for him, and only a few of them worked out. So it's not the first time."

Karen was relieved to learn she wasn't the first one to run into trouble with Charlie's clients. She was in good company if Charlie's own son had the same problem. She put Arnold Hays out of her mind and went back to her files.

Tuesday, Karen's phone rang twice, but when she answered it, no one was on the line. "Who was that calling me, Belinda?" Karen asked, but Belinda wasn't sure. "Was it Arnold Hays?"

"It might have been. I couldn't swear to it either way, Karen."

Karen put the obese man out of her mind and returned to work.

The following morning, Belinda buzzed Karen again."There's a lady on the line. She asked for 'that nice young woman' who works here, and I assume she means you."

Karen was puzzled. Who would be calling, asking for her? Karen had barely met any clients yet, and the few Charlie had introduced her to–like the loathsome Arnold Hays–had all been male. "Okay, I'll take the call," she told Belinda.

The woman on the line sounded elderly and uncertain. "Hello, miss? Is this the nice young lady I spoke with a year or two ago?" she asked.

A year or two ago?

"No, I'm sorry. This is Karen Clark. I've only been working here a short time."

"Oh. Are you sure?"

Karen stifled a laugh. "Yes, I'm sure. Can I help you?"

"Well, are you a lawyer, like the other young lady?"

"Yes. I'm a lawyer." Who was this other "young lady" the woman kept talking about?

"That's good. Then maybe you *can* help me."

"I'll certainly try. Do you want to begin by telling me your name?"

"Oh, surely. Forgive me. My name is Ruth Swenson, Mrs. Ruth Swenson."

Karen jotted down the name. She waited for the woman to say something else, then realized that Mrs. Swenson was waiting for Karen to say something first. "And you're calling about a problem?" Karen said tentatively.

"Yes, I certainly am!"

Again, silence on the line. "Do you want to describe your problem to me?"

"Well, the other young lady...she knew all about it. I can't remember her name. It was a Swedish name, like mine, but...it's gone now. I can't remember things the way I used to."

"Well, can you tell me what the problem is?" Karen was puzzled and exasperated at the same time. She was rapidly losing patience with Ruth Swenson.

"Well, you see, a few years ago, I had an accident. Fell down the stairs in a restaurant in Green Bay. My back's never been the same, and I get a lot of pain in my left leg when...."

Karen interrupted. "I see. But how can I help you with this problem?"

"Well, Mr. Chase handled my lawsuit for me, and he told me I would get a lot of money for my injuries and for my pain and... and...now what did he call it?"

"Pain and suffering," Karen said.

"Yes, that's it. Pain and suffering."

"And...?"

"And I got some money a while ago, but it was just five hundred dollars. Not the thousands of dollars Mr. Chase said I'd get."

"I see. When did you get the five hundred dollars?"

"Oh, about three years ago. I don't remember the exact date."

"And you've had nothing since then?"

"No. But that nice young woman with the Swedish name, I talked to her about it. She said she'd get the rest of it for me."

"I see." Karen hesitated. It sounded like a simple matter of getting some insurance company to cough up some bucks. Just another case mired in the paperwork on a desk somewhere.

"Well, I can look into it for you again, Mrs. Swenson. I'll speak to Mr. Chase about it as soon as I can and get back to you." Karen took down Mrs. Swenson's phone number, the date of the accident, and the approximate date of the payment of five hundred dollars, then hung up. She left her desk in search of Harold Chase, but his office was empty.

"He's gone out," Belinda said. "A meeting at the bank, I think. I'm not sure when he'll be back."

Karen decided to get Ruth Swenson's file in the meantime. "Can you help me, Belinda? I need to find the file on Ruth Swenson. A personal injury case from a few years ago."

"Ruth Swenson? That name doesn't sound familiar. But I'll check the files."

Twenty minutes later, Belinda entered Karen's office, a baffled look on her face. She had searched every file cabinet in the office, including the ones in Harold's office. But she couldn't track down a file for Ruth Swenson.

"Thanks," Karen said finally. "I'll ask Harold about it when he gets back."

"Okay, dear. Sorry I couldn't find it."

Belinda returned to her desk, and Karen put aside the file she was reviewing, puzzled by Belinda's failure to find the Swenson file. It must have gotten lost. Maybe it had been thrown out by mistake, or fallen behind some piece of furniture, like those letters that get lost in the post office, then get delivered thirty years later.

Karen knew she could wait, could talk to Harold when he returned to the office. But she wanted to do something about Ruth Swenson while the woman's problem was fresh in her mind. She would write an interoffice memo to Harold. That way she could describe the situation in writing, right now, before she forgot anything.

She left the memo on Harold's desk and returned to her office and the piles of file folders Charlie had stacked there. By the time Harold returned on Thursday morning, Karen had forgotten all about Ruth Swenson.

As Karen rode to work on Friday, her bike abruptly stopped five minutes short of the Walden city limits. She got off the bike and checked the tires. One of them was undeniably flat. Karen's heart sank.

Damn! It's finally happened! What if I can't get this bike repaired? I don't want a car. Not yet.

Karen walked slowly towards town, pushing the bike, wondering once again what she was doing in this town, in this life, pushing a rusty bike to work at a two-bit law firm, instead of hailing a cab on Madison Avenue and zooming down to Wall Street in style. The sun was hot on her shoulders, and she could feel sweat on her back, under her red rayon blouse, dripping into the waistband of her navy blue skirt.

She passed an Arco station. That looked promising. She pushed the bike past the pumps, to the open door of the station's office. A grizzled fellow in an Arco cap was sitting behind a battered metal desk. "Can you fix a flat tire on a bike?" she called out.

"Sure can, young lady. Let's see it." The man jumped up and approached Karen. His craggy face was weather-beaten from too many years spent peering inside and under Walden's cars, but it appeared to be kind, maybe even honest. He took a quick look at the bike, and they struck a deal. The flat would be fixed and the bike ready for riding by five o'clock.

Karen, still sweaty, walked the rest of the way to the office building on Main Street. The burden of the bike was gone, but the hot sun and humid air made the walk a steamy, sticky ordeal nonetheless.

Entering the office building, she ducked into the women's room to wash her face and comb her hair. The cool water felt good on her face, red and blotchy now from the heat. She removed her blouse, moistened some paper towels, and sponged her neck, her back, her armpits. Finally she felt cool enough, presentable enough, to walk through the door of Fuller, Fuller & Chase.

As Karen entered, she sensed that something was different. The air-conditioned atmosphere felt charged somehow. Belinda wasn't at her desk, and Martha Morgan wasn't at hers either.

Karen heard a low hum of voices from one of the offices and walked towards the hum. It was coming from the other corner office. Not Charlie's. Chad's office. Had Chad returned?

Chad. She'd wondered about him ever since she'd seen his name at the bottom of a letter, a letter she'd read in another city, in another life.

Everyone had gathered inside the doorway of Chad's office. Suddenly Belinda turned and noticed Karen. "Karen! C'mon in!" Belinda stretched out her arm and put it around Karen's shoulder. "Come meet Chad!" She ushered Karen into the office, the others stepping aside. "Now Chad, this is Karen Clark, our new associate," Belinda said, smiling.

Karen looked up at Chad. He was every bit as handsome as the photographs on the wall had hinted. Tall, blond, with a broad smile and beautiful deep-blue eyes. Blond curls fell onto his forehead, darkly tanned from his weeks in the sun.

"Karen! So we meet at last! What a pleasure!" Chad thrust a large tanned hand towards Karen and gripped her hand in his.

"Thanks," Karen stammered. "I'm happy to be here."

"Great, great," Chad said, still smiling broadly. "I understand my old man has you working pretty hard."

Karen smiled, unsure what kind of response to make. "Pretty hard," she said finally, nodding her head.

"Well, don't let him work you too hard!" Chad laughed. "*I* don't!"

Everyone laughed. "You sure don't," a sardonic voice added.

Karen turned around to see who had spoken. Harold Chase. When she turned back to look at Chad, he was glaring at Harold, his smile gone.

"You should know, Harold," he said.

The men exchanged hostile glances.

"Now, now, boys," Charlie Fuller spoke up. "Chad's just back from vacation. Let's try to keep things harmonious around here." Charlie pulled Harold aside and began walking out of the room, putting his arm around his derisive partner. "Don't start up with him now, Harold...," Karen heard him muttering as the two men left.

"Well, I guess it's back to work," Belinda said, glancing around the room. Karen nodded and turned to leave behind Belinda and Martha.

"No, wait, Karen," Chad called out. He had seated himself behind his massive oak desk. "Come back. Tell me how you're getting along here. You've been here what? Two or three weeks?"

Karen turned back toward Chad, uncertain whether to stay or not.

"It's okay, don't worry," Chad smiled. "You're allowed to talk to me. Don't let my relationship with Harold bother you. That's strictly between him and me."

Karen felt uncomfortable, caught between the two men. They clearly were on bad terms with each other. But then, why should that concern her? She walked back toward Chad's desk and seated herself in a chair facing his.

"So what is it now? Two weeks?" Chad asked again.

"Almost three," Karen answered. "I began here three weeks ago next Monday."

"And how's it going?"

"Fine. I like the work I'm doing. Mostly wills and real estate."

"My father giving you his work to do? Or did you get stuck with Harold's stuff?"

"It's your father's work," Karen answered. "He must have been overwhelmed without any help. He's got a pretty substantial caseload."

Chad nodded. "He does, he does. It's amazing how much work the old guy pulls in." He smiled. "Just avoid working with Harold if you can. The guy's a real bastard."

Karen smiled back at Chad. "I've barely spoken to him. Or perhaps I should say he's barely spoken to me."

"That's Harold," Chad said, nodding again. "A real cold fish. But my father likes him. Maybe even feels some sort of loyalty to him. Harold was here, helping the old man, before I joined the firm. So I think he feels he owes him something. Even though Harold hardly carries his own weight around here."

Karen thought Chad's view of Harold was probably colored by the personal animosity between them. If Charlie was satisfied with Harold's work, it had to be all right.

Suddenly Karen remembered Ruth Swenson. "I *did* have something come up the other day. An old case of Harold's. A client called me about it. But I couldn't find the file."

"Typical," Chad smirked. "What was the problem?"

"A personal injury case. The woman said she never got the money Harold told her she'd get."

"Also typical. Harold's a real slacker. Did you ask him about it?"

"No. He was out when she called, so I wrote a memo and left it on his desk. I forgot about it till just now."

"Well, don't worry about it. He probably has the file squirreled away somewhere."

"Probably."

"But let's not talk about Harold. I want to know more about you. How are you doing in that house of yours?"

"You know about my house?" Karen was surprised to learn that Chad knew anything about her house.

"Sure. I helped Belinda find it. At least, I checked out what was available in town. Nothing you'd have liked. I saw a couple furnished places, but they were really run down. The old Parker place is a thousand times nicer. We finally tracked it down just before I left on vacation."

"Where did you go?"

"Fishing up north. I go every summer. It's paradise up there–no phones, no clients, no suit and tie." He paused. "And no Harold!" He laughed.

Karen joined in the laughter, thinking how unpleasant Harold was, siding immediately with Chad in his feud with the older man. Still, she had to get along with Harold, too. In fact, she had to ask him about Ruth Swenson. Karen stood up to leave. "I'd better be getting back to...."

"Okay, okay. We all have to get back to work. But drop in here now and then to let me know how everything's going, okay?" Chad got up and came around his desk to take Karen's hands. Karen noticed that he had something of a paunch, a slight ballooning around his middle. So the "thin Chad" photos were the older ones. He had definitely put on a few pounds since then.

"Now, Karen," Chad said, holding onto her hands, his deep blue eyes looking steadily into hers, "don't work too hard. My father can be something of a slavedriver. Just don't let him push you too hard."

Karen felt a bit overwhelmed by Chad's interest in her. "Okay," she said, at a loss for any other words. His hands felt soft and sweaty. Were they sweating because he was nervous, holding her hands in his?

"Promise?" Chad asked, his blue eyes twinkling.

Karen nodded.

"Okay, then," Chad said, releasing her hands. "Keep me posted."

Karen turned and walked to her office. She realized as she fell into her desk chair that her heart was beating much faster than normal and that her hands were suddenly sweaty, too.

CHAPTER NINETEEN

When Karen knocked on Harold's open door a minute later, he looked startled to see her. "Yes?" he said coldly.

"Harold, it's about that memo I wrote the other day. The one about Ruth Swenson." Harold had not yet invited Karen to come into his office, and she remained standing awkwardly in the doorway.

"Memo? What memo?"

"Ruth Swenson. The woman who was injured in Green Bay. She phoned to ask about her settlement."

"Oh, the Swenson woman," Harold said, nodding, apparently remembering the memo at last. "Come in, come in."

Karen entered the office. It was barren. Like Harold. No artwork, no photographs or plaques on the wall, no signs of life except a small framed photograph of a curly-haired little boy on Harold's desk.

"Is that your son?" Karen asked, hoping to get some sort of response.

"Yes, yes, sit down," Harold said, waving in the direction of a chair. He obviously had no desire to discuss his family, even the adorable tousled-haired child in the photograph. Karen sat down, feeling uncomfortable opposite the older unsmiling lawyer. "I remember now," Harold said. "You got a call from my client, Mrs. Swenson, is that right?"

Karen nodded.

"How did she come to call you? Why didn't she just leave a message for me?" Harold's tone verged on belligerent, as though Karen herself was responsible for the phone call.

"Belinda put the call through to me. I'm not sure...." Karen suddenly recalled Mrs. Swenson's words. "Oh, I remember now. Mrs. Swenson asked for 'the nice young woman' who works here. But she apparently meant someone else, another woman who was here a couple of years ago. Someone with a Swedish name, she said."

Harold screwed up his face, concentrating. "Laura," he mumbled finally.

"Laura?"

"Laura Hanson. That's who Ruth Swenson meant. We had an associate named Laura Hanson here a couple of years ago."

"Oh." Laura Hanson. An associate who had apparently left the firm. "Well, this Laura Hanson must have assured Mrs. Swenson that she'd get her settlement money quite a while ago, and she's wondering why she hasn't gotten it."

"I see," Harold said. His face had become the usual impassive mask again. "Well, you can stop worrying your pretty little head about it now." Patronizing bastard. "I'll take care of it. And I'll instruct Belinda to put Mrs. Swenson's calls through to me, or else to take a message. I don't want you to get involved in this old case. I have everything under control." Harold rose, clearly indicating that their meeting was over.

Karen followed his lead and rose from her chair, turning to leave. She looked back at him for a moment, expecting some words of thanks, or goodbye, or something. But Harold was already seated and completely absorbed in the work on his desk.

Karen returned to her own office and shut the door. What a strange bird, she thought. Thank God I'm working with Charlie, and my contact with Harold is minimal. If I had to work with that man, I wouldn't last another week in this firm.

The phone on Karen's desk rang, disturbing her reverie. "There's a John Smith on the line, Karen," Belinda said when Karen picked up the phone. "Do you know a John Smith? Sounds a little funny to me."

Karen searched her mind. John Smith? Was this a prank? She didn't know anyone in Walden well enough to inspire any pranks. "I'll take the call, Belinda. I'm sure it's all right."

A cheery male voice came on the line. "Karen? It's Jon."

"Have we met?"

The voice laughed. "Yes, we have. You came to my party last week, remember?"

Suddenly Karen remembered the party, remembered arriving at the house, remembered the house with the sign in front:

Medical Office
L. J. Smith, M.D.

She hadn't really thought about it before. The "Jon" she'd met was Jon Smith.

"Sorry, Jon! I didn't put two and two together. I didn't remember your last name."

"Yeah, I got stuck with a great name, didn't I?" He laughed again. "My name's really Lowell Jonathan Smith, Jr. But my father was always called Lowell, so they called me Jonathan. Then that became Jon. And now I'm stuck with the incredibly distinctive name of Jon Smith."

"That must be a problem for you," Karen said sympathetically.

"Sometimes. Like now."

Karen laughed.

"Well, I might as well tell you why I called. I got your number from Nedra, and I'm calling to find out if you'll be in town this weekend. You're not leaving, are you?"

"No. Why would I?"

"It's a holiday weekend. Labor Day. Don't tell me you didn't know it's Labor Day weekend, Karen."

"I didn't," Karen admitted, feeling embarrassed to be out of touch with things like holiday weekends. "Thanks for telling me. I was all set to come into work on Monday."

"You mean no one in your office mentioned the holiday?"

"No, not yet." Karen supposed that Belinda was planning to mention it before she left for the day. But it was strange that no one had mentioned it to her till now. Strange, too, that Chad returned to work on the eve of a holiday weekend. Unless he had some reason to come back to Walden for the weekend. Some holiday gathering. Or a special date with a special someone.

"Karen? Are you still there?"

"Yes, yes." Had she missed something Jon had said?

"I was asking you about Monday."

"Sorry, Jon. I was distracted for a moment."

"I was just saying, if you're not busy on Monday, would you like to go swimming with me?"

"Swimming? Where?"

"At the lake."

"The lake?"

"There's a small lake a few miles out of town. Lake Allison. It's a lovely little lake, great for swimming. I know a quiet spot along the water that very few people know about, so it's not usually invaded by the hordes."

"Where do the hordes go?"

"They're usually at the beaches. There's a couple of small sandy beaches. That's where the families go. The little kids like to play in the sand, and the parents go where the kids can play." That made sense. "So what do you say, Karen? Do you like to swim?"

Karen wasn't a strong swimmer. Two summers' worth of lessons in Camp Alpine's pool hadn't helped very much. But she figured she could manage well enough in a small lake. Besides, what else did she have to do on Labor Day? "Okay. Sounds great."

"Terrific. Nedra told me where you live. The old Parker place, right?"

"Right."

"I'll pick you up about eleven Monday morning, if that's okay with you. That'll give me time to see any emergencies at my office and throw together a picnic lunch before I pick you up. Okay?"

"I could make lunch...," Karen began.

"Nope. I'm doing the inviting, I'll do the food. Just be ready about eleven."

Karen heard a baby begin to cry at the other end of the line.

"Gotta go, Karen. One of my patients...."

"I understand."

"See you Monday." Jon hung up.

Karen replaced the receiver and sat back in her chair. Jon Smith. A dashing new beau in hot pursuit.

Things were looking good. A swimming date with Jon, and gorgeous Chad Fuller just down the hall. Who needed New York and Jason Singer's chin?

CHAPTER TWENTY

Leaving work that afternoon, Belinda popped her head into Karen's office. "Want a ride home today, Karen? It's nearly 90 out there. I could cram your bike into my station wagon somehow."

"My bike! I just remembered. It's at a gas station getting fixed."

"Flat tire?"

"Right."

"Okay," Belinda said, "we'll stop off there. You can bike home, or ride the rest of the way with me."

"Thanks, Belinda. You're really...."

"C'mon, honey, let's go."

Karen checked her watch. "But isn't it too early to leave? It's only 4:30."

"That's okay. Charlie said we could leave early today. Holiday weekend."

Karen grabbed her things and left the office with Belinda. Once in the station wagon, Belinda asked, "Have any plans for the weekend? If not, you could come over to my place Monday. Fred and I are having another barbeque. Just a few friends. Nobody from the firm."

Belinda's great, Karen thought. So kind to invite me. But I'm sure she doesn't really want me at her barbeque. She feels sorry for me, that's all. Thank God I finally met Nedra. And thanks to Nedra, I've met Jon. "Thanks for the invitation, Belinda. But I have a date."

"You do? Wonderful!" Belinda looked immensely relieved. "Do I know him?"

"Jon Smith. The fellow who called today. He's a doctor in town."

"Jon Smith, Jon Smith. Oh, *that* Jon Smith. I know who he is. My cousin Marge swears by him."

"Does she?" Karen couldn't keep a smile from creeping over her face. She was going out with a doctor Cousin Marge swore by.

"She does. Now how did you meet him, Karen?"

"At a party."

"So you've been partying here, and I didn't even know it." Belinda smiled broadly at Karen.

"Do you know Nedra Bailey?"

"Nedra Bailey." Belinda thought for a moment. "She the one taking over Joe Featherstone's accounting firm?"

"That's right." Did everybody in Walden know everybody else? "She invited me to go to this party at...."

Belinda swerved suddenly and pulled into the Arco station. "Isn't this the place, honey?"

Karen jumped out of the car and approached the gray-haired attendant, who was pumping gas into a beat-up Cadillac. "Is my bike fixed?"

The man looked up. He looked puzzled for a moment, then his face cleared. "Oh, right, you're the young lady with the bike. Sorry, sis, it's not fixed yet." The man grinned, trying to smooth things over. "I had a couple rush repairs to do before the weekend."

Karen was not amused. "What am I supposed to do now? That bike is my only means of transportation!"

"Now, now, sis, don't get upset." The man finished pumping gas and took some money from the driver of the Cadillac. "Let's see.

I...I can give you an old car for the weekend. One of my loaners. Do you have a driver's license?"

"Of course I do," Karen said hotly.

"Okay. You can have the old Plymouth over there," he said, pointing at a battered brown Plymouth parked next to the men's room. "It's got some gas, and it runs pretty good. If you show me your license, I'll get you the keys."

Karen hesitated. She had two driver's licenses, for two Karen Clarks. Which one should she use? She didn't resemble the photo on K.B.'s license, but her own New York license revealed her Manhattan address.

A horn blared nearby. Karen and the attendant both looked up. Belinda was honking, her head halfway out of the driver's seat window in the station wagon. "What's the problem, Ed?"

Ed and Karen approached Belinda together. "Hi there, Belinda," Ed said. "The bike's not ready. I'm gonna give this little lady a loaner car if she's got a driver's license."

"Do you have your license with you, Karen?" Belinda asked. Karen suddenly saw a way out of her dilemma.

"Not with me, Belinda. I haven't needed it, with no car here...."

"I'll vouch for Karen, Ed," Belinda said. "She's working in our office now. You won't have any problem getting your car back."

"If you say so, Belinda." Ed turned to Karen. "Well, I guess you're all set, sis. Just follow me."

Karen bent towards Belinda. She could feel the heat emanating from Belinda's car. The air conditioner was pounding, pushing more heat into an already overheated world. "I can't thank you enough, Belinda."

"Don't mention it, dear. Have fun this weekend. I'll see you Tuesday." Belinda rolled up her window and drove off.

Karen ran to catch up with Ed, waiting by the side of the Plymouth. "Okay, sis, you got wheels. Now don't forget to drive real careful. Holiday traffic, ya know. Lotsa nuts on the road."

Karen climbed into the Plymouth. It felt like an oven and smelled as though something had actually been baking inside it. Karen caught a glimpse of a half-eaten hamburger bun on the car floor. She quickly opened the windows, took the car keys from Ed, and inserted the ignition key. After pumping the gas pedal a few times, she heard the engine start. "Thanks," she told Ed. "I'll be back for my bike on Tuesday."

Karen drove out of the gas station carefully, slowly turning onto the highway, making sure she was headed in the right direction. Then she floored the accelerator, delirious with the brand-new freedom she suddenly possessed behind the wheel of the Plymouth.

Saturday and Sunday were a delightful change of pace. Karen used a well-thumbed map she found in the glove compartment and drove the Plymouth for miles in every direction, exploring Walden and its neighboring towns and villages. The Plymouth's motor coughed and wheezed as she steered the old car down one Main Street after another, noting their invariable sameness: drug store, hardware store, insurance agency, and the inevitable greasy spoon. "Fungible towns," she thought. But she liked the quiet, the smallness, the realness of these little towns, so unlike the crowded impersonal chaos of the big city.

With a car to call her own, she shopped till she nearly dropped. She was especially grateful that she could stock up on groceries, hoping to avoid as many deliveries by creepy Tim Brennan as she could.

And now that she had a better notion of what she needed, she returned to Patricia's, buying a bathing suit for Monday and a few things for the fall and winter weather that loomed ahead. I can use these things no matter where I live, she thought. But in her mind's eye, she saw herself wearing them in Walden–striding down Main Street, autumn leaves swirling at her feet, or seated at her desk at the firm, looking out her window at the snow-covered rooftops of Walden.

Driving north along a little-traveled road, Karen discovered Lake Allison. She parked the Plymouth nearby and took a long look at one of the sandy beaches Jon had described. It had indeed been invaded by the hordes. Hordes of sunburned fathers with paunches and frazzled mothers coated with sunscreen. Hordes of kids making noise and sandcastles and splashing each other in the clear blue water.

Karen recalled the beaches in the Hamptons, where the sun-worshippers were, if not younger, far more affluent. Where even the kids on the beach were dressed by Saks and equipped by F.A.O. Schwarz. The families at Lake Allison looked happy, content with their lives in small-town Wisconsin. Their swimsuits came from Penney's instead of Saks, the sand molds from Sears and the beach balls from Kmart, but their faces glowed with a kind of well-being Karen had rarely seen in New York.

CHAPTER TWENTY-ONE

Monday morning dawned cool and overcast, but by eleven o'clock the sun had broken through. Labor Day would be a glorious and fitting end to summer. Karen dressed, feeling slim in her new bathing suit. The Parker house didn't have a scale, but she was sure she had dropped a few pounds in her nearly three weeks of biking to work. As she combed her luxuriant hair in the bathroom, she felt healthy, strong, beautiful. She looked at her radiant reflection in the spotted bathroom mirror. Life in Walden certainly appears to agree with you, Karen Clark.

She heard a knock at the front door and ran down the stairs to open it. Jon was waiting on the porch. An inordinately happy look crossed his face when he saw Karen. She invited him inside, and he surveyed the living room while she collected her things for the afternoon. "Nice house," he said, nodding in approval. "But you're a little isolated out here, aren't you?"

"I guess I am," Karen admitted. "But so far, that hasn't been a problem."

"Have you met any of your neighbors?"

"No...the other houses are pretty far from here."

Jon nodded again, walking to the window and gazing outside. "A friend of mine in high school used to live up this way, on the farm next to you. Nice folks. Maybe they still live there, you could get to meet them."

"Maybe."

"You know about this house, don't you?"

"This house? No, I really don't. All I know is that everyone calls it 'the old Parker house.'"

"Right," Jon said, "the Parker family used to live here. Generations of them. But the last one left a few years ago, and no one wanted to buy the place. So some real estate agency took it over. Andrews Realty, I think. They've been trying to rent it for a long time now."

"Is there some secret I should know about the house? Like someone being murdered here? Ghosts haunting the place or something?" Karen's tone was light, but in truth, the idea of some worrisome secret attached to the house had crossed her mind.

Jon laughed. "Hardly! It's just another boring old house. Don't worry. No ghosts are going to jump out of the woodwork at you." Jon's smile suddenly faded. "But I don't know if it's such a great idea for you to live alone out here, so far from town, no neighbors close by."

"So far it's been okay. In fact, I love the peace and quiet out here." Karen said. "But I do feel a little nervous sometimes," she admitted. "Maybe I should look for something else. Something in town. The people at my law firm–they said they couldn't find anything for me in town, but maybe...."

"Nothing in town? That's hard to believe." Jon looked skeptical. "Why don't I look around for you, see what I come up with?"

"That would be great!" Karen said.

"In the meantime, let's get going. I want to stake out a place at the lake before anyone else gets there." Jon ushered Karen out her front door and into his car, an almost-new Ford minivan.

As the Ford made its way to Lake Allison, Karen asked Jon about himself and his life in Walden. Jon was happy to fill her in on his background. He had grown up in Walden, the son of a doctor. He'd gone off to college at Harvard, then returned to Wisconsin for medical school. After a residency in pediatrics in St. Louis, he'd joined his father's medical practice. He took over the practice a few years later, when his parents retired to Sarasota.

"So the sign outside your house isn't yours? It was your father's?"

"Right. That's why there's no 'Jr.' on it. But when I took over, I figured, why bother changing it?"

Karen smiled. She felt relaxed, talking to Jon. They had something in common–several years spent at Harvard–and they proceeded to discuss life at the university for the rest of the bumpy ride to the lake.

Karen was grateful she could keep Jon talking about Harvard and steer him away from other areas of her life. Unlike Belinda and the others at the law firm, Jon didn't know anything about K.B. Still, Karen worried that he might reveal to someone, somewhere, a bit of information, a small piece of biography, that would expose her. She had put off creating a new persona, a Karen Clark who would somehow match up both with herself and with the dead K.B. Her failure to deal with it hadn't caused any real problems yet. But she had to face up to it sometime....

Jon turned off the highway and onto a dirt road. The minivan bumped and bounced for half a mile before it turned again, this time onto a smaller dirt road surrounded by woods. After a minute, Jon pulled over and stopped the engine. "We're here!" he announced, grabbing a wicker picnic basket and a tattered cotton quilt from the back of the van. "Let's have lunch."

Karen followed Jon into the woods. Suddenly he stopped at a postage-stamp-sized clearing and began to spread out the quilt. Karen looked around, catching her breath when she spotted the lake, a brilliant turquoise blue, stretching out several hundred feet away. Jon had found the perfect spot for their picnic. Secluded, thickly surrounded by trees, yet near the edge of the lake. "How did you find this place?" she asked him. "It's gorgeous."

"Found it when I was hiking once, years ago. Luckily, very few people know about it. Besides, most people come to the lake with their families, and this place isn't good for kids. No sand, and the water gets deep fairly fast. Most folks go to the sandy beaches on the other side of the lake."

Karen nodded. She'd seen those beaches, crowded with families, the day before.

"Want to have a quick swim before we eat?" Jon asked.

"Sure," Karen answered, slipping out of her t-shirt and shorts. Jon gave her swimsuited body an admiring glance while he pulled off his own shirt and pants, revealing a slim, well-muscled body. His tan was uneven, concentrated on his arms and neck. Too many hours spent in examining rooms instead of out in the sun, Karen thought.

Down to his swimsuit, Jon grabbed Karen's hand and led her to the water. Together they plunged into the clear blue depths, splashing and swimming, cooling off in the late summer heat.

Laughing and dripping, they left the water and returned to the cotton quilt, ready for food. While they talked, learning more about each other, Jon opened the wicker basket and brought out a feast: cold turkey sandwiches on hearty whole wheat bread, hard-boiled eggs, carrot and celery sticks, cut-up fruit, iced tea in a large thermos.

Karen had skipped breakfast and hadn't realized how hungry she was till she saw the food, spread out on the quilt. She ate greedily, the carefully-prepared meal satisfying her hunger. Smiling, Jon watched her eat.

"I like watching you eat," he said finally. "You enjoy it so much."

Karen felt embarrassed, both by Jon's stares and by his teasing comment about the food. "I do enjoy eating. And this lunch is delicious. Thank you!"

"My pleasure." Jon moved closer to Karen and took her hand. "Karen, I feel so...so lucky to have met you. You're extraordinary."

Karen flushed, embarrassed again by Jon's words. She was unsure of her own feelings, unsure of the words to say in response. Jon was wonderful–bright, thoughtful, generous. She probably should feel lucky, too. But everything was happening so fast. She hardly knew what she felt.

Jon was moving even closer to her. Suddenly his arms were around her. In her wet bathing suit, she felt almost naked, vulnerable, but she didn't move away. She felt the curly brown hairs on his chest against the tops of her breasts, tickling her skin, making her laugh. At once Jon stopped her laughter, pressing his lips against hers, kissing her hard, eagerly, as though he had waited a long time to kiss someone this way.

Karen felt herself responding to him, kissing him back, almost breathless now, her heart beating wildly inside her chest. Who was this man, this Jon Smith? She hardly knew him, but it felt right to be kissing him like this. His lips were sweet, the sugared iced tea still on them, her mouth eagerly opening to let in his searching tongue, flavored like his lips by the sweet tea.

Slowly, Jon pressed Karen down on the tattered quilt, kissing her neck, her breasts above the bathing suit, stroking her arms as he lowered her gently, lovingly. His hand slowly pulled down the top of her suit. He cried out "Oh!" when he saw her breasts, then kissed them greedily, taking the nipples into his mouth.

"Jon...," Karen began, but his mouth was back on hers, his hands exploring her breasts, then tugging at the suit to lower it still more. Karen felt herself melting, melting in Jon's arms.

She thought briefly of Jason. It hadn't been like this with Jason for a long time. The breathless excitement of exploration, of discovery. The careless self-abandon, inhibitions suddenly cast away. It hadn't felt like this for a very long time.

Karen heard hushed sounds in the woods around her. Squirrels or rabbits in hot pursuit of each other. Did animals feel what people felt, or was it pure instinct? Did animals feel the heart-pounding excitement she was feeling right now?

Jon was breathing fast. His hands trembling, he helped Karen remove the rest of her bathing suit, then slipped swiftly out of his own. His hands covered her body now. He seemed to know all the right places to caress, all the right buttons to push. There was no going back now. Karen opened herself up to Jon and felt him enter, felt him thrust inside her. She closed her eyes, feeling nothing but his thrusting, his raising her to dizzying heights, waiting till she cried out in a throbbing climax of sensation, then ending with his own.

Jon kissed Karen on the lips again, then collapsed beside her, his chest heaving, his face glowing with satisfaction. He looked over at Karen. "You're wonderful. I feel incredible with you."

Karen felt herself glowing, too, filled with emotions she hadn't felt in years. Since the first few months with Jason. But these feelings were suddenly chilled by a cold blast of reality. It had all happened so fast. Too fast. Maybe she should have pushed Jon away, waited a while before she had sex with him. What would he think of her, meeting her one weekend, having sex with her the next?

Jon read her thoughts. Looking at her, he grabbed her hand. "Don't worry, Karen. I know you aren't the kind of woman who goes to bed with every man she meets. This was different. It was right. We both knew it was right."

Jon's face was honest, sensitive, caring. Karen knew he was telling the truth. There *was* something extraordinary about the way they felt. A spark of electricity between them, a responsiveness she never could have predicted. She curled up inside his arms.

They lay there together for an hour or more before swimming again, laughing and chatting again, then leaving the lake, encircled in each other's arms.

CHAPTER TWENTY-TWO

When Karen and Jon arrived on her front porch late Monday afternoon, she was still glowing, still harboring the on-top-of-the-world feeling a new romance always engendered in her. But a few small doubts had begun to creep into her consciousness. Jon seemed like the ideal beau–attentive, sensitive, clearly mad about her–but who was he really? She had leapt headlong into this relationship, into intimacy with Jon, without knowing very much about him.

You'd better go slow, Karen. No, you can't change what you've already done, and you probably wouldn't want to if you could. But don't plunge any deeper into this relationship for now. Wait, wait, till you find out more about Jon.

Her uncertainty made Karen's body stiffen when Jon put his arms around her on the porch. "What's wrong?" he asked, pulling back.

"Nothing. Nothing's wrong. It's just that everything's happened so fast. Let's...let's put on the brakes for a while. Go a bit slower."

Jon carefully examined Karen's face. "Okay. If that's how you want it. Things did...move pretty fast down at the lake. I think I understand how you feel. But I don't want to lose you, Karen."

Karen smiled. "I don't want to stop seeing you. I just need some breathing room. . . ."

"I understand," Jon said, pulling her back inside his arms. "I'll say goodbye for now." He kissed her gently, then released her and walked back to the minivan. "I'll call you tomorrow," he shouted as he drove off.

Karen went inside, hugging herself in the small kitchen, trying to figure out how she felt. About Jon, about Walden. Things had worked out pretty well so far. But so many things were still unresolved.

If she stayed in Walden, she would have to arrange for packing and sending all her things from New York, close her checking account there, notify her father and stepmother of her new address. And she would have to sort out her feelings about Jon.

But I don't have to make any decisions yet, she thought. I've got time. Plenty of time. No need to decide anything like that right now.

Still, one thing she *had* decided. She had to have a car of her own. After a weekend of driving the battered brown Plymouth, she couldn't go back to riding a bike to work every day and depending on others to take her shopping or make deliveries. With colder weather approaching, and with it the threat of rain, even snow, she needed a car.

She couldn't afford much of a car, of course. Not until she transferred her funds from her bank in New York. And she wasn't ready to do that. But there was one possible alternative. Maybe Ed would sell her the old Plymouth. It was in working condition, and she was already accustomed to its idiosyncrasies. It would suit her needs for now.

When she broached the subject Tuesday morning, Ed happily agreed to sell her the car. "That'll be $400 in cash," he said.

Karen hesitated. "What about the brakes? They need some work."

"I'll do what I can with the brakes, sis. Throw in a lube and oil job, too. I'll start work on it this afternoon."

"Okay," Karen said. "I'll take it." She was relieved that buying the old Plymouth had been so easy. Now all she had to do was get the $400 in cash from Belinda.

Belinda had explained at the outset that Karen would be paid monthly, beginning at the end of her first month. Because Karen needed some cash right away, Belinda had already advanced her a few hundred dollars. Karen was sure she would advance another $400 for the car.

Luckily, Karen was right. Belinda agreed to get the money from the bank at lunchtime. The Plymouth would be Karen's that afternoon.

Karen finally settled down at her desk about 9:30. Attacking the mound of files in front of her, she was quickly immersed in the world of leases and wills.

A few minutes later, Belinda buzzed her. "Charlie wants to see you in his office. Sounds important."

Karen walked swiftly to Charlie's office. He looked up and smiled when he saw her. A wooden smile, but a smile nonetheless. "Got a problem for you, Karen," he said, thrusting a file in her direction. Karen took the file and began to leaf through it. A typed will appeared to be the most significant document in the file.

"Testator in this case died a couple of weeks ago." He paused. "A woman. Years ago, we used to say 'testatrix' for a woman. Not anymore, thanks to the women libbers," Charlie cackled, enjoying his little joke.

Karen nodded, remembering her first-year Property Law course at Harvard. How she had despised her arrogant, obnoxious professor. He spent nearly the whole year talking about antiquated, centuries-old property law instead of the modern law the students needed to know. She remembered "testatrix" all right.

"Nobody says it anymore," Charlie repeated. "Everybody's a 'testator' now." He looked back at the file, remembering why he had called Karen in. "We prepared this will, the one there in the file."

Karen nodded again.

"Sit down, sit down," Charlie impatiently waved Karen into a chair. "It's a long story. You might as well get comfortable." Karen seated herself opposite Charlie. "I got a call late Friday afternoon, after you left." Karen remembered leaving the office early on Friday. Was she going to be held to account for it now? Fortunately, Charlie didn't mention her early departure.

"Mrs. Cameron–Darla Cameron–left everything to her daughter in that will," Charlie continued. "She disinherited her son Hecky. I wasn't surprised. Hecky always was a problem kid. He went off to Chicago a while back and got into the drug scene there. Even got arrested once. Didn't get convicted, though–some smart lawyer down there got him off." Another wooden smile.

"Now Hecky's turned up again. Heard about his mother's death and came up for the funeral. Then he found out about the will and talked to a lawyer in Chicago. That call Friday, that was from the lawyer down there. Hecky, he wants to contest the will. He's going to claim his mother was incompetent when she made it."

Karen nodded again, wondering what part she would be asked to play in the unfolding drama. People got very emotional about wills; she knew that already. But where was this particular struggle headed?

"I went and called Elizabeth, the Cameron daughter, after I spoke to Hecky's lawyer," Charlie continued. "She'd already had words with her brother but didn't know where to turn. After talking to me, she decided to retain us to defend the will.

"Now here's what I want you to do," Charlie said. "Check out the witnesses to the will. It should be simple enough: their names and addresses are right on the document. They appear to be a married couple. Elizabeth thinks they were friends of her mother's. People she knew at church or neighbors, something like that. Call them and make a date to interview them. Take one of the secretaries along and get a statement from them. Their testimony will be the basis of our defense."

Karen nodded again. If the married couple testified that Darla Cameron was mentally competent at the time she signed the will, that testimony would be powerful evidence in Elizabeth's favor. Of course, it would also be helpful to interview others who knew the dead woman–anyone who could counter whatever evidence Hecky would try to produce.

"Should I try to contact others? Darla's doctor, for instance?" she asked.

"Not yet, not yet. Contact this couple first. What's their name?"

Karen flipped through the will until she found the page with the witnesses' signatures. "Ruddy. John and Catherine Ruddy."

"Yes, that's it. Call them right now. Don't waste any time." Charlie's patience was beginning to wear thin.

"Right, Charlie. I'll do it right away." Karen rose from her chair. By the time she walked out the door to his office, Charlie was already delving into other documents on his desk.

Back at her own desk, Karen looked through the file more carefully, starting with the will. She read it over slowly, digesting its important features. Interesting. Darla Cameron hadn't merely ignored her son when she distributed her assets. She had explicitly disinherited him, stating clearly in the will, "Because my son Harlan has been a disappointment to me, turning to a life totally opposed to the values both his father and I have always stood for, he shall take nothing from my estate after my death."

Pretty outspoken. Darla Cameron certainly seemed to know what she wanted. If that statement was any indication of her thinking at the time she made her will, there wasn't much question that she was mentally competent, fully in control of her mental faculties at the time. That she had what the law called "testamentary capacity." Hecky would have a tough row to hoe if he were going to prove otherwise.

Karen flipped through the other materials in the file. Someone had done an extensive interview with Darla Cameron and made notes based on that interview. Karen didn't think she needed to review those notes, not right now. But the name of the lawyer at the top of the first page suddenly leapt off the page at Karen: Laura Hanson.

There was that name again. Laura Hanson. Karen looked quickly through the rest of the file. It appeared that Laura Hanson was the lawyer who had interviewed Mrs. Cameron, prepared the will, and appeared at its signing in front of the two witnesses.

Laura Hanson. Karen wondered again who she was. A young woman lawyer, she knew that much. But when had she come to work at Fuller, Fuller & Chase? When had she left? And why?

Karen heard a telephone ring somewhere else in the office. It brought her back to the business at hand. She had to put aside her questions about Laura Hanson and get to work instead. She pulled out the Walden telephone book, looked up John Ruddy, and picked up her phone to place the call.

CHAPTER TWENTY-THREE

"John Ruddy?" the voice asked. "I'm sorry, Mr. Ruddy's deceased. Can I help you?"

"Deceased? John Ruddy has died?" Karen asked.

"Yes, I'm afraid so. About a year ago. This is his daughter, Barbara Simon."

"Well...I'm very sorry about your father...." Karen was at a loss for words. She hadn't expected to hear that one of her witnesses was dead. "My name is Karen Clark. I'm a lawyer representing Darla Cameron's daughter. Your father was a witness when Mrs. Cameron signed her will, and I was hoping to talk with him."

"Darla was a neighbor. Lived down the street somewhere. I don't remember exactly where...."

"Well, perhaps I could speak to your mother. She was also a witness."

"My mother?" Barbara's voice changed, and Karen thought she could hear a quiet sob on the other end of the line. "Mother passed away, too, three months ago."

Both witnesses dead? Now what? "I'm terribly sorry, Ms. Simon. What a great loss for you."

"Yes, yes, it has been. First Dad died very suddenly, then Mother. She didn't seem to want to go on living after he was gone. It's been a terrible time for me."

"I can imagine." Karen tried to think. Was there anything she could ask Barbara Simon before she hung up? "May I...may I ask you a question?"

"Sure."

"Did you know Darla Cameron?"

"Not really. I haven't lived in this house for years. I was just going through some of Mother's things this morning. I'm planning to put the house up for sale next month, and I left the phone connected just in case I...."

"Of course," Karen interrupted. "But about Darla Cameron...."

"Oh. As I said, I didn't know her very well. She moved here when I was in high school, oh, about twenty years ago. I never got to know anyone in the family before I got married and moved out."

"I see."

"I'm sorry I can't help you very much. But I've been...."

Karen interrupted the garrulous woman again. "Well, thanks for the information. Again, I'm sorry about your parents." Karen hung up.

Both witnesses to the will-signing were dead, barely two years after the will was written. An unusual occurrence but certainly not unheard of.

Wisconsin law required only two witnesses to the signing of a will. Surely there were other cases of both witnesses dying before the testator. She would research Wisconsin case law to see where to go from here. No doubt Darla's doctor, her other friends, could provide evidence of her competence. Certainly her lawyer....

Her lawyer.... Of course! Her lawyer was Laura Hanson. One thing Karen could do immediately: track down Laura Hanson and get a statement about Darla's competence from her.

Karen left her desk and headed for Belinda's. Belinda would have a forwarding address for Laura Hanson.

Belinda looked up as Karen approached. "Yes, dear? What can I do for you?"

"I need Laura Hanson's address. Her telephone number, too, if you have it."

"Laura Hanson?" Belinda hesitated. "You mean the Laura Hanson who worked here a few years ago?"

"Yes." Karen was puzzled by Belinda's response. Why the hesitation?

"I don't have it," Belinda said, shaking her head.

"Didn't she leave a forwarding address when she left the firm?"

Belinda shook her head again. "No, Karen, sorry. She left rather suddenly, as I recall. Just left a memo for Charlie, something about moving back to California. We never did get a forwarding address for her."

Karen stared at Belinda in disbelief. A lawyer who didn't leave a forwarding address? "What about her mail? What did you do about that?"

"We saved it for a while. I thought we'd hear something eventually. But we never did, so I finally threw it all out." Belinda seemed to be as surprised by Laura Hanson's behavior as Karen was. "I know it sounds crazy, Karen, but that's what happened."

Karen continued to stare at Belinda.

"Charlie knows more about it than I do," Belinda volunteered. "Maybe you should talk to him."

Karen nodded. "Yes. Of course." She walked to Charlie's office and knocked on the open door.

"Come in, come in," Charlie said, waving her in.

Karen sat in the chair facing Charlie and filled him in on developments in the Cameron case. With both witnesses dead, she wanted to get a statement from the lawyer who prepared the will. Laura Hanson.

"Oh, so it was Laura who did it. I'd forgotten."

"There's just one problem, Charlie. Belinda doesn't have an address for Laura."

"No address? You mean she never sent us an address?"

"I guess not."

"Well, the circumstances of her leaving *were* rather unusual," Charlie began, leaning back in his large leather chair. "She seemed pretty happy here, all things considered. Worked here, oh, about two years. Bright girl, good worker. Everything seemed okay. Then one Monday morning I come into the office and find a memo from her on my desk. She had decided to go back to California. She had her folks out there, and she talked once in a while about going back. Especially during the winter. She talked about the beautiful California winters. Tried to adjust to the cold weather here but never quite got...."

Charlie was rambling. Who cared about the beautiful California winters? Karen tried to get him back on track. "What about this memo she left you. What did it say?"

Charlie's blue eyes looked startled for a moment. Then he resumed talking. "As I recall, she said she missed her family and the weather out there, and decided to go back. She said she'd let us know her new address when she found a job there. I always assumed she did."

"What about her work here? Her cases? Did she just drop everything in your lap?" Karen couldn't believe that a lawyer would suddenly pull up stakes like that, leaving work for her colleagues to handle after she was gone.

"The three of us divvied it up. We were all familiar with her cases. She had assisted us, after all. Not dealing with clients directly very much, mostly helping us with our work."

Sounds like my job description, Karen thought. Clearly Karen had assumed the same role Laura Hanson had held at the firm a few years earlier. "Her affidavit would really help us on the Cameron case. Should I try to track her down?"

Charlie paused, thinking. "Check with Belinda, see if we still have her old employment file. That should have her résumé, law school transcript, that kind of thing. If Belinda can't find her file, forget it. Start contacting Darla's doctor, her neighbors, people like that."

Karen nodded. A reasonable approach. She left Charlie's office to look for Belinda. After wasting her time on the Ruth Swenson case, Karen felt bad about saddling her with still another search, but this time the request was Charlie's.

"No problem," Belinda said when Karen explained what Charlie suggested. "I keep all the personnel files together so I know just where to find them. Should have thought of it myself. I'll have Laura's for you in a jiffy."

Karen returned to her office and leafed through the Darla Cameron file while she waited. Laura Hanson had done a good job; the file was in excellent shape. Laura had even noted the name of Darla's doctor, Roger Huggins, M.D. Karen would place a call to him that afternoon.

Karen looked up. Belinda was in the doorway, shaking her head. "I can't find it, Karen."

"You can't find it?"

"I can't imagine where it is. All my personnel files are in that drawer. Everyone who's worked here for the past umpteen years. But Laura's isn't there."

Karen felt a sudden chill. This was too odd to be coincidental. Laura Hanson's name had popped up twice. First, in connection with Ruth Swenson's claim. Belinda had been unable to find the file for that case. Although Harold Chase had assured Karen that he would "take care" of it, his behavior regarding Ruth Swenson seemed odd, as though he were trying to cover up something.

Now Karen had been handed another case involving Laura Hanson. And this case was too important to set aside. Finding Laura was vital to the Cameron case. Other testimony would be useful, sure, but in the absence of the two witnesses to Darla Cameron's signing, it was absolutely essential to talk to the attorney who handled the will and was herself present at the signing.

Karen had to find Laura Hanson.

Belinda turned to leave. "Wait, wait a second," Karen said. "Sit down, please. Maybe you can remember something about Laura. Maybe I can track her down without that file."

Belinda took a seat opposite Karen. "Sure. What do you want to know?"

"Charlie said she was from California." Belinda nodded. "Did she ever say what city she was from?"

"Ummm...let me think." Belinda's face screwed up as she tried to remember. "I think she mentioned some small town. I'd never heard of it before. Sorry, I can't remember it now."

"Did she ever mention wanting to work in San Francisco? Or L.A.? San Diego?"

"Not that I recall. She...she just talked about 'California.' How nice the weather was, especially in the wintertime. That kind of thing."

"Did she ever go back there for vacations?" Think, Belinda, think.

"I don't honestly remember, Karen. It's a while ago now."

Karen nodded.

Belinda stood up to leave. "Sorry I can't...."

"Wait, Belinda. Do you remember where she went to law school? I could contact the alumni office, get her current address that way."

Belinda looked down at the floor, thinking hard. "Law school, law school. No, I don't remember. It was a pretty good one, I think. But the name's totally gone. Maybe one of the lawyers remembers."

Yes, of course. The lawyers would remember. She'd ask Charlie first. "Thanks, Belinda. I'll ask Charlie."

"Okay. I'll get back to work then." Belinda hurried off to her desk.

Karen sat back, thinking. She'd ask Charlie, maybe even Harold and Chad if they remembered Laura's law school. Then she'd phone the alumni office. Those offices kept tabs on their alumni, soliciting donations to the old school, if nothing else. Karen was familiar with Harvard's efforts. They were constantly writing her, sending magazines, sponsoring luncheons and dinners, asking for money at least once or twice a year. Laura's school certainly did the same.

Karen had a sudden inspiration. Maybe Laura had gone to Harvard, too? She remembered now, there'd been a woman named Hanson in the class ahead of her. Charlie had made contact with K.B. through the Harvard placement office, and if he made a practice of doing that, he might have hired Laura the same way.

Karen did a mental computation. The woman a year ahead of her would have graduated four years ago, just about the time Laura Hanson arrived at the firm. Perfect! Karen placed a call to Harvard and got through to the alumni office immediately.

"No," came the response a few minutes later, "there was a Rebecca Hanson in that class. No Laura Hanson."

"Oh." Karen's bubble had burst. "Well, are there any Laura Hansons? In any other classes, I mean?"

"Just a minute. I'll check." After another minute, the voice came back. "There was a Laura Hanson in the class of '57."

Class of '57. That meant she was much too old to be the right Laura Hanson. "She's listed in our records as a judge in Atlanta, Georgia, for the past fifteen years. Would that be the woman you're looking for?"

"No, I'm afraid not."

"Well, do you know where this woman is working?"

"California, I think."

"You might try the State Bar out there. They keep excellent records on their members. And if she's practicing in California, she has to be a member of the bar."

Of course! Karen hung up and called Directory Assistance, finally getting through to the State Bar's offices in San Francisco. An employee gave her the names and addresses of three members of the bar named Laura Hanson. Karen took down the information, got the three phone numbers, and began calling.

Her first call, to a public defender in Los Angeles, was inconclusive. The woman was in court and would have to return Karen's call. Karen left her name and number and a short message: "It's urgent that you call me as soon as possible."

The second Laura Hanson was an associate with a patent law firm in San Francisco. Karen reached the lawyer's secretary and explained that she was looking for a Laura Hanson who had worked for a law firm in Walden, Wisconsin, two to four years ago. "Ms. Hanson has been at this firm for the past six years," the secretary responded. "Sorry."

Karen's third call went to a number in El Cajon. Where in California was El Cajon? Could it be the little town Laura Hanson came from?

A harried woman's voice answered. "Hello?"

Karen could hear a baby crying in the background. "My name is Karen Clark. I'm a lawyer in Wisconsin. Is this Laura Hanson?"

"Yes." The voice sounded wary.

"Ms. Hanson, have you ever worked for a law firm in Wisconsin?"

The woman's voice changed. "Me? Wisconsin? I've never even been *in* Wisconsin." The woman laughed. "And I've never worked for a law firm either. I worked for the federal government before I had my baby, but I left when she was born."

"Oh. Well, sorry to have bothered you." Karen hung up. Her last hope was the public defender in L.A. But she would have to wait for a return call on that one. In the meantime, she had a pile of work she had put aside.

Karen attacked the pile with as much energy as she could summon. The morning's efforts had exhausted her, but she kept plugging. For one thing, she wanted to call Darla Cameron's physician, Dr. Huggins. She finally reached him at four o'clock and quickly described the reason for her call. Dr. Huggins agreed to meet with her at his office late Friday afternoon, promising to review Darla's medical records before the appointment.

Karen struggled through the rest of the day, staying a bit later than usual in hopes of getting the call from Los Angeles. At last she had to leave, afraid she'd miss Ed at the gas station if she waited too long.

She walked briskly to the station, looking forward to driving the Plymouth home. But when she arrived, Ed looked embarrassed. "I didn't get to the Plymouth yet. I'll have it for you tomorrow." Karen was too startled, too angry to speak. "But the bike's ready, sis," he said quickly.

The Plymouth clearly had priority over the bike. Didn't the old fool realize that?

She hopped on the bike and rode off in silence. She would ask Nedra for a ride in the morning. Surely the Plymouth would be ready by the afternoon, and she would never have to bike to work again.

CHAPTER TWENTY-FOUR

At home Tuesday evening, Karen eagerly waited for Jon's call. It never came. Fleetingly, she considered looking up Jon's number and calling him, but she couldn't bring herself to do it. He had promised to call. She would wait.

A thousand questions danced crazily in Karen's head. Had it been a mistake to let things go so far with Jon? She barely knew him. But at the lake she'd been swept away by his adoring glances, his passionate embraces. She had sensed that he was genuinely taken with her and desired a serious relationship. Had she read the signals all wrong?

Looking back, Karen was appalled by her own eagerness to make love, to surrender herself so quickly to the closest possible kind of intimacy. She felt like a tart, or worse, like a vulnerable single woman desperate for a man's attentions. She'd never felt that way before. All of her previous relationships had built more slowly, leading gradually, step by step, to the inevitable conclusion. But this, this was different. Karen felt as though she had virtually leapt into Jon's arms, giving herself to him almost without hesitation. Was she really so desperate, so needy, that she had come to this?

Karen finally put her thoughts of Jon aside. She had a more immediate problem. She couldn't face taking the bicycle to work one more day; a ride the next morning was essential. She made a quick phone call to Nedra and arranged to be picked up at 7:30. She would get to work and make progress on her files in the quiet early morning before anyone else arrived.

"How was your weekend?" Nedra asked when she picked up Karen the next morning. "I was going to call you about getting together, but my parents phoned and asked me to come home."

"It was...it was really good, Nedra. Jon asked me to go swimming with him at Lake Allison. We...we had a great time." Karen's heart began to beat a little faster as she thought about the afternoon at the lake. In spite of Jon's failure to call, she had to admit that her recollection of their afternoon together excited her.

"Jon? Jon Smith? Terrific! I thought the two of you might hit it off," Nedra said, turning to Karen, then looking back at the road. She was wearing a pale yellow summer suit, and her long brown hair was pulled up into a professional-looking bun. "I dated Jon myself at one time. He's a great guy, but after a while he...he just stopped calling." Nedra looked wistful for a moment, then changed the subject. "How are things going at your firm? Charlie Fuller treating you all right?" she asked with a smile.

Karen hesitated for a moment. In truth, Charlie did treat her pretty well. "No complaints so far," she said.

"And have you met Chad yet?"

"As a matter of fact, I have. He finally showed up last Friday."

"And...?"

"And...he's everything you said he was. You called him a hunk, right? Well, he seems to be a gen-u-ine, Grade-A hunk!" Karen laughed.

Nedra joined in the laughter. "Isn't he ever? Yum! I'd love to get my hands on that guy!"

"Well, why don't you?"

Nedra giggled. "He never asked!"

"Does he date anyone?" Karen asked.

"I don't know," Nedra said, her face turning serious again. "Someone told me he talks about a 'ladyfriend' in Madison, a woman on the faculty there, but that's all I know."

"Hmmm....I'll see what I can find out. You're really interested, right?" Karen felt she owed Nedra something. For befriending her, for taking her to Jon's party. Nedra had, after all, introduced her to Jon and seemed sincerely happy that Karen and Jon had gone out together. Now Nedra was nodding her head, indicating her interest in Chad. I'll say something to Chad, Karen decided, something to get him thinking about Nedra.

Karen felt a sudden pang at the thought. Wait a second, she told herself, I'm not ready to give up on Chad myself just yet. Maybe Jon has a good excuse for not calling, and maybe the relationship with him really is going somewhere. But I'm not sure, can't be sure, about Jon. And I'm not ready to forget about Chad.

Suppose this "thing" with Jon didn't last. That gorgeous tan, those blond curls, that perfect smile–Chad was a very appealing guy. Karen didn't want to cut herself off from anything that might develop with him in the future.

Still, it wouldn't hurt to do a little digging. She would do exactly what she promised Nedra. Try to find out about Chad's purported "ladyfriend." The result would be useful, whether for Nedra's benefit or for her own.

Nedra's Lumina pulled up in front of Karen's office building. "Thanks, Nedra," Karen said, waving goodbye. She used her key to enter the deserted building. The hallway was still dark, almost eerie. Karen couldn't find a light switch and climbed the stairs carefully, reaching the door to the office in the light from the dirty double-sash window on the landing.

She let herself into the office and turned on the lights. A wonderful early-morning silence greeted her as she walked to her desk.

Only the overnight heat build-up disturbed the pleasant peaceful feeling. Karen found the air-conditioning switch and turned it on, enjoying the comfort the familiar hum immediately began to produce.

Back at her desk, she pulled out the Darla Cameron file again. I hope I hear from that public defender in L.A. today, she thought. But it's too early–only six o'clock in the morning out there. I'll have a long wait.

Six o'clock there and–what?–nine o'clock in New York. Karen suddenly had a mental picture of Garrity & Costello, all the secretaries rushing in to work about now, saying "Good morning," getting a cup of coffee. Just about now, she would be asking Melissa for coffee and sitting down with it at her desk.

Melissa. Melissa Cohen. Oh, no. Karen had a sinking feeling in her stomach. She'd never called Melissa back, not once, not after that call the first Monday morning in Walden. Melissa had to be frantic, worried about Karen, wondering what to tell Phil Hendrix about Karen's long absence from the office.

How could I have forgotten to call Melissa? I must have suppressed everything about New York, buried it in the farthest corner of my mind, eager to forget everything and everybody there. How else could I have forgotten to call Melissa?

Now Karen ransacked her brain, trying to remember Melissa's phone number at Garrity & Costello. The firm, New York, Melissa–all of it seemed a million miles away. Finally the number came back to her, and she picked up the phone.

"I'll accept the call," Melissa told the operator.

Hearing Melissa's voice, Karen pictured her secretary in her mind's eye. The curly red hair making a halo around her pink, freckled face. The face itself radiating cheerful good humor. But how cheerful would Melissa be after such a long time?

"Karen! Where *are* you? I've been worried sick. No word from you all this...."

"Melissa, I'm okay, I'm okay."

"Well, why haven't you called? Where have you been?"

Karen had to come up with a reasonable explanation. "I...I had a relapse and...I had to go back to the hospital for a while."

"What? A relapse? You went back to the hospital? Oh, my God...."

"But I'm all right now, Melissa. I really am."

"You sound okay. But Karen, I'm worried about you. Besides which, Phil Hendrix has been on my back for the last three or four weeks, however long it's been."

"Didn't you tell him to give my work to somebody else?"

"Yes, I told him. But he wanted to wait, to see what we heard from you. He's been asking me almost every day."

Oh, God. That bastard. "Melissa, I'm really sorry. I would have called you earlier if I could," Karen lied. "I just couldn't."

"Okay, okay, I understand," Melissa said. "I'm really sorry to hear you've been so sick. What do the doctors say?"

"The doctors?"

"When do they say you can come back to work?" Melissa asked.

"Oh. Well, they're not sure, Melissa. They can't give me a date. I have to rest more. They'll know in a month or two."

"A month or two?" Karen could picture Melissa's agitated face turning even pinker, her bright brown eyes opening wide. "Are you serious?"

"Perfectly." A month or two would give Karen some breathing space. October, November. She could come to some sort of decision by then. "The doctors say they won't know till then. They don't want me to leave town in the meantime."

"Are you back at your cousin's?"

My cousin's? Karen paused, trying to remember what she had told Melissa that first Monday morning. At last she remembered. "Yes, I'm back at my cousin's."

"Can you give me the number there?"

"No, Melissa, I can't. She's really hyper about it. I'll just have to call you."

"Okay, Karen, if that's the way it's gotta be." Melissa sounded resigned to the situation. "But what am I gonna tell Hendrix?"

"Just tell him I've been very sick and that..." Suddenly Karen remembered the ploy she'd decided on weeks before. "Tell him I need to go on medical leave. I'll prepare a letter to that effect and send it to you." Karen grabbed a pencil and jotted down a note to herself: HENDRIX LETTER RE MEDICAL LEAVE! Then she buried the note under the Cameron file, where no one else would see it.

"Good. That should take care of him for a while. But Karen, there's...there's something else." Melissa's tone changed. She sounded reluctant to broach this new problem.

"Yes?"

"It's...it's Jason Singer."

"Oh." Jason.

"He's called me several times, and last week he came by my desk. He...he keeps asking me what to do with your stuff."

"My stuff?"

"Yeah. Karen, look, this is none of my business, but I guess you never called Jason, and he keeps trying to find out about you through me."

"Sorry, Melissa. I didn't think...."

"That's okay. It's just that he keeps asking about your stuff. The stuff you left behind in the apartment."

"Oh." Karen closed her eyes, trying to shut out the image of the apartment, of Jason, that had just popped into her brain.

"Karen?" Melissa was saying. "From what he said, I got the impression that someone else has moved into the apartment, and he needs to clear out your stuff to make room for this other person."

Of course. Joan. Joan Granger had moved into the apartment. She was sleeping in Karen's bed, pawing through her things. Probably wearing her clothes, using her cosmetics, reading her books. The thought made Karen feel ill.

Melissa's voice came back on the line. It was softer, gentler, almost apologetic. "Karen? What should I tell him?"

"Let me think for a minute." Melissa had nothing to apologize for. It was Jason who was the bad guy, not Melissa. Karen was oddly happy, almost grateful she had discovered what Jason was really like before she wasted any more time on him.

But what about her things? Suddenly Karen knew what to do. "Just tell Jason to pack up all my stuff. He can get packing cartons at a liquor store. He can use the suitcases I left behind, too. Tell him to pack up everything."

"Okay," Melissa said, sounding relieved that Karen had reached a decision. "Do you want him to send them to your cousin's place?"

"No, no." My cousin's place meant Chicago. How could she give Melissa an address in Chicago, an address that didn't even exist? She had to think of some other solution. "She's had problems with deliveries here. Things have been stolen. Let me think another minute."

Finally Karen realized there was no way to get her things without revealing her location and her new identity. "You know, I don't need those things right now. And I won't need them again till I'm completely recovered. Just tell Jason to put everything into storage somewhere. As soon as I'm better, I'll pick it up. And tell him I'll pay the storage bill."

"That sounds good. I'll tell him."

"Great. Thanks, Melissa. Now I've got to hang up. My cousin needs to use the phone." Karen was amazed at her new competence at lying. It got easier and easier every time she did it.

"Oh, okay. Listen, take care of yourself. And call me! Don't wait so long next time!"

"Okay, I promise." Karen hung up. Now she could forget about New York again, for a little while at least. Melissa would take care of everything.

The rest of the day went by swiftly. When she didn't hear from L.A. by four o'clock, she tried phoning the public defender's office again. Once more she was told that Laura Hanson was in court. And once more she stressed to the voice at the other end just how urgent her call was.

At five o'clock Karen left the office, walking through town to Ed's Arco station. A cool breeze grazed her face as she walked, looking in shop windows, gazing at her reflection in the shiny glass. After a block or two, she found herself in front of The Gift Hutch. Peering inside, she could see Jackie Berlinghof standing next to a customer in front of a tall display case, pointing at a small collection of glittering crystal bowls.

Jackie was animatedly chatting with her customer and didn't notice Karen. But seeing her reminded Karen of Jon's party, where Jackie had clearly viewed Karen as a threat, a rival for Jon's affections. Maybe the two of them were a couple, and Jon had called Karen only for the sake of a little variety.

A wave of nausea hit Karen. She felt dizzy remembering how quickly, how easily, she'd given herself to Jon at the lake. What a colossal mistake! I must have meant nothing to him but an easy lay.

Now he's probably returned to Jackie, picked up where they left off without missing a beat.

Karen straightened her shoulders and began walking again, reaching Ed's station after a few minutes. "No bike today?" Ed asked when he saw her. She shook her head. "Well, the Plymouth's ready. As ready as it'll ever be," he laughed, walking with Karen to the car.

"Don't expect miracles now, sis. It's an old car with a lotta problems. It'd cost a fortune to fix it up right. But it's good enough now for your purposes. You're just going to drive it around town, right? No long highway trips?"

"Right," Karen answered. All she needed was basic transportation. Something to get her to work and back, to Brennan's, occasionally to the shopping mall. No long trips.

"It'll be okay, then. That's 400 bucks, sis."

Karen peeled the bills out of her wallet, and Ed handed her the car keys. At last! A car of her own! Karen jumped into the Plymouth and drove off, free again to go where and when she wanted.

Just now, that place was home.

CHAPTER TWENTY-FIVE

Karen fixed a light supper and ate it on the front porch. She always felt calm, peaceful, sitting in one of the white wicker chairs on the porch, gazing at the huge old trees surrounding her. A gentle breeze blew her hair away from her face, making her feel sleek and cool, refreshed after the long day. She could hear the crickets tuning up for the evening's performance.

This life—this life in Walden. She had to admit that it came close to her fantasies of small-town life. To the kind of existence she'd hoped to find when she made her impulsive decision in a Chicago hotel room a month before. She had cottoned to the pace of life here, to the ease of small-town living, to the slow measure of her work at the law firm.

Talking to Melissa that morning had brought New York back to her consciousness. The stress, the distress. The meanness of the city and of the people she had known there. Not Melissa, of course, but others, like Phil Hendrix. Like Jason.

Escape from New York. The movie title popped into her head again. That was, after all, exactly what she had done. Escaped.

And I owe it all to K.B. To Karen Beatrice Clark.

Karen had tried to keep from thinking about K.B. Assuming the other woman's identity was unlike anything else she had ever done. It was totally foreign to her to lie, to be evasive, to pretend to be anything other than what she was. But coming to Walden had forced her to make that her everyday routine. The easiest way to forget all the lies, she had found, was to shake off thoughts of K.B. whenever they arose.

Now the memory of K.B. suddenly surfaced again, resurrected after weeks of denial. K.B.'s heart-shaped face, her shiny dark hair, her light-hearted laugh flashed through Karen's brain, flooding her mind with memories of the dead young woman with her name.

K.B. had been excited about coming to Walden, about starting her first real job. Her excitement had led Karen to start her own new life in Walden.

I'm sure now that I was right to take K.B.'s place, Karen thought. It sounds bizarre, but I think I was meant to come here. K.B.'s death liberated me–liberated me from my miserable life in New York, allowed me to begin a new one here.

The phone rang, and Karen hurried inside to answer it.

"Karen?" Jon's voice. Her heart began to pound at the sound of it.

"Yes."

"It's Jon. I want to explain about last night."

"Go ahead."

"I had an emergency. A patient who nearly died."

"Oh. Really?" A good excuse. The best excuse. What could be better than a patient who nearly died? If it's true.

"Really, Karen. She nearly died." Jon paused. "Can I come over to see you?"

"Now?"

"Karen, you're angry, aren't you?"

Karen was silent.

"You're angry because I didn't call last night. I...I want to tell you why. In person, if I can."

Karen hesitated. Maybe it was better to keep her distance, to hear the explanation over the phone. Once she saw Jon, once he came near her, she wasn't sure she could listen to his story and doubt one word of it.

"I don't think so. Can't you just tell me now, over the phone?"

"I could, but I want to see you. I think I can explain the situation better that way. I hate telephones. I...I want to look into your eyes when I tell you what happened."

"Well...." Karen's resolve was eroding fast.

"Please, Karen. It's important to me. I don't want anything like this to come between us. It could happen again. I want you to understand exactly what can happen."

The sincerity, the pleading in Jon's voice were too much for Karen. "All right. I guess it's all right."

"I'll be there as soon as I can."

She pictured Jon hanging up, dashing out of his house and into the minivan, speeding down the streets of Walden on his way to her. She liked that picture, the notion of Jon making a beeline to her house, to her. She went inside to prepare for his visit.

Applying a fresh coat of lipstick, Karen looked at herself in the hall mirror. How do I really feel about Jon? Where is this relationship going? My heart's pounding like crazy, so there must be something there. But what?

In the kitchen, where Karen made a pitcher of cold lemonade, she heard a sound outside her kitchen window. Could that be Jon already? She rushed to the front window, but no cars were in sight.

A minute later, while Karen was putting the lemonade on the porch, the minivan arrived. Jon bounded out of the van and ran up the stairs, scooping Karen into his arms. His warm mouth pressed against hers, and he hugged her close to him. "Karen!" He backed off a little and looked into her eyes. "I know you must be upset about last night. Let me explain."

Karen extricated herself from Jon's arms. "Sit down," she said, pouring him a glass of lemonade, seating herself in one of the wicker chairs.

Jon sat down and sipped the lemonade. "I was going to call you last night, right after dinner. But before I could, I got a call myself. From Roger Huggins. Another doctor in town." Karen nodded. "He was desperate, calling from a farm outside town. He went to help a woman deliver her child. She'd never been to see him or me or any other doctor. And she turned out to have a difficult delivery."

If Jon was making this story up, it was a good one. His agitation seemed genuine, and the story was plausible. Besides, she could always check it out with Dr. Huggins on Friday.

"We have no obstetrician here in Walden," Jon went on. "The town's too small to support a specialist like that. So Huggins and I and a couple of others do the obstetrical cases in this area. It's a tremendous burden on us, and the women don't get to see a specialist, but we manage."

Karen nodded again. It sounded awful, not only for the doctors but for the delivering mothers as well. A definite drawback to small-town life. She had always imagined delivering her babies in a high-tech state-of-the-art hospital with at least one superbly-trained specialist at her side.

"This patient last night had a complicated delivery. Huggins hadn't seen one like that in a long time, and he's getting a little worn out anyway. He called me just about the time I was finishing my dinner. Naturally, I dropped everything and went out there to help him."

Naturally. Karen nodded again, more sympathetically this time. The story rang true, she was sure of it.

"Anyhow, we were there all night. I didn't get home till about six this morning, and then I tried to get a little sleep before I began seeing my own patients again." Jon paused. He put down his lemonade and grabbed Karen's hands. His hazel eyes looked directly into hers, imploring her to believe him. "If you can forgive me, I'll...this sounds corny, but I'll be the happiest man on earth."

Karen stood up and, still holding Jon's hands, moved closer towards him. He stood up then, too, and put his arms around her. "Karen, Karen...."

They kissed, and Karen felt herself melting again, just as she had at the lake. This "thing" with Jon, it was all the old slogans she had heard all her life. Chemistry, kismet, a match made in heaven. All those corny slogans she'd heard and laughed at. Now they suddenly seemed to make a lot of sense.

Karen felt Jon's warm lips pressing hers, then nuzzling her ears and neck. "I want you, Karen. I want you so much," he whispered into her ear. Arm in arm, they walked into the house and up the stairs to Karen's bedroom. Karen felt as though she were floating, Jon's arms never leaving her, then his hands gently pulling at her clothes and hers tugging at his.

In bed, she felt the way she had felt at the lake. This was right. She and Jon were a team, a pair. They moved together the way a team moves until, at the exultant final moment, they were joined, their bodies throbbing, every nerve tingling, screaming out in pleasure at the sheer joy of it.

Later, lying still and peaceful in her bed with Jon, Karen could hear the crickets singing, could hear the animals moving around outside, brushing against the twigs and grass beneath her window. The whole world approves, she thought. Every living creature salutes Jon and me and the magnificent team we make. She looked over at Jon. He had fallen asleep, exhausted. Karen kissed his bare shoulder and drifted off to sleep beside him.

Karen awoke at seven. Jon was rushing around the room, picking up the clothes he'd shed the night before. "Jon?" she said sleepily.

"Hi, gorgeous," he answered. "I've got to get out of here. Got to get to the office to see my patients. Do you mind?"

"Of course not." Karen wanted him to stay, to climb back into bed with her, but she knew she couldn't ask him to.

Jon was dressed now. He came over to the bed, sat down next to Karen, and took her hand in his. "Karen, I won't be in town for a while. I have to leave tonight, in fact. I'm going up to Minneapolis to see my sister, then over to Rochester for a medical conference."

Karen was silent. After their splendid reunion, she hated the idea of his leaving town, even for a little while.

"I want to see you again as soon as I get back," he said. "And I'll phone while I'm gone. But don't make any plans for a week from Saturday. We'll go to the game together."

"The game? What game?"

"The football game. The first football game of the season."

Football game? In Walden? Karen couldn't imagine what sort of football teams would show up to play in a town like Walden.

Jon laughed at the bewildered look on Karen's face. "Everyone here goes to the high school football games. It's a big deal every fall. The whole town practically shuts down."

Karen smiled. She'd heard about the phenomenon of small-town high school football games. Now she'd have a chance to experience the phenomenon herself.

"The first game is a week from Saturday at 3:30. If you want to go, I'll pick you up here about three o'clock. What do you say?"

"Sure," Karen said, smiling. It sounded like fun. Good clean fun. Karen liked the prospect of everyone in Walden turning out to cheer the high school football team.

"Great. I'll call you in the meantime from Minnesota." Jon swept Karen into his arms, kissing her gently on the lips. "Till then, love."

"Till then," Karen answered.

She wasn't ready to say "love." Not yet. But hang in there, Jon, she thought as she watched him leave. Maybe next time.

CHAPTER TWENTY-SIX

After Jon left, Karen tried to doze off again, but thoughts of him raced through her head. Finally she gave up the notion of any more sleep. She jumped out of bed and threw on some shorts and a shirt, then laced on her jogging shoes.

She warmed up in the kitchen, then ran down the front stairs and out onto the highway. It felt wonderful to stretch her muscles again, to pace herself against the trees and the cornfields that surrounded her. She felt strong, strong and healthy. Able to leap tall buildings in a single bound.

Some wildflowers caught her eye as she ran along the highway in the early-morning light: brown-eyed Susans and Queen Anne's lace and some luminous purple flowers she couldn't name. Sturdy cattails were bending in the breeze, waving their furry brown spikes at Karen, welcoming her to their patch of ground. Even the flowers here are friendly, Karen thought, smiling as she ran.

Back home, she ran up the stairs for a shower before dressing for work. She couldn't help grinning at herself in the bathroom mirror. You're doing all right, kid, she told her reflection. A month or two away from New York, and you've got a great job, a house of your own, and a terrific guy–a doctor, no less. A doctor who just called you "love." Not bad, kid.

Karen emerged from the steamy bathroom in search of something to wear–something fabulous to match her exuberant mood. Naked, she approached the closet, then sensed that someone else was in the room. Was that breathing she heard behind her? Oh, my God! Who...? She froze, too terrified to turn around.

"Karen!" Jon leapt out from the shadows in the corner of the room and, approaching Karen from behind, put his arms around her. His hands went quickly to her breasts, while his mouth began to nuzzle her still-damp neck.

"Jon!" Karen gasped. She turned and pushed him away. "You frightened me! What are you doing here? Shouldn't you be...?"

Jon laughed, trying to cover up his fumbling attempt at playfulness."You'll never believe this, but I drove all the way home before I remembered I have a light schedule today. I told Beverly not to make any morning appointments so I could pack. And my beeper never went off, so I guess there aren't any emergencies, either."

Karen's adrenaline was still pumping, her nerves jumping. Trying to calm down, she went to her closet to get some clothes to cover her nakedness.

Jon followed her and, before she could move away, he put his arms around her body once again. "What are you doing?" he said. "Don't you want to go back to bed?"

"Not now," Karen said, pushing him away. A hint of irritation crept into her voice. "Look at the time. I have to be at work in a half-hour."

"Do you really have to leave now? Why don't you call in sick and stay here with me?" Jon smiled and reached for Karen again.

"If you hadn't run out of here so fast an hour ago, maybe I would have," Karen said coldly. She moved away from Jon again and went back to the closet. She pulled a beige dress off a hanger and slipped into it, giving Jon an icy stare.

Jon was silent for a moment before speaking. "I'm...I'm sorry I frightened you. I really screwed up, didn't I? Blundering into your room like this.... It was a stupid thing to do. Please tell me you forgive me."

His abject, stricken look melted Karen's iciness. "Just...just don't ever surprise me like that again. I don't like it."

"I don't blame you," Jon said, tentatively approaching Karen, taking her hands in his one more time. "Your door wasn't locked, and I thought it would be fun to surprise you. But it was really stupid, I see that now." He embraced Karen again, and they kissed.

Karen wished now she didn't have to leave for work, wished she could stay home all morning in bed with Jon. But she was dressed now, and she had other things on her mind. The Laura Hanson in the L.A. public defender's office might call, and Karen wanted to be in the office if she did. Karen was frantic to know if she was the right Laura Hanson, and damn, that woman was hard to reach!

Karen and Jon had a bite of breakfast together before Karen headed out for town in the Plymouth. She was running late and arrived at the firm about 9:30. Belinda smiled as Karen tiptoed past Harold's office, hoping he wouldn't notice her late arrival.

"You don't have to worry about seeing Harold today," Belinda called out. "He's gone on a hunting trip. Taking a long weekend."

Karen exhaled in relief. She hadn't seen much of Harold lately, but learning he was out of the office for the rest of the week was welcome news. Ever since her run-in with him over the Ruth Swenson case, Karen had felt even more uncomfortable around him than before.

"Charlie's out of the office, too," Belinda added. "Went to see his aunt in the rest home. She's doing poorly, he said. Won't be back for the rest of the day."

Karen nodded calmly, trying not to betray her inner joy. Things would go swimmingly around the office today, with neither Charlie nor Harold around to look over her shoulder. She wondered, then, about Chad.

Belinda read Karen's mind. "Chad's here, though. For a change." Karen pondered Belinda's comment. She was right. Karen hadn't seen Chad in the office since last Friday, when he'd returned from vacation. Must be nice to be the boss's son, she thought. Come and go as you like. What a deal.

Karen entered her office and shut the door, determined to plow through a lot of work today, without the distractions of Charlie and Harold to interrupt her. But when she saw the stack of work on her desk, she sighed. The stack seemed much larger than before; Charlie must have put some new files there before he left.

She picked up the file sitting on the top of the stack. A new one. Karen groaned softly, thinking of the additional work. Still, she reminded herself, it was nothing compared to the burden she'd shouldered at Garrity & Costello.

She sat down and opened the file. Another case of Harold's, but Charlie had stuck a Post-it note on the top page:

Karen, take a look at this. Client called.
Never got a penny of his settlement.
Check it out and get back to me.

Another Ruth Swenson? She began to leaf through the file. Her guess proved accurate; the file looked a lot like the Swenson case. Another p.i. case, even older than Swenson's. The client had been injured in a car collision and, after several years of stalling, the insurance company had finally agreed to settle. The agreement by now was five years old. Why didn't the client have his money yet?

Suddenly Karen had a sobering thought. There was only one explanation: Harold was playing fast and loose with his cases. Boring, dull, impassive Harold was appropriating his clients' funds, money that was rightfully theirs, and using it for his own purposes. The worst possible violation of professional ethics.

He could be disbarred for this, and worse. He could be liable to every client he had cheated for whatever he owed them, plus interest, plus the possibility of punitive damages on top of that.

Karen wondered about the firm's liability. She searched her mind, trying to remember what she knew about the law on this point. If Harold was culpable, his partners in the firm might be culpable, too.

Karen wouldn't be affected; she was just a salaried employee. But if she remembered correctly, Charlie and Chad could be targets of a lawsuit by the client. The firm was a partnership, and they could be held personally liable for their partner's wrongdoing. The firm–Charlie, Chad–could be wiped out financially. She would have to let the two of them know, now, before Harold did any more damage.

Karen hesitated. She had a hunch that Charlie, not Chad, was the one to talk to. She would wait till Charlie was back in the office. In the meantime, she'd review this file, make sure she had her facts right.

Had Harold handled this case by himself? Karen checked the file carefully. No, apparently he'd been assisted by another lawyer, someone named Hope Shimkus. Karen had never come across the name before. She was sure she'd have remembered it, an unusual name like that.

Hope Shimkus. She'd worked on the case six years ago. She was Laura Hanson's predecessor, then. Another woman lawyer who'd come to Fuller, Fuller & Chase to assist the partners. What had become of her? Had she disappeared, like Laura Hanson?

Karen dismissed the idea immediately. No doubt the woman had moved on to another firm. Young lawyers moved around a lot, trying to find the right professional fit. They switched firms, went from corporate law to litigation, from the EPA to the IRS and back. Nothing strange or unusual about it.

Karen's phone rang. She answered immediately, her pulse accelerating.

"Ms. Clark?" The woman's voice was brisk, no-nonsense, pressed-for-time. "This is Laura Hanson in Los Angeles. I have two messages from you, and they're both marked 'urgent.' I came in early to call you before I go back to court this morning. Could you please tell me what this is about?"

"Oh, yes, yes. Thanks for returning my call, Ms. Hanson," Karen said quickly, her heart thumping. "I'm...I'm trying to track down a Laura Hanson who worked in Walden, Wisconsin, a few years ago. I believe that she's living in...."

"Sorry," the no-nonsense voice interrupted. "I can't imagine how you got my name. I've lived in Los Angeles all my life, and I'm 43 years old."

"Oh, I see." Karen's disappointment was palpable. This was the call that was supposed to resolve her problems with the Darla Cameron case. This was supposed to be the right Laura Hanson. "I'm very sorry to have bothered you."

"That's quite all right. Good luck with your search."

Karen heard a phone slam down somewhere in downtown Los Angeles. Now what? She was back to square one, with no Laura Hanson and no idea how to find her.

Someone knocked at Karen's door. "Come in," she called. Belinda stuck her head in the door.

"Long distance from Los Angeles? What was that all about?" Belinda's tone was friendly, not reproachful, and Karen didn't mind her questions. Long distance calls from L.A. didn't happen every day at Fuller, Fuller & Chase.

"I'm still trying to find Laura Hanson. For that Cameron case, remember?"

Belinda nodded. "Right. I remember. You called Los Angeles for information?"

"Actually I called three lawyers in California named Laura Hanson. But none of them was the right one."

"Well, maybe she didn't settle in California," Belinda offered. "Maybe after she went back there for a while, she took a job someplace else."

Belinda's idea made sense, but where would it lead her? The state bar of every state in the country? Karen knew she couldn't devote that much time or expense to the search for Laura Hanson. Maybe it was time to drop the whole idea and simply focus on people in Walden. People like Roger Huggins, M.D.

"Did you ever ask the other lawyers about her law school?"

Karen looked up. "What was that? Sorry, my mind was wandering."

"I just asked about her law school. Remember, you said something about finding out which law school Laura went to. Then you'd call the school and ask about her."

Right! Belinda had resurrected Karen's idea, an idea she herself had forgotten. She was supposed to ask the other lawyers about Laura's law school.

Karen had phoned Harvard and gotten nowhere, but one of the lawyers probably remembered where Laura had attended law school. That was something lawyers were unfailingly aware of: where their colleagues had gone to law school and how high in the pecking order of law schools it was. Karen couldn't help making a mental note of the law school each of her friends and associates had attended. Everybody did it. Lawyers were constantly appraising each other, and their law school backgrounds were part of that appraisal.

"Brilliant!" Karen said. "I'd totally forgotten. I'll talk to Chad about it now." The two women left Karen's office together, Belinda beaming in the glow of Karen's praise.

Karen walked the few steps to Chad's corner office and peered inside. Chad was standing at his window, staring out at Main Street, humming to himself. A real bear for work, Karen thought. He wouldn't last a week at Garrity & Costello. "Chad?" she ventured.

Chad turned around and faced her, a startled look in his beautiful deep blue eyes. "Oh, Karen. What can I do for you?"

"Well...," Karen began.

"Have a seat, Karen." Smiling broadly, Chad waved Karen into a chair and seated himself behind his desk. "Now what is it?"

"Do you remember Laura Hanson? She worked here a few years ago."

Chad's smile faded almost imperceptibly. "Yes, of course, I remember Laura. She left here rather suddenly, as I recall." He looked pensive, remembering Laura.

"I'm trying to locate her in connection with one of Charlie's cases. She handled a will that's being challenged, and it would really help if I could get a statement from her."

Chad nodded, the pensive look still covering his perfect features. "How can I help you? I barely knew her."

"Do you remember which law school she went to? I thought if I knew her law school, I might be able to learn her whereabouts from the school."

"Good idea," Chad said, nodding in approval. "Let me think. It was a fairly large law school, one of the state universities, I think. Midwest, but not Wisconsin. Illinois maybe, or Michigan. Or was it Iowa?"

Not very helpful. Karen couldn't see herself calling the alumni office of every large Midwestern law school. If only Chad could narrow it down some more.

"You can't be any more definite than that, can you? It would be a big help."

Chad shook his head, his blond curls drifting back and forth across his tanned forehead. "Nope, sorry. Have you checked her employment file? Belinda keeps those in a file drawer somewhere."

"She already checked," Karen said. "The file is missing."

"Missing?" A look of concern crossed Chad's handsome face. "We'll have to speak to Belinda about that. Our files should be complete. Sounds like Belinda's falling down on the job." Chad looked concerned for an instant longer, then suddenly smiled again. "So tell me, Karen, how are things going otherwise?" Chad leaned back in his chair, his whole demeanor changing. Karen felt as though she'd just been transported from a small-town law office to a Manhattan singles bar. Chad was actually beginning to flirt with her.

Seize the day, she thought. Sure, Jon was terrific, but he wasn't the only man in town. Why not get to know Chad better?

"Okay, I guess," Karen answered. "I really like Walden, and I like the work I've been doing here." No harm in earning a few Brownie points while she was at it.

"Great, great," Chad said, nodding in approval. "And how's the house?"

"Very nice, thanks. I'm really happy with it. Maybe you'd like to come over to see it sometime," Karen added. Well, why not? It was a perfectly innocent invitation. An innocent invitation that just might lead to something else.

"Thanks," Chad said, nodding again. "Remind me to take you up on that sometime."

Oh, great, Karen thought. Now the ball's back in my court.

"Do you ever feel a bit creepy out there?" Chad suddenly asked.

"What?" Karen was startled by Chad's question. "Creepy?"

"There are rumors about that house, you know," Chad said.

"Rumors? About what?" Karen's pulse started jumping again. What was he talking about?

"Well...they say that the Parkers left in a big hurry. Nobody's sure why," Chad said, looking serious. Was he genuinely serious, or...was that a mock-serious expression on his face? Karen couldn't tell.

"Can you tell me more about it?" Karen asked. Maybe there was something to this "old Parker house" business she kept hearing about.

A smile began to play around Chad's lips. "Don't worry, Karen. There's nothing to worry about."

"What?" Now Karen was confused.

"I was just kidding. You're perfectly safe in that house."

"But you said something about rumors. What did you mean?"

"I'm just pulling your leg, Karen. There aren't any rumors. And there's nothing wrong with that house." Chad looked sheepish, sorry that he'd ever said anything about rumors. "Just forget I said it."

Karen took a deep breath. "Okay," she said. She couldn't help wondering, though, why he'd done it. The way he talked about rumors, about the house being creepy, then dropped the subject right away–that was strange. Why did he bring it up in the first place?

Chad began swiveling in his desk chair, going from side to side the way a little kid, plunked down in an adult-sized chair, would. He was just like a little boy, Karen thought. An adorable little boy.

"You know, I'd love to show you around town," Chad was saying. "Take you up to the lake sometime."

Karen's heart began to beat faster again. An afternoon at the lake with Chad? That sounded promising. "I'd love it, Chad," she said, smiling what she hoped was her most fetching smile.

"Unfortunately, I'm involved with someone else right now. Someone pretty special. So I'm not exactly a free man these days," Chad laughed.

Karen nodded rapidly, trying to get her heart back to its normal rhythm. So Nedra was right; Chad did have a girlfriend.

"Does she live in Walden?" Karen asked.

"No, no, she doesn't. She's on the faculty at Madison. A professor, no less."

"What does she teach?" Karen tried to keep her tone light, friendly. She didn't want to make Chad think she was pumping him for information.

"Teach? She teaches German," he said, smiling. "The lovely Marlene Dieckmann of the German Department," he added, using a German accent when he pronounced the name. "*Achtung!*" he said, then laughed.

Karen had never found jokes about Germans to be particularly funny. She'd read too many books about the Holocaust, seen too many documentaries featuring children in Nazi death camps, bodies being thrown into mass graves. Looking away, avoiding Chad's laughing face, her eyes fell on the framed photograph on his desk. "Is that the...the professor, Chad?" Karen pointed at the silver picture frame.

Chad's eyes followed Karen's hand. He raised his eyebrows in surprise when he saw where it pointed. "Oh, no," he said, his tone changing immediately. "That's my mother."

Karen stood and walked towards the desk to get a closer look at the photograph. A woman in her early thirties looked back at her. Her blonde hair was in a '60s flip, her lime-green dress an A-line miniskirted number. The woman's face was lovely; Karen saw immediately where Chad had gotten his good looks. "She's beautiful, Chad."

"She *was* beautiful," he corrected her. "She's dead. Been dead for twenty years."

Karen remembered now. Belinda had mentioned that Charlie was a widower. "I'm sorry. She must have been lovely."

Chad nodded and looked away, gazing out the window again. He seemed terribly disturbed by his mother's death, even twenty years after the fact.

A few awkward moments of silence passed, and Karen realized that her conversation with Chad was over. He was still gazing out the window when she whispered "Bye, Chad" and walked quietly out of his office.

CHAPTER TWENTY-SEVEN

Karen returned to her case files, putting aside the Laura Hanson problem for the moment. But her mind kept returning to the new case, the one Charlie had left for her. Another client of Harold's who had never received the settlement he was supposed to get.

When Charlie came back Friday morning, Karen would have to tell him her painful suspicions about Harold. But she dreaded the prospect, dreaded the role of messenger of this particular bit of bad news. Harold had been a trusted partner of Charlie's for a dozen years before she showed up. What would Charlie say when she accused his partner of wrongdoing?

Karen was troubled by something else as well. She had stumbled across the name of another woman, Laura Hanson's predecessor, and now she couldn't get the name of Hope Shimkus out of her mind. Who was Hope Shimkus? How long had she worked at Fuller, Fuller & Chase? Where had she gone when she left? And wasn't it odd–an incredible coincidence, really–that two women lawyers had put in time at the firm, then disappeared?

Wait a minute, Karen. You're jumping the gun. You don't know that Hope disappeared. You haven't even asked Belinda about her; she might know where Hope is this very minute. You have to talk to Belinda and get this straightened out. Now.

Karen looked for Belinda in the outer office, but her chair was empty. Martha Morgan's chair was empty, too. Coffee break, Karen figured. Playing hooky while their bosses were out of the office. Can't say I blame them. Who wouldn't escape from the 9-to-5 grind any chance she got?

Returning to her desk, Karen suddenly heard women's voices coming from Charlie's office. So that's where they are, she thought. They must have gone in there to look at Charlie's files.

She took a few steps towards the voices, then stopped in her tracks. She couldn't hear every word, but the discussion certainly wasn't all business. She distinctly heard Martha say, "Charlie's so screwed up it's...." Then Martha's voice drifted off and became inaudible.

Karen stopped breathing for an instant. Should she keep listening? This was personal stuff, stuff that wasn't meant for her ears. She looked down the hallway to see if Chad was around, but no one was there.

Karen's curiosity got the best of her. She leaned against the wall in the hallway outside Charlie's door and listened.

"I know what you're going through, Marth," Belinda was saying.

"No, you don't!" Martha responded. "You have no idea."

"I was single once, too, you know."

"Belinda! That was thirty years ago!" Martha said.

"I still know what it's...."

"You have no idea, so don't tell me that, Belinda. You don't know how it feels to be my age and alone and so...so lonely that you go to bed with a shit like Charlie Fuller."

My God! Karen thought. Martha's sleeping with Charlie?

"No, that's true," Belinda was saying. "I guess I'm pretty lucky to have Fred. But...." Belinda paused. She seemed to have run out of comforting words. Karen thought she heard some sniffling, then genuine crying. She felt guilty, overhearing the conversation, and now listening to Martha cry. Maybe it was time to tiptoe back to her own office and try to forget what she'd just heard.

Then Belinda began speaking again, and Karen decided to stay where she was. I'll feel better if Martha gets through this okay, if I know Belinda has managed to help her, she told herself.

Yeah, right, Karen. Face it, you just can't tear yourself away. It isn't every day you overhear tabloid sex at Fuller, Fuller & Chase.

"C'mon now, Marth. Things aren't that bad," Belinda was saying. "Why don't you just break up with Charlie?"

"I would, I really would. But I told you, Charlie's so warped, he's so fucked up–sorry, Belinda–I don't know how he'd react. He treats me like shit, then he tells me I'll be sorry if I walk out on him. What's that supposed to mean?"

"I don't know what to tell you," Belinda sighed. "I just don't know. I wish I...."

Chad suddenly emerged from his office at the other end of the hallway. Karen looked up, startled. Noticing Karen, Chad waved and called out, "Karen, tell Belinda I'll be back tomorrow!" Karen nodded stiffly, frozen to her spot outside Charlie's office. But Belinda would exit Charlie's office now, after hearing Chad's voice. Karen began moving toward her own office.

Sure enough, Belinda strode out of Charlie's office an instant later, nearly running into Karen. "Was that Chad leaving?" she asked.

"Yes, yes, it was," Karen said. She felt shaky, guilty that she had eavesdropped on Martha's revelations, frightened by what Martha had revealed.

Belinda looked grim, but she straightened her shoulders and returned to her desk. Finally she noticed that Karen hadn't moved, was still standing outside her office, looking glassy-eyed at Belinda.

"Honey?" Belinda said. "Is there something you want?"

Karen pulled herself together and tried to remember why she had come in search of Belinda ten minutes earlier. It was hard to push Martha's words out of her mind, but she finally remembered. "Belinda, do you have a minute? I have another job for you. Finding someone else in your personnel files."

"Okay. Who?"

"Do you remember a lawyer named Hope Shimkus? She was here a few years before Laura Hanson."

"Of course I remember Hope," Belinda answered. "She was... she was a very interesting girl."

"Interesting?"

"Sit down." Belinda pointed to the empty chair next to her desk. Karen sat down and turned to listen. "To be truthful, Hope was...well, different. She was from New York, as I recall. She came here to get away from the East and her family and all that." New York. Karen's heart skipped a beat. Another expatriate New Yorker who fled the big city for the Midwest. "But she never really fit in here."

"What do you mean?"

"Oh, I don't know. I guess when Charlie hired her, he explained how things would be. But she had a different picture of it all, and she just...she just never seemed very happy. She didn't like the work he gave her. And I don't think she liked Walden. She didn't last very long here."

"How long was that?"

"Oh, not much more than a year, I guess. She complained about everything. The weather. The work. The town."

"Why did she come here in the first place?"

Belinda squinted her eyes as she tried to remember. Then she began shaking her head. "I don't honestly know. Maybe Charlie remembers. It must be five, six years ago now."

"Do you have her personnel file?"

"Let me see," Belinda said, rising from her chair. "It should be here in the file drawer," she said, pulling out a drawer near her desk and thumbing through it. "Hmmm...I don't see it right off. Give me a minute to look for it."

"Sure," Karen said. "Let me know when you find it."

Back at her desk, Karen had trouble concentrating on her work. She was trying to cope with the news that Hope Shimkus was another transplanted New Yorker who had tried life in Walden. Like Karen, she must have seen the small Wisconsin town as a refuge, as a simple, unspoiled alternative to life in the congested, competitive East.

But what happened to her? Did she return to New York after getting her fill of the bucolic life–a life she thought she'd like but instead grew to despise? Or was she somewhere else entirely? Another town, another city, where she'd finally found the right combination of satisfying work and appealing lifestyle?

Karen puzzled over the whereabouts of Hope Shimkus for the rest of the day. As her mind wandered from Walden to New York and back again, her halfhearted efforts to focus on her files didn't get anywhere. Then, just before the end of the day, Belinda buzzed her. "Karen, I'm having trouble finding that file. But I haven't given up. Not yet. I have to finish up some letters now, but first thing in the morning, I'll look some more."

Karen left the office a short time later, suspicions hurtling through her mind. What had happened to these women? Both of them had worked for Harold. Was working for him the key to their departures? Had they uncovered, as Karen now had, his unethical conduct, his schemes to pocket his clients' funds?

Karen felt frightened as she drove home. She got through dinner quickly and went to bed. The usual noises outside her bedroom window suddenly seemed more ominous than before. Was it merely animal noises? Or was it a person, Harold maybe, creeping around outside?

Karen jumped out of bed, terrified, and turned on the light. In the glare from the ceiling fixture, she had to laugh at herself and her ridiculous fears. You're really going off the deep end, she thought. It's the usual assortment of squirrels and rabbits outside. Can you imagine Harold, bespectacled Harold, climbing around outside your window? Get serious.

Nevertheless, Karen remembered what Jon had said about living alone in this isolated location. Maybe he was right about finding another place. She would start looking for something in town as soon as Jon returned to Walden.

Karen turned out the light and got back into bed. Once again, she listened to the sounds from outside. Now the insistent singing of a choir of crickets drowned out the other noises, soothing her. What had frightened her so? A couple of rabbits? She felt silly to have worried about it and finally drifted off to sleep.

CHAPTER TWENTY-EIGHT

But in the morning Karen felt uneasy again. She had to approach Charlie today and try to pump him for information. She would tell him what she had learned about Harold. In exchange, she would ask Charlie about Hope Shimkus.

Karen entered the office with a sick feeling in her stomach. She dreaded her confrontation with Charlie. Am I really prepared to tell him my suspicions? He's worked with Harold, trusted him, considered him a partner in every sense of the word. How will he react to my accusations?

"I need to talk to Charlie," she told Belinda as she approached the secretary's desk.

"Go right in," Belinda said. "He's expecting you. And Karen, I'm going to look for that file again this morning."

Charlie looked up when Karen reached his doorway. His lined face was frowning. "Come in, Karen. Sit down. Got something for me?"

Karen hesitated, then reminded herself that Charlie always looked stern and forbidding. She couldn't let that stop her.

"You find out something on that old case I gave you? Merv Robbins is really getting antsy, wondering about that settlement. Did you talk to Harold?"

Karen sat down opposite Charlie. "Harold's away on a hunting trip. He was gone yesterday. Won't be back till next week."

"Oh. He didn't mention it to me." Charlie looked disturbed by the news. "Well, I guess we can't get very far without talking to Harold."

Looking at Charlie, Karen couldn't help thinking about Martha Morgan's stunning revelations the day before. In the office, he was curt, gruff, strictly business. But if what Karen had overheard was the truth, in Martha's bedroom he became something much worse–abusive, demanding, a lover who offered sex without a hint of love. Karen found it difficult to imagine Charlie and Martha entwined in bed, with or without a spark of romance, but maybe that's what happened in small towns. Maybe you settled for what you could get.

Karen suddenly realized that Charlie was staring, almost glaring at her. Was he waiting for her to say something else? This was her chance: take it and run with it. "Charlie, I...."

"Yes?" Charlie was still glaring, his impatience beginning to break through.

"I think this case may not be the only one of Harold's where... where the client hasn't...hasn't...."

"Spit it out, girl! What are you trying to tell me?" Charlie broke in.

"I know of two clients...Merv Robbins and someone else...who haven't received the money they should have gotten."

"What?"

"I came across another one last week. Ruth Swenson."

"What are you telling me?" The impatience on Charlie's weathered face had evolved into a full-fledged scowl. He looked almost fierce, a vein throbbing on his forehead.

"I'm...I'm not sure, Charlie," Karen stammered. "All I know is that there are two cases where Harold's clients haven't gotten the settlements they should have. One's a woman named Ruth Swenson. She called to complain that she never got all the money she's entitled to. When I mentioned it to Harold, he said he'd take care of it."

Charlie stared at Karen in silence. Finally he spoke. "Maybe he has." Charlie looked unwilling to believe that Harold was guilty of any wrongdoing.

"Maybe. But now you've got this other client with the same story. An even older case. I...I just thought you should know...."

"Okay, okay, I get your drift." Charlie seemed suddenly eager to drop the subject. "I'll discuss it with Harold when he gets back. Don't trouble yourself about it any longer. That was Ruth Swenson, right?" Charlie began writing on a yellow legal pad.

"Right."

"Okay, that's all I need to know. You can get back to work now." Charlie dismissed Karen with a wave of his hand.

Karen didn't move. "There's something else, Charlie."

"Something else?" The impatient tone was creeping back into Charlie's voice.

"Can you tell me about Hope Shimkus?"

"Hope Shimkus?" Charlie looked puzzled, then appeared to recognize the name. "Oh, of course. Hope Shimkus. Why do you ask about her?"

"I came across her name in Merv Robbins's file. Would it help if I could contact her?"

"About what? Merv's case?"

"Yes."

Charlie paused. "Maybe. Maybe. Get her number from Belinda. It must be in a file somewhere." Charlie looked back at the papers on his desk.

"Charlie," Karen said, "I already asked. Belinda's having trouble finding Hope's file. Just like Laura Hanson's."

Charlie looked up quickly. "What's that?"

"Belinda hasn't been able to find her file."

"Well, then, drop it. You don't need to call her anyway." He looked down at his papers again.

"If I just had something to go on, I'd like to try to reach her." Karen couldn't really justify her need to find Hope Shimkus. The Merv Robbins case would proceed with or without Hope. But if she just kept pushing, nagged Charlie just a little longer....

Charlie bristled with impatience. "What the hell...?"

Karen refused to give up. "Can you remember something, anything about her?"

"Okay, okay," he said reluctantly. "Let me see...." Charlie narrowed his eyes, thinking. "She was a New Yorker. New York City. Went all through school there, I think. Then she decided to leave the East Coast. I think she had some family in Wisconsin, so she sent her résumé to some law firms out here. When it landed on my desk, we had just been talking about hiring someone. So I called her in New York and we worked out an arrangement. She came out here right after she graduated. But it...well, it never worked out."

"In what way?"

"She missed New York. City life, her friends. She was a good lawyer, she did the work all right, but she never seemed to fit in here. She started talking about leaving after the first couple months. She stuck it out a whole year, as it turned out. But that summer, she went on vacation and never came back."

"Never came back? Wasn't that odd?"

"No," Charlie said brusquely, shaking his head. "She'd threatened to leave a dozen times. When she went home on vacation, she wrote me she wasn't coming back. Asked me to close up her apartment and give her things to charity. I had Chad go over there and clean up the place. He told me she didn't have much stuff anyway. Guess she never planned to stay."

Karen remained skeptical. "But isn't that a strange way to leave a law practice?"

"Well, it didn't seem that strange at the time. You have to understand, Hope never seemed happy here, so her leaving didn't surprise any of us." Charlie seemed to have long ago resolved any questions he might have had about Hope's departure.

"She went back to New York then?"

"As far as I know," Charlie nodded. "But I doubt if it would do you any good to contact her about Merv Robbins. She probably forgot about that case years ago." Charlie was frowning again, beginning to shift uneasily in his chair.

Time to go. Charlie had said as much about Hope as he ever would. "Thanks, Charlie," Karen said. "I'll get back to work now."

But Karen had trouble focusing on her work. She considered calling New York, trying to learn Hope's current whereabouts. But where to begin? She had to have some leads, some way to get started. But she couldn't think of a thing.

A few hours later, Karen's phone buzzed, startling her. "Karen," Belinda's voice said, "I have something for you."

Karen bounded out of her chair and arrived at Belinda's desk in seconds.

"I never did find Hope's file," Belinda began. Karen's heart sank, then jumped back wildly. Why should Hope's file, like Laura's, be missing? Had someone deliberately removed them from the file drawer?

"But that bothered me," Belinda continued. "That file should have been there. So I did a complete search of all the files in the drawer. Every one of them. And I finally found something." Belinda picked up a paper from her desk and waved it in the air.

"What is it?" Karen asked.

"Hope's résumé. The original résumé she sent Charlie, it looks like."

Karen grabbed the paper.

"It was in someone else's file. I must have misfiled it. Years ago."

"Thank God you did," Karen said, scanning the résumé. It had Hope's home address in Queens and her entire educational background, culminating in attendance at New York Law School in Manhattan. At the bottom were the names of two references, both law school professors. Now Karen had something to go on, even if it was a six-year-old résumé, prepared by Hope when she was still a law student in New York.

"Belinda, I'm going to go into my office and close my door. I'll be making a couple of long-distance phone calls. Please don't let anyone disturb me."

"Sure," Belinda smiled, pleased to have helped Karen once again.

Karen closed the door to her office and, gazing at the faded résumé, picked up her phone. She put the receiver down a moment later, uncertain which number to dial first. Hope's old phone number, the number Hope had listed as her home telephone number in Queens? Or the law school? If she called the school, who should she ask for? The alumni office, or one of the two professors Hope had listed as references?

Karen's head began to ache. What if Charlie found out what she was doing? He wouldn't approve of her making a lot of calls to New York instead of doing the work he was paying her to do.

Suddenly Karen had a flash. She didn't have to place a lot of calls to New York. She would have Melissa Cohen do it for her. Karen quickly dialed Melissa's number.

"Karen! How are you?" Melissa sounded happy to hear Karen's voice again.

"Much better, thanks. Listen, Melissa, can you do something for me?"

"Sure. What is it?"

"My cousin needs to get in touch with an old friend of hers in New York." Karen felt a blaze of remorse, hoodwinking Melissa again. She was getting a lot of mileage out of her fictitious cousin. "Could you make a few calls to find her?"

"Oh, Karen...I'm really busy right now. Hendrix gave me Gary Goldberg's work to do. I've got to finish typing a long memo he just gave me."

"Well, uh, when do you think you could do it?" Karen asked, surprised by Melissa's response. She had expected Melissa to drop everything and make the calls immediately.

"Is it important? I could try to get to it later."

"It's pretty important."

"Okay, give me the information. I'll do the best I can. I'll call you back as soon as I know something. What's your number?"

Karen caught herself just as she was about to blurt out her number at Fuller, Fuller & Chase. "I'll have to call you back. Remember?"

"Oh, yeah. Now who's this friend?"

Karen gave Melissa all the relevant information. She asked Melissa to call the phone numbers on the résumé first, then try the phone book and the New York state bar association. Karen promised to call Melissa back by five o'clock New York time and hung up.

Karen glanced at her watch. She had only a few minutes to get to her appointment with Roger Huggins, M.D., and she suddenly felt famished. She rushed out of the office and headed for Huggins's address, grabbing a greasy burger at the Tastee Freez on the way.

CHAPTER TWENTY-NINE

Roger Huggins's medical office turned out to be, like Jon Smith's, in a big old house on the edge of town. The white frame Victorian stood on the corner of a quiet intersection, surrounded by tall maple trees that lent their leafy shade to the house and lawn. Karen rang the doorbell, and a short, slight man in his late sixties or early seventies answered the door a moment later. A thick gray mustache covered his upper lip. "Ms. Clark?" he asked.

Was this small man Dr. Huggins? "Yes. Please call me Karen."

"All right, Karen. Come in, please." The diminutive doctor, his shiny pate covered by a few wisps of gray hair, led Karen through a small waiting room into a private office. The walls displayed a collection of diplomas and certificates attesting to the professional competence of Roger Huggins, M.D.

"Have a seat, Karen." Dr. Huggins waved Karen into a chair facing a large walnut desk and seated himself behind it. "You wanted to ask me about Darla Cameron, is that right?"

"Yes," Karen said. "Darla Cameron was a client of my law firm. We drew up her will about three years ago, and she signed it in front of two witnesses and an attorney. Unfortunately, both witnesses have died, and we haven't been able to find the attorney who handled it."

"You can't find the attorney?" Dr. Huggins looked surprised.

"Yes. I know that sounds unusual, but she left the firm a couple of years ago, and we aren't certain where she is."

"That surely is unusual," Dr. Huggins said.

Karen nodded in agreement. "In any event, we now expect a challenge to the will. From Mrs. Cameron's son. He was expressly disinherited in the will."

Dr. Huggins nodded. "That would be Hecky. Always was a troublemaker. Got into drugs in Chicago, last I heard."

"That's what we've heard, too. Now, because he's challenging the will, and the witnesses are both dead, whatever you can tell us about Darla Cameron has become very important."

"I understand. Well, I got out my records on Darla and looked them over." Huggins patted a folder on his desk. "I think I can help you out. I saw Darla once or twice the year before she died. Then she had a massive coronary, and she died before any medical help could get to her."

"And her mental state?"

"Well, I'd say she was in pretty good mental shape until the end."

Karen paused. Pretty good shape until the end. She needed more precise information than that. "What exactly do you mean by that?"

"Well, the trouble with Hecky really got to her, you know. After he was arrested, she started to go to pieces."

"When was that?"

"Three or four years ago, I guess. Darla seemed all right for a while after his arrest, but in the last year or two, I began to see more and more deterioration."

"That was well after she made the will, of course."

"If the will was made more than a year or two ago, yes." Huggins smiled reassuringly at Karen.

"I'm glad to hear that," Karen responded. "Then we can count on your testimony if this matter should go to trial?"

"Surely," Huggins said, smiling. As he sat back in his chair, however, the smile began to fade. "But to be honest, I probably should add something. I've found that when someone breaks down mentally, even after a traumatic event that appears to be the reason, the origins of the breakdown are usually deep-seated. Darla must have been having emotional problems even before Hecky's arrest."

What was Dr. Huggins saying? Was he hinting that Darla might not have been mentally sound even before her son was accused of a serious crime? Even at the time she wrote and signed her will?

"But didn't you just say she was in good mental shape at the time she made the will?" Karen asked.

"Yes, of course. And I do believe she was. Still, when a woman like Darla falls apart like that, it raises some questions in one's mind. If she had been completely stable emotionally before the trouble with Hecky, she might have held up better afterwards."

What Dr. Huggins had just said disturbed Karen. If he were a sworn witness in court, he would testify that he believed Darla to be mentally competent at the time she made the will. But if he were pressed during cross-examination, he would probably say exactly what he had just told Karen: it was possible that Darla was emotionally unstable when she signed her will.

That testimony could be viewed as inconsistent with his earlier statement regarding her competence. Any half-baked lawyer could get Huggins to make these inconsistent statements in court and could then try to discredit Huggins as a witness. Then, if Hecky and some of his friends testified that Darla was mentally unsound, the case could easily tip in Hecky's favor.

The only question, after all, was Darla Cameron's soundness of mind, her "testamentary capacity." If Hecky's lawyer could cast doubt of any kind on her capacity, that would jeopardize the possibility of a judgment in favor of Hecky's sister, Elizabeth.

In other words, Huggins was not a wholly reliable witness. Karen wondered just how damaging his testimony would be. Damaging enough for the firm to recommend to Elizabeth that she settle with her brother?

Some sort of compromise, allowing him to recover a portion of the estate, might satisfy him. But Karen suspected that Elizabeth would be loath to disregard her mother's explicit instructions, loath to turn over even a portion of the estate to a son who was such a shocking disappointment.

If only I could get in touch with Laura Hanson. She prepared the will, she held Darla's hand while she wrote it. Her testimony would be far more detailed than Dr. Huggins's. It could therefore carry more weight than the conclusions of an elderly doctor who had seen his patient only once or twice in the year before she died.

Everything kept coming back to Laura Hanson. But there were so many obstacles to finding her. Karen sighed.

"Is something wrong, Karen?" Dr. Huggins was looking intently at her. "Did what I say disturb you?"

"In a way, yes," Karen admitted. "But you have to be honest with me. It wouldn't do me any good if you said something today to make me happy, then said something else in court. I need to know exactly what you think."

Huggins nodded.

"My problem is that I don't have much in the way of witness testimony that can help us," Karen said. "Some of Darla's friends, I suppose. But her daughter has a stake in this, and the witnesses to the will-signing are dead, and Laura Hanson is missing."

"Laura Hanson?"

"She's the lawyer who handled this case."

"Hmmm...." Huggins sat back in his chair again and peered up at the ceiling. "That name sounds...I think I may remember her. She may...may have been my patient."

Karen shot upright in her chair. "You remember Laura Hanson?"

Huggins nodded. "I think so."

"Would you have her medical records?"

"If she was my patient, I certainly would. Anyone who's been a patient in the last ten years or so, those records are here in the office."

"Could you find Laura's?" Karen asked.

"I'll check. What would you want to know? I can't reveal any confidential medical information, you know."

"Oh, no, of course not. What I need is something, anything, that would help me find her. At first I thought she was in California, but all my leads out there have fizzled. If you could find something in your files that might give me a clue, an idea where she might be, that could be very helpful."

"Well, I'll surely try." Dr. Huggins took down Karen's home phone number and promised to call her as soon as he discovered any useful information. "Now try to forget your work for the rest of the weekend," he added, smiling. Small yellow teeth appeared behind his gray mustache. "Relax and enjoy yourself. You look like you need some rest."

"Thanks, Dr. Huggins." Karen looked at her watch. 4:15. She had told Melissa she would call fifteen minutes ago. She stood up to leave, then remembered something that was troubling her. "By the way, I heard *you* didn't get much rest the other evening. Tuesday evening."

Dr. Huggins looked puzzled.

"I heard you were busy delivering a baby all night Tuesday."

"Tuesday, Tuesday. Let me think." Huggins paused, then smiled again and nodded his head. "That's right, I was. Now who told you that?"

"Jon Smith. He told me he assisted you." Karen mentally crossed her fingers, hoping Jon had told the truth about Tuesday night.

"Yes, yes, Jon was there. I don't know what I'd have done without him." Karen felt an enormous wave of relief. So Jon hadn't lied, hadn't been with Jackie Berlinghof or anyone else Tuesday night. Just Dr. Huggins and the laboring mother.

"Is Jon a friend of yours?" Huggins asked.

Karen nodded. "Yes, he is."

"A wonderful young man, Jon. I knew his father very well. We and a couple of others were the only doctors in town for a long time. Then Jon came back here after medical school. Wanted to be a specialist–pediatrics, I think. But the old man talked him into taking over his practice, and God knows, we're lucky to have him. Walden needs more young doctors like him."

"Yes, I'm sure you're right." Karen was beginning to feel awkward, still standing, still wanting to call Melissa. It was nice to hear Dr. Huggins praise Jon to the heavens, but she had to get out of there fast.

"Well, you go on your way now," Huggins said, sensing her discomfort. "I'll check my records tonight, and if I find anything, I'll give you a call."

Karen thanked Dr. Huggins and hurried out of the white frame house.

It was nearly 4:30 by the time she called–5:30 New York time–and she got Melissa's voicemail. Karen left a message, but Melissa probably wouldn't check her voicemail over the weekend. Damn! Karen didn't have Melissa's home number and didn't remember exactly where she lived.

Damn, damn, damn! But cursing wouldn't help. No matter how many "damns" she muttered to herself, Karen knew she'd have to wait till Monday to talk to Melissa. A long weekend's worth of waiting to find out what Melissa had learned about Hope Shimkus. If she had learned anything at all.

CHAPTER THIRTY

Saturday morning Karen awoke to a gray sky that threatened rain. No matter. She'd already resigned herself to a quiet weekend. With Jon out of town and Chad preoccupied with his German professor, no male companionship was in the offing. But maybe Nedra Bailey was free. Karen made a mental note to call Nedra before lunch.

The overcast sky was growing darker. Karen hurried into sweats and jogging shoes to get in a run before the rain began. She took a different route this time. About a quarter-mile from her house, the highway led to a small dirt road she'd never taken before. She turned off the highway onto the small dirt road, running after a few minutes into a thickly wooded area. The heavily-leafed branches of the tall trees alongside the road made a cool green canopy over her head as she ran.

Suddenly she heard the sound of raindrops hitting the leaves above her. She turned and retraced her path, returning to the highway just as the rain began in earnest. Karen sped up, hoping to get home before she was drenched, but the rain increased its pace as well, and she was dripping when she leapt up her rain-slick stairs onto the front porch.

Soaked to the skin, she dashed inside and ran upstairs to change into dry clothes. From her bedroom window, she watched the rain come down in sheets, the dry earth around the house thirstily drinking up the much-needed moisture.

The driving rain reduced her options. Bicycling, poking around outside the house–those options were out. Karen picked up the phone and dialed Nedra's home number. No answer.

Could Nedra be at work on a Saturday morning? Karen looked up Nedra's office number and tried it. Nedra answered after one ring.

"Nedra Bailey."

"It's Karen. Are you working today?"

"Yep. When I heard the weather forecast this morning, I figured it was a good day to work. What's up?"

"Absolutely nothing," Karen said. "I was hoping we could get together. When will you be finished?"

"I'm in the middle of something messy right now. What did you have in mind?"

"Lunch, maybe. Or dinner. I'm free all day."

"Dinner sounds great. Have you been to Hutter's yet?"

"No." Karen remembered hearing about Hutter's her first day in Walden. Belinda Binnington had called it the best restaurant in town.

"Let's go there then. Should I pick you up?"

"No, no, I can drive myself. I've got a car now."

"Okay, let's meet at Hutter's about seven o'clock. Do you know where it is?"

Karen got directions to Hutter's from Nedra, then hung up and went back downstairs. Taking stock of her nearly-empty kitchen cabinets, she realized she couldn't put off another shopping trip to Brennan's any longer.

But now that I have the Plymouth, I can buy everything I need and carry it home myself. No deliveries by geeky Tim Brennan anymore, thank God.

She whizzed through Brennan's, hoping to avoid seeing Tim. Roy was working one of the cash registers, and she settled her bill with him before leaving the store with her shaky, overloaded grocery cart. The rain had stopped, but the pavement was still slippery, and she pushed the cart slowly to keep it under control.

Loading the grocery bags into her car trunk, she suddenly sensed someone beside her. She looked up. Gawky, pimply Tim stood next to her, his head bobbing, a nervous smile on his quivering lips. "Oh, Tim. Hi," Karen said, returning to bag-loading.

"Can I help you?" Tim asked. He thrust his arms out, grabbing a bag before Karen could stop him.

"No thanks. You'd better get back inside. Your dad'll be looking for you," Karen said, trying to sound pleasant. The kid made her nervous. She wished he'd leave her alone.

"That's okay. I'm supposed to help customers load their cars." Tim was gaining confidence now. He touched Karen's arm. "Can I help you unload this stuff at your house?"

Karen pulled her arm away. That was going too far. "No thank you. I can manage," she said stiffly. The bags were all in the trunk now. She closed the trunk, opened her car door and dove inside, slamming the door in Tim's face as he came around the side of the car. Karen drove off, grinding her teeth.

What a creepy kid. New York clearly had no monopoly on weird characters like Mr. Mehlman. Even little Walden had one or two.

Her kitchen shelves stocked again with jams and cereal and spaghetti sauce, Karen retreated to the living room and a comfortable chair. She had brought down some of the books she found in the attic. Now, her feet up on an old ottoman she'd discovered in a corner of the basement, she plunged into "Moby-Dick." She'd always meant to read Melville's classic, had even started it once or twice, but never got around to finishing it.

I can finish it now. With colder weather approaching, I'll have plenty of time to read. Not just "Moby-Dick," but some of the other classics I've always wanted to read. Austen, Dickens, Tolstoy....

The phone rang, and Karen hurried into the kitchen to answer it.

"Karen? Dr. Huggins here." The elderly doctor had a surprisingly youthful voice. Over the phone he sounded like a man of thirty.

"This is Karen." Her pulse began to speed up. Had Huggins uncovered something helpful about Laura Hanson?

"I found Laura Hanson's records last night," Huggins began. He paused. "Looking at them refreshed my memory. I remember her very well now. But...but I'm not quite sure how much I can tell you."

Karen didn't say anything. Huggins clearly knew something, but he was wrestling with his conscience, trying to decide how much he could reveal to someone else.

"Laura consulted me in May, two years ago," he said finally. "If she left Walden two years ago, then she must have seen me a short time before she left."

Karen wasn't clear on the dates involved. She would have to check with Belinda to find out exactly when Laura had left.

"Karen?"

"I'm here."

"I know you need to find Laura because of Darla Cameron. You need her testimony, am I right?"

"Yes, that's right."

"But is there anything else I should know about?"

"Anything else? I'm not sure what you mean."

"I mean...I mean, are you concerned about her welfare in any way? Are you concerned about what may have happened to her? Aside from her helping you with Darla's will, I mean."

"Well, yes, I suppose I am." Karen wasn't exactly sure how to respond. What was Huggins getting at? "I suppose I'm curious about her. The way she left the firm so suddenly, that was kind of strange. I guess I'd like to know why."

"In that case...I do have some information for you," Huggins said. His words came out slowly, reluctantly. Karen waited. "This is a breach of professional ethics, of course, and I hope you'll keep this strictly between the two of us," the doctor said.

"Of course," Karen said hastily. Her heart had begun to pound. Why all this secrecy?

"Laura came in for a check-up that May. She hadn't been feeling well. She described her symptoms: nausea, bloating, fatigue, that sort of thing. I suspected what it was even before I examined her." Huggins paused again.

"Yes?" Karen prompted.

"She was pregnant. About two months along, as far as I could tell."

Pregnant. Laura Hanson was two months' pregnant in May, and she disappeared a short time later. "How did she react? Do you remember?"

"I do remember," Huggins said. "She was surprised, almost shocked. She apparently didn't realize that her symptoms indicated a first-trimester pregnancy. I remember thinking that was odd, coming from a well-educated woman like her. A teenager, that's different."

"Did she seem happy about it?"

"Happy? That's hard to say. As I recall, she tried not to show any emotion. Once the initial shock wore off, her face became a blank. She seemed to be trying to hide how she felt."

Maybe Laura didn't want to have the baby. If so, she might have asked Huggins about terminating the pregnancy. "Did she ask you about...about an abortion?"

"I don't honestly remember. My notes don't indicate anything either way. Because of her situation, being unmarried and working at the law firm, I might have hinted around about it. But I didn't write anything down, so I can't be sure."

"I see."

"I...I shouldn't be telling you this, Karen, but I feel I can trust you. Am I right?" Huggins's voice was shaking. He took his oath of confidentiality very seriously. Karen rushed to reassure him.

"Of course you are. Don't worry. This is between you and me. I won't tell anyone."

"That's good." Karen thought she could hear a soft sigh of relief at the other end of the line. "Now, as for any other information, I'm afraid I don't have much. She gave her local address, a place on Oak Street, and she listed her employment at the Fuller firm. She had no health insurance. There's just one other thing: I have her social security number. I always get those, for administrative purposes."

A social security number. Would that be useful? Karen took it down, wondering what she could do with it. Contact the Social Security Administration in Washington? Try to find out if Laura had reported any income in the last two years? Karen wasn't sure she could get that kind of information over the phone. She'd check on Monday morning.

"That's all I've got. I hope it helps." Huggins's voice had returned to normal.

"I'm sure it will. I can't thank you enough, Dr. Huggins. I'm very grateful." Karen's own voice was quavering with excitement. She finally had some concrete information on Laura Hanson, something to check out that might lead to the missing woman. She hung up and began to pace around the kitchen, thinking.

According to Huggins, Laura Hanson had learned she was pregnant in May, and a short time later (when? June? July?) she had left Walden. Abruptly, leaving only a memorandum on Charlie's desk. Why?

Had she really been startled to learn she was pregnant? Maybe. But once she knew, then what? Did she confront the father and find out that he didn't want her to have the child?

If she wanted to have the baby, maybe she had fled to California. To give birth surrounded by loving family and friends who welcomed her home again, happy to have her back regardless of her unmarried condition.

Or was she afraid to return home? Did she have the kind of parents who couldn't accept her if she was pregnant and unmarried? Did she fly elsewhere, nervous, terrified? Seeking a new home where she could raise her child alone and unashamed–one more single mother among thousands, maybe millions of others in late-twentieth-century America.

There was another possibility. Laura might have left Walden to have an abortion. In Milwaukee or in Madison, somewhere where no one knew her. She might have planned to return to Walden, but something happened. She took ill, maybe even died, as a result of the surgery. Deaths from abortions were extremely rare, but they did occur.

Karen's mind was racing. The abortion could have plunged Laura into a massive depression. That was possible, too. Alone and depressed, she couldn't face returning to Walden. Instead she stayed on in the new city, or moved on to Chicago, working at whatever jobs she could find until she could get back on her feet.

Karen felt dizzy as the jumble of ideas swirled around in her head. She headed for the bathtub, trying to put herself into Laura's shoes. What would she do if she suddenly found out that she herself was pregnant?

The thought disturbed her, as always. Abortion was a last resort, of course, but the thought of giving birth alone, no loving husband by her side, was troubling, too. She'd been lucky that her romantic liaisons had never resulted in pregnancy. Not yet.

Well, I've been careful. I've made sure that Jon used a condom each time, even at the lake. No single motherhood for me. Maybe, at 40, with my biological clock about to wind down, I'll consider it. But I still have a dozen years to go.

Karen's mind returned to Laura Hanson. Just how had she reacted to the news that she was pregnant? Karen could only guess.

Leaning back in the tub, soaking in the warm water, she tried to put thoughts of Laura Hanson aside for a while and concentrated instead on what she would wear for Saturday night dinner at Hutter's.

The restaurant was crowded when Karen arrived in a navy silk dress she'd bought on impulse at Patricia's on Labor Day weekend. Searching the crowd for Nedra, she finally spotted her at the bar, her long straight brown hair hanging below her shoulders. Large silver hoop earrings peeked out from under the brown locks.

Karen grabbed the stool next to Nedra. She turned and smiled brightly at Karen. "It's a good thing I made a reservation. Look at this place! It's always like this on Saturday nights. Can you believe all the people here?"

Compared to the mob at Karen's usual haunts in Manhattan, the Saturday night crowd at Hutter's was barely worth mentioning, but Karen didn't want to insult Nedra. Nodding, she ordered a white wine spritzer and carried it with her when the hostess led them to their table a few minutes later.

The menu listed several French dishes, including *canard,* and Karen felt a sudden chill, remembering K.B. and their Saturday night dinner at the Maison Carrée in Chicago. But as Nedra pointed out some of Hutter's specialties, Karen cleared her head, and a moment later Karen and Nedra both settled on prime rib, the house salad, double-baked potatoes, and a carafe of Bordeaux.

Waiting for their food, Karen looked around, evaluating the restaurant. Hutter's wasn't outstanding by New York standards, but it was a damned sight better than the Walden Cafe. White tablecloths, candlelight, fresh flowers at each table.

"So what have you been up to, Karen?" Nedra asked brightly. "I haven't seen you in a while."

Karen paused for a second, then plunged into the history of Laura Hanson, telling Nedra only those details she felt comfortable revealing. Nedra thought she remembered meeting Laura once or twice, but she wasn't sure where. She tried to get a handle on what was troubling Karen.

"So whatever she can tell you about that woman, that Darla Cameron, is really important? You want to find her so she can help you win that case, right?"

"That's a big part of it, Nedra. But it's gone beyond that. Now I'm just so damned curious. I want to know what happened to her." She was tempted to tell Nedra about Laura's pregnancy but resisted the temptation. She owed Dr. Huggins that much.

Nedra nodded. "I wish I could help you. But you don't have a clue where she is?"

"Well, I checked the California state bar, but not much else," Karen admitted. "I guess I could start calling all the big state law schools in the Midwest. Chad seems to think she went to one of them."

"Her address in Walden wouldn't help much either. The post office doesn't forward mail for more than a year anymore. What else have you got?"

"Not much." Suddenly Karen remembered something else Dr. Huggins said. "I've got her social security number...."

"You do?" Nedra's face came alive. "Karen, *that's* something. You can get lots of information from that."

"I can?"

"Well, *I* can anyway. One of my good friends from college works for the IRS. He can plug in a social security number and come up with lots of good stuff. It's against the rules, of course, but I think he'd do it for me if I asked."

"Really? That would be terrific," Karen said, her pulse rate picking up. "I've got the number at home. I'll call you later."

They finished eating and said their goodbyes in the parking lot. Driving home in the dark, Karen felt buoyed by Nedra's promise of help. Maybe Laura's social security number would lead somewhere. It was the first hopeful news she'd had since she started her search for the missing woman.

Suddenly Karen noticed the headlights of another car immediately behind her own. They were coming closer, closer, almost on top of her now.

A drunk driver, leaving Hutter's after one too many. The police are never around when you need them, she thought.

The other car stayed right on top of her, even when she pushed the accelerator to speed up. Then she felt a sudden jolt. The other car's bumper had struck hers. Karen screamed and floored the gas pedal, hoping to escape the other car.

Oh my God! What's happening? Why is this car bumping me?

Karen speeded ahead, barely able to breathe. Finally the other car swerved to one side and zoomed past her, scraping the side of the Plymouth as it went. Karen glanced inside the other car as it drove past, but she couldn't make out anything more than a good-sized driver behind the wheel. She couldn't tell if it was male or female.

Karen's adrenaline was still pumping when she reached her driveway. She bolted up the stairs, locked the front door, and ran upstairs. She threw herself onto her bed, still wearing the navy silk dress from Patricia's. After a few minutes, she began to relax. It was only a drunk driver, or some goofy teenager trying to spark a drag-race. Nothing to worry about.

Safe in her own room, drowsy from the wine she'd consumed, she fell asleep a few minutes later.

CHAPTER THIRTY-ONE

When Karen awoke Sunday morning, the weather had turned sunny but cooler, a portent of autumn and the colder temperatures it would bring. She jogged again, returning to the shady wooded area she'd discovered the day before, enjoying the lush greenery, knowing that in two or three months the woods would be covered with snow. She'd try to do more jogging before the long winter began. She suspected that once the harsh winter weather arrived, she just might want to hibernate till spring.

Back home, Karen climbed the attic stairs to survey the pile of dusty books again. She remembered seeing one or two more she wanted to bring downstairs. Passing the old chest of drawers, she was suddenly drawn to it, remembering the letters she had seen her first week in the house. Maybe they would make more sense to her now.

She pulled a batch of letters out of the drawer. The faded ribbon holding them together tore as she tugged at it. She looked eagerly through the yellowing letters, searching for one that would explain the secret, if there was one, about the old "Parker house."

But most of the letters were just folksy family news–Christmas newsletters from cousins and aunts, birth announcements from relatives in other small towns in Wisconsin. Finally Karen came across one that looked different–a crudely hand-printed letter with a cryptic message: "Don't say anything. You'll be sorry if you do."

What did that mean? Karen scanned the envelope. It was addressed to "Gerry Parker" and postmarked in Walden, but Karen couldn't make out the date.

Karen looked quickly through the rest of the letters. At the bottom of the pile was another hand-printed envelope addressed to Gerry Parker. Inside was another, even shorter, crudely-scripted message: "Remember what I said."

Karen shuddered. Someone had been threatening Gerry Parker, warning him that he'd be sorry if he said something. What? And when? Were the warnings somehow related to the fact that the house, the "old Parker house," had stood vacant for so long?

Karen returned the letters to their hiding place, then scurried back downstairs to phone Nedra at home. When she answered, Karen rushed to ask her what she knew about the house.

"Sorry, Karen, I don't know a thing about it. But I can ask Joe Featherstone."

Karen suddenly felt foolish. Why should she be so agitated about some yellowing letters she found in an attic? The people involved were long gone, and the threats were long forgotten. She certainly didn't want Nedra talking to her boss about it.

"No, no, I'm probably making too much of it. Just forget it," she said. "But I do have that social security number for you." Karen gave her friend Laura Hanson's number, and Nedra promised to phone back as soon as Ron, her friend at the IRS, found out anything.

Karen took a long hard look at her kitchen floor. It was filthy. Time to scrub it, Karen thought, as she replaced the receiver. In New York, she and Jason had occasionally hired a cleaning service to do the really heavy cleaning jobs, and Karen hadn't scrubbed a kitchen floor for years. Now, she found a pail and scrub brush under the sink, got down on her hands and knees, and started to scrub.

Karen almost welcomed the hard work, watching the warm soapy water scrubbing away weeks, maybe months of accumulated dirt. When she was finished, she felt as though she'd truly done an honest day's work, and headed upstairs for her reward: a long, relaxing soak in the tub.

Lying back in the tub, Karen closed her eyes and tried to relax all of her muscles. But she was too wired to completely relax.

I can't stop thinking about Laura Hanson. And there's that other woman, the one who worked at the firm before Laura. Hope Shimkus. I have to remember to call New York tomorrow, to ask Melissa what she found out.

Suddenly Karen heard a noise outside. Twigs snapping again. Startled, alone in the bathtub, she jumped out quickly and grabbed a towel.

When will I get used to these noises? Never, probably. As soon as Jon gets back, he'll help me find another place.

When *would* Jon be back? Karen had to think for a moment. Next Saturday. Almost a whole week away. In time for the big football game.

Karen smiled at the thought of the whole town turning out for "the big game." Turning out to see a bunch of muscle-bound high-school kids, a team the whole town pinned its hopes on every year. Karen couldn't imagine ever getting excited over a group of adolescent athletes. But maybe, after a year or two in Walden....

Drying off, Karen thought she heard the phone ringing downstairs. She threw on some clothes and dashed downstairs. "Hello?" she said breathlessly.

"Is this Karen Clark?" Karen didn't recognize the coarse male voice.

"Yes. Who's this?"

"My name's Hecky Cameron. I'm calling from Chicago."

Hecky Cameron. Karen grabbed a kitchen chair and fell into it. "Mr. Cameron, you really shouldn't be calling me. I can't talk to you. The rules of ethics...."

"Fuck the rules of ethics," he interrupted. "I just have a few words for you, babe."

Karen was shocked into silence, but she knew she couldn't have this conversation. He was the client on the other side of her case, and it was against the rules to talk to him without his lawyer. She had to stop him before he went any further.

"Mr. Cameron...."

"Listen, I hear you're working for my sister Lizzy. That's not very smart. You don't want to have any trouble with me, like that cute little babe Laura, do you?"

"What?"

"I know how Laura worked, how she got my mother to write me out of her will. You female lawyers make me sick, all of you. A little bitch like you brought criminal charges against me here in Chicago. But she couldn't make 'em stick!" Hecky laughed, a loud, arrogant laugh. Then the laugh stopped. "Now get your cute little ass out of my mother's case. I mean it."

Hecky slammed down the receiver, and Karen heard the dial tone a second later. Her heart was pounding.

How does Hecky Cameron know I'm working on this case? I haven't done any work on it. Not yet. All I've done so far is talk to that woman, the witnesses' daughter, whatever her name was, and to Roger Huggins. And try to track down Laura Hanson.

Karen tossed and turned in bed Sunday night. Why had Hecky Cameron called?

Did he think he could frighten me into dropping the case? Or merely tear away at my confidence so I would screw up things up? And what does he know about Laura Hanson?

More questions popped into her head.

What should I do now? Go to Charlie and tell him about the call?

Maybe it's better to keep quiet right now, she thought. I'll make a few notes, memorialize the call, in case I need to document it later. That ought to be enough.

Karen grabbed a note pad she kept on the nightstand and jotted down what she remembered of the call. After much more tossing and turning, she finally fell asleep.

Monday morning Karen let herself into the office a few minutes before eight o'clock, welcoming the early morning silence. She would have nearly an hour to call New York before anyone else showed up.

She dreaded the thought of facing Harold, due back from his hunting trip today. Putting ugly thoughts of Harold aside, Karen pulled Hope Shimkus's faded résumé out of her top desk drawer and looked at it again. A lot of information there. Too bad it was six years old.

She picked up the phone and, placing the résumé on her desk where she could see it, called New York precisely at eight. Melissa was always at her desk by nine o'clock.

As Melissa's phone rang, Karen suddenly had the horrible thought that her former secretary might have gone on vacation. Melissa always took a week off in the fall, heading for Vermont with her mother to see the leaves change color.

"Melissa Cohen. Can I help you?" Melissa's New York nasality sounded like sweet music to Karen.

"Melissa, it's Karen. I tried reaching you Friday afternoon, but you'd already left."

"Sorry, Karen. I stuck around till quarter after, but I couldn't...."

"I know, don't worry about it. Just tell me if you made any progress with that name I gave you."

"As a matter of fact, I did. I couldn't get to it right away, because of Gary Goldberg's work, but...."

"Melissa! Just tell me what you found out!"

"Okay, okay. Hold on a second while I find my notes." Karen waited, her patience disintegrating, while Melissa searched. Finally she came back on the line. "I found out quite a bit, actually." Karen's hopes soared. "Not from the law school alumni office, though. They lost contact with her years ago, right after she graduated. That's what Professor Young said, too. One of her references. He hasn't heard from her since she left school."

Not terribly unusual, Karen thought. I haven't contacted any of my law school professors since graduation either.

"Then I tried the state bar people. They have no record of her. I made them do a complete search of their files. Turns out she never took the bar exam in New York."

Another dead end.

"Then I started calling numbers in the phone book," Melissa continued. "There aren't that many people named Shimkus in New York. A couple in Manhattan, three in Brooklyn, and two more in Queens."

And? And?

"I didn't even get to the Bronx or Staten Island 'cause I hit pay dirt in Queens. You gave me a number in Queens, remember? It was disconnected, I forgot to tell you that, but I tried all three numbers in the Queens phone book, and one of them was this girl's uncle."

Hope's uncle. Huzzah! Karen could barely contain her excitement. "What did he say?"

"Well, he gave me her mother's number in Miami. He said she'd moved there a couple years ago. I called the number a few times and finally got through."

"You spoke to her mother?"

"Yeah. Nice enough lady. Couldn't understand why I was asking about her daughter, though. She said they had a fight years ago and didn't talk much after that."

That bit of news didn't sound good. "When did they talk last?"

"Well, she knew Hope had gone out West somewhere. I asked her where exactly, and she said she thought it was some little town in Wisconsin. I guess that's not too far from where you are, huh?"

"What?" Karen wasn't *near* that little town in Wisconsin. She was *in* it.

"I was pretty good at geography in school, and I seem to remember that Wisconsin is somewhere near Chicago. Am I right?"

"Oh, yeah, sure," Karen said. She'd almost forgotten that as far as Melissa was concerned, she was still in Chicago. "You're absolutely right. So what happened after Hope moved to Wisconsin?"

"Well, her mother said that after a couple calls from her the first few months, she never heard from her again."

"What? Her daughter didn't call after the first few months?"

"Yeah. That's what she said."

"And she didn't come back to New York?"

"Not as far as her mother knows."

"Well, isn't she worried about her? Doesn't she wonder what happened to her?"

"I got the feeling she wasn't worried exactly. More like hurt that her daughter had stopped calling. She said they weren't on such great terms anyhow, so when she stopped hearing from her, she just figured her daughter forgot about her, living so far away and all. I think she feels hurt more than worried."

"So she has no idea where her daughter is now? Whether she's still in Wisconsin, or back in New York, or somewhere else entirely?"

"She doesn't have the foggiest, Karen. At least that's what she told me. All she has is some old address in some little town in Wisconsin. I could probably call her back and get it."

"No, don't bother. But save the phone number just in case, okay?"

"Okay. Is that it, Karen?"

"I guess so."

"Any word on when you can come back?"

"Not yet. I should know soon, though."

"Well, just be happy you're not here right now. There's a transit strike threatened for tomorrow, and you know what that means."

Karen pictured massive gridlock on the streets of Manhattan as every Tom, Dick, and Mary tried driving or cabbing to work the next morning. "Sounds awful."

"Plus we're having a heat wave, record temperatures for September. And the garbagemen are threatening to strike again."

Karen said a silent word of thanks to whatever gods had conspired to set her down in Walden.

"Karen...?"

"Yes?"

"Hendrix told me Friday he never got that letter from you. You know, that letter about medical leave."

The letter about medical leave. Karen had totally forgotten about it. The note she'd written to herself, the reminder to write Hendrix, was buried somewhere on her desk. "Thanks for reminding me. I'll send it out today."

"Good," Melissa said. "He's flipping!"

Karen thanked Melissa for her help and hung up. She stared at the résumé in front of her, reading and re-reading the words on it, trying to glean one more salient fact she could use to track down Hope Shimkus. Finally she gave up, replacing the résumé in her top drawer. It was 8:45, time to settle down to work.

Suddenly Karen tore the drawer open and pulled out the résumé. There it was, right under Hope's name and her six-year-old address in Queens. Her social security number. If Nedra could use Laura Hanson's number to learn her current whereabouts, couldn't she use Hope's number as well?

Karen called Nedra immediately, relaying Hope's number to her. Nedra hadn't reached her friend Ron yet. Now she'd give him both numbers and call Karen as soon as she heard anything.

Karen hung up the phone again, her heart pounding. Nedra seemed pretty sure that Ron would turn up something. Now all Karen could do was wait.

CHAPTER THIRTY-TWO

Karen used Belinda's typewriter to type the almost-forgotten letter to Phil Hendrix. It had been a jolt to see Belinda using a typewriter, instead of a word processor, that first week in Walden. "Don't you have computers here?" Karen had asked.

"Oh, Charlie's been after me to get a computer, Karen," Belinda answered. "But Martha and me—we're making do with our typewriters." And they did. Karen was no longer surprised to see the quality of the work Belinda and Martha managed to produce on their twenty-year-old IBM Selectrics.

Now Karen typed out a short letter, stating that she'd been injured in an accident in Chicago and required medical leave for an indefinite period, until she could recover completely from her injuries. She stuffed the letter into an envelope, then wondered what to do with it next. She couldn't drop it into a mailbox in Walden. She was requesting medical leave in Chicago; a postmark from Walden, Wisconsin, would almost certainly raise questions.

I'll decide what to do about it later, she thought. She went back to her office and stuck the envelope into her shoulder bag.

She thought she heard a sound in Harold's office. I can't face seeing him yet, she thought, and went to shut her door. But all she heard now was silence. Maybe Harold wasn't there after all. Karen walked slowly toward the door to his office and glanced inside. No one there.

I could take a quick look around his office, she thought. Maybe I'll find something to show Charlie, something that will back me up on Ruth Swenson and Merv Robbins and the money they never got. She tiptoed quietly into Harold's office.

Oh, don't be silly, she told herself. No one's here yet; you don't have to creep around like this. She strode toward Harold's file cabinet in the corner. He probably stashes his private papers here, keeping them separate from the files in the outer office. She grabbed the handle on a file drawer and pulled.

A large number of file folders were crammed into the drawer every which way. Karen thumbed through them quickly. Andrews Realty, Baxter & Co., Dillons Garage, Frankenthaler Farm. Just a bunch of client files, as far as she could tell. No files for Ruth Swenson and Merv Robbins, though.

She turned around to look at Harold's desk. Except for the small framed photograph of his son, the desktop was completely empty, devoid of any clue about its owner. Karen reached for the top drawer–nothing but pens, a cheap plastic staple-remover, some white-out, some Wrigley's gum. She pulled out another drawer–a stack of yellow legal pads, nothing else. Sighing, she bent over and opened the bottom drawer. A pile of empty file folders teetered on top of something else, something uneven at the bottom of the drawer. Karen pushed the folders aside and felt beneath them.

Something cold and metallic touched her fingertips. Karen peered beneath the empty folders and saw a gun. A small silver-and-black gun, something like the one she'd found in K.B.'s suitcase.

Once again, Karen felt a chill run through her. Another gun. And once again, she felt stupid, totally ignorant, knowing nothing at all about guns. Was this one any more menacing than K.B.'s? Less? She had no idea. Was it the kind of gun Harold would use when he went hunting? Karen rather doubted it. Didn't hunters use bigger guns–shotguns, rifles, whatever they called those things?

Suddenly Karen heard voices in the outer office. Belinda and Martha were arriving. She closed Harold's drawer and scurried to the door of his office, hoping the other women wouldn't suspect that she'd been prowling through Harold's things. She made it back to her own office before they noticed her.

She could hear Belinda discussing her weekend; then she heard Martha mention Charlie again. Something about his getting "a little too rough this time." Karen closed her ears, not wanting to hear any more intimate details of Martha's relationship with Charlie.

The women sat down at their typewriters and began to work. A short time later, Karen heard Belinda greeting Harold when he walked in.

Harold. Harold, gun-enthusiast. The proud owner of a silver-and-black gun stashed in his desk drawer. Karen couldn't put off talking to him much longer. She would approach him as soon as he settled down at his desk.

"Harold?" Karen stuck her head into Harold's office about ten minutes later. "This a good time to talk?"

Harold grimaced. "Not really. What is it?" He looked up at Karen, light bouncing off the lenses of his wire-rimmed glasses.

"A couple of things," Karen said, sitting down opposite him. "While you were gone, Charlie got a call from a client named Merv Robbins. He asked me to look into it. It seems Mr. Robbins never got the insurance settlement he was supposed to. Something like the Ruth Swenson case." Karen watched Harold's face carefully to see how he would react. So far his face remained impassive, his eyes staring back at her, expressionless as ever.

"I'll talk to Charlie about it. You can just forget about it, now that I'm back," Harold said. "I'll explain everything to Charlie."

"Fine," Karen said. "There's just one other thing." Karen thought she detected a slight twitch, barely noticeable, under

Harold's left eye. "I've been trying to track down Laura Hanson." No reaction. "She used to work here. You even mentioned her name to me once." Harold nodded, and Karen went on. "Her information about a will-signing would be very helpful, but I can't seem to find out where she is."

Harold shook his head. "I can't help you. Have you asked Belinda to check the files? We ought to have some record of her forwarding address."

"Yes, we should. But her file is missing."

Harold paused. "That's strange," he said coldly. "But, as I just said, I have no idea where Laura is. She left some sort of memo for Charlie when she took off, but she didn't leave any word for me, and I never heard from her again. Never."

There was that twitch again, right below his left eye. Was Harold upset because Laura had left without saying goodbye, without leaving him so much as a note to say farewell? Or was he simply angry, irritated with Laura for taking off and dumping her work on him?

Maybe, Karen thought, he's angry with *me* because I've dredged up a painful episode he forgot about long ago. It was impossible to tell what he was thinking. But Harold did seem, at long last, to be having some kind of emotional reaction,.

"You wouldn't happen to know what happened to Hope Shimkus either, would you?" Karen tried to inject an ingenuous tone into her voice. Just asking, Harold. That's all.

Harold's eyes widened at the sound of Hope's name. "Hope Shimkus?" The twitch was beating out a rapid tattoo now.

"I came across her name in the Robbins file, but I haven't had any luck finding her either."

Harold shifted uneasily in his chair. He had begun to look genuinely agitated. What had stirred him up? Was it the name of

Hope Shimkus, or was it the accumulated stress of Karen's questions, probing him in a sensitive spot?

"I haven't heard anyone mention that name in years. Good God, I'd forgotten all about Hope," he said. "She's another one. Just like Laura, walked out of here one day and never came back. Never said goodbye to me, either. Just like Laura."

Harold no longer looked angry. A look of dismay had replaced the hint of anger he had shown moments before.

Karen tried to hide how surprised she was by Harold's reaction. For the first time since she'd met him, bland boring Harold had begun to reveal some feelings, some semblance of emotion. For him, it was the equivalent of someone else's primal scream. He appeared to take the disappearance of the two women as a personal affront, a deliberate blow to his ego. They had left the firm, left Walden, without so much as a fare-thee-well to Harold, and he seemed genuinely disturbed by their abrupt departures.

Or was he too clever for Karen? Was there something else he wasn't telling her, something he was covering up with the appearance of a bruised ego?

Harold leaned back in his chair, staring at Karen again. Karen began to feel uncomfortable. Suddenly Harold spoke. "You know, you remind me of Hope," he said.

Karen was startled. "I do?"

"Yes, you do. You're from the East, aren't you? New York, Boston, one of those places?"

Karen nodded, hoping he wouldn't delve into any particulars.

"Hope was from New York. She was different from the girls who grow up around here. More aggressive. More outspoken. You're a lot like her."

"And Laura Hanson? Was she like that, too?"

He took the bait. "No, no. Laura was from California. She wasn't like that at all. 'Laid-back,' I think they call it." He emitted a short bark of a laugh. "Everyone got along great with Laura." His eyes glazed over as he remembered her, but it was impossible to know what he was thinking.

Karen decided to disturb his reverie. "Hope, I take it, didn't fit in quite as well." Would Harold bite again?

He did. "No, she didn't. Oh, it wasn't a case of being at each other's throats all the time," he added hastily. "She had an occasional run-in with one of us now and then, but nothing serious. Hope...she was a hard worker, and she got along here most of the time. But she never seemed terribly happy. So I wasn't really surprised when she left that summer and never came back."

"And you've never heard from her since?"

Karen's luck ran out. "No, I haven't," Harold said abruptly. The impassive mask had returned. His face, once again, revealed nothing. "And now I think it's time we both got back to work." He looked away from Karen, focusing intently on the papers on his desk. The interview was over.

Karen rose and returned to her office. She made a stab at doing her work, but Harold's words kept running through her head. He'd described Hope as aggressive, outspoken, never terribly happy in Walden. By contrast, Laura was laid-back, likable, a California girl.

But both of them had disappointed Harold. They'd taken off and left Walden–and him–in a cloud of dust. Was he angry? Or just annoyed? Indifferent? Or heartbroken?

Harold was a tough nut to crack. Karen wondered if she would ever find out precisely how he felt about Laura and Hope and their unceremonious departures from his life.

CHAPTER THIRTY-THREE

Karen began counting the days until Jon's return. His absence left a gaping hole in her life, and she now realized just how much she had come to care for him. He phoned several times from Minnesota, and his long chatty calls left her feeling even closer to him than before.

Meanwhile Karen was making calls of her own, calling Nedra every day to learn what her friend Ron at the IRS had come up with. Every day, Nedra had the same response. "I can't pressure him, Karen. He'll get back to me eventually. Just be patient."

Karen would hang up after talking to Nedra and pace her office, trying to stay patient. When would they hear from Ron? What exactly could he tell them?

And if Ron came up empty-handed, then what? Karen could try more phone calls–to other law schools, to other state bar associations, to the ABA, to the NLA, to city and county bar associations all over the country. But where would she make all these calls? If she made them from the office, sooner or later Charlie would find out. Karen could imagine how he would react: livid, furious, ready to kick Karen out the door.

No, she couldn't justify to Charlie–or even to herself–making dozens of phone calls to find two elusive women lawyers. Darla Cameron's will would be litigated without Laura Hanson, and absolutely no one needed to know where Hope Shimkus was. Hope's own mother had given up on her.

Karen wondered sometimes why she herself had gotten so caught up in this whole business. It was stupid, really. To have stumbled across the names of these two women, then proceeded to conduct a frenzied search for them. No one else seemed to care.

Finally, just before lunch on Thursday, Nedra called. "Karen, I have news for you." Her voice sounded strangely flat, unlike Nedra's usually animated tone.

"Terrific! What is it?" Karen whooped.

"Let's get together for lunch. I'll tell you then."

"Lunch?" Karen couldn't imagine waiting a moment longer to learn where Laura and Hope had settled.

"It's pretty confidential stuff, Karen. I don't want to talk about it over the telephone."

"Oh. Okay." Karen felt suddenly subdued. "Where do you want to go?"

"How's the Walden Cafe–in fifteen minutes?"

"Sure. Fifteen minutes." Karen grabbed her bag and got up to leave. As she approached Belinda's desk, a young man entered the outer office, nodded cursorily at the secretaries, and rudely brushed past Karen. He pushed open the door to Harold's office, then slammed it shut.

"Who was *that*?" Karen asked.

"Oh, that's Andy. Harold's son."

Karen remembered that Harold had a son. Now she'd finally had a glimpse of him. No longer a curly-haired little boy, he was a grown man–medium height, wire-rimmed glasses, brown hair, pasty complexion. A younger version of Harold.

"What's he like?" Karen asked.

"Oh, Andy's all right," Belinda said. "Kind of a nervous type, but he's all right. You've never met him?"

"No."

"He's in and out of here all the time. But I guess he hasn't been around much lately."

Karen nodded, still puzzling over Andy's rude behavior. "What does he...?" she began.

Belinda stopped her in mid-sentence. "Weren't you on your way to lunch?" Belinda asked. "I overheard you on the phone, something about lunch in fifteen minutes."

Andy's arrival had distracted Karen, almost made her forget her date with Nedra. "Thanks!" she said, flying out the door and down the stairs. She headed for the Walden Cafe, her excitement building again. What was it Nedra had said? She had "news"? Nedra must have learned something concrete. Maybe the puzzle of Laura and Hope was finally solved.

Karen entered the cafe and looked around for Nedra. Her friend waved at her from a red leatherette booth near the window. Karen walked quickly to the booth.

A tired-looking waitress immediately approached with a pot of coffee. "Coffee, ladies?" Both women nodded and ordered sandwiches. "I'll get that for you in a minute," the waitress said, filling their coffee mugs before turning away.

"Finally! Now tell me everything," Karen said, her face shiny with excitement.

"It's not...what you think."

"What do you mean? Ron found out something, didn't he?"

"Yes. But it's...it's not very helpful." Nedra's large brown eyes were wide-open, serious, silently asking Karen to slow down for a minute.

"Okay, Nedra. What are you trying to tell me?"

"Ron plugged in the two social security numbers you gave me as soon as he could. Yesterday, I think. He couldn't do it any earlier because his boss was around. What he did, getting this information, is illegal, you know."

"I know, I know. But what did he find out?"

"Just listen. I'm going to tell you, okay?"

"Okay." Karen sat back in the booth and sipped her coffee.

"He discovered that the IRS has put both women on 'uncollectible status.' That's what they call it when taxpayers stop sending in returns but the IRS can't find them."

"So what does that mean?"

"It's like this, Karen," Nedra said. "When a taxpayer has a record of filing returns, then stops filing, the IRS starts sending notices. Sometimes they send out an investigator to talk to former employers, relatives, even neighbors. If the IRS is still getting 1099 forms from banks, stuff like that, they may go ahead and composite a return and send out a bill to the taxpayer. But if they don't get any response, and can't track the guy down, the taxpayer gets put into this 'uncollectible' status until the IRS learns something else."

Where was all this IRS mumbo-jumbo going? Was Nedra leading up to something? Otherwise, this was all a big waste of time. "But what exactly does this mean for Laura and Hope?"

Nedra's mouth tightened. She swallowed hard and looked away for a moment. Then she turned again to Karen. "Ron thinks it means...something bad may have happened to them. He thinks, with both of them in this status, he thinks they may both...both...."

"What, Nedra? What?" Karen almost shouted. Why was Nedra dragging this out? There had to be some simple explanation.

"Well, when people just disappear like this, women who've held responsible jobs, Ron says the chances are pretty good that they've met with foul play."

"Foul play?"

"That something terrible has happened to them, Karen. They may even be...dead."

"Dead?"

"There's been no official report filed with the IRS, of course. No official word that either of them has actually died. But Ron says that in most of these cases, the taxpayers have either left the country, or...or...they're dead. And the chances that both of these women have left the country are, well, pretty remote."

No, no, Nedra, he's wrong. Laura and Hope—they must have both left the country. Maybe they'd had their fill of the good old U.S. of A. Right now, I bet they're both doing Europe on the cheap, hopping trains with heavily-laden backpacks, accompanied by sexy Italian lovers with day-old stubble and a month's supply of lambskin condoms.

Karen smiled and shook her head. "It's very clear to me what's happened. They've both left the country. Anyone can see why they'd...."

"I think we have to be realistic, Karen. It's much more likely that they're both dead."

There was that word again. "Dead." The air in the restaurant suddenly felt icy cold, and the seat beneath Karen became fluid, gelatinous. She was floating on red leatherette, her whole body bobbing as it floated. She felt dizzy, disconnected.

Dead. The word reverberated through her head, bouncing around inside it.

Karen swallowed and tried to breathe. She hadn't figured on this.

Nedra was staring at her. "Are you all right?"

"Yes. I'm...I'm all right."

"I know it's a terrible shock," Nedra said, taking one of Karen's hands. "You're trembling. Let me take you home."

"No, no," Karen said, withdrawing her hand. "I'm okay. I don't want to go home. I'm fine." Karen's heart was still pounding, but the booth had stopped floating, and she thought she could get through lunch and the rest of the day at work. "Can you tell me anything else?"

"No, sorry. That's all Ron could find out. He'd have to go through a pile of paperwork to get anything more. And he can't do that without getting into all kinds of trouble."

"So we don't know if they actually died. Or when. Or where."

"Right."

"But they're probably...probably... dead."

"Yep."

"But how? Who...?"

Nedra attempted a nervous half-smile. "Maybe some disgruntled client did them in."

Karen considered that possibility. Nedra was right. Lawyers were often targets of unhappy clients, clients who decided that their lawyers weren't smart enough, weren't honest enough, or hadn't moved heaven and earth enough to win their cases. A few madmen had even shown up in big-city law offices with guns blazing, ready to kill anyone in sight, culpable or not.

Was that what had happened to Laura and Hope? It hardly seemed likely in sleepy little Walden. But there was that call from Hecky Cameron. Was he angry enough to have harmed Laura? Was there some other client with a grudge against Hope?

The waitress arrived at the booth and dispensed their sandwiches. Karen couldn't look at her tuna salad sandwich, much less eat it. She started to get up.

"Wait, Karen. Have something to eat, you'll feel better."

"No, I can't. I've got to go."

"Where? Back to the office?"

"Sure. Why not?"

"I think you should call in sick. Go home and lie down. You're not in any shape to go back to work right now."

"I have to go back, I want to go back. I can't just take off because...because of this."

Nedra took Karen's hand again. "Okay, but promise me you'll go right home at five o'clock and try to get some rest."

Karen nodded. The two women sat a while longer in the booth, sipping coffee. Karen left her food untouched while Nedra picked at hers, upset by both the news and her friend's reaction to it. Finally, both women got up to leave.

"I'll walk you back to your office," Nedra said, taking Karen's arm.

"You don't have to do that. I'm fine," Karen insisted. But she was still shaky, and a million thoughts raced through her head as they walked. When they parted at the corner office building, and Karen climbed the stairs to her office, she finally had a chance to think without Nedra hovering over her.

Okay, imagine the worst. Both of them dead. Why? How?

Was it happenstance? A weird coincidence? Karen wanted to believe that, but it was hard to accept. How could two young women who had worked at one small law firm in one small town have both disappeared, then met with death a short time later, by sheer coincidence?

Then what *did* happen?

CHAPTER THIRTY-FOUR

Karen felt unsteady as she entered the firm's outer office. Belinda looked up at her with a smile. "Everything okay? You look kind of pale."

"I'm fine, thanks," Karen said, wondering whether Belinda knew anything that could help her. She walked slowly into her office. The aura of two dead women engulfed her. Laura, Hope—both of them had probably used this office, sat at this desk, looked out this window. Karen fell into her desk chair, trying to stop shaking.

Suddenly her blood ran cold.

Maybe I'm a target now.

Karen Clark, third in line. Third in line behind Hope and Laura.

No, no. The two deaths were unrelated, had to be unrelated. Hope had gone back to New York, remember? She'd written Charlie to tell him that. She must have become ill there, seriously ill. Something incurable that killed her within a year or two. Or she was the victim of a mugging that went terribly wrong, like the famous "Central Park jogger." Karen had always been careful to jog in safe areas, but maybe Hope was a jogger who wasn't so careful. Lots of things could have happened to her back in New York. There were countless ways she could have died, alone and unidentified.

Laura's situation–that was entirely different. Karen already knew about Laura. She'd been pregnant when she left Walden. She must have fled because of the pregnancy. She wanted to have the baby somewhere else and...and what? Give it up for adoption? Or raise it as a single mother, in a larger city where single motherhood was more acceptable than in small-town Walden?

Maybe she had chosen a third alternative: not to have the baby. To abort it, under a phony name, in a city where she could begin her life again, away from the prying eyes of Walden.

If the father had wanted to marry her and raise their child together, then Laura surely would have stayed. But maybe he was already married. Or maybe he had rejected the notion of marriage, or maybe he was a rapist and Laura couldn't face having his child....

Oh, Karen, aren't you getting a bit carried away? The idea seemed so preposterous, she nearly laughed.

Still, something had clearly happened to both women. Each one had wound up dead. Their deaths were probably–no, surely–unrelated. Still, Karen was desperate to know what had happened to each of them.

Where, how could she find out? Maybe talk to Charlie again. After all, he was head of the firm, and both women had communicated with him when they left Walden. If there had been a disgruntled client, say, Charlie might remember him.

But Charlie was so impatient, so easily irritated. Karen was reluctant to pounce upon him with her questions.

What about Harold? He remembered both women. They had assisted him in some of his cases, and he didn't seem all that reluctant to talk about them. He was much more reluctant to discuss the cases themselves, cases where the clients' settlements were still unpaid.

Harold's stand-offish personality was an obstacle, of course, but the last time they'd talked, Karen had felt some sort of breakthrough with him. Maybe his initial reticence was wearing off. Maybe he had finally come to view her as his colleague.

Yes, I'll talk to Harold. Right now. I'll tell him I've learned that both Laura and Hope are dead. I'll say, 'Harold, do you have any idea how each of them might have died?'

Karen stood up and straightened her shoulders. She left her office and walked next door to Harold's. Empty. She turned to the outer office. Belinda had gone to lunch, but Martha Morgan was at her desk, typing. "Martha, do you know where Harold is?" she asked.

Martha looked up, annoyed by Karen's interruption. "Harold's at a funeral this afternoon." Martha looked back at her typewriter, flashing her white roots at Karen. "Won't be back till tomorrow morning."

Karen felt dashed but recovered quickly. "Someone in his family?" Maybe she was expected to go to the funeral, too, or to commiserate with Harold at his home tonight.

"No. One of his old clients." Martha grudgingly looked away from her typewriter. She pushed around some papers on her desk and finally found a handwritten note. "Somebody named Ruth Swenson."

The name hit Karen like a punch in the stomach. "Ruth Swenson?"

"That's what this note says. He left word when and where the funeral is, in case we need to get in touch with him. Do you want me to try to reach him?"

"No, no. Thanks." Karen turned toward her office. She had to sit down, fast.

Another death. This time Ruth Swenson, a client Harold had probably cheated out of her rightful settlement. The hypocrisy of the man, going to her funeral, as though nothing untoward had happened!

Karen stumbled toward her desk and sat down heavily. This shock, on top of Nedra's news, was more than she could handle. Her mind raced, trying to deal with all of the day's assaults. She jumped when her phone buzzed and Martha came on the line. "Charlie wants to see you. Right away."

Charlie. Maybe this is my chance to talk to him, Karen thought. He's summoning me for some reason or another; maybe I can divert him long enough to ask about Hope and Laura.

Karen found Charlie packing up his worn leather briefcase. "I'm on my way to a meeting, Karen," he said brusquely, "but I want you to do something for me tomorrow."

There'd be no chance to talk to Charlie today.

"I need to file some important documents with the state Supreme Court tomorrow. I want them hand-delivered, just to be safe. You have a car now, am I right?"

Karen nodded.

Charlie was rifling through the papers on his desk, stuffing his briefcase with every third or fourth one he glanced at. "Good. I thought you might like to drive down to Madison and file the papers for me. You haven't been to Madison yet, have you?"

"No," Karen answered.

"Great town. You'll enjoy the trip. It's just a few hours from here. Here are the papers," he added, handing her a file folder. "You need to file them with the clerk of the Supreme Court."

Karen nodded, taking the file folder. She supposed she could get a map and find her way to Madison all right. It might even be good to get out of Walden, to put some distance between her and the disturbing developments that swirled around her.

"Fine, Charlie. I'll be happy to do it."

"Good. Now I'm off to my meeting." Charlie scooped up his bulging briefcase and brushed past Karen on his way out of the office.

"Tell anyone who calls I'll be back in the morning," he shouted to Martha as he walked out the door.

Karen remained standing in the doorway of Charlie's office, leafing through the file folder. Some sort of petition for leave to file an appeal in one of Charlie's cases. Fairly routine. Suddenly she was aware that someone was approaching her. She looked up.

"Karen, long time no see." Chad had sidled up next to her, smiling his devastating smile. "How are things?"

"Fine, fine," she stammered.

"My father keeping you on your toes?"

"Yes, yes, he is, Chad." Karen tried to smile as she said it.

"I hope you're having a ball outside the office, too," Chad said, cocking his head, looking flirtatious. "All work and no play makes Karen a dull girl, you know."

Chad's demeanor suddenly struck Karen as inane, and she had to work hard to stifle a laugh. His idea of flirting was to throw a bunch of clichés at her. For a great-looking guy, his approach was remarkably unsophisticated.

"Going to the game this weekend?" he asked.

"The game?"

"The football game. The Walden Warriors." He looked surprised that she hadn't grasped immediately which game he meant.

"Yes, I *am* going," she answered.

"With a date?"

"Yes," Karen nodded, wondering whether he would have asked her to go with him if she didn't have a date.

"Anyone I know?"

"Jon Smith. Do you know him?"

"Sure, I know Jon," Chad answered, nodding. His smile had vanished. "Nice guy. Have a good time, Karen."

Chad turned and walked quickly back to his office. So he *had* planned to ask her to go to the game with him, and now he felt rejected.

If he wanted to take me to the game, she thought, he could have asked a week or two ago. Why didn't he?

Just then, Belinda walked in. She took a long look at Karen, still standing in Charlie's doorway. "Hey, you don't look too good, hon. Why don't you take off the rest of the day? Charlie and Harold won't be around. Go home and get off your feet."

"I'm okay, Bel...," Karen began.

"Charlie's sending you to Madison tomorrow, isn't he?" Belinda interrupted.

Karen nodded.

"Well, go home and get some rest. You're not used to all that driving."

Belinda was right. Karen felt exhausted, and now she had a perfect excuse to go home early.

Karen drove home carefully, concentrating on her driving for fear she might run off the road. After a glass of cold water at her kitchen sink, she fell into bed and sank into a restless sleep.

CHAPTER THIRTY-FIVE

A bell was ringing somewhere. Karen stirred in her sleep. Was it the telephone downstairs? She jumped out of bed and raced down the stairs to answer it.

"Karen? Are you all right? Did I wake you?" Jon had interrupted Karen's sleep, but she was deliriously happy to hear his voice. He was the anchor in her suddenly pitching, lurching life.

"I...I was napping for a moment, but I'm awake now."

"It's just nine o'clock. I didn't think you'd be in bed yet."

"No, no, it was just a nap. I'm glad you called." Karen could hear the crickets singing outside, background music for their conversation. "How's the conference going?"

"Winding down. I may decide to cut out early and come home tomorrow. I'll call you if I do."

"Good. I'd like that."

"How's everything there?" Jon asked.

Karen paused.

"Karen, is everything all right?"

"No, not really."

"What is it?" Jon's voice was filled with concern.

"There were these two women. Two lawyers who used to work at my firm. They've disappeared."

"What?"

"Two women have disappeared. And both of them worked at my firm."

"Both...both of them disappeared?"

"Yes." Should she add that both of them were probably dead?

Suddenly she realized that Jon might have known the missing women. "Did you know them? Their names were Laura Hanson and Hope Shimkus."

Jon hesitated. Finally he said, "I knew Laura. But I didn't know the other woman. Hope, was it?"

"Yes, Hope." Jon was silent. But there was something he'd already said. "How well did you know Laura?" she asked.

"We...we knew each other very well."

"Do you remember when she left town? She left very suddenly, a couple of years ago."

"Yes, I remember when she left." Jon paused again. "Karen, I think I'd rather talk about this when I see you."

"Why?" Silence again. "Why can't you talk about it now?"

"It's not that I can't talk about it. It's...well, it's a long story, Karen...."

"A long story?"

More silence. Then Jon spoke, haltingly, his voice shaking. "Laura and I were engaged."

"Engaged? Engaged to be married?"

"Yes."

Karen's mouth went dry. Jon, her Jon, engaged to Laura Hanson. Another shock in an already shock-filled day.

"Karen? Are you still there?" Jon's voice was tremulous.

"Yes, I'm here."

"I'll tell you about Laura now, if it's important to you."

"It's very important," Karen said slowly. "It's...."

"All right, I'll tell you." Jon cleared his throat. "Laura and I met a few months after she moved to Walden. We...we hit it off right away. The way you and I did, Karen." The line was silent for a moment. Then Jon spoke again. "After about six or eight months, we got engaged. But she wanted to go back to California to get married. We had trouble scheduling when that would be, so we just went along for a while without making any wedding plans.

"My folks had moved to Sarasota by that time, and I went down to visit them for a week. I wanted Laura to come with me, but she begged off. Said she had too much work to do."

Jon cleared his throat again. "When I got back to Walden, she was gone. She had moved out of her place and left town. She didn't call me, just left me a letter saying she was going back to California. Said she wasn't happy in Walden. Maybe...maybe that's why she postponed making wedding plans for so long, I don't know." Jon sounded melancholy, reviewing events he had tried hard to forget. "I checked with Charlie Fuller. She'd left him a note, too. Same story. She wanted to go back to California. No forwarding address. No new phone number. And...that was it."

"Did she ever call you?"

"No, never."

"And she never wrote again either?"

"No. No, she didn't."

"How awful."

"It was, it really was."

"Did you try to find her, to get in touch with her?"

Jon paused. "I wanted to, of course. But I didn't know exactly where her family lived in California. She was always pretty vague about it. Besides, I felt so hurt, I just couldn't pursue her. It really hurt, the way she left."

"Yes, I'm sure it did," Karen said softly.

"After a few months, I got over it. Put it behind me. I had to. What else could I do?" Jon's tone had changed. He started to sound stronger, more secure, more like the Jon she knew. "And then this summer, you came into my life. My beautiful, wonderful Karen."

Karen didn't say anything. Jon finally spoke again. "Laura...she's just a memory now. A painful one. But just a memory."

"I see. I really do." Karen and Jon said a quick goodbye, and she hung up the phone. Then she began to pace in the small living room, back and forth, back and forth. Suddenly she stopped.

She felt rooted, unable to move. Subconsciously, her mind had connected two sets of facts. If Jon had been engaged to Laura, then the baby Laura was expecting was almost certainly Jon's.

But if Laura and Jon were engaged when she became pregnant, why had she left Walden? Jon would undoubtedly have welcomed the child. And he would have married Laura right away, to spare her any embarrassment. That was the sort of thing a man like Jon would do.

Or was it? Maybe Karen didn't know Jon as well as she thought she did. Maybe he didn't want to have a child just then, and he urged Laura to have an abortion. If she didn't want to abort the child, she might have fled Walden, determined to keep her baby and raise it herself.

Or maybe they had argued over something. A serious argument, serious enough for Laura to flee Walden, to have the baby somewhere else. Somewhere where Jon couldn't find her. Maybe she was afraid he would challenge her for custody if he knew where she was.

Or maybe.... Karen shuddered, but she had to consider another possibility.

Maybe Jon was lying. Maybe he and Laura had a fight that got out of hand. She said things that made him turn violent, he took a swipe at her, and....

No. No. Karen couldn't even imagine it. Not Jon. He'd never turn abusive and physically strike out at a woman, no matter how provoked he might be. There had to be another explanation. Jon was–had to be–totally innocent of any role in Laura's death.

Karen tried to think of other scenarios. Maybe Jon didn't even know that Laura was pregnant. She had sought out Roger Huggins, not Jon, when she felt ill. What if she only feigned surprise when Huggins told her she was pregnant? She may have suspected all along that she was pregnant, making an appointment with Huggins to confirm it, keeping her pregnancy a secret from Jon.

Yes. That was it. Laura had never even told Jon she was pregnant. She must have decided she didn't want to marry Jon after all. So she left Walden and returned to California to have her child, free of any need to tell Jon about the baby. If she didn't tell him, she could avoid the hassle of arranging visitation and all the other problems Jon might have caused if he'd known he had a child.

That was the most likely scenario. That would explain everything.

But suddenly Karen had another startling thought. What if someone else was the father of Laura's child? If there was another man in Laura's life, that would mean a whole new set of possibilities.

Karen sighed and walked into the kitchen. She poured herself a tumblerful of wine to help her get back to sleep. She faced three or four hours of driving the next day, and she had to get some rest.

But, despite the wine, sleep didn't come. All night Karen tossed in bed, then arose and went downstairs to pace again. Another glass of wine, back to bed, then back downstairs. She went over and over in her mind the same few facts, the only facts she knew, trying to put the crazy puzzle together.

Okay, she thought, I've come up with a logical scenario–even two or three of them–that explain Laura's disappearance. But what about Hope? Did she simply go back to New York, the way she said in her letter to Charlie? According to Melissa, Hope never even took the New York bar exam. Why would she return to New York, then fail to practice the highly-paid profession she had trained for? It didn't make sense.

Karen finally fell asleep at five in the morning. The alarm clock woke her, groggy and headachey, three hours later. She stumbled into the bathroom and quickly got ready for the drive to Madison.

She didn't want to miss her date with the clerk of the Supreme Court of the sovereign State of Wisconsin.

CHAPTER THIRTY-SIX

Two brimming cups of coffee later, Karen picked up a map at Ed's Arco station and set out for Madison with an eagerness she hadn't anticipated. After six weeks in Walden, she relished the idea of seeing a city again, even a small city like Madison. Besides, Madison wasn't your run-of-the-mill small city. It was the state capital and the home of the main campus of the University of Wisconsin. She hoped it would offer a vibrant mix of interesting shops and restaurants, the kind she hadn't encountered since leaving Chicago.

The drive went quickly. Karen concentrated on the road, not allowing herself to think about Laura Hanson and Hope Shimkus. She resolved, in fact, not to think about them at all right now. Not until she returned to Walden.

Once or twice the Plymouth seemed to lose momentum, scaring Karen. She feared the kind of car trouble that would leave her, stranded and alone, on the road between Walden and Madison. But the Plymouth came back to life and made it into Madison about 10:30 in the morning. Getting directions from a couple of college-age pedestrians, Karen located the state capitol building and parked nearby. It took only a few minutes to file Charlie's petition, and Karen fled the court clerk's office to spend the rest of her day in the city.

She left the Plymouth where it was and set off on foot to see what Madison had to offer. From the capitol building, she walked up State Street, stopping to look in the shop windows. In one small shop, she bought herself a pair of cleverly-designed silver earrings, sophisticated enough to please even a jaded Manhattan shopper.

Then, in a bookstore, she browsed for nearly an hour. She hadn't realized how much she had missed bookstore-browsing in Walden. Hungrily, she leafed through volume after volume. She came across two novels she thought Jon might like, one about a small-town doctor, another set in St. Louis, and ended up buying both, along with a couple of books for herself.

Karen left the bookstore and emerged into the hazy September afternoon. She passed Antony's, a small Italian restaurant, and overwhelmed by the smells emanating from it, went inside and ordered a dish of pasta shells stuffed with ricotta in a light marinara sauce. Heavenly. Something else to add to the list of things she missed in Walden: Italian food. The closest Walden came to Italian cuisine was a mom-and-pop pizza joint on Highway 195.

Suddenly Karen thought about K.B. and the lunch they'd shared at an Italian restaurant in Chicago. If K.B. had made it to Walden instead of me, would *she* be here right now, eating lunch at Antony's?

Karen sighed. It was pointless to speculate about K.B. K.B. was dead.

Karen looked at her watch. Still plenty of time before she had to leave. She didn't trust the Plymouth, she knew she had to get back to Walden before dark, but that still left another hour or two to look around Madison. She decided to keep strolling up State Street till she reached the campus. She hadn't looked around a real college campus for years, not since she'd left law school over three years before.

The campus was huge and bustling, not surprising for a large state university, but considerably different from the smaller private schools Karen had attended. Gazing at the vast number of buildings, she felt overwhelmed. All around her, hundreds, maybe thousands of students were rushing by.

And all of them seem to know exactly where they're going, Karen thought. Unfortunately, I don't.

Tired of wandering aimlessly around the campus, Karen decided to head for a specific destination. I'll try to find the law school, she thought. I might even take a quick look at the library. I've always liked poking around in a law library.

Maybe I'll even try to find the answers to a couple of those questions Charlie asked me last week. It was impossible to find definitive answers in the miniscule law library at the firm. If only Charlie would pop for a few more books....

She stopped a shaggy-looking male student and asked for directions. He wore a faded Bucky Badger T-shirt, and Karen couldn't help wondering how many jokes the Wisconsin team mascot must have inspired over the years.

"Uh, I think it's over there," the student said, pointing off to the left. Karen wasn't terribly optimistic, but she set out in the direction of the student's finger. Walking briskly up a small hill, she noticed a large pink granite building off to her left. Could that be the law school? Karen approached the building and the weathered bronze plaque to the right of the main door. The plaque read:

DEPARTMENT OF GERMAN

DEPARTMENT OF ROMANCE LANGUAGES

Karen abruptly stopped walking. Why did the ornate plaque make her feel oddly nervous?

Suddenly she remembered. Chad had mentioned that his "ladyfriend" was a professor in the German department. His use of a heavy German accent when he mentioned her had made Karen feel uneasy.

But now she had to admit she was curious. What sort of woman was this German professor?

I could spend a couple of minutes looking for her, Karen thought. Chad would never have to know. What the hell, this could be a lot more fun than a trip to the law library. I'm right here, and I might as well try to find this woman. The law school can wait.

She entered the building and searched for some sort of faculty directory. Down a narrow corridor, she found a list displayed on the grimy wall. The building appeared to house the offices of several different language departments, and Karen scanned the list till she came to members of the German department.

Now what was that woman's name? Something that reminded me of an old movie star. What *was* it? Karen's eyes went up and down the list of professors' names, finally stopping at Dieckmann, Marlene.

That was it, wasn't it? Marlene Dieckmann. I remember now: The name reminded me of the German actress Marlene Dietrich, the one who starred in that old movie, "The Blue Angel."

Professor Dieckmann was in Room 203-A. Karen found a stairway and climbed to the second floor. After wandering up and down several confusingly similar corridors, she finally located 203-A. The door was open, and Karen peered inside. An older woman, gray hair pulled back into a severe bun, was seated at one of the two massive desks in the large office. Karen knocked on the open door. The woman turned around and smiled. "Yes?"

"I'm looking for Professor Dieckmann," Karen said.

"Come in, please, and sit down," the gray-haired woman said, her German accent modified by her gentle tone of voice. Behind tortoise-shell glasses, her bright eyes were friendly.

Karen entered the office and looked questioningly at several empty chairs, unsure where to sit.

"Here, sit down here," the woman said, pointing to the chair next to her desk. "How can I help you?"

"Can you tell me when Professor Dieckmann will be back?"

The woman laughed. "She's here now."

"Really? Where?" Karen looked around the office. It was empty except for herself and the older woman.

"I'm Professor Dieckmann," the woman said, smiling. "Now how can I help you?"

Karen stared at the older woman. This woman was Marlene Dieckmann? The girlfriend Chad had talked about, the woman he said he was involved with? Impossible!

The long silence was becoming awkward. Karen had to explain, to say *something*. "I...I just came in to say hello to you. Someone I work with mentioned your name, and...I. . .I just wanted to meet you," she said. It sounded lame, but it was the best she could come up with.

"Who's that?"

"Uh...Chad Fuller. Charles Fuller, Jr." Chad had to know this woman. He hadn't just imagined her. There had to be some connection between them. But what?

"Chad Fuller?" Professor Dieckmann closed her eyes, searching her memory, trying to summon up Chad's face from the thousands of students' faces she'd encountered over the years. "Oh, yes, Chad." Professor Dieckmann nodded. "He was a student of mine years ago. He still writes to me at Christmas every year. Once in a while, he'll even drop in to see me. How nice of you to drop in, too."

Karen was still puzzled. "Was he a special student of yours in some way? Especially good at German?"

"Not really. He...well, he latched on to me for some reason."

What did she mean by "latched on to"? And for what sort of "reason"?

Professor Dieckmann was looking at Karen's face, evaluating her. "Do you know Chad very well?" she asked Karen.

"No, no, I don't."

"Well, maybe I shouldn't tell you this, but...I think I know why he became so attached to me." Marlene Dieckmann's eyes began to glitter behind her tortoise-shell glasses. "He once told me that his mother was German. She died when he was young, and I think he was looking for a mother-figure. Do you know what I mean? Someone to replace his mother, in a sense. When he was assigned to my German class, I think he saw me as that mother-figure.

"I didn't encourage it," she said, shaking her head. "But he would seek me out after class, come up to see me here in my office, write me little notes. He seemed to get a lot of pleasure out of it, and it was harmless enough, so I never put a stop to it." Professor Dieckmann's eyes still glittered. She seemed to find it amusing, even flattering that a handsome young student had taken such an interest in her.

"I see," Karen said, nodding. But she didn't really see. Sure, she could understand a close relationship with a beloved teacher, a teacher Chad came to view as a mother-substitute. Certainly women students fell in love with their male professors all the time, and some of that was the appeal of a father-figure. Male students were entitled to the same weakness.

But why had Chad described Marlene Dieckmann as something more? As a woman he was involved with, in a relationship that precluded his getting involved with Karen or any other woman?

Karen didn't understand that at all. But there was no point in sticking around here. It would be awkward, trying to make conversation, peppering the German professor with even more questions. She had already told Karen everything she knew.

"Well, it was nice to meet you," Karen said, getting up to leave.

"Thank you for coming by. It was a pleasure, Ms..., Ms...? I'm sorry, I didn't catch your name...."

"I...I have to go now," Karen stammered, heading for the door. She had no desire to start explaining who she was. "Goodbye," she called as she exited the office and walked quickly to the stairs and out of the building.

She headed back to her car, too disturbed now to look for the law library. Her whim to see Chad's girlfriend, just to check her out, had left Karen's head spinning. With all the other startling facts swimming around in her head, now she had one more to deal with.

Karen walked blindly through the campus, unaware now of the students rushing past her, and finally realized she was totally lost.

Where am I? What am I doing? I have to find my car, get in my car, try to get home somehow.

She grabbed a woman student, literally grabbed her, and begged her for directions to the state capitol building. The frightened student blurted out something intelligible, and Karen finally found the street where she had parked her car. She climbed into the Plymouth in a haze, her emotions churning. Her hands were shaking too badly to drive, and she sat behind the wheel, breathing hard, trying to make sense of everything.

What kind of place was Walden anyway? She had envisioned it as an idyllic spot, a place where she could forget the tensions of New York City and live a tranquil, unchaotic life. But life in Walden had not turned out the way she'd imagined.

Instead, everything was so damned confusing. She'd been plunged headfirst into the turbulence at Fuller, Fuller & Chase. Two missing women lawyers, both of whom she suspected were dead. Three unpleasant male colleagues: one hot-tempered; one stand-offish and probably corrupt; one a liar with a warped attachment to a mother-substitute.

And Jon. Karen didn't know what to make of Jon anymore. He'd been engaged to Laura Hanson, and Laura Hanson was dead. Was his involvement with her as innocent as he tried to make it sound?

Maybe Jon was a murderer. Maybe he had murdered Laura and covered it up somehow. Jason Singer was a scum-bag, but at least he hadn't murdered anybody.

For this, for all of this tension, this stress, I left my life in New York? My job with a prestigious law firm, my friends, my apartment?

Okay, okay, things in New York weren't so great. I admit it. I had my reasons, good reasons, for leaving. But Walden is far, very far, from the utopia I expected.

A light rain began falling as Karen drove out of Madison. Still agitated, she clung nervously to the steering wheel of the Plymouth for the next two hours. As the rain became heavier, Karen inched along to avoid an accident with the old car, whose tires were frighteningly slippery on the wet pavement.

As she neared Walden, the car began to wheeze and cough, scaring Karen. Could it get her all the way home?

A mile and a half from her house, she got the answer to her question. The Plymouth gave one final cough and died.

CHAPTER THIRTY-SEVEN

Karen stumbled along the dark rain-slick road for nearly an hour, slipping twice but picking herself up, uninjured, both times.

Slipping like this, falling on my face—it's just like the night I fell in Chicago. The night K.B. was killed. The night everything changed.

Finally Karen made out the outline of her house up ahead. She staggered into the house, dead-tired and soaking wet, and pulled off her wet clothes. The phone began to ring just as she slipped into a warm nightgown, pulling a fuzzy robe around her to dispel the terrible chill she felt after an hour in the pouring rain.

Jon's voice. "Karen, where have you been? I've been calling for hours."

"I had to drive to Madison for Charlie. Then my car broke down, and I had to walk the rest of the way home. I just got here...."

"Are you all right?" The concern in Jon's voice cheered her.

"Yes. Yes, I'm all right."

"Karen, I miss you."

"I miss you, too," she said. She did miss Jon. Her doubts about him, about his relationship with Laura Hanson, suddenly seemed foolish. "When are you coming home?"

"I was planning to leave this afternoon. But now I can't. I met some people here today, and I want to talk to them first thing in the morning."

"Oh." Why did Jon want to spend another night at the medical conference when he could be back in Walden, spending the night with her? "When can you leave?"

"Probably by ten, eleven at the latest. I should get back to Walden by early afternoon."

"What about the game? Will you be back in time?"

"Sure. It doesn't start till 3:30. I should get home in time to pick you up by three, the way we planned."

"Then you'll be here around three?"

"Right. Listen, I'm sorry I can't get back tonight, but we'll make up for it when I see you."

Karen was silent.

"Are you okay?" Jon asked.

"I'm okay. Just tired, that's all. I drove to Madison and back, and...." Karen was tempted to tell Jon about Madison, about Chad and his warped relationship with Marlene Dieckmann. About Harold and how she suspected him of wrongdoing. Then she dismissed the idea. She'd see him tomorrow. That was soon enough.

"No wonder you're tired. Go to bed now, and get a good night's sleep." Jon's voice was strong, authoritative, but Karen heard the undertone of caring in it.

"All right," she said. "I will."

Jon paused. Then he spoke again. "Karen, I love you."

Karen hesitated. She didn't feel ready to say those words, to commit herself irrevocably to Jon. Not until she saw him again, felt his arms around her. Maybe then.

Finally she said, "I think I love you, too." That much was true.

"See you tomorrow, three o'clock."

"See you." Karen hung up and walked into the kitchen for something to eat. Too exhausted to cook, she poured herself a glass of milk, ate a bowl of Cheerios, and dragged herself upstairs to bed. The long drive, the lack of sleep for several nights' running, the bewildering events in Madison had left her completely drained.

She fell into bed, into a deep sleep, and didn't awake until late Saturday morning.

When she finally arose, it was close to eleven o'clock. The rain had ended, and the sun was shining, creating a picture-perfect autumn day. The ancient toaster was recalcitrant, but after shaking it a couple of times, Karen revived it and feasted on rye toast and cherry preserves with her coffee.

She had to do something about the Plymouth. It was sitting alongside the road somewhere, a mile or two from the house. She called Ed's Arco station and asked him to tow it there. She'd decide what to do with it later. Then she dusted and swept, washed dishes and did some laundry, trying to shape the general disorder of her surroundings into a more presentable form. The hard physical work kept her too busy to think about Chad and Harold, Laura and Hope.

By one o'clock, she'd had enough of domesticity. There was just enough time to go out for a run, then shower and dress, before Jon arrived at three. She changed into comfortable jogging clothes–shorts and her favorite yellow polo shirt–and was out the door and down the stairs, emerging into the glorious sunshine, five minutes later.

Karen felt restored by her long, deep sleep, felt that she could run for hours. She returned to the dirt road that led to the wooded area she had discovered. Once in the woods, a cool, green calm descended on her. The elms and maples, the birches and evergreens, were like old friends who welcomed her into their emerald-green home. It was easy to forget that outside this lovely green home was another world, a far less benevolent one, where women disappeared and men went balmy over teachers who reminded them of their mothers.

Glancing at her watch, Karen knew she couldn't stay long. She reluctantly left the woods at two o'clock, running home to freshen up for the football game.

As she bounded up her front stairs and entered the house, Karen sensed that something was different. She couldn't put her finger on it, but the house didn't seem the same. Had someone been there while she was gone?

She searched the first floor, but no one was there and nothing seemed changed. Still, Karen tried to think why the air in the house seemed charged, as though someone else was lurking there.

Maybe Jon had gotten back to Walden earlier than expected and, eager to see her, had come directly to the house. Maybe he'd planned to surprise her, the way he did the day he left. But he discovered that she wasn't there. After waiting for a while, he finally went home to shower and change.

That was logical. That explained it.

Karen ran upstairs to shower, heading for her bedroom to shed her sweaty jogging clothes. First, the yellow polo shirt, next....

"Hello, Karen."

Karen whirled around.

It was Chad. Chad Fuller. He was standing by the doorway to her bedroom, smiling his devastating smile.

CHAPTER THIRTY-EIGHT

"Chad! What are you doing here?" Karen's heart began to pound. Why was Chad in her house, in her bedroom? She grabbed her yellow polo shirt and clutched it against her bare chest, covered only by a lacy white bra. She felt exposed, violated by Chad's uninvited presence in her bedroom.

"I came to have a little talk with you, Karen," Chad said, smiling. His smile was devilishly appealing, as always. "Let's go downstairs. I want to show you something." He waved a large tan envelope in Karen's face.

Still clutching her polo shirt to her chest, Karen moved woodenly out of the bedroom and down the stairs. What did he have in that envelope? Her heart beat wildly as she entered the living room and seated herself on the shabby sofa.

"I've got some pictures to show you," Chad smiled. "Some photographs I've taken." He opened the envelope, extracted some photos, and spread them on the coffee table. "I think you'll find these very interesting," he said, his eyes glittering.

Karen picked up two of the glossy black-and-white photographs and gasped. They were photos of her. In her bedroom, alone. In her bedroom, with Jon. And at the lake, on Labor Day, in the secluded spot where she and Jon had made love.

Karen looked up at Chad, her face flushed, her heart beating violently. "What...? What is this? I don't understand."

Chad was standing across the room, facing her, smirking. "You don't understand, Karen?" His voice was heavy with sarcasm. "Don't you recognize yourself in these pictures?"

Karen said nothing. She could hardly breathe, let alone speak.

"Maybe *you* don't understand, Karen," Chad said, his perfect features assuming a grim look, "but I do. I understand very well."

He paused.

"I understand you, Karen. I understand women," Chad said, his mouth tight and unsmiling now. "You're all a bunch of whores, every one of you. Starting with my dear departed mother." He laughed, a short bark of a laugh.

Karen's eyes widened at the mention of his mother.

"Yes, Karen, my mother was a whore, just like the rest of you. I know that better than anyone." Chad's mouth hardened now into a rigid narrow line.

My God! All women are whores? Instinctively, Karen knew she had to say something. Chad was giving off vibrations that frightened her. He was seething with anger, and he seemed unhinged, off-balance.

She had to get him to talk. To keep him from acting out his anger. She swallowed hard and took a deep breath.

"Chad, why do you say that?"

"Why do I say what?" he said, crossing his arms in front of him.

"What you just said, about your mother." Karen's voice shook as she spoke.

Chad stared at Karen, his lips curling now into a half-smile. "That's an interesting story. Want to hear it?"

Karen nodded. God, he looked weird, staring at her this way, his usual good looks distorted, warped by the demented half-smile on his face.

Chad moved towards a chair near the window and eased his body into it. "My father tells everyone my mother is dead," he began. "That she died while we were on a trip to Canada. He even put together a big memorial service for her when we got back home. Told everyone she slipped while we were hiking. Fell down a rocky cliff. That no one ever found her body. But that's not what really happened."

Chad's eyes glazed over. Where was he? Not in this living room. Somewhere else, somewhere with his mother.

Finally he looked back at Karen. His mouth opened, then closed again.

"What *did* happen, Chad?" Karen asked.

Chad struggled to focus once more on Karen. When he did, his eyes were icy-cold. "First things first, Karen. First, I've got to tell you about my father."

Charlie Fuller. Of course. First things first.

"You know my father, Karen. What do you think of him?" Chad sat back in the chair and waited for Karen's response.

"Your father? He's...he's...." she stammered.

"He's a bastard, isn't he, Karen?" Chad said, cutting off her response. "A miserable bastard...cold, unfeeling...."

I'll go along with that, Karen thought. "Always has been, always will be," Chad went on. "When I was a kid, he never showed me any love. Never. I never got the feeling that he cared about me for a minute. Oh, yeah, he'd take me out fishing once in a while, or toss a ball back and forth a couple of times. But he never hugged me, never told me I was a great kid. Nothing like that."

It figures, Karen thought. People usually treat their kids pretty much the way they treat everybody else. It figured that Charlie would be as indifferent, as unfeeling toward Chad as he was to the rest of the world.

"He treated my mother the same way," Chad went on. "She was a sweet little woman, but Charlie, he gave her a hard time. There wasn't any love in our home, Karen. No love between that ice-cold bastard and little Gretchen. That was my mother's name–Gretchen."

Gretchen. A German name. So Marlene Dieckmann was right.

"My mother had a lot of love in her," Chad said. "And she showered it all on me. No husband to give it to, no other kids. Just me.

"Then, that summer, the summer I was eleven, she changed. She still made a big fuss over me, but she didn't seem to mind so much when I went to a ball game with my friends, or I went fishing with Charlie. She almost welcomed it, and she'd never done that before.

"I was going to school in Clarion that summer, working on a project for the science fair. Every morning, about five of us kids from Walden took a schoolbus to Clarion, the only town around here with a summer school."

Karen shifted uneasily on the sofa. Where was Chad going with this? Summer school and science fairs–what did they have to do with his mother?

Chad was looking down at the floor now. "One day I got sick at school," he said to the floor. "I threw up a couple times, and my teacher, she didn't want me to wait for the bus. So she got someone at the school to leave early and drive me home."

Chad suddenly looked up again. His eyes bore into Karen's. "When I got home, I saw my father's Buick in the driveway. He never came home from work during the day. What was his car doing there?

"Then it dawned on me. I was old enough to know that grown-ups did things in bed together, and I thought he'd come home to do it with my mother. So I tiptoed into the house and up the stairs. But I was kind of scared. I didn't know what to expect."

The grim look returned to his face. He stood up suddenly and began to pace around the room. "When I got to the top of the stairs, I saw my father. But he wasn't inside his bedroom. No. He was standing outside the door."

"Outside?" Karen asked.

"Outside the bedroom door. It was partly open, and he was looking through the crack. He was watching what was going on inside."

Oh, no, I don't want to hear this, Karen thought.

"I could hear noises coming from the bedroom. It was my mother, crying out in pleasure. I'd never heard a woman doing that before." Chad paused. "She was making love, Karen. She was fucking someone, and my father was watching."

Chad turned and stared at Karen. She stared back at him, wide-eyed with shock. "Suddenly my father stormed into the bedroom, shouting at the top of his voice, 'You whore, you whore!' Then I heard her crying. I got closer to the door, and I could hear her saying, 'You don't love me, you never loved me!' Then my father shouted back, 'And Leo does?'

"When I heard that, I crept up to the doorway and looked inside. My mother was in bed with my Uncle Leo, my father's younger brother. The two of them were sitting up in bed, holding onto each other.

"All of a sudden my mother noticed me standing there. She screamed and jumped out of bed. She came running toward me, telling me she didn't love my father, she loved Uncle Leo instead.

"I ran away from her and down the stairs. I could hear my father calling her a whore again, and it sounded like he hit her and she fell down, hard, on the wooden floor in the bedroom. I ran out of the house as fast as I could...."

Chad sat down again. His eyes looked moist. "I stayed away for hours, in the woods, till it got dark. I remember crying and crying, feeling so scared, not knowing what to do. Finally, I walked home. Charlie was sitting at the dining room table, all alone, drinking a big glass of scotch. He told me my mother had gone away somewhere with Uncle Leo.

"He said she didn't love us anymore. She didn't love him, and she didn't love me. Uncle Leo was more important to her than we were. I didn't want to believe him, but what else *could* I believe? I ran upstairs and looked for her, but she wasn't there. She'd left us. Just like that.

"When I went back downstairs, Charlie sat me down and told me he had a plan. He was going to tell everyone she died. 'It'll be better if people think she died,' he said. 'Nobody'll ask us any questions, and the kids at school, they won't make fun of you.' I didn't say anything, just watched him while he made a bunch of phone calls, telling people we were going on a trip. That all of us were going away, Uncle Leo, too. We left a few hours later.

"After a week up north, we came back home. He told everyone my mother and Uncle Leo were dead, that they slipped and fell while we were hiking on some mountain. Then he put on a big show, a memorial service, pretending that he cared. The long-suffering widower. What a crock!"

Karen stared at Chad. In minutes, he'd changed from a hostile, sarcastic bully to a frightened, spurned child, a child whose whole life had been warped by what his parents had done that day. She felt genuinely sorry for him.

Chad leaned back, a confused look on his face. "I'm still not sure what really happened that day. Sometimes I think my father lied to me. She loved me, I know she did. She left us because of *him*, not me."

Chad paused for a long time. The room was so quiet, Karen could hear herself breathing. "You know," Chad said finally, "sometimes I think Charlie killed her."

Karen stopped breathing for a second. *Charlie Fuller, a killer?*

"Maybe when Charlie hit her, and she fell on the hard floor, that might have killed her. People can die when they fall down and hit their heads."

Karen nodded.

"I ran out of the house just then, when she fell. Maybe she never got up." Chad looked sad. Was he thinking that he might have saved his mother if only he'd stayed in the house instead of running away?

"There's something else, Karen. Charlie had a shotgun. He could have killed her, killed both of them with that gun. He could have shot them both dead and got rid of their bodies while I was off in the woods."

Karen nodded. Maybe Chad was right. Maybe his mother loved him too much to leave him. Maybe she *was* dead.

Chad was nodding, too. "Sometimes I think that's what happened. Because she never came back to see me. If she was alive, she would have. At least she would have written or called me sometime. I know she would. She loved me."

Chad paused again. "Do you think Charlie killed them, Karen?"

Karen didn't answer. Whatever answer she gave could be the wrong one, could set off his anger again. It was safer to say nothing.

"I don't know what to think," Chad said. "Maybe the old man didn't lie. Maybe it really was the way he said. Maybe she *didn't* love me, and she ran away with Uncle Leo and forgot all about me, the way Charlie said."

Karen's mind was racing. She was beginning to understand why Chad was so screwed up. Any half-baked student of pop psychology could figure it out. Chad's mother had left when he was eleven, a vulnerable age. He'd been deeply scarred by her departure, especially after seeing her in bed with his uncle. His father led him to believe that his mother didn't love him, that she had abandoned him.

But Chad couldn't accept that. In his heart of hearts, he wanted to believe that his mother hadn't abandoned him. That his father had killed her.

Chad had begun to pace the room again. Karen felt sorry for him, now that she knew why he behaved so oddly, but she couldn't help thinking he might be dangerous. His demeanor was so menacing, so strange....

And he had taken those pictures, those pictures of her and Jon. Was that how he got his kicks? Maybe his childhood trauma made him incapable of any kind of real relationship with a woman. Maybe the only way he got his kicks was by taking pictures of women having sex, pictures of women like me.

He was looking at her, his deep blue eyes searching her face for some reaction to his story. "You can see why I'm a bit cynical about the fairer sex. If my mother was a whore, the rest of you are no better. You're all a bunch of whores. Even you, Karen. You...and the others."

Karen's heart skipped a beat. "Others? What others?"

"Oh, don't play the innocent, Karen," Chad said, sneering. "You know who I mean. The lovely Hope Shimkus, for one."

"Hope Shimkus?" What did she have to do with any of this?

"Yes, Karen. Hope. And Laura."

Hope and Laura. What did he mean?

"Karen, you look confused. Maybe you *don't* understand. Let me explain it to you." Chad sat down again, his smirk back, his tone of voice condescending. He was going to enjoy making this explanation.

"My father hired Hope Shimkus just before I came home to Walden," he began. "Once I got back, I found myself fascinated by Hope. She was everything I'm not: confident, aggressive, full of energy.

"And my father adored her. Thought she was the greatest thing since sliced bread. Me? I didn't work hard enough, I didn't bring in any new clients, I didn't get along with Harold. Well, *of course* I didn't want to work very hard. That's why I left Milwaukee! Why not get some mileage out of being the boss's son, right?" Karen nodded.

"Still, I got tired of his criticism, his constantly comparing me to Hope. So I decided to start checking up on her. I wanted to know if she really was the paragon of virtue my father thought she was."

Chad paused. Smirking again, he went on. "Guess what. She was a whore."

Karen felt her face turn ashen. "I followed her after work," Chad said. "It was easy. She had no idea anyone was interested in her life. She'd go back to her place and wait for him. Andy. You know Andy, don't you?" Karen shook her head. "Harold's son, Andrew Chase."

Andrew Chase. Karen recalled the pasty-faced young man she'd seen in the office on Thursday.

"Hope had the hots for him," Chad continued. "He'd come over almost every night, and they'd jump in the sack together. They went at it pretty good, too. She was aggressive in bed, just like everywhere else. They'd do it two, three times before Andy would leave, going home to Harold's house, innocent as a baby. Harold never even knew.

"But I did. I watched. Her bedroom was on the ground floor, and her blinds were never closed all the way. They liked to leave the light on, too. It was easy to stand outside her bedroom window and watch."

Karen's stomach was churning. She pictured Chad outside the bedroom window, watching Hope, just as his father had stood outside the bedroom door watching his mother.

"Then one night I brought my camera along. I've always liked taking pictures. Maybe you've seen some of the enlargements we've got hanging in the office?" Karen nodded. "I've got a lot of great equipment. A darkroom, too.

"So I brought a camera with a zoom lens to Hope's one night. She was going on vacation, back to New York or somewhere the next day. I got some great shots of her and Andy in bed. Then I went home and developed them.

"Later that night I went back to her place and rang the bell. Andy was gone by then. Hope was surprised to see me, but she let me in. I showed her the pictures. Then she was even more surprised." Chad laughed. "She didn't like my pictures very much. She started screaming at me, and...and I had to stop her, of course. Someone might have heard her." He stopped talking. He seemed to be reviewing the events of that night in his mind.

Karen waited, her heart pounding. Finally Chad began talking again. "I slapped her to shut her up," Chad said. "I said I was going to show the pictures to my father, see what he thought of his precious Hope then. She started to tear up the pictures, so I grabbed her arms and pulled them back behind her. She started screaming again, so I hit her again, harder. She fell and hit her head on the corner of a table. Then she was quiet. Very quiet.

"I picked her up off the floor. She wasn't breathing anymore. So I panicked. You can see why, can't you, Karen?" he asked. A vein on his forehead had begun to throb.

Karen nodded again. "Sure, Chad. I understand. You didn't mean to kill her."

"That's right. That's exactly right," he said. "But I didn't want to deal with all the accusations and the explanations. All the shit that would come around. So I wrapped up her body in her bedspread. Appropriate, huh?" He was smirking again, the vein still throbbing as he spoke.

"I carried her body out of the house and buried it in the woods. Then I went back to her place and cleaned up. I found some stationery and an old typewriter in her bedroom, and I wrote my father a letter. I wrote one to Andy, too. I told them I–I mean Hope–had decided to go back to New York and stay there. I said someone should take care of her things, give them to charity."

Chad began to laugh. "My father really helped me out on that one. He loves to tell me what to do. After he read her letter, he told me to go to her house and look through her things. What a joke! That meant I could check everything, make sure I hadn't left anything behind. Can you believe it? Charlie giving me orders to remove the evidence of my own crime!" Chad corrected himself immediately. "Not that it really was a crime, of course." Chad shook his head vigorously. "It was an accident."

"Yes, of course, Chad," Karen said, rising slowly from the sofa.

He looked up sharply. "Where do you think you're going?" he snarled.

"I just need a glass of water, Chad. I'm just going into the kitchen for a glass of water. Want one?" Karen used a gentle tone of voice, trying to sound as unthreatening as possible.

"Sure, sure, get me a glass of water," he said.

Karen left her yellow shirt on the sofa, walked into the kitchen, and filled two glasses with water from the tap. She glanced at the kitchen clock. 2:30.

If I can just keep him talking for another half-hour, I'll be okay. Jon will be here by three o'clock. Just keep him talking, Karen. That shouldn't be too hard. He seems eager to talk, eager to recount every detail of what happened between him and Hope.

Karen returned to the living room with the water. The moment she got back, he started talking again.

"A couple years later, my father hired another smart bitch. You know who I mean. Laura Hanson." He took the glass of water from Karen and gulped it down thirstily. "A California girl this time. A prize package, just like Hope." Chad smiled. "Charlie thought she was terrific. Pretty soon he started comparing me to Laura, just the way he'd compared me to Hope. She worked harder, she was smarter, all that shit. So I started following her, the way I followed Hope.

"She was different from Hope, though. She didn't drop her drawers so fast. For a while, I thought I had come across the world's most endangered species: a virtuous woman," he said, smirking again. "So I stopped watching her. I figured there was nothing to watch.

"But then she met your boyfriend, Karen. The dashing young Dr. Smith."

Karen felt a sudden wave of nausea. Chad knew about Jon's relationship with Laura. What ugly revelation would come next? Karen didn't want to hear it. She got up and began moving towards the front door. Chad reacted quickly. He leapt in front of her and grabbed her arm.

"Where do you think you're going, Karen? You already got the water." He pulled her back towards the sofa, tightly clutching her forearm. "Now sit down and listen, or I'll have to do something you won't like. Understand, Karen?" His voice dripped with sarcasm.

"Laura and Jon. The perfect couple," Chad went on, finally releasing her arm. "At first it was completely innocent. A few quick goodnight kisses at her door. But that didn't last very long. After a month or two, they were hopping into bed together every chance they could." Karen didn't want to hear about Laura and Jon. She put her hands over her ears, trying to keep Chad's words from penetrating her consciousness. But Chad pulled her hands away and smiled wickedly as Karen looked up at him, furious.

"I watched them," he said.

No! Karen could believe that one woman's bedroom blinds were conveniently left half-open. *But two?*

"Yes, Karen, I watched," Chad protested. "Laura lived in one of the few apartment buildings we've got in Walden. On the second floor. She must have thought no one would ever come up the back stairs and look inside her bedroom window because she never closed the drapes or blinds at all.

"I crept up the back stairs one night and waited on her back porch. I had a story all ready in case anyone noticed me. I'd say I was there to do some emergency repairs. But you know what, Karen?" He paused. "No one ever said a thing." He laughed. "A couple times people passed the building and saw me standing there on the porch, looking into her room. But no one ever said a thing." He laughed again, the vein throbbing in his forehead. "Everyone in Walden is so honest, so trusting. So stupid. They'd never dream that someone like me was looking through a bedroom window, watching a slut spread her legs for some man."

Nausea gripped Karen again. She couldn't listen to any more of Chad's sick, twisted stories. She closed her eyes, hoping, praying he would stop.

"There's more, Karen," Chad went on. "Don't you want to hear about the pictures I took of the two of them? Terrific shots. No blinds in the way this time. Laura...she wasn't as aggressive as Hope. But good old Jon was aggressive enough for both of them.

"But then you know that, too, don't you, Karen?" Karen opened her eyes. Chad was smiling his weird half-smile again. Karen felt scared, so scared she rose from the sofa and made another dash for the door. Chad was after her in a flash, grabbing her by the arm again, slapping her across the face. "Sit down!" he shouted.

Karen's head was spinning. The force of the slap made her ears ring, and her head begin to throb with pain. Chad threw her back onto the sofa. "Now sit down and listen to me!" he shouted.

It has to be 2:45 by now. Jon will be here any minute. If I can just last till then....

Chad was watching her closely now. "One night, when Jon was out of town, I went to see Laura. I showed her my pictures. Told her she was nothing but a cheap whore, just like Hope. She got really crazy. Started throwing things at me. I grabbed her and...there... there was another...another accident."

Chad wasn't smiling any more. "I...I grabbed her hard. Around her neck. I must have grabbed her too hard because...she...she stopped breathing right away. Much faster than I thought she would."

Karen took a deep breath and tried to calm down. I see everything clearly now, she thought. Chad has convinced himself that Hope's and Laura's deaths were accidental. Unplanned rough stuff that got out of hand. He isn't culpable, not in his eyes. He just wanted to teach them a lesson, make them squirm, get them to admit they were the whores he thought they were.

But Chad was guilty of murder. Manslaughter at the very least. Two women were dead because of his weird, sick mind.

Hope and Laura. Two women who'd made the same mistake. Each had entered into a normal, loving relationship with a man she cared about, and each had done it within the perverted view of Chad Fuller.

"I handled Laura's disappearance just like Hope's," Chad was saying. "A letter to Jon, a memo to my father. Everyone thought it was strange, but nobody did anything about it. Assholes! Hope had disappeared only a couple of years before. I was sure someone would call the police, demand an investigation, when Laura disappeared the same way. But nobody ever did!"

Chad sounded amazed that his duplicity had never been challenged. Karen wondered herself at the ease with which he had managed the two women's deaths. It had been too easy. Much too easy.

"And now we come to you, Karen," Chad said. Karen slowly lifted her head to look at him. "The latest addition to my father's harem of brilliant young female attorneys." He laughed. "I really had high hopes for you," he went on, shaking his head. "I thought you were going to be different.

"But I was wrong, wasn't I?" Chad's face was contorted now. "I started watching you from the very first night you got here."

The first night? No, that wasn't possible.

"Yes, Karen," Chad went on. "I found this house for you, you know. Belinda wanted to get you someplace in town, so I volunteered to look. Told her I couldn't find anything. This place was much more convenient for me."

Karen's mind raced back to her first night in Walden, the night Belinda brought her to the house. Belinda had said nothing was available in town. Later Chad said the same thing. Now Karen knew why.

"Besides, I liked the idea of renting the Parker house for you," Chad said. "It was a nice touch somehow."

The Parker house? What did that have to do with anything?

Chad noticed the puzzled look on Karen's face. "Oh, that's right. You don't know about the Parkers, do you?"

Karen shook her head.

"Gerry...Gerry Parker, he was my Uncle Leo's best friend. After Leo and my mother disappeared, he got suspicious. I overheard him talking to Charlie a couple times. He told Charlie he didn't believe they had died on that hiking trip. He hinted around that he might even go to the police. Finally Charlie got sick of Gerry's threats. He decided to ruin him."

"Ruin him? How?"

"He used his influence in town to ruin Gerry's business. His little two-bit insurance agency. Business dried up, and Gerry couldn't make a living any more. He finally gave up and moved away a couple years ago. The poor jerk, I almost felt sorry for him, the way my father gloated over it."

Another life touched–and destroyed–by Charlie Fuller.

"I liked the idea of your living here, where Gerry used to live. I kind of hoped Charlie would say something about it, but he never did." Chad looked wistful. His efforts to get back at his father had somehow missed their mark.

"Anyway, the old man asked me to pick you up at the bus station that night, but I begged off. I told him I planned to leave town for a fishing trip," Chad said, chuckling to himself. "The old fart believed me. Told Belinda to get you.

"But I was here, Karen, waiting for you. I started watching you that first night."

Karen stopped breathing for a moment. Her mouth was suddenly dry, and she couldn't swallow. "But how...?"

"I rigged up a way to climb the wall outside your bedroom window. Just some ropes and pegs, nothing fancy. It worked pretty good, too," he said, grinning, proud of his ingenious contraption.

Oh my God. I saw those ropes, hanging from the roof in the back of the house. I assumed they belonged to some workmen. Roofers or painters.

And those noises I heard, from the beginning. How stupid I was to think they were animal noises, made by chipmunks and squirrels, when all the time it was Chad, creeping around outside my house.

"I'd drive out here and park down the road, behind some trees. Then I'd come over here and climb up those ropes. No one ever noticed me. Not even you, Karen." Chad was smirking again. "It wasn't too interesting, watching you at first. Not much happened. But I liked to watch you take your clothes off and go in for a shower. You take a lot of showers, Karen."

Karen felt another wave of nausea ripple through her stomach.

It has to be three o'clock by now. Where are you, Jon? You should be here right now to rescue me from this man. This monster.

"Then you met Jon. Wonderful, wonderful Dr. Jon Smith," Chad sneered. More of his sickening sarcasm. Karen took a deep breath and tried to smile, trying to hide her fear from Chad.

Chad began talking again. "I hate the guy. Do you know that, Karen?" He seemed to be waiting for some response. She shook her head. It began to throb again, pulsating with pain.

"Well, I do. Always have. We were in school together, Jon and me. He was always smarter than me, better at sports, better at everything–everything except looks. I was better-looking, and you'd think...you'd think the girls would have wanted me. But they didn't. They all stayed away from me, especially after my mother died.

I mean, after my mother *left*, don't I, Karen?" He paused. Karen nodded, tight-lipped, grimacing in pain.

"No, I never liked Jon. But you sure fell for him, didn't you? The first time you went out with him, that day at the lake, you couldn't wait to fuck him, could you, Karen?"

Karen bent over now, nauseated, barely breathing. She felt as though someone had just punched her in the stomach.

"I have some pictures of you at the lake, see?" Chad leafed through the photos on the coffee table and selected one. He waved it in Karen's face.

"Please, Chad, don't. I feel sick," she pleaded.

"You know what, Karen? You make *me* feel sick," he said. His face was grim again. She had to get away from him somehow.

"Can I get some more water?" Karen held up her empty glass. "Please. I...."

"Okay, okay. Get me some, too." Chad thrust his glass at Karen as she passed him on her way to the kitchen. "And make it fast!" Chad stood up, walked over to the window, and glanced outside, his eyes squinting in the sunlight.

CHAPTER THIRTY-NINE

Karen hurried into the kitchen and looked at the clock. 3:10. *Where was Jon?* Shaking, she approached the sink and turned on the water.

Where was he? He should have been here by now.

She was frightened, terribly frightened. Any minute now Chad would finish his spiel, and then what? Another accident? And this time the accident victim would be....

Say it, Karen. It would be me. It would be me who winds up dead.

She looked desperately around the kitchen while she filled the glasses with water. She couldn't wait for Jon to show up. She had to do something, now, to save herself.

Her eye fell on the basement door. Was that a way to escape? No, it would be a dead end. Literally.

There had to be another way. She glanced around. A back door would have made a perfect escape route. Why wasn't there a back door in this dreadful house?

Think, think! You've got to do something!

Karen remembered, for an instant, the gun–K.B.'s gun–sitting in her nightstand drawer upstairs.

But I don't know how to use a gun. I don't even know if it's loaded. And I could never get up the stairs without his grabbing me and....

There had to be some other way!

She glanced around the kitchen one more time. Suddenly she put the water glasses down and picked up the shiny antique toaster. It felt heavy in her trembling arms.

"Hurry up, Karen! What's taking so long?" Chad shouted from the living room.

"I'm coming!" she called, pulling the plug out of the wall.

She tiptoed into the living room carrying the heavy chrome toaster. Chad was still standing by the window, looking outside. He began to turn when he heard her coming.

Approaching him slowly, taking careful aim, she hurled the toaster at Chad's head. He jerked his head, fast enough to miss the brunt of the toaster, getting only a glancing blow on his forehead.

It was enough to stun him for a moment. Karen saw her chance and ran for the front door. She flung it open, leapt down the stairs, and ran out onto the road.

She glanced at the empty driveway. No Plymouth to jump into. Not anymore.

She turned and began to jog down the highway. This jog was unlike any other she'd ever run.

This time she was running for her life.

CHAPTER FORTY

Karen raced down the highway, Chad's horrific story echoing in her brain. Hope and Laura. Both victims, innocent victims, of Chad's twisted, tortured mind.

And now? What about me? I'll be next. Unless I can outrun Chad. Outrun him and find someone, anyone, who can help me.

Karen swallowed hard and kept on running. She felt alone and friendless as she ran along the deserted highway.

Where was Jon's minivan? It should have been on the highway, coming up the road to her house. But she saw nothing. Oddly, there was no traffic at all.

There were always two or three cars on the highway on a Saturday afternoon. Where were they? Suddenly Karen remembered the football game. It had to be 3:20 by now. Everyone in town was already at the game.

Earlier in the week the shops in town had all posted signs: "Closing Saturday at 2 p.m." Even the yellow-and-black sign at the all-you-can-eat chicken restaurant said "Closed 3 to 6 on Saturday." Walden would be a ghost town for the next few hours, its small-town mania for high school football literally making the football game the only game in town.

But where was Jon? Why had he never called to say he'd be late?

Karen turned her head and looked back down the road. Her heart sank. Chad was running down the highway some distance behind her.

So he's recovered from the blow to his head, recovered enough to set out after me, Karen thought. At least I slowed him down. At least he hasn't caused another "accident." Not yet.

She turned again to look back at Chad. He was gaining on her. She concentrated on running faster, faster.

Thank God I was still wearing my running shoes when he showed up, Karen thought. If I had been barefoot, or wearing other shoes....

She couldn't even complete that thought; it was too terrifying. Now, at least, she could run efficiently, speedily. But the absence of her polo shirt was somewhat disturbing. She realized that she must have left it back at the house. Running along the public highway without a shirt, a bra the only thing covering her upper body, she felt almost naked, vulnerable.

Karen glanced back again. The distance between her and Chad had narrowed even more. She looked ahead and saw the dirt road coming up, the one that led to the emerald-green woods she had come to love.

Should I turn off the highway and take that road?

Karen's eyes searched again for the minivan, but the highway was empty in every direction. Her best chance lay in the woods, the woods where she had run just this afternoon. Was it only two hours ago? It felt like days ago, weeks ago.

Karen turned off onto the dirt road, looking back once again at Chad. He seemed to have lost some ground. Was she mistaken, or had his pace slackened off? She continued running, as fast as she could, reaching the woods after a few minutes.

Surrounded by the trees, Karen considered her strategy. Should she keep running, or try to hide among the trees? She wasn't sure exactly where the road led. It might turn into terrain where Chad would have the advantage somehow.

I'll run just a bit farther down the road, then try to find a heavily wooded area, one where I can hide behind a group of trees. Maybe Chad will lose sight of me and give up the chase.

She ran a bit farther, then turned. Chad was still falling behind, struggling to keep up his pace. Karen suddenly remembered the photographs hanging on his office wall and the bodily change in Chad they'd revealed. He'd put on weight over the last few years. His youthful slenderness had evolved into the beginnings of a paunch.

Those extra pounds work to my advantage, she thought. Too many beers? Too many hamburgers and fries? I don't know, and I don't care. All that matters is that Chad's added weight has hurt his endurance. I stand a better chance against him this way.

Up ahead, Karen spotted a group of birch trees that stood close together about twenty feet from the side of the road. She headed for it, hoping Chad was so far behind he couldn't guess where she was going. Reaching the trees, she plunged into their welcoming embrace and sank down, very low to the ground. The lower she was, the closer to the ground, the less chance that Chad would see her. She lay very still now, breathing hard, her heart pounding.

After a few minutes, Karen's breathing became almost normal. She raised her head to get a view of the road. A few hundred yards away, Chad was limping up the road. He'd clearly fallen down somewhere along the way. His pants were ripped near one knee, and his face was smudged with dirt. Karen stopped breathing for a moment, hoping he would keep going, limping past her. Then she'd make a run for it.

Instead, Chad slowed down as he approached the birch trees. "Karen!" he called, nearly breathless with exhaustion. "Karen, I know you're here! I saw you run into these trees."

He knows I'm hiding here.

Karen slowed her breathing as much as she could. Otherwise she was perfectly silent.

Chad stopped short in the dirt road and looked around. Karen raised her head again for a second. Did he detect the movement? He started to stumble towards the birch trees, approaching her safe haven.

It was no longer safe.

Sunlight dappled through the leaves, creating shadows everywhere. If I can move slowly enough, she thought, I might be able to get away. First, I'll move away from these birch trees. Then I'll creep out of the woods and back to the road. If I run fast enough, I can outpace Chad again and get away, get to safety somewhere.

She began to move slowly, very slowly. A gentle breeze came to her aid, moving the branches of the trees. The changing shadows, the rustling sounds gave her some camouflage. She could get away, she was sure of it. She was glad now that she had abandoned the yellow polo shirt. It would have been a bright yellow flag, announcing her exact location.

Creeping along near the floor of the forest, she looked up for a second. Chad was staring in her direction.

Does he see me? Is he watching me move?

He started coming directly toward her.

Should I make a run for it?

He was moving closer to her. She had to do something. She stood up and began to run. Chad called out, "Karen! Stop!"

Running through the trees, her heart beating wildly, Karen thought she could outrun Chad. Just keep going, Karen, she told herself. You can do it.

Suddenly her foot struck something in her path, and she fell, sprawling on the ground ahead of her. She felt dazed for a moment, then quickly turned to look for Chad. He was approaching rapidly, maybe a hundred feet away.

Karen glanced down. She had tripped over a small boulder, its lower portion stuck in the damp earth. Karen put her hands around the boulder and began to tug at it.

It didn't move.

She looked up. Chad was now about fifty feet away. With renewed energy, she dug her fingers into the ground around the boulder and scraped some of it away. Then she tugged at the boulder again.

It moved!

Chad was closer now. He'd be at her side in a matter of seconds. Karen managed to free the boulder from its muddy moorings and pulled it out. It was heavy, maybe eight or ten pounds. She stood up now, waiting for Chad to get even closer. Her aim had been pretty accurate when she threw the heavy toaster. She hoped for even better aim now.

Karen hid the boulder from Chad's eyes, holding it beneath her waist. Then she turned and watched him approach.

"Karen! Don't move! I...I just want to talk to you!" he was shouting.

Just talk to me? Sure, Karen thought. The way you talked to Laura and Hope?

She stood very still. Chad's head was a moving target, but now that she'd stopped running, he was moving much more slowly. Karen calculated where his head would be in ten seconds, then five. Summoning all her remaining strength, she hefted the boulder and hurled it at his head.

Chad looked startled, his eyes widening, watching the boulder sailing through the air. He stopped dead in his tracks, paralyzed.

After what seemed like an eternity, the boulder struck his head, and Karen saw him stagger, then collapse. She heard him groan as he fell to the ground.

Karen emerged from the patch of trees, onto the dirt road, running fast, running toward home. She turned, only once, to look behind her. No one was there.

CHAPTER FORTY-ONE

Two hours later, Karen was once again sitting on the shabby sofa in her living room. She could hear the two sheriff's deputies in her kitchen, arguing in loud voices. They'd arrived at the house an hour earlier and been sparring ever since. One of them, Deputy Carter, was on the phone now, trying to reach Sheriff Gates, whom no one seemed able to find.

Karen was still trembling, her nervous hands repeatedly rubbing her face, then her arms, then her face once more. She was wearing her yellow polo shirt again. She had slipped it on just after she made it back to the house and called the sheriff's office, hysterical, stammering, trying to explain what had happened to her, first in the house, then in the woods.

The other officer, Deputy Helm, left the kitchen and sat down heavily on the sofa next to Karen. He picked up the photographs Chad had spread out on the coffee table and began looking through them. He looked up at Karen, then back at the photographs. "Miss...?" he began.

"He took those. I told you, he was sick, he followed me. He took those pictures. He took pictures of the other women, too."

Helm nodded. She stared at him. Underneath his gruff exterior, he had a kind face, and Karen wondered what he was thinking as he looked at the photographs. She'd already gone over her story several times, but neither deputy had scrutinized the photos until now.

Helm held the photos up to the light, squinting to get a better look. Karen felt violated, the way she had when Chad first showed them to her. The photos would be evidence now. Everyone in Walden would learn about them, learn how she and Jon....

"Here's some coffee, Miss." Deputy Carter had emerged from her kitchen and tried to hand a cup to Karen.

Karen's stomach revolted at the thought of coffee. "No, no, I don't want any," she said, shaking her head and pushing the cup away. Carter retreated to the kitchen.

Someone knocked on the front door, left open since the deputies arrived. "May I come in?"

Karen looked up. Jon stood in the doorway, staring at her.

She stared back at Jon. He rushed in and grabbed her hands.

"Who's this?" Helm asked.

"I'm Dr. Smith," Jon answered immediately. "Karen's friend. And her physician."

"Okay, okay," Helm said, backing off. "Maybe you'd better examine her, Doc. I think she's in a mild state of shock. Didn't want us to call anyone, though." Helm stood up and walked into the kitchen, letting Jon take his place on the sofa.

"Karen, what's going on? What are these guys doing here? And where *were* you this afternoon?" Jon said. "I waited for you. I waited at the gate for an hour before I finally went home."

"Gate? What gate?"

"The gate at the football field."

What was Jon talking about? *He* was the one who hadn't shown up where he was supposed to. "You...you were supposed to pick me up here at three o'clock. But you never came!" Karen's heart was pumping hard, her anger with Jon welling up inside her.

If only Jon had been here....

"But I had that message on my answering machine," he said.

"What message? I didn't leave you any message."

"No, that's right. You didn't. Chad Fuller did."

"Chad!"

"Yes, Chad." Jon's face looked puzzled. He clearly had no idea what had happened. "He said you had to finish something at the office today, and you'd asked him to call me. He said you'd meet me at the game, at the entrance gate, at 3:30."

Karen tried to make sense of what Jon said. This message from Chad–Jon had never arrived because of a message from Chad?

Suddenly she remembered. Chad had asked her on Thursday about the game, and she'd cheerfully volunteered that she was going with Jon.

Chad must have figured I'd be alone in the house this afternoon, getting ready for the game. Then he cleverly steered Jon away by leaving that phone message. He'd planned well, that miserable sick bastard.

Jon was staring at her, waiting for a response. "I wasn't at the office, Jon. I was here, waiting for you. Chad left you that message to keep you from coming here. Then he came here instead." Karen slowly finished telling Jon her story.

When Karen stopped talking, Jon leapt off the sofa and accosted Deputy Helm, seated at the kitchen table, filling out a form. "Do you know what happened here?" he demanded. "Have you picked this maniac up yet?"

"Okay, Doc, calm down," Helm said. "We know the whole story. We picked up Fuller an hour ago and sent him to the hospital in Clarion. The doctors say he may have brain damage. They aren't sure he'll make it."

Jon rushed back to Karen's side and took her hands in his again. "Karen, you can't be alone here, in this house. You'll come and stay with me tonight. I'll take care of you."

Karen listened to Jon through a mist of shock and fear. Finally she nodded, agreeing with him that she couldn't stay alone in the house overnight. But she couldn't stay with Jon.

In a day or two, everyone will know about the pictures. Those horrible pictures. I can't move into Jon's house when everyone will know....

"I'll go to Nedra's," she announced, standing up for the first time since she'd phoned for help. She felt dizzy as she walked to the phone.

Karen reached Nedra right away.

"I thought I'd see you at the game," Nedra said. "I just got back. Where were you?"

Karen told Nedra what she needed to know, stumbling over her words. Nedra reacted with shock, horror. "Of course, you can stay here!" she said. "Should I come get you?"

Karen looked over at Jon. "No. Jon will drive me."

"Okay, Karen. I'll be here," Nedra said.

The sheriff's deputies had gathered up their papers and moved toward the door. "Our investigation's just about complete," Helm told Karen on his way out. "We finally got in touch with the sheriff, and we're heading back to headquarters to write all this up. We'll tie up any loose ends with you in the next day or two. You'll be in town?"

Karen told Helm where she'd be staying, then looked over at Jon. He looked somber now, dejected. But Karen knew she couldn't stay with Jon, not right now. He'll just have to deal with it, she thought. He'll have to deal with what happened to me, just the way I'm dealing with it. One day–no, one hour at a time.

Still shaky, Karen moved toward the staircase, and Jon jumped up to help her walk upstairs. Together, they threw a few things into Karen's suitcase, the same suitcase she had packed for a weekend in Chicago two months before. In Jon's car, he rummaged through his medical bag and stashed a small bottle containing two sleeping pills in her suitcase. "Take one of these if you have trouble sleeping," he said.

On the way to Nedra's, neither of them spoke. But when they arrived at Nedra's house, Jon took Karen into his arms before he left her at the door. "Remember, Karen, I love you. I know you have to work this thing out for yourself, but I'll be here to help you any way I can. Remember that."

"I will," Karen said, too numb to say anything else. She couldn't look ahead any further than tonight, to the bed she would find at Nedra's, to the long sleep she desperately needed.

CHAPTER FORTY-TWO

Karen rang the bell, then turned and looked at Jon one last time. Nedra opened the door, and Karen fell into her warm embrace. "Oh, Karen, come inside, have something to eat...."

"All I want to do right now is sleep," Karen said. She swallowed one of the sleeping pills with a glass of water at the kitchen sink, and in Nedra's spare bed, she fell into the deep, drugged sleep she longed for.

Karen awoke late on Sunday, startled to find herself in a strange bed, her head aching, her muscles stiff and sore. Nedra was watching her from a chair next to the bed.

"Karen? Are you all right?" Nedra's face was lined with concern.

"I guess so," Karen answered.

"I just called the sheriff's police," Nedra said, looking solemn. "Do you feel ready to hear what happened to...to Chad?"

"Of course! Tell me! Does he have brain damage?"

Nedra paused for a moment, evaluating Karen before she spoke. "Karen, Chad's dead."

"He's dead?"

"He regained consciousness for a short time, long enough for the police to question him. Then he lapsed into a coma and died a few hours later. Massive brain hemorrhage, they said."

Karen shuddered.

I killed a man. But he might have killed me if I hadn't killed him first.

Nedra was staring at Karen, waiting for her to speak. "Do the police want to talk to me again?" she asked Nedra.

"I don't think so. Deputy Helm, he said Chad told them enough before he died to...what do you call it? To support your story. There's a legal term for it, isn't there?"

Karen searched her brain, trying to find the right word. "Corroborate. That's the word."

"Yes, that's it. He corroborated your story. The police know you were telling the truth."

At least no one would challenge Karen's story now. No more questions, no more dubious looks, like the ones she got when the two deputies first arrived at her house. They'd been incredulous at first. Chad Fuller–the scion of a prosperous, well-regarded family, a partner in one of Walden's law firms–a perverted killer? She'd repeated her story, over and over, trying to convince them of the truth.

Now there'll be no more queries, no one impugning my credibility. Chad Fuller is dead, but luckily for me, he lived long enough to confess his terrible, ugly secret.

"Karen," Nedra said, "I don't want to do anything to upset you, but...."

"But what?"

"I don't know what really happened. You told me a little bit on the phone yesterday, and I heard some bits and pieces from the police, but I don't think I really understand. Chad came after you? He wanted to kill you?"

Karen dreaded the thought of repeating her story one more time, but she owed it to Nedra to explain everything. Slowly, quietly, she reviewed the surreal unfolding of events in Walden, not merely over the past few weeks but over the twenty-odd years since Chad Fuller watched his father looking through a crack in the bedroom door.

Nedra should know what happened, Karen thought. She lives here in Walden; she needs to know what kind of monsters grow up here. She has to know about Charlie, too, not just Chad.

Nedra sat quietly and listened as Karen went over everything she knew, everything that had happened in Walden to turn Chad into the crazed pathological killer he became.

Nedra carefully absorbed Karen's words. "I understand now about Chad," she said. "But Charlie? Do you think he killed his wife?"

"I wouldn't put anything past Charlie. He could easily get violent if he's pushed hard enough." Karen closed her eyes for a second, remembering Martha Morgan.

"And the photographs?"

"What?" *Oh, God, the photographs. I'd almost forgotten about the photographs.*

"Why did he take those pictures, of you and the two other women?"

Karen hesitated before answering. "I'm not sure. Maybe he used his camera to try to connect with people. Especially women. Even though he was so good-looking, I don't think most women could stand him. He was so uneasy, so uncomfortable around women. I sensed that myself.

"Look, he had to invent a relationship with his college German teacher just so he would appear halfway normal. Maybe...maybe taking pictures of women...taking pictures like that...was a way to control them...to force them to have some kind of relationship with him."

"Taking those pictures of you...it's sickening...," Nedra said.

Karen felt somehow comforted that Nedra shared her horrified reaction to the monstrous photographs Karen had described. But she had to probe her friend about them. "Nedra," she began hesitatingly. "Do you think...do you think everyone will hear about those pictures?"

Nedra paused. "I wish you hadn't asked me that. Do you really want to know?"

Karen nodded.

"Well, then, yes, I'm afraid they will. Sooner or later, everybody will know about them. In a small town like this, word gets around. I'm...I'm sorry, Karen. Truly sorry." Nedra looked down at the floor, unable to face her friend.

The somber look on Nedra's face told Karen exactly what she had feared. Everyone would know about the photographs, sooner or later. It would be impossible for her to go back to a normal life in Walden, with the photographs burning a hole in her brain every day she stayed.

Jon began calling Nedra's at ten that morning, but Karen refused to take his calls. Nedra told him, over and over, that Karen wasn't ready to talk to him yet. The truth was that Karen felt almost paralyzed when she heard Jon's name. She was drawn to him, his kindness, his love. But she knew he would urge her to stay in Walden, to build a life with him in his home town. She couldn't face that prospect right now.

It's better not to talk to Jon at all, she decided. I don't have the strength to debate him, to counter all the arguments he can muster. Maybe in a week, a month. I'll talk to Jon eventually, talk about our future, but for now, he'll just have to wait.

CHAPTER FORTY-THREE

After a supper of cheese omelets in Nedra's kitchen, Karen slept in the spare bed again Sunday night. She slept fitfully, tossing about, confused and frightened and uncertain. But by the time she climbed out of bed early Monday morning, she had reached a decision. She would leave Walden. It was the only real option.

I'll go back to New York. By next week, I can be back at my desk at Garrity & Costello.

Thanks to Jason Singer, she thought, I'll have to move to a new apartment. But at my Wall-Street-law-firm salary, finding a new place won't be hard.

She felt relieved to have made the decision. To know she would be leaving Walden and the horrific events of the last few days behind her.

I'll miss Walden, Karen admitted to herself. I'll miss the placid pace, the civility of the townspeople, the warmth and openness of a friend like Nedra. Above all, I'll miss Jon.

Jon was radiant and loving, a sparkling and stimulating presence in her life. An extraordinarily caring and sensitive man, especially compared to most of the men she'd known in New York. Karen would miss him terribly. She knew that. But she also knew she couldn't stay in Walden another day.

Nedra drove Karen to the corner office building about ten o'clock. "Are you sure you don't want me to go in with you?" she asked. Nedra's face was anxious; she desperately wanted to help Karen any way she could.

Karen shook her head. She had resolutely forbidden Nedra to accompany her to the offices of Fuller, Fuller & Chase. She would face everyone there alone.

"I'm sure," Karen said, forcing a smile. Her shaky voice betrayed how nervous she was. "Don't worry about me. I'll be fine." Karen climbed out of the Lumina, determined to appear confident, steady. She turned back to smile again at Nedra.

Nedra smiled a reluctant smile. "Okay, but remember, call me if you need me. I'll pick you up whenever you want." Karen nodded, and Nedra drove off.

Karen entered the old corner building for the last time, thinking as she ascended the stairs how terrified and unsure she had been on that first Monday morning weeks before. She felt unutterably calm now. Certain that what she was doing was the right thing, the only thing, to do.

Karen walked through the office door. Belinda's and Martha's heads shot up simultaneously, and Belinda ran quickly to Karen's side. "Karen! Are you okay? We heard...we heard everything yesterday. It must...it must have been terrible for you!"

Karen nodded. "It was. It was terrible." Numbly, she began to walk in the direction of her office. "I'm going to pack up my things now. Do you have any empty cartons I can use?"

Belinda stared at her for a moment. "You're leaving us?" she asked sadly.

Karen turned to face Belinda. "I can't come back to work here now. With Charlie here, with Chad's office down the hall...."

Both women were silent for a moment. Belinda's eyes searched Karen's expressionless face. "I feel...I feel so bad, Karen. Maybe if one of us had realized.... If we had only put two and two together. But Chad...Chad was so smooth, he had an explanation for everything. None of us suspected a thing." Belinda clutched Karen's arm as she spoke.

Karen hesitated before responding. She yearned to make Belinda feel better, and she chose soothing words. "He covered his tracks very well. He was a smart man, and he knew exactly what he was doing. You shouldn't feel guilty, no one should. Chad did it. No one else should feel responsible for what he did."

But even as she spoke, Karen couldn't help thinking that maybe someone *could* have figured it out. Maybe it *didn't* have to happen. If someone like Belinda had just tried to track down Hope, maybe Laura would have escaped her sickening end. Even after Laura disappeared, if only someone had tried to find her....

Belinda nodded. "Well, I'll go and find some cartons for you. Let me know if I can do anything else to help...." Belinda released Karen's arm and turned away to look for packing cartons.

Karen entered her office and sat down heavily at her desk. She felt exhausted, drained of her usual energy. But she had to look through her files now, get them into some kind of shape before she left. She would also have to pack up her personal items, put them into cartons, then ask Belinda to send them to her in New York in a week or two.

New York. The reality of it came crashing into Karen's consciousness. She wanted to leave Walden, leave today, but where would she go in New York? Jason was living in the apartment with Joan Granger. Where could she stay? A hotel? With a friend from work?

Melissa Cohen's face suddenly popped into Karen's head. Plump, lovable Melissa Cohen. I can call Melissa. She'll know of a place to stay, even put me up at her own place, the one she shares with her mother, if I'm really desperate. Karen picked up the phone and dialed Melissa's number.

"Karen!" Karen's spirits soared when she heard Melissa's voice. "Am I glad to hear from you! Hendrix is boiling mad, says he never got that letter from you. Now he wants my head. He can't understand why I don't have a phone number for you, and he's steaming...."

"Wait a minute, wait a minute," Karen interrupted. "I've got news for you. I'm coming back to New York, today, if possible."

"Coming back? Really? The doctors say you're okay now?"

Karen had almost forgotten her original deceit. "Yes, yes, they tell me I'm fine. You can tell Phil Hendrix that's why I never sent the letter. They...they told me last week I was recovering faster than they expected. And now I'm all better, and I'm coming back."

"You don't know how happy I am to hear that!" Melissa said, her voice bursting with excitement. Karen pictured her, seated at her desk, her bright red curls bouncing as she talked. "When will you get here?"

"I'm not sure yet. Have to call the airlines. I called you first." Karen felt suddenly depressed at the thought of all she had to do. She knew she had to start making the kind of calls she hated making, to find out when the next bus for Milwaukee or Chicago left Walden, then to coordinate its arrival with a flight to New York.

"Can I help at all?"

"As a matter of fact you can. I need a place to stay when I get to New York. Can you book me a hotel room?"

"Hotel room?" Melissa sounded confused. "Don't you have an apartment on 86th...?" Melissa stopped in mid-sentence. She'd remembered about Jason, about Karen's things being packed up and stored. "Listen, you don't have to stay in a hotel room. You can stay with me and my mom. If you don't mind staying in Queens, that is."

"Thanks. I may take you up on that offer. I'll call you back when my plans are more definite, okay?"

"Sure thing. I'll be here till five or so. And maybe you should have my home number."

Karen jotted down Melissa's number, then hung up quickly. Belinda had appeared at her office door, carrying an armload of empty cartons. "Thanks, Belinda. Just put them down anywhere."

"Can I do anything else?"

Karen hesitated. Why not ask Belinda to make some calls? It might make her feel better if she thinks she's somehow helping me, Karen thought.

Karen described the sort of information she needed, and Belinda returned to her desk to place the calls. While Belinda was busy calling, Karen looked through her files, then began filling the cartons with books and papers, everything she'd accumulated since mid-August. The detritus of her ill-fated stay in Walden.

The office was strangely quiet. Charlie was clearly absent, and Chad was dead. It looked as though Harold had concluded that he should absent himself from the office as well. Even Belinda and Martha seemed to be doing little more than handling the intermittent phone calls coming into the office. Their typewriters were silent, mute witnesses to the sudden, shocking dismemberment of the law firm.

Her packing done, Karen left the files and cartons on her desk and strode toward the outer office. Belinda was just hanging up the phone. "I did the best I could on such short notice. You can take a bus to Chicago this afternoon and catch a 6 p.m. flight to New York. You'll get there about nine o'clock. Is that okay?"

"That's fine."

"Now what else can I do?"

Karen thought for a moment. "Can you drive me home?" she asked.

"Your car...?"

"It broke down on the way back from Madison. Nedra Bailey drove me here just now, but I thought...."

"Of course I'll take you! It's just, I didn't know about your car and all...." Belinda grabbed her handbag and took Karen by the arm. "I'll be back in a little bit, Martha. You'll be okay alone here?"

"Sure, go ahead," Martha said. "And Karen...good luck."

"Thanks, Martha," Karen said. Martha waved farewell as Karen and Belinda left the office together for the last time.

Ten minutes later, Belinda pulled her station wagon into Karen's driveway. "I'll just come inside and help you pack," Belinda said, turning off the ignition.

"Oh, no, thanks. I don't need any help, really." Karen's protests stopped Belinda, who had begun to climb out of the station wagon.

"Are you sure?" Belinda said, turning to face Karen. "I'm happy to help...."

"I know that, and I'm grateful. But it's better if I'm alone right now. Sorting out everything, packing it up, that's something I have to do myself. You understand."

Belinda nodded. "Okay, I'll go. But what will you do with all your stuff?"

"I'm not sure. Probably leave most of it behind. Take some things with me. I have a big old suitcase somewhere."

K.B.'s suitcase. A small case was still at Nedra's, and there were a couple of other cases somewhere in the house, but Karen doubted that she'd need them. She didn't plan to take very much. Once she got back to New York, she didn't want any reminders of her stay in Walden.

Belinda gave Karen a hug and drove off. Slowly, Karen climbed the wooden stairs and entered her house. She glanced quickly around the living room where Chad had terrified her two days before. The police had drawn the shades Saturday night, and they were still down, keeping the morning sunshine from brightening the room.

Chad Fuller, you bastard, you sure got what you wanted, Karen thought. You scared me away from Walden, away from my peaceful new life here. From Jon and the love we might have shared if you hadn't intervened. You killed Hope and Laura, and you nearly killed me, too. Thank God you're dead.

Karen headed up the stairs in search of K.B.'s suitcase. Where had she stashed it?

She found it in a corner of the attic, a couple of cobwebs clinging to one side. Karen brushed them away and carted the heavy battered case downstairs to her bedroom. Looking in the closet, she wondered what was worth packing. The beige dress, maybe, and the navy blazer. But the gray....

Suddenly Karen heard a noise downstairs. Oh my God, no! Noises again?

Well, at least I know it's not Chad, she told herself. Her heart pounding, she crept to the bedroom doorway, then to the top of the stairs. It was quiet again.

Then what did I hear? Am I imagining things, imagining noises like the ones I used to hear in this house? She walked back inside the bedroom and looked out the window. The ropes were still there. Chad's ropes. But they were empty. No crazy Chad Fuller hanging from them, peering into the bedroom.

Okay, then, what *was* it? Karen tiptoed back to the stairs and slowly crept downstairs. The dark house was silent now, but she felt compelled to search the first floor anyway.

Maybe it's Nedra with my suitcase, she thought. Or Belinda's back, unable to tear herself away without helping me somehow.

Karen stepped off the bottom stair and turned toward the kitchen. A flash of light in the living room stopped her. She turned back to see what it was.

"Hello, Karen." Harold Chase was sitting in a chair by the window, holding a gun. The gun Karen had come across in his bottom desk drawer. The silver on the gun was glinting, catching the few rays of light that filtered into the room beneath one of the window shades.

Karen gasped and stumbled toward the living room. "Harold! What are you doing here?"

"Waiting for you."

"But why? Why are you waiting for me?" A dozen crazy thoughts sped through Karen's brain. He's on his way to go hunting, and he's looking for his son Andy, and he thinks I might know where he is, and....

"I'm very angry with you," Harold said, his voice cold, threatening.

"But...but...why? What have I done....?"

"Don't bother playing Little Miss Innocent. You know damn well what you've done." Harold raised the gun and pointed it at Karen. "You found out about two of my clients, and you–you went to Charlie. He tried talking to them, to Merv Robbins and to Ruth Swenson's daughter, but they weren't satisfied. They went to those pricks at the bar association. Now I'm up to my ass in trouble." Harold's face was filled with rage. Even in the dim light, Karen could see the agitation, the murderous look in his eyes. "I'll probably be disbarred. Because of you, you little bitch!"

I can't believe this is happening. Another madman in my living room, scaring me to death, this one pointing a gun at me. I can see it in his face–he's so full of hate and anger, he genuinely plans to kill me. He blames me for ruining his career, even though he's the one who....

"Put the gun down, Harold." A piercing woman's voice called out from the kitchen doorway. "Put it down!" Karen and Harold both turned toward the kitchen, searching for the owner of the voice.

Karen saw a heart-shaped face and felt herself stop breathing for an instant. It was Karen Beatrice Clark, and she was pointing a gun at Harold Chase.

CHAPTER FORTY-FOUR

"K.B.! You...you're alive!" Karen gasped.

"Who the hell is *this*, Karen?" Harold asked. He was still holding his gun, still pointing it at Karen.

"I said, put the gun down, Harold," K.B. repeated. "I know how to use this weapon. I can kill you right now."

Harold hesitated, then slowly placed his gun on the floor next to his feet. "Karen...," he began.

"It's...it's a woman I know, Harold. Now just stop talking for a minute," Karen said. She walked towards K.B. "I thought you were dead. I thought you died in Chicago...."

K.B. smiled. "Now what made you think that?" Her hand on the gun was steady, the gun still pointed at Harold.

"You...you were hit by that car. You were unconscious.... I went running for help...."

"Well, help must have come, Karen, because here I am." K.B.'s grin evolved into a laugh. "Here I am!"

"But there was that article in the newspaper...."

"What article?" K.B. looked mystified, her laugh cut short.

"It said...it said they found a body...."

"What the hell is all this about?" Harold suddenly shouted, rising from his chair. "What the hell is going on here?"

"None of your goddamned business," K.B. said, her gun still pointed at him. "Sit down, you miserable shit. You're nothing but a thief, taking your clients' money like that. You're the kind of lawyer who makes every other lawyer ashamed. You know what? You *deserve* to die."

"What?" Harold suddenly sounded breathless. "How do you know about that? Where....?"

"It's my job to know about it, Harold. Now just tell me one thing: Did you do it to save your son's business? Or did you do it for your own selfish ends?"

Harold groaned and fell back into the chair, plunging his face into his hands. Karen thought for a moment that he had begun to weep, but then he raised his head and spoke again. "Parents are supposed to look out for their kids, help them out when they get in trouble." He looked pleadingly at the two women.

"Look," he continued. "Andy's always been a problem kid, that's why I set him up in business in the first place. I didn't think he could make it on his own. The real estate business looked like a good thing for him. He'd learn the business and maybe make a go of it. If Andrew's Realty had worked out, he could have made a decent buck on his own."

So Andrews Realty was really Andrew's Realty, Karen thought. I should have figured that one out. "But it kept losing money," Harold went on. "Lots of money." Harold was shaking his head now. "I had to help him. He's my kid. I had to prop him up, just for a while, just till he could get on his feet. But every cent...every cent I put in that damn business went down the drain."

He was looking at the two women, first one, then the other, hoping for some acknowledgment of his desperate situation. "Andy, he doesn't have a head for business. He wouldn't listen to me, wouldn't take my advice. After a while, I stopped giving him anything. But by that time, I'd already borrowed some of my clients' money...."

Now Karen understood. Andrew's Realty was a money-losing proposition, and Harold had wound up throwing good money after bad. Until he finally ran out of cash. Then he blithely "borrowed" his clients' funds, probably intending to pay them back when he made a few extra bucks at the law firm. Only those few extra bucks never happened.

She almost felt sorry for Harold. Sure, he'd stolen money that didn't belong to him, but to his credit, he was the kind of father who cared about his kid. Whose instincts were to help his own flesh and blood. Not like Charlie Fuller....

Karen looked over at K.B., who appeared to be studying Harold's face, trying to decide whether to believe his poignant story. K.B.'s right hand still held her gun, but she had relaxed and was no longer pointing it at Harold.

Harold suddenly bent over and grabbed his own gun from the floor. "Okay, miss, now it's your turn to put the gun down," he shouted at K.B., rising from the chair, this time pointing his gun at her instead of Karen.

K.B. looked around, evaluating her situation. "Okay, okay," she said, carefully laying her gun down on the coffee table in front of the sofa. She raised her hands in the air. "How's this?"

"Fine, f...fine," Harold stammered. K.B.'s immediate relinquishment of her gun seemed to take him by surprise.

"Now what?" K.B. said.

Harold looked around the room wildly, as though he'd forgotten why he'd come there in the first place. His glance fell on Karen, and he seemed to remember that he'd come to settle his score with her. "You," he said, aiming his gun at Karen again. "You're the one who started all the trouble. If it hadn't been for you...."

"Oh, but that's where you're wrong, Harold," K.B. interrupted. "The trouble started with your friends Charlie and Chad, not with Karen. Right, Karen?"

Karen couldn't think of anything to say that would mollify Harold, get him to put the gun down again. "I...I...yes," she stammered. "Charlie. And Chad...."

Karen glanced at Harold. He looked furious, and Karen feared he would pull the trigger that instant. *Pull the trigger.* Her throat was constricted and she couldn't speak. She looked over toward K.B. again, but K.B. had stealthily moved behind Harold while his gaze was fixated on Karen.

Suddenly K.B. threw her right arm around Harold's neck and pulled him down, knocking the gun out of his hand. The chair toppled over on Harold, and his gun hit the wooden floor, going off with a shockingly loud noise.

The bullet shattered one of the living room lamps, and shards of green glass flew through the room. Harold was on the floor, shrieking, as K.B. calmly picked up first his gun, then her own. Pointing both of them at Harold, she told Karen to call the police from the kitchen phone.

CHAPTER FORTY-FIVE

Karen stood on her front porch, next to K.B., watching two sheriff's deputies cart Harold Chase away. K.B. had flashed some sort of ID at them, after which they carefully listened to everything she said. Now she turned to Karen. "So, where do you want to talk? Inside?"

Karen hesitated. "Let's just stay here, on the porch."

"Don't feel like going back in there, huh?" K.B. grinned. "I don't blame you." K.B. seated herself in one of the wicker chairs, and Karen sat down beside her.

Karen was struck by K.B.'s demeanor. In Chicago, K.B. had seemed so different. Quieter, more diffident, nothing like this confident, aggressive young woman who now sat next to her on the porch.

K.B. was looking at her, but Karen hardly knew how to begin.

K.B. began for her. "You're wondering what I'm doing here, right?"

Before Karen could respond, K.B. continued. "I'm a cop, Karen. Well, not exactly what most people think of as a cop. I came here to find out what happened to Laura Hanson and Hope Shimkus."

"You what?"

"Don't look so shocked, Karen. You must have realized that I...."

"I don't know the first thing about you," Karen said. "I only know what you told me in Chicago. You said you had a clerkship in San Francisco that fell through, and you took a job in Wisconsin at the last minute because you...."

"Hold on, hold on," K.B. said. "That's all you know? You don't know about the IRS and...." K.B. stopped. "Okay, okay. I'd forgotten what I told you, but I remember some of it now. I didn't level with you in Chicago. It's all starting to come back...."

Karen's heart began racing again. What was K.B. talking about? She didn't level with me in Chicago? And what did the IRS have to do with anything? Did this have something to do with Nedra's friend Ron, and the information he pried out of the IRS?

"Okay," K.B. said. "I'll begin at the beginning. There's a lot you don't know. To be truthful, when I met you in Chicago, I told you a pack of lies." Karen's eyes widened. "Sorry about that, kiddo." K.B. smiled. "I had to. And some of it was true. I did go to Oberlin, and I was a paralegal in Cleveland. But I never went to Harvard–couldn't get in. I went to B.U. instead."

"B.U.? Boston University?"

"Right."

"But the story about your clerkship, and Judy Montana, and the call to the placement office...."

"Lies, Karen, lies. Well, I did meet Judy Montana at a party while I was a student at B.U. That was lucky, as things turned out, because later Judy really helped me with.... But let me explain this, okay?"

Karen nodded.

"When my third year of law school rolled around, I just couldn't see working for a law firm. I'd been a paralegal in a big firm in Cleveland, and as far as I could tell, the lawyers there weren't all that happy. So I thought I'd try something different. I'd worked in D.C. that summer and liked it, so I interviewed with some of the big government agencies. And the job that really interested me turned out to be with the IRS."

"Doing tax law?"

"No," K.B. said, shaking her head. "I never liked tax that much. All those regs, and the Tax Court rulings–boring stuff. Not for me."

"Well, what else is there at the IRS?"

"Oh, there's lots of other stuff. What I picked was the CID."

"The CID?" Karen had never heard of it.

"The Criminal Investigation Division."

"Oh."

"I really liked it, too. I could tell, from my first day, that I'd made the right choice. My work was related to law, but it wasn't all that boring research, figuring out what some judge said somewhere, then writing a ten-page memorandum telling somebody else what I found."

Karen nodded again. K.B. had just described the usual fare of first-year lawyers. "But how did you wind up in Chicago?"

"Okay, let me finish. As my first year went along, the CID started this new program. Checking out professionals who haven't filed tax returns. You heard about it?"

"I think I heard something about it. . . ."

"Yeah, it's gotten some publicity lately," K.B. said, smiling. "Anyhow, one day my supervisor gave me a stack of files from Wisconsin. I began looking through them, and I nearly fell out of my chair when I came across one of the names."

"Why?"

"It was Laura Hanson's file."

Laura Hanson! "But why were you surprised to see her name?"

"Because I knew Laura."

"You knew Laura Hanson? The Laura...the Laura who worked at Fuller....?"

K.B. nodded. "Yes."

"How did you know her?"

"You remember I said I was a paralegal in Cleveland?"

Karen nodded. That was one of the few truthful things K.B. had told her.

"Well, one summer, just before I left for law school myself, Laura worked at my firm as a summer associate. We became pretty friendly. She had one more year at Penn, and she gave me advice about law school, stuff like that."

So Laura Hanson had gone to Penn. Not a Midwestern state university, as Chad had said, deliberately putting Karen on the wrong track.

"So you two became friends?" Karen asked.

"Right. And after Laura went back to Penn, and I started at B.U., we kept in touch. Not phone calls so much, but letters back and forth every couple of months. I was going through law school on a tight budget and tried to keep my phone bills low. But it was easy enough to type a letter to Laura now and then, and she did the same.

"That year, she got an offer to go back to the firm in Cleveland after graduation, but she didn't want to live there. She didn't want to go back to California, either. She'd lived in a small town in Wisconsin till she was ten, and she wanted to try that kind of life again. Lots of fresh air, open space, all that stuff. So she wrote to some firms in small towns in Wisconsin and got several job offers. For some reason–I don't remember what it was exactly–she picked the firm in Walden. The next thing I knew, she was out there and working at Fuller, Fuller & Chase.

"We kept writing for the next year or so. About halfway through the first year, she started mentioning some guy she'd met. A doctor, I think."

Of course, Karen thought. Jon.

"She got pretty involved with this guy. Decided to marry him. So when I didn't hear from her for a while, I figured she was busy with wedding plans, then with her honeymoon and with getting settled. But when six months or so went by with no word from her, I tried phoning. Only there was no listing for a Laura Hanson in Walden, Wisconsin. I tried to find her old letters, see if she mentioned the doctor's name, but I'd thrown them all away."

"And?"

"And I never heard from her again. After a while, I just decided to forget about her. People come and go in your life, and you have to accept that, right?"

"Right."

"So I finished law school and wound up in D.C. in the CID, and there's her name on my list of non-filers. Laura Hanson. Last-known address, Walden, Wisconsin."

"What did you do then?"

"Well, I started investigating. The best I could from D.C. That's when I discovered there was another woman lawyer from Walden who hadn't filed in several years."

"Hope Shimkus."

"That's right!" K.B. looked surprised. "So you know about Hope, too?"

Karen nodded.

"I did some more digging and learned that both Laura and Hope had worked at the same firm. The odds of that happening were enormous–way too much to be a coincidence. I figured something was going on, and I went to Steve–that's my supervisor–and asked him to let me come out here. Go undercover and try to find out what happened. It looked like more than just a couple of non-filers to me. It looked like some kind of serious criminal activity.

"After a few days of arguing about it, Steve agreed to let me go undercover and come out here. That's when I contacted Judy Montana."

"Why Judy?"

"Remember, I'd met her in Boston, at a party. I knew she was head of placement at Harvard. So I called and asked if she'd help me with my undercover investigation. Of course, she said yes. So we created this new identity for me. She made up a transcript for me, like I was a third-year Harvard student with great grades," K.B. said, laughing. "Then she called the Fuller firm and told Charlie Fuller that Harvard had a new program where selected students went to firms in small towns to experience life as a small-town lawyer. She told him she had the perfect candidate for his firm, and she described me. Or at least the new me that we'd created.

"We figured the firm wouldn't be able to resist hiring a brilliant young Harvard graduate. And we were right. Charlie Fuller snapped at the bait right away, said he'd be delighted to have me join the firm. It only took one phone call," K.B. said, laughing again. "It was even easier than Judy and I expected.

"So then Steve and I got the IRS to put together some fake documents for me. Massachusetts driver's license, social security card, all that stuff. I went to the Salvation Army and put together a dumpy wardrobe, clothes I thought a serious but money-strapped Harvard student might wear. Then I picked out a couple of beat-up old suitcases and a pathetic-looking patent leather purse. All of it disappeared when I had that accident."

"I have it," Karen said quietly.

K.B. nodded. "That's what I figured. Anyhow, on the way to Wisconsin from D.C., I flew into Chicago. I had a bus ticket for Walden in my purse." K.B. looked at Karen. "But I guess you know about that, too." Karen nodded. "I planned my trip so I'd have a couple of days to see Chicago–I'd never been there–so I booked a room at a hotel for two nights. It turned out to be the headquarters for the NLA convention. In between sightseeing, I decided go to a couple of seminars that sounded interesting. That's when I ran into you."

"That must have been a shock."

"What?"

"Coming across someone with the same name."

"A shock?" K.B. paused. "Yes. Yes, it was. Especially because my name isn't Karen Clark."

"*What?*"

"My real name is Sandra Webster. My friends call me Sandy."

Karen could hardly speak. She had taken the place of a Karen Clark who wasn't really another Karen Clark. A Karen Clark who was really Sandra Webster. Karen looked at this woman and shook her head. Sandra Webster. Her friends called her Sandy.

"But you're right," Sandy was saying, "I *was* startled when you came over and said your name was Karen Clark. I have no idea why Judy Montana picked your name for me. She must have known who you were. But I guess she figured you were settled in New York and would never get near Walden, Wisconsin. As things turned out, it was a pretty big mistake, wasn't it?"

Yes, it was, Karen thought. If I'd known your name was Sandy Webster, I maybe wouldn't have....

"Anyway," Sandy was saying, "I liked the idea of having dinner with you that night. I thought it would be more fun than going to that banquet, or going somewhere by myself. But when you started asking me all those questions about Harvard, and where I was going to work, I had to think fast. I concocted that story about a judge, made up the name, because I didn't think you'd believe that anyone from Harvard would go to a little town in Wisconsin without some last-minute catastrophe like that."

"People from Harvard go everywhere. Not very many go to small towns, but a few do. You didn't have to make up such an elaborate story."

"Well, maybe I was wrong about that. But I was pretty thrown by some of your questions, so after a while, I pretended I was getting drunk from all the wine."

"You mean you weren't really…?"

"Nope," Sandy said, laughing. "But I did such a good job of acting that way, I ended up getting hit by a car, or whatever it was. I blacked out immediately, and I have no idea what happened next. I was in a coma for five weeks."

"Five weeks?"

"Right. I didn't wake up in Cook County Hospital till a couple of weeks ago. As soon as I felt better–and remembered everything that happened–I called Steve and tried to find out what was going on. He checked and discovered that another Karen Clark had shown up in Walden when I was supposed to. He was totally baffled, but I knew who it was. I knew it was you."

Karen nodded. She was trying to sort out everything Sandy Webster had said. "So when you set out for Walden, you were coming here as an undercover detective, trying to find out what happened to Laura and Hope?"

"Right."

"And you had a gun–I found it, it's in the nightstand upstairs–and you knew how to use it to protect yourself."

"Right again."

"So if you had come here instead of me, you would have been on guard. You...you suspected that something had gone wrong here, that something terrible might have happened to Laura and Hope, and you were prepared to track down whoever was responsible and...."

"Where are you going with this, Karen?"

"*Where am I going with this?* Don't you know what happened here? Don't you know how Chad Fuller showed up at my house, the way he showed up at Hope's, and then at Laura's, and that I nearly, I nearly...."

"Yes, Karen," Sandy said quietly. "Forgive me. I know what happened here. The sheriff filled me in on everything when I talked to him this morning. I...I'm really sorry about it. Sorry I wasn't the one who was here to deal with Chad. Things might have turned out very differently...."

"You're damned right they would!" Karen said hotly. "I was so stupid, so...unaware, not knowing a thing about this place...." Karen rose from her chair and began pacing the porch. A cool breeze had come up, and she was suddenly shivering, her whole body shaking, thanks to the cool air and the revelations by Sandy Webster, CID.

Sandy walked over to Karen and put her arms around her. "It's okay now. You survived. Chad could have killed you, but he didn't. *You* killed *him*, remember?"

A phone began ringing somewhere. Karen felt paralyzed, unable to move. "I'll get that," Sandy said. She released Karen and walked toward the door. "By the way, Karen, my middle name really is Beatrice." She pronounced it "Bay-ah-tree-chay," just as she had in Chicago.

Karen fell into the wicker chair and stared straight ahead, at the road and at the field beyond it. Everything Sandy said, everything is so different, Karen thought. So different from the way I thought it was. *Her name wasn't even Karen Clark....*

A black dot appeared at the end of the road. It got larger and larger, approaching the house. After a minute, Karen knew it was Jon's minivan.

More trauma, more emotional overload. *What will I say to him? What can I say to him?*

Karen rose and turned to enter the house, but Sandy was just coming through the doorway. "That was someone named Belinda calling. To remind you about the bus leaving soon. I told her I'd tell you."

"Thanks," Karen said. *The bus...the bus is leaving soon. But I'm not ready to go, I've barely begun packing....*

Just then, Karen heard a noise. Jon's minivan had pulled up in the driveway next to the house.

CHAPTER FORTY-SIX

Jon leapt out of the minivan and raced up the stairs to the porch. He stopped short, noticing a strange woman standing next to Karen. Then he turned to look at Karen.

"Karen, I..." he began. He reached out for her hands and grabbed them. "Karen, you've got to talk to me."

Karen pulled her hands away. "Jon, this...this is Sandy," she said, turning to Sandy. "Sandy Webster."

"Hi," Jon said. He nodded perfunctorily at Sandy, then turned back to Karen. "Can we sit down and talk for a minute?"

"Uh..., why don't I go inside?" Sandy said. "I've got to call Steve. Can I make a long-distance call from here, Karen?"

"Sure, go ahead." Karen walked to the edge of the porch, refusing to look at Jon, as Sandy entered the house. What was there to say to him? She was leaving Walden this afternoon.

"Karen," Jon said, approaching her. "Won't you look at me? I need to talk to you." He put his arms around her, then turned her around. His hazel eyes implored her to say something, anything, to him.

"Okay," Karen said. "We can talk for a minute. But not for long. I have to pack. I'm leaving this afternoon."

"Leaving? Leaving Walden?"

"Yes," Karen said. She seated herself at the top of the porch stairs. Jon sat down next to her.

"I guess I owe you an explanation," she said.

Now Jon was silent. Karen took a deep breath before she spoke again. "Jon, I'm not who you think I am. I'm not the Karen Clark who Charlie Fuller hired."

"What?"

"I didn't just finish law school this year, the way I told you, when I was pretending to be the other Karen Clark."

"Who? What other Karen Clark?"

Karen glanced at her watch. She didn't have time to explain that there was no other Karen Clark. That it was Sandy Webster, using the name of Karen Clark.

"I've been out of law school for three years, Jon, working in New York. I met her, this other Karen Clark, in Chicago, and when she..." Karen's voice broke for a moment. This was much harder than she had expected.

"When she died–I mean, when I thought she died–in an accident, I...I did something crazy. I decided to take her place and come here to Walden. I hated my life in New York. I thought I would escape from New York, try life somewhere else, get away from everything I hated...."

"Karen, stop," Jon interrupted, taking her hands in his again. "I don't know what you're talking about. But whatever it is, it doesn't matter. I don't care if there *was* another Karen Clark. I don't care if you...if you took her place. It doesn't matter. I fell in love with *you*, Karen. That's all I care about." Jon paused. "I fell in love with you, and I want to be with you."

Karen sat on the steps of her porch, listening to Jon's outpouring of emotion. She didn't say anything for a long time.

"Karen?" Jon said finally. His voice was husky. "I mean it. About wanting to be together."

Karen swallowed hard. "I've decided to go back to New York. I have a job there, and I have friends, and I can pick up my old life where it left off. I can't stay in Walden. I think you know why." She pulled her hands out of Jon's grasp and pressed them together in her lap.

Jon hesitated before responding. "Okay, Karen, you don't want to stay in Walden. And I know why. But don't you want to be with me? Maybe even marry me?"

Karen was silent. What did he mean? Marrying Jon meant staying in Walden.

Jon spoke again. "Karen, listen to me. If we could...if you and I could live somewhere else, would you marry me then?"

Live somewhere else? But Jon would never leave Walden. His practice was here, his father's practice that now was his, and the people in Walden needed him. Roger Huggins would probably retire soon, and the town would need Jon more than ever.

"I don't understand, Jon. You'd never leave Walden."

"Yes, I would, Karen. The truth is, I've even done something about it."

Done something...?

"At the medical conference last week, I stayed over Saturday morning, remember?"

"Yes, of course I do." If Jon hadn't stayed in Rochester, if he'd come back to Walden Friday night, the nightmare with Chad–those hours Karen spent with that pathetic, deranged killer, waiting for Jon to show up—might never have happened.

"I was talking with some doctors from Chicago. Pediatricians with a busy practice there. They want to add a couple new people to their practice. I told them I was interested, and they just called me. They want me to come down to see them as soon as I can."

Karen's heart skipped a beat. It wasn't possible. It couldn't happen.

"But you can't leave Walden, can you? Your father's practice? Your patients?"

Jon smiled. "That's not a problem. I called my dad in Sarasota yesterday. He told me to do whatever makes me happy. Not to feel tied to Walden if it isn't working out for me." Jon grabbed Karen's hands again. "To be honest, I think the old guy feels guilty that he made me give up pediatrics. He pressured me to come back here and take over his practice. I think he sees now that was a mistake."

"Well, what about all your patients? Won't it bother you to leave them without a doctor?"

"But I wouldn't be doing that, Karen," he said, squeezing her hands gently. "Roger Huggins has been advertising for someone to take over his practice. He told me a few weeks ago he heard from a married couple in Pittsburgh, both docs. They want a small-town practice, and Walden's just the kind of place they're looking for. He's negotiating with them right now. So even if I go, I won't be leaving Walden short of doctors."

Karen's heart was thumping now. Jon could leave Walden, would leave Walden, to join a pediatrics practice in Chicago. Something he wanted to do anyway. That meant that being with Jon didn't mean staying in Walden.

"Karen, I understand why you don't want to stay here," Jon continued. "I understand. With everything that's happened...."

"That's why I decided to go back to New York."

"But you don't want to go back to New York. You weren't happy there. We can go to Chicago instead.

"Come with me, Karen. We can get married, or not. It's up to you."

Maybe it was too soon to talk about marriage. But either way, she could be with Jon.

"You can find a good job in Chicago–big firm, little firm, no firm–whatever you want," Jon was saying. "We can make a new life there. Together."

Chicago? The idea of living in Chicago struck Karen as hugely ironic.

If I hadn't gone to the convention in Chicago, I never would have met the other Karen Clark. We never would have gone to La Maison Carrée, and I never would have fallen down and woken up as someone else.

I never would have, on a crazy, dizzy impulse, boarded a bus for Walden, Wisconsin, and found myself in a world of small-town lawyers who were demented, dishonest, or worse.

And I never would have met Jon Smith.

All of those "never would haves."

Maybe, after everything that's happened, going back to Chicago is the right ending here. Maybe that sudden, impulsive break with my life in New York–that crazy inspiration to fly to Chicago in August–was meant to be final. Irrevocable.

Now. . .now I can try again. Try to get it right this time. With Jon. We can start over, make that new life together. In Chicago.

Karen looked at the field across the road. The sun was brilliant overhead, and fat golden leaves drifted slowly from the branches of the trees to the ground below.

Jon suddenly put his arms around her and pressed his lips against hers. She felt herself melting again. Chicago...Jon...it suddenly seemed possible.

"What do we do now?" she asked.

"I'll call Chicago. We can drive down there tomorrow and see how it goes. What do you say?"

She thought for a moment longer, then threw her arms around Jon. "Let's do it," she said.

Karen B. Clark, attorney at law, Chicago-style.

Why not?

Yes, Karen admitted to herself, it was another impulsive decision.

Another impulsive decision. But this one just might work.

THE END

ABOUT THE AUTHOR

Susan Alexander is a graduate of Harvard Law School who has devoted much of her career to working as a lawyer in the public interest. She has also served as a federal judge's law clerk, an arbitrator, a law school professor, and a consultant on legal writing, in addition to working at three Chicago law firms.

Susan now focuses primarily on writing. Her writing has appeared in a wide array of publications, including the San Francisco Chronicle, the Chicago Tribune, the Chicago Daily Law Bulletin, and a host of other professional and mainstream publications.

Susan lives in San Francisco. *A Quicker Blood* is her first novel.

Made in the USA
Lexington, KY
26 January 2010